JESUS

MAN, NOT MYTH

A NOVEL

JESUS

MAN, NOT MYTH

A NOVEL

PETER D. SNOW

BOOK PUBLISHERS NETWORK

Book Publishers Network
P.O. Box 2256
Bothell • WA • 98041
Pʜ • 425-483-3040
www.bookpublishersnetwork.com

Printed in the United States of America

10 9 8 7 6 5 4 3 2 1

LCCN   2010934496
ISBN10   1-935359-49-5
ISBN13   978-1-935359-49-4

Editor: Lori Zue
Cover Designer: Laura Zugzda
Typographer: Stephanie Martindale

DEDICATED TO

Lisa, my wife

Hilary, my daughter

Howard and Julian, my sons

The four people who give the most meaning and
purpose to my life.

The time is coming—indeed, it is already here—

when worshippers

shall worship the Father in spirit and in truth.

St. John 4:23

CONTENTS

Preface xi

Author's Note to Reader xiii

Part 1: Signs and Symbols

1. Nightmares 3
2. Repudiation 10
3. The Baptizer 17
4. Jonathon 23
5. Jesus 30
6. Conversations on the Road to Galilee 33
7. Galilee and Nazareth 42
8. The Return Journey 49
9. The Beginning of Jesus' Ministry 60
10. His Ministry by the Jordan 65
11. Nicodemus 82
12. Makers and Shakers 88
13. Annas' Diary 102
14. Dreams and Terrors 107
15. Return to Jerusalem and the Pool
    of Bethesda 115
16. Disturbing the Peace 120
17. Tensions and Reflections 129
18. The Samaritan Woman 131
19. The Wedding at Cana 141
20. Arrest of the Baptist and Moves Against Jesus 146
21. Confrontation 156
22. Healing the Blind Man 171
23. Raising of Lazarus and the Way North 186
24. The Official Response 195

Part 2: The Kingdom of God

25. The Way North 205
26. The Call 215
27. Moving Through Galilee 235
28. Personal Reflections 247
29. Disciples' Discussion 256
30. Parables of the Kingdom 261
31. Feeding the Five Thousand 266
32. A Night on the Water 276
33. Sermon on the Plain 284
34. Visits to Tyre and Sidon 293
35. Transfiguration and the Way to Jerusalem 304
36. Gathering the Threads 315
37. The Last Week 322
38. Annas' Quandry 328
39. Teaching in the Temple 332
40. Final Preparations 343
41. The Last Supper and Jesus' Arrest and Trial 349
42. The Trial 360
43. The Crucifixion 376
44. The Burial 391
45. The Resurrection 399
46. Galilee 414
Epilogue 419
About the Author 421

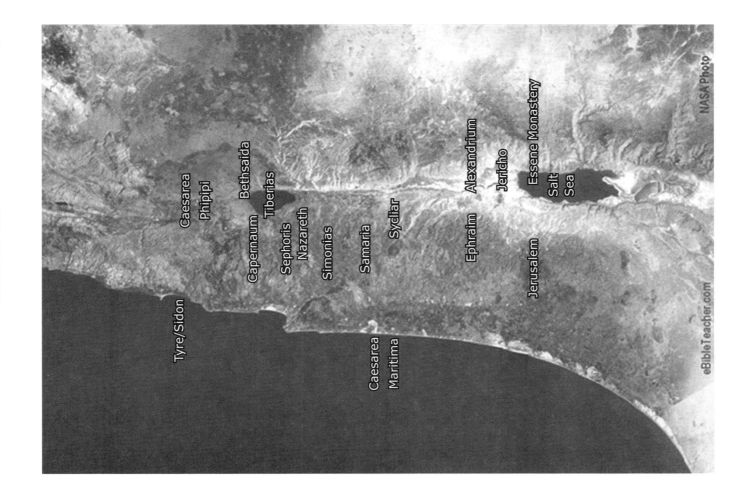

Tyre/Sidon

Caesarea Phipipi

Bethsaida

Capernaum

Tiberias

Sephoris

Nazareth

Simonias

Samaria

Sydiar

Caesarea Maritima

Ephraim

Alexandrium

Jericho

Jerusalem

Essene Monastery

Salt Sea

NASA Photo

eBibleTeacher.com

Preface

PREFACE

All we know about one of the most important people in the history of the world is contained in four gospel stories about the person of Jesus of Nazareth. Sorting out the story of Jesus and defining his teaching is like putting together a jigsaw puzzle from a box that's missing 20 percent of its pieces and has pieces from other puzzles tossed in too. Theologians have done a good job of sorting the pieces into piles but putting the puzzle together is difficult.

Writing a novel about Jesus and his teaching has given me license to speculate, imagine and make intuitive connections that our present-day demand for certainty and accuracy would otherwise not permit. With this format, I explored questions that scholars ask but have difficulty answering definitively. For the sake of the person in the pew, I have written an account that gives plausible scenarios and emotionally believable support to the gospel story.

Here are a few questions I wrestled with as I wrote the story.

- **What was Jesus' mission statement?** I chose to see Jesus' mission statement as his intent to destroy not the physical Temple building but the Temple's system of sacrifices, the priesthood it supported and the notional beliefs that maintained people's superstitions. I chose this mission statement because, in their writings, the members of the early church often described their experience of salvation as a replacement for or an alternative to the ancient practice of animal sacrifice centered at the Temple in Jerusalem.

- **If the sacrificial system of the Temple was to be overthrown, with what did Jesus intend to replace it?** I describe Jesus laying out for the people of Galilee a full program that leads them to holiness by a different path. Like others before me, I refer to it as "The Way." Taking the disjointed accounts—the puzzle pieces—I assembled them into a description of a coherent path to holiness for both an individual and a community of that time period.

- **What were the dates of Jesus' ministry, i.e., how long did he lead a public life?** We have conflicting information. Gospel stories (Luke and John) describe Jesus' ministry as beginning as early as 26 CE and lasting seven years until Jesus' death in 33 CE. At least half of this time he spends in the Jerusalem area. However, other gospels (Matthew and Mark) tell of his ministry as lasting between only one and three years, with him confined to Galilee except for the last week of his life, which he spent in Jerusalem.

- **Why should John, the Beloved Disciple, be telling the story?** St. John's Gospel, in spite of its editorial material, contains several very convincing eyewitness accounts. The cleansing of the Temple, the walking on water, Jesus' trial and the resurrection are examples of firsthand accounts. Its author is traditionally thought to be the Beloved Disciple and the person closest to Jesus during the story's time frame. His familiarity with Jerusalem and its institutions suggested to me he was a resident of Jerusalem rather than of Galilee.

My descriptions of healings and the encounters other people had with Jesus are taken from my own experiences. The words I quote and the actions I describe are often those of people I have been privileged to work with during my ministry.

I wrote this book for all those who demanded of me believable answers to their thoughtful and intelligent questions. With or without me, these people so often found themselves in the presence of Jesus of Nazareth, their Lord and their Christ. He was and is to them, the man Jesus, before the myths made him remote, incomprehensible and unapproachable.

AUTHOR'S NOTE TO READER

This is a novel—a fictional description of Jesus' ministry. This novel is not supernatural fantasy, but an attempt to portray Jesus as a man who has both feet on the ground and casts a shadow.

Much of what I have written references teachings, miracles and happenings within the gospel stories as we find them in the New Testament. I use events found in other contemporary sources to support the historicity of Jesus' story. To learn where, exactly, in the Bible and other sources you can find more information about the happenings and people described in this book, please visit www.jesusmannotmyth.com to see an extensive list.

As you read this book, you will also find descriptions of a few miracles I invented, together with many conversations that are, by necessity, fictional. I urge you not to accept these as fact but to enjoy them, speculate about them, wonder about the questions they pose—and, in the end, know the whole story is a fictional rendering of Jesus' ministry.

Peter D. Snow

Part I

SIGNS AND SYMBOLS

NIGHTMARES

I couldn't sleep again. I awoke, startled, from a nightmare with the screams of my people ringing in my ears. In vivid colors, I had seen them again, dying, as they were butchered in the town square or standing before their executioners, awaiting the sword, the garrote or worse.

Drenched in sweat and trembling throughout my body, I put my hands over my ears to block out the screams, and I closed my eyes so I could not see the blood…but the blood and screams were on the inside.

They are sights and sounds I could not rid myself of even as they happened; I could not look away. Since that terrible time, there has been no escape; the gruesome memories return unbidden, and often when I least suspect it. Twenty-nine days since my worst fears had come true.

And, to tell the truth, I don't want to stop those sights and sounds, because they are all I have left of those I saw die in the persecution in Ephesus.

Early this morning I stood outside on the cool patio tiles, staring out over the sea towards the mainland, just discernible on the horizon. The coastal mountain range was nearly hidden by low morning mist, and I could only see its summits. I looked where Ephesus had to be and saw in my mind's eye—as clear as day—the city Forum and the rows of columns marching on either side of the street towards the square where that monstrous effigy of the Emperor Domitian stood.

At the thought of that blind, deaf staring mass of marble, I trembled all over again. I remembered Marcius as he was dragged before the effigy and asked to worship the image. He stood there, bloody, cut and beaten and refused. Three times he was asked, and three times he refused. Finally he was condemned to die in the theatre. Onlookers slavered as they anticipated the spectacle of his slow death.

As the scene again unfolded before my eyes, a scream rose in my throat. *No!* I shook my head to force the images away. Then, as if the whole scene were a fragile pot, it shattered into pieces and dropped away.

I was still standing, alone, in a home not of my own, looking at the sea from my perch on the island of Patmos.

Collapsing on the low stone wall separating the patio from the steep slope leading to the valley below and the sea beyond, I wept afresh in the chill gray light of dawn. As I rocked back and forth, arms wrapped around myself in a futile attempt to contain my grief, I slowly chanted the names of all those who had died.

They had been mine. My people.

They had obeyed the law and were loyal to the Emperor. They prayed for him and the authorities daily as Jesus, the Master, taught us. Yet they were desecrated, tortured and inhumanely put to death to satisfy the lusts of the people in that cursed city.

I cursed the goddess Diana and her bloody Temple. I hurled curses at the horizon on all who entered that cold mausoleum of man's depravity.

I wished I were with my people. I could not bear the pain anymore.

I tried to pray my Lord's own prayer but I fumbled to a stop when I reached the words 'forgive us our sins as we forgive those who trespass against us.' I could not forgive those murderers. How could I pray? I was full of sorrow, anger and, yes, hatred. So far was I from Jesus' one command, I could no longer remember how to forgive or even why I would want to.

"Dear Lord, help me." I could not forget, I could not forgive, I could not hope for this world or for the people in it. I wanted to see it smashed. I wanted to see this world and the people in it utterly destroyed, and our people avenged. I couldn't help myself. In spite of all Jesus had taught us, I wanted violent vindication.

Covering my face with my hands, I wept the bitter tears of absolute despair and cried aloud, "Lord, help me to pray."

I had a nightmare again last night. The memories of my people's murders at Ephesus have evolved into a nightmare which repeats itself over and over. I know it's a vision of my hatred and rage visited upon the world, and the world is destroyed as punishment for the terrible persecution of us here and in Rome. The methods of this destruction and the forces involved change from one dream to the next.

The first dream of this sort occurred a week ago. Seven seals were holding back the punishment awaiting all those who had persecuted my friends and the faithful everywhere. The seals were broken one at a time, and disaster was visited upon the world. Four horsemen, representing the wrath of God, poured forth from the seals to battle against this savage world. The last seals were my cry for vindication, mixed with the voices of all the slaughtered faithful.

The very next night, I had the dream again, but this time there were seven trumpets, and they heralded, in turn, the destruction of the sky, sea, rivers and earth. Everything was in flames, which consumed this wretched world. Then, out of the abyss, huge locusts came, sought out men and stung them, and then stung them again.

In my sleep, I screamed my approval. I wanted the destruction to go on and on, but I awoke to the silence of the night. My waking dream, in which I relive my friends' death, began again to flicker before my eyes. There was no escape in sleep or in wakefulness.

Three nights ago was the same conflict. The powers of this world were waiting to devour anything good, anything that the Almighty sought to bring about. In my dream a child was to be born, and a dragon representing the seven empires of the world waited to devour it as soon as it was born. The child was whisked up to heaven before the dragon could snatch it. *Yes!* I wanted to scream in triumph. I wanted to shout out loud, "He will be back to rule the earth and conquer Satan. All the powers of evil and their henchmen will be obliterated, and there will be no hiding from Him. Nero's name will be printed on all their foreheads. No one will be able to deny their complicity. They will all get what they deserve!

Last night my dream was once more of seven great chapters of destruction, but this time it was seven bowls from the altar. One by one they were emptied on the earth. I saw the people afflicted, and I screamed my approval. I saw the sea and rivers turned to blood. The sun exploded and burned people up. Total darkness fell, the rivers dried up and the air was destroyed. All the Kings of the earth had joined together at Meggiddo to war against God and His anointed one, but it wasn't going to do them any good. I even saw Rome picked up by a great angel and thrown into the sea, as easily as you might skip a stone.

I awoke and lay imagining what tortures they all deserved; kings, all their officers, their citizens and the lustful crowds baying like mad dogs eager to see innocent blood flow—all deserved the suffering they had inflicted on the innocent.

The innocent…the innocent in my nightmares reminded me of my friends. Their deaths were no dream, and to forestall the images of their last hours I quickly forced myself up and onto my feet. Yet I still felt the scream rise in my throat again, and I held my head in my hands in hopelessness.

When I could move again, I sought the open air and the gray light of early morning, and labored to get control of my mind. I was consumed by impotent rage. The evil I so opposed was obliterating everything Jesus had ever taught me.

I couldn't breathe. I was drowning.

My attempt at prayer was fruitless; I could only form enough coherent thought to beg, "Lord, help me."

At last, I turned to the prayer He had taught me. "Thy Kingdom come, Thy will be done…" The prayer died in my throat. Reluctantly, I admitted that the prayer I wanted to pray was for the whole world to melt in hell.

I am John.

I used to be known as the beloved disciple, but now I am an old man full of despair.

I was the closest person to Jesus back then, but now I am far from his love and grace.

I want to die, but I cannot. I want to join those I came to love. Why should I be the only one left of all those who walked with him?

Yet just the thought of Jesus helps. Yesterday morning, when I sought the open air and stood in this very spot, trying to wrest my mind from the depths it had sunk, I could swear I felt his hand on my shoulder while I tried to pray for my own soul and those of our friends.

"They are all mine, John. They are all mine." His words were clear, his hand was comforting and those long gone days didn't seem as distant.

"That's right," I thought. "They were, indeed, his people." I bowed my head. "I must remember they were his people, not mine. Our people, *his* people, are with him now. Could that be true?"

The sun was up, and I could smell the thyme, sage and other herbs that covered the hillside. The soft morning light made the mist translucent and, for a moment, I saw my savior treading down the sun's rays, flooding the earth with His presence. My nightmares and waking dreams felt distant, and, for a few moments, I saw all my friends who had died in Ephesus now swept up in his presence.

The vision faded but as I sat there in the warming sun, memories I had not visited for years began to stir. The images calmed me, and cherished memories began to squeeze out the shattered shards of suffering that littered my head. Nerve-wracking and exciting days in Jerusalem, contemplative days down by the Jordan with John the Baptist, followed by illuminating days walking in the company of Jesus.

When was that? How did it all start? Gazing across the sea once again, I knew exactly when it had begun: more than fifty years ago, not long after the aqueduct was built.

I returned to my room and sat looking at the disorganized mess of dumped manuscripts of one kind or another. They had been hastily gathered up in Ephesus before I was hurriedly forced into exile here, one step ahead of a pack of vigilantes. My friends—those who were still alive—bundled me off to a small cove south of Ephesus and smuggled me aboard a boat belonging to one of them.

That was more than a month ago.

Before I left Ephesus, my students—my disciples—asked me to write what I remember from the early years. As I surveyed the mess before me, I could not summon the energy or even the desire to take on that task. I sat at the desk and stared at the wall. Blank numbness pervaded my mind, and after a long time I shifted my unfocused stare to the window opening, and back again to my desk.

I took my pen in my fingers and weighed it there. "Write!" I heard Jesus' voice in my head. "Your healing is in the memories of all those years, not in these last few months."

Write!

Could I do it? Could I go back to the beginning, when I first met Jesus?

In those days, I was a twenty-something young man who wanted to see the world turned upside down, and I was prepared to help do it. Every generation of young men longs to do the same, and there were plenty of us back then. I blushed, embarrassed, as I remembered how little we actually knew of the world. How naïve we were! I let my thoughts wander over those early days when we were so full of hope.

Already, my heart was calmer, my pulse slower, as I silently reminisced about those early years during the reign of Tiberius Caesar Augustus. Pontius Pilate was governor, or Prefect as he was called, for Judea. The Temple still stood, and life in Jerusalem was as it had been for decades—fractious, disputative and insipiently violent.

Somewhere in the jumble on my writing table, I recalled, was an enlightening series of old writings. I searched for the collection of tattered sheets and scrolls that made up what I had come to think of as the Diary of Annas, the High Priest during those years. Buried under my aborted efforts to write lessons for my disciples in Ephesus, I plucked them out and shuffled them into some semblance of order.

I read for hours, reliving those turbulent, exciting and fecund years with Jesus that I wouldn't have missed for all the sweet nectar in Galilee.

Annas' written musings helped me put in perspective what I had witnessed so recently in Ephesus. That tragedy, while all-consuming and life-changing for so many of us, was nothing new in the overall scheme of the world. Nothing had changed; the world still cannot see good when it is displayed or the powers of this world will try to extinguish it, but what I have witnessed born into the world will never be overcome.

These terrible memories, that today tear me apart, are simply a part of all the cruelty and violence ever practiced upon the innocent. Violence is not new, but as old as mankind.

We were, all of us, contentious in our own ways. The various blocks of power vied for control; old debts and animosities were carefully rehearsed and remembered.

Into this corrosive environment came the Christ. The man we knew as Jesus.

I have decided to write what I know of the emergence of the light that challenged the violent darkness we lived with on a daily basis. I helped introduce many friends to that light, and it illuminated my friends in Ephesus. And, in spite of the darkness that haunts my dreams, that same light still calls me back to itself.

Annas' diary came into my possession only after the Temple and most of Jerusalem were destroyed. Who saved it from the flames I don't know, but it passed into my keeping two years ago, along with other bits and pieces salvaged from the wreck of our city.

The pages contain years of daily entries and follow the tortuous turns of that man's mind. Reading some of the entries was my own form of self-torture; I banged my fist on the table more than once at the blindness of Annas and all the others in authority who had refused to see what was in front of their noses. The world then, like now, had no clue how badly it needed grace.

Pausing for nourishment, I sipped water from a chipped cup and slowly ate three figs. Where to begin? I was ready to write, but didn't know where to start. Even after I ate a couple pieces of sweet bread my neighbor's wife had delivered yesterday, I was still stumped.

Maybe I should begin with the High Priest. Annas. He was utterly ruthless. People who were opposed to him would suddenly disappear. He had men murdered, or had accidents happen to them and their kin that terrified friends and foes alike. So extreme were his measures that even the Romans found his violence intolerable. The Roman Prefect, Gratus, forced Annas into retirement yet the wily man retained most of his power by covert means, namely, by setting one group against another and creating suspicion and distrust among all. His malign influence over Temple politics created the foreboding backdrop to the ministry of Jesus. The one we call the Christ.

Sipping sage tea and feeling the sunset's warm rays on my face, I realized the beginning—for me—was not when I met the man named Jesus, but before that, during the time of my own turmoil and loneliness.

Without family or friends to connect me to the earth, I had been adrift, and didn't understand why I was unhappy and restless. I had no purpose beyond running my father's business in the city, nor did I have any sense of where I fit in the world. I went through the motions of living, of getting up, working and going to bed at night, with no idea why I was doing it.

Yes. That is where my story begins. Inspired, I rose from my perch on the stone wall, rinsed my cup, lit two candles, and started writing.

REPUDIATION

By the time I was in my twenties, I had experienced a number of reverses and frustrations in my business and personal life. I lived alone, and my sense of alienation from those around me had been developing over the previous two years or so. The crisis came one day when, in a somewhat jaundiced mood, I made my customary monthly visit to our Temple.

Begun by Herod some forty-five years before, the Temple now stood as a magnificent witness to our faith. I had often speculated at the irony of a non-Jew building such a beautiful expression of our religion. I grudgingly admitted to myself, if not to my friends, that the building was indeed beautiful, and it was the one thing we Jews had left to us. The Temple was the center of our nation. Those who lived strewn around the shores of the Great Sea saw Jerusalem and its Temple as the place they ultimately belonged. They saved for years to make a pilgrimage here. They stood in the courts of the Temple, offered their sacrifices and returned home with a sense of belonging, their beliefs cemented by the vision of Herod's building at the very heart of their nation.

On that day I had come to the Temple to make my obligatory sacrifice of two turtledoves: one for purification and one as my sin offering. I waited in the crowd for my purification offering—the first dove—to be received and processed. The second dove, representing my sin, was taken and—as is typical—had its head torn off and its entrails pulled out so it would be ready to offer unto the fire and burned to ashes. My whole burnt sacrifice, as we called it then, represented the purging of my sins. We all edged towards the altar area where the clouds of smoke from the sacrificial fires billowed up into the blue of the sky. In those billows of smoke, life was returning to whence it had come. We were all rendering homage and recognition to the source of our existence.

The attendant who took my two offerings was dressed in a tunic stained with blood, both old and new. The man made no attempt to hear my reason for the offering, but took the turtledoves from my hand and ushered me towards the altar area where more men stood witnessing the drama of the sacrifice.

I made the ritual ablutions by washing my arms and hands from the elbows to the tips of my fingers in the lavers that were provided. Water ran into stone basins and splashed out into a channel that took it away, along with my impurity. The great stone containers were filled from a hollowed-out stone conduit. I wondered if this water was courtesy of the Romans and if it had traveled the length of their aqueduct, all the way from the Bethlehem area.

Grimacing at my unruly thoughts, I returned my attention to the task at hand. I looked around me and felt a sense of alienation swamp me. The smell, the sight of those filthy attendants, and the sweaty mass of the crowd conspired to plunge me into a resentful and cynical attitude. We all stood on a polished black area that rose slightly towards the altar. The customary sickly sweet smell that permeated this area of the Temple turned my stomach. In the midday heat, the black floor turned sticky. I moved off to the side a little to better get a view of the proceedings and felt the clinging glutinous surface of the pavement reluctant to let my sandaled feet go. The floor was covered in dried blood from centuries of sacrifices. The shiny blackness of it filled all the spaces in the stone paving and created a smooth, polished look to the courtyard. It was inches thick.

The smell I had always associated with sanctity was from the layers of blood from thousands of sacrifices offered daily. Bullocks, heifers, goats, sheep and birds formed a daily procession to end here in this courtyard of death. They left behind only this stain, and the ancient blood was added to every day, year in and year out.

My irreligious thoughts sprang at me, and before I could stuff them back as I had always done, I allowed the revulsion I had experienced at finding my feet stuck in the decomposing blood of all that death to become a full-flooded objection. My stomach roiled so I quickly extricated myself from the crush and stood by the wall, trying to get control of my stomach and its contents.

This was not the way the Temple should administer its sacrifices. I looked around at the repulsive men who acted as assistants, and I saw the priests on the high platform going about their duties. They laughed among themselves as they slit the throats of the animals, carelessly splashed the blood into the receptacles that were supposed to catch it all, and handed the dying animal over for more processing before being racked for roasting.

I thought of all the hopes and prayers of people from a thousand miles away who had struggled to come here, in anticipation of the moment when they could see their sacrifice be made here at the center of our nation. What they got, instead, was a careless, unceremonious nonchalance from men who processed the people with as much feeling as they dispatched the animals.

What a waste.

If I could, I would have taken back the doves I had offered. What would I do with them? This was the only show in town. This was the only place a sacrifice could be offered. Maybe I should just let them go.

Sickened, I turned my back on the spectacle that these most holy acts had become. The acts of sacrifice, enjoined on us by our God, were being gutted of meaning just as surely as those so-called priests gutted the animals they were given.

As I left I watched a procession of clergy bearing the roasted remains of the sacrifices towards the areas off-limits to us ordinary folk. There, the clergy would consume the meat. As I watched, one man stopped another going the other way and reached out and plucked a morsel from the silver salver the other bore, and pushed the hunk of meat in his mouth. He returned to the altar area, the juice from the meat dripping down his chin as he masticated the flesh of someone's offering.

That gluttonous and unthinking act fed my outrage and I grew more disgusted by everything I had witnessed. That was the final straw.

I hurried down the steps away from the Temple courts, and plunged through the crowded stalls that lined the already narrow street to my own apartment. It was small, and part of two other buildings. Thankfully, there was a courtyard with one small lemon tree in it, because the apartment had no roof garden or other amenity. The location was good, the size fit me, and it was quiet. Noise and heat did not penetrate the thick stone of the walls.

I threw my satchel in one corner and slumped down on a low divan. Feeling contaminated rather than cleansed by my experience at the Temple, I got up again. Taking my own stone laver, and using a stone-hewn jug, I poured enough water to fill the laver to overflowing. I plunged my arms in beyond the elbows, paused, and thrust my whole face down into the water and rubbed my hair and beard with the cool liquid. I needed to be clean from that cloying stink. Water splashed all around my feet but there was not enough to wash away what I had witnessed.

Later that evening I sought a friend of mine. Tobias was a bright, intelligent person whose presence I enjoyed because he thought for himself, and yet he was not irreverent about our religion. He was married, was part of his father's business venture as I was, and was always ready to find me a wife.

His wife set before us thin slices of hard bread and a small bowl of cumin-laced garbanzo bean spread. Tobias poured me a cup of red wine that he said his father had just imported from Cyprus. He offered water to add to it, but I shook my head. I didn't want to drink it as a cordial, but as fortification against my own alienation.

He studied me. "So, what is on your mind? For you look as if you've lost a whole talent and found a denarius."

I smiled at his simile. "Maybe you are right. That is just what has happened, although for the life of me I don't know why it happened today, and right out of the blue."

He waited for me to go on, looked up at me through his long dark hair that had fallen across his face, and fixed me with an inquiring look. Tobias waited, spreading some of the paste on a piece of bread, and studied it before beginning to eat it.

I sat back, sipped my wine, and told him of my experience that afternoon. "Look, I've been there every month for most of my life. I have made countless offerings, so why suddenly do I hate the smell and see fakery everywhere I look? This is our Temple I am talking about, and the rites expressly laid out by Moses and those who followed him." I took another piece of bread and helped myself to more of the bean spread. "Tobias, I don't think I can go back there. You were right. I have lost a whole talent, as it were, and I don't know where to look for it."

Tobias munched on his bread and gazed out through the open doorway to the cramped courtyard still lit by the setting sun. "Well, you are not the only one to feel like that. How many people there, were from Jerusalem and how many were pilgrims? How many of our friends avoid the Temple except on the festivals? How many of us to arrive at this point. "I don't know why it took you longer than the rest of us to arrive at this point. Personally, I pay my Temple tax, ignore the goings-on there, and go about my business. I observe our law, and my wife and I enjoy all the rites of every Jewish household. We love the Sabbath…which reminds me, how about joining us this week?"

"Thank you, I will. But, Tobias, we can't just walk away from the central pillar of our nation." I set my piece of bread down uneaten, "The Temple is the center of Jerusalem, Jerusalem is the center of our nation, and the place to which our people turn constantly."

Tobias nodded. "Yes, I know, but you try to do anything to reform that bunch of thieves up there on the mount, and you are likely to find accidents happening to you and yours. Let me tell you what happened when we tried to get licensed to operate our business within the Temple precincts. Our applications got lost, the man we needed to see was gone for a month, and then no licenses were being considered at that time. Then, we had a mysterious fire in one of our warehouses. We caught it in time but after that we got the message. So, we are expanding elsewhere. Caesarea is a growing market and Gentiles appreciate good, honest dealings. So, am I turning my back on our people?" Tobias stuck the knife in the bread board to emphasize his point. "No, but I am not going to waste my strength on bucking that gang on the hill.

"Now you talk of the deficit of sanctity, and the loss of effectiveness in our religious institution. It's one and the same. I don't know what to tell you, except you are not alone. He sat back and shrugged his heavy shoulders, "No, John, you are most certainly not alone."

After a pause he went on to say, "I have heard that the Essenes have opened up their way of life to everyone. A friend of mine, do you know Jared?" I shook my head. "No? Well, anyhow, he went down to Jericho or somewhere near there, and met with a group of men who are talking about developing a profound response to the kind of questions you've just raised. He was full of it when he came back."

I sat in silence and considered what I wanted to do. Above all else, I desired to belong to something. The experience today had destroyed my one fixed point that I had counted on for years. The Temple was always there. When I needed to be with people I could immerse myself in the anonymous crowds there, but now I didn't think I could go back there. I certainly needed to think about this.

The conversation took a new direction as I asked about Tobias' father, and other aspects of our daily lives we had in common. Tobias soon brought the conversation back to what we'd discussed earlier.

"John, you are all alone. You are running your father's office here with only old Aholiab for company, whilst your parents are living it up in Caesarea Maritima. You are on your own too much. You need to belong. We don't see you enough, and you don't go out of your way to join in."

That much I could agree with. "Maybe you are right about my being alone too much. I don't know what I am looking for. Maybe those men you mentioned might be a place for me to start. Where can I find your friend Jared? I would like to at least speak to him."

Two weeks later, I caught up with Jared and we made our way down the road to Jericho. On the way, Jared, described the man we were to meet. "You will find John the Baptizer something else! There is nothing phony about him. All of us who come down to listen to him go away charged up. I've been down here a good seven or eight times and I never tire of listening to him."

Crossing the Jordan, we found the Baptist's camp. My first response to him was relief. He manifested no fake piety or sanctimonious unction, but looked and sounded like I imagined one of the old prophets of our traditions. He stood gaunt and bearded, covered in a rough garment cinched around his waist with a piece of leather that looked like either a piece of the reins from a camel or maybe part of a pack strap.

He roared at all of us. "You think our nation is the victim of all the injustice in the world, well, I tell you we are not! We have turned to other nations for strength and protection, and we have sold our independence for security. Did not the prophets Isaiah and Jeremiah warn our nation to not put their trust in Egypt or Babylon but in our God? What happened last time we put ourselves into the hands of foreign powers? We were banished from our land for a hundred and fifty years. If we go on doing as our fathers did, we will end up the same. Turn to our God, and make him the center of your life, not that heap of stones built by an unclean man with unclean hands. Turn to Him who is Lord of Life and not to the priests and clergy who prey upon you and take your offerings and eat them with defiled hands."

I wanted to stand and shake my fist and yell my agreement, but I didn't. I sat, mesmerized.

He plowed on. "Those who profess sanctity don't believe what they profess; they think running water over themselves will wipe away contagion and uncleanness, but all it does is remove the dirt. I say more is required. Purify your thoughts and act according to our laws. Ready a place for our God to make a home among us. Look to him as the power from whom our security flows." At this he entered the river and walked into the shallows. Facing us, he gestured to the flowing water. "You want ablutions? Then here is enough for all your sins and the sins of the whole of Israel!"

Yes! I wanted to shout in response to John's challenge. As I saw John standing in those waters that had been so much a part of the story of our nation, a flood of approval rose in me. John was using those same waters to call people back to begin anew. Abraham had crossed those waters as he entered the land of Canaan, and since then everyone who had come from the east had had to first cross those waters before entering our land. I was ready to join John in the river right then, but, as usual, I held back. I needed to digest everything I'd heard and seen.

A month later I went back to the Jordan. In the interim, I had sat and talked with Jared at length, visited with Tobias and met several others who all shared my need for a new center for our religious lives. I decided to return to the Jordan and ask John to baptize me. I needed to belong with others who were having the same thoughts as I, and who sought a new loyalty to our God.

Yes, above all, I needed to belong. I had allowed myself to be solitary too long.

THE BAPTIZER

For some, the experience was heavily emotional and represented some turning point in their lives, but for me, my baptism by John was more in my head.

I nominally rejected what I had experienced at the Temple and dedicated myself anew to obedience of the laws of our God. I studied the law as well as I could and extended my day-to-day observance of it. I sought out some of the Pharisees who were always willing to teach others their exacting standards. For the first time I felt I had a purpose beyond the marketing of imports and the haggling over the price of our exports. I would prepare a place for the living God, and in my small way create a highway for him just as John had described.

I remember one typical weekend I journeyed down to where John was baptizing. I greeted several of the other disciples whom I had gotten to know. I went over to the little crowd that surrounded the Baptizer, and I sat there and listened. I had grown accustomed to his railing against the authorities and watched with approval as he denounced their practices.

Today he was speaking more insistently to those who listened. "I know you love to listen to me cry aloud at the terrible misuse of power by those in Jerusalem, but none of you are innocent either. You go along with their beliefs and allow them to bamboozle you into compliance. Are you not as complicit in their sins as the worst of them? How many of you think that if you offer a little sacrifice, one that is as small as you can get away with, you will be held innocent of any offence and clean of any contamination? Is that what you believe? Do you believe that will protect you from bad luck? Or do you think maybe because you have cleansed yourselves on the outside God will not notice what you are on the inside?

"Do you think their ablutions or sacrifices will save you from misfortune? Will the pestilence we all fear avoid you because you have just come from the Temple? No, I say. None of this will protect you from the wrath to come.

"Do you think listening to me will save your hide? Does the fact you have come all this way to hear me count in your favor? No, I say. Unless you repent and change your ways you will suffer just as the worst sinner.

"Clean up your life, take the law of our fathers, Moses and Aaron, and let it be an expression of your hearts. Obedience is not what is wanted, but a whole hearted expression of those laws. Delight in obeying them, shun and turn aside from evil. Avoid the evil or dishonest man. Desire good as the only thing in your life. That way you will be making a highway for your God, an oasis for Him who alone is Holy."

I lingered for a while and watched as some came to John and entered the water to be baptized. I was aware that I watched with detachment as they came up out of the water. What I wanted was to see our God move or declare Himself, so that we would know. That's what I wanted above anything else. I wanted to see the God of Israel *do* something.

Oh, I believed in the God of Israel, but I wanted more than belief. I wanted to know Him like the old prophets knew him. I wanted to know him as David knew him and talked to him. I thought to myself that what I wanted was like trying to hunt a lion in the wilderness. Once when Jacob, a hunter friend of mine, had insisted on me going for a few days into the wilderness to hunt antelope we had sat hidden from everything for most of a day. Although we had heard the roar of a lion early on as we moved towards the area Jacob sought, we looked and looked but could not see him.

As we lay still under the prickly branches of a desert shrub, we watched an antelope cross our line of vision. I motioned to Jacob, but he shook his head, and put his finger to his lips. I lay still and watched. Then I saw what I thought had been a rock detach itself from the desert background and begin a silken, stealthy stalk of the antelope. How long had the lion been there? His camouflage was so well adapted to this desert environment that until he moved I had no inkling of his presence. Jacob whispered, "See? The lion of Judah. You can't shoot him 'til he moves. Marvelous!"

That was how I began to think of my problem of seeking our God. However would I see Him if He did nothing? How could I recognize him if he didn't move? Like the lion in the desert, He was too well camouflaged for me to recognize. I wanted to believe in our God, but how does one do that?

I did not find my baptism to be the answer I had hoped. Inside, I was awash with the disquiet of someone who felt outside the group because I had not had the experience I was supposed to have. Everyone else was so sure of themselves and positive about their experience. I began to think there was something wrong with me. My regular appearance down by the Jordan automatically made me one of John's disciples, and I was welcomed as such by the rest of those there. I had never dared articulate my thoughts out loud and more and more I felt at times I was an interloper or there under false pretenses.

As usual I had brought food down with me and took it out to share. Others had done similarly, and what little there was we passed round. Eleazor, whom I had met before, asked me for news of the city. I shrugged, "It's hot, dirty and full of people. I thought I would rather spend my Sabbath with you."

After a long silence I tried to address some of my concerns and ideas. "Eleazor, you have been here with John some months now, do you think he could be the Messiah?"

Eleazor spat an apricot pit into his hand, weighed it there as he thought, then answered, "No, he has said as much. But there are plenty of us who think he is. John says he is just a voice crying in the wilderness, 'Prepare the way of the Lord,' but more and more people are coming. He has been teaching us how to observe the law and for our diligence in its observance to be an expression of who we are rather than merely an enforced obedience. He has been teaching us how to accept the events in our lives with thankfulness instead of fighting them. He has been beating into us that the disasters that befall us are fate, and it is up to us to take what happens and accept it as God's will."

I shook my head, "Yes, I was here when he was talking about that earlier, but I have a problem with that. Is fate God's will? If that is so, then we are back to the old issue of why does God allow his faithful people to perish in such terrible ways."

Eleazor warmed to the discussion and energetically rounded on me, "That is just the point. If we try to understand why these things happen then we are wasting our breath. They are the mysterious will of the living God, and we, by our unquestioning acceptance of them increase our faith in the living God."

Another voice chimed in. "I disagree. If that is true why can't he mysteriously stop things happening? I would believe in him just the same, in fact I would believe a whole lot more."

Eleazor replied, "Fate means nobody deserves what they get, so you have to learn to accept things the way they are. That way you learn to rejoice whatever the situation. At least accepting whatever happens helps get over things and get on with life. The opposite idea that disaster happens to people because someone sinned, maybe a hundred years ago, has never made sense to me. If I don't know what I did or my grandfather did, then how can I do anything about it? It doesn't matter how hard I try, misfortune can still catch me out. No, I prefer fate."

A voice chimed in from the fringe of the group that lay in various attitudes on the sparsely grassed gravel bench that bordered the river at that point, "Maybe when the Messiah gets here he will straighten things out. The Baptist has been ratcheting up his expectations this last three months. When we do see the Messiah we can ask him. I have a number of questions for him."

"Me too," a young man added. "How about all the foreigners? We are not a nation of Jews any longer. There are people building settlements on our land and displacing good farmers. Our people have to move to the city or sell themselves to one of the new landholders. What is the Messiah going to do about that?"

"Seems to me there are a number of different things he is going to tackle. There is the Temple, there are the foreigners as you called them, then there is the moral decay of our own citizens. Did I mention the Romans? Well there are those too. How will he do it all?" asked a heavily bearded man lying on his back looking up at the cloudless sky.

"I like what he is saying about us preparing a highway for our God. I can identify with that. That is what I want to do. Everything else is so confused and there is no center to our nation any more. I long for God's word to be heard loud and clear, that everyone knows where it is coming from and what it means," reflected Phinias, sitting next to me. Then in a louder voice he said, "We have to be a nation again. We don't have any one to speak for us, we have foreigners rule us, make our laws for us, and they appoint our kings for us. Such kings they are too. None of them are truly Jews. They care little about our faith except some of the superstitions they pander to in order to protect themselves from our God's displeasure. I tell you, they have even stolen our God and reduced the Almighty to the status of one of their gods they think they have to placate or humor. These are not our people."

I sensed the mood change as we delved into this subject. Suddenly we were not discussing ideas but were touching on a violence that underlay every man there. Was this why they were here? I found myself swept up with the ardour of our suppressed nationalism. I lay back and the drone of conversation went on about me. I thought, "I want to feel as if I belong here in my own country, my own nation with its history."

I looked out over the Jordan Valley to the steep cliffs on the other side and imagined Abraham travelling in hot pursuit of those raiders who had captured Lot. I imagined him galloping up the valley with his small raiding party, looking in my direction and even almost two thousand years ago, seeing what I now saw.

I redoubled my efforts at preparing myself and ordering my life more strictly according to our laws. We were going to make a difference!

During those months many came down to the Jordan to enjoy the show John put on. Some, who had come to jeer, stopped to listen. There were frequent visits from his friends in the Essenic monastery further down the coastal plain by the Dead Sea or the Salt Sea, as we knew it. He used to belong with them and was even brought up by them there in the desert. This was not unusual, for the Essenes were well known for raising other people's children in their traditions.

When I first met Essenes, I toyed with the idea of joining them. I even went as far as talking to one of the council members. However, what they would require of me went beyond what I could ever hope to handle. Right off the bat they would require three years of living in their community, during which time I would be a novice. They would not even take my possessions and mingle them with the community's possessions. In other words, I would not be a part of their group for at least three years. After that I would have to be rigorously examined, on goodness knows what, and only if everyone was in favor would I be received as an initiate. At that time I would be included at their sacred meals and be a member of their community; yet I would still be on trial and always under the authority of those above me.

No, that would not work for me. I can imagine lasting maybe a month before I found their petty rules and procedures intolerable. I needed to belong, but not at that cost.

John certainly knew the people who came because he called them by name sometimes. Also they all spoke the same language as well as shared the same ideas. I gathered John had taken their personal lifestyle and purpose, left their community and applied their message to the whole of Israel. I got the impression they were not too pleased with him. To everyone including the men from the monastery down south he spoke as if we were all the lost sons and daughters of Israel. There were no elect. I think this did not sit well with those Essenes who had worked so hard on their own act, for they definitely saw themselves as such.

We did not have much of an organization, but John taught us how to pray, fast and discipline our bodies. We even gave up our own life plans to become servants of the coming kingdom. I was unmarried, and though I had been thinking of finally bowing to my parents' desires and allowing them to find a wife for me, once I became involved with John the Baptist I postponed the idea of marriage indefinitely. As with other aspects of my life, I went overboard, and I struggled to purify myself inside and out. I even got good at it.

Most weekends when I was there a good number of representatives from the Temple in Jerusalem would be there listening to him and demonstrating their outrage. We were fool enough to laugh at their alarm and delighted in further outrageous statements. We loved tweaking the lion's tail. Little did we know how deadly a game we were playing.

John was, of course, outrageous. He called out to these Temple representatives, "You vipers, who warned you to flee from the coming judgment? The axe has already been laid to the roots of the tree. You will all be caught like rats in a trap. You are too late. There is nothing worth saving there."

The crowd loved it, for most of them had come for the entertainment value and to see the sparks fly. They came expecting to hear a crazy prophet, only to find themselves touched by his not-so-crazy rhetoric. We Jews can't separate our nation from our religion. Therefore, our nation's future was bound up with our own morality. The two were connected. Whether they were pious or not, Jews from all over felt within them a surge of hope for their nation when they listened to John.

Jonathon

During one of my extended visits to sit at the feet of the Baptist, I was surprised to see my friend Jonathon. We had often met in Jerusalem and shared a meal every now and again. His parents knew mine and so our history went back a long way. I liked his mother and father. They were solid, common-sense types, and very moral, sensitive and deeply respectful people.

He greeted me with surprise, "John, what are you doing down here? Am I glad to see you. All the rest of my companions are here to jeer. Have you been down here long?"

I told him a little of what had been happening for me. We moved off towards the river bank where some of my friends and I had set up a little camp. The fire we had used for cooking still smoldered and I put on some more driftwood we had collected earlier. Early evening was a comfortable time to sit and be with friends so we found ourselves a convenient rock and a trunk of a tree, both brought down by floods. Jonathon sat in silence for a while then picking up a stick began to studiously draw in the sand.

Finally, without looking up, he said, "John, tell me, do you think the Baptist knows something about the Messiah? I've heard in Jerusalem John is predicting his arrival any day now."

I cautiously nodded my head. "If you are around him long, you begin to look at every crowd that assembles and expect to see someone step out and say, 'Here I am.'"

"Really? You don't think that is how it is going to happen?"

"No, but we are all on edge now. Of course we get it from the Baptist, but if you stick around here long and listen to him you will catch the bug."

"So what is his main thrust?"

"His call to all of us is to clean up our act. Prepare a pathway for the Messiah. In other words, adopt the kind of lifestyle our own scriptures describe. He talks about a purity that is not just outward but also inward. In particular he wants to see us put away all corruption and dishonesty. Power-grabbing and hypocrisy are absolutely anathema to him."

Jonathon shook his head slowly, "Hmm, I can understand why old Annas sent me down here. Everyone else he has sent comes back dismissing John as an offensive nobody. They will never tell Annas what he says."

I smiled. "I can imagine why nobody will tell Annas the truth. Just listen to him talk about the Temple and how it is desecrated by the present holders of office. He is quite specific. The Temple is his main illustration of what is wrong with our nation and represents to him how the center has to be ripped out and rebuilt. That is a job for the Messiah."

"Oops, no wonder the reports Annas gets are just generalizations. By the way, do you know who really runs the Temple?" asked Jonathon.

I thought for a moment. "I suppose Caiaphas. After all he is the High Priest."

"You are in good company because even Caiaphas thinks he is running the operations of the Temple, but the person who knows every little thing that goes on and manipulates those he cannot directly control is Annas. He may have been fired or rather deposed by the Romans, but he is not gone. I know, because I see everything that happens there. In fact I soon realized I saw too much for my own good."

Jonathon paused for a moment as if considering whether he wanted to go on, or maybe that he had already said too much. I think he felt far enough away from Jerusalem that he could talk, but his reticence came back for a moment and he looked out at the gathering shadows beyond the fire light as if to assure himself we were alone.

Finally, he continued, "When I took the job I thought I was going to be helping the old man write his memoirs and look after his library. What I am really doing is keeping a set of books on the whole operation just for Annas. He keeps tabs on everything that goes on. He sits in his office studying reports he gets from all kinds of sources, sends for Caiaphas and grills him on what ever is currently of concern to him.

"He has contacts with some very odd people. I have seen men visit him after dark that I would not like to meet even in daylight. I know he has contacts among the sicarii terrorists, and he has his informers at Herod's court. As for Pilate's office, I know he keeps an eye on everything there, and he has an open channel all the way to Rome. He trusts no one, suspects everyone and takes nobody into his confidence. Even when he talks to himself, he only mumbles, as if his thoughts might be overheard. I do know he writes all his thoughts down every day. He expects me to catalogue the pages of his journal and store them with his other papers.

"Annas scares me. I do not know what he would do if he knew I was talking like this to you. Maybe I would just be fired, but I am not sure he would stop there. I would probably never get another job. Disloyalty never has to be proven to him; all he needs is to suspect it. He tells Caiaphas what to do, appoints family members to every office he can, and crushes any opposition he suspects."

I said, "He sounds like something you find under a rock in the desert."

"You bet," said Jonathon. "Let me give you an example. I read up on all this the other day when I was looking back in one of Annas' journals. It happened a couple of years ago.

"Pilate developed a scheme to bring water right into the center of the Temple precincts and empty into the cisterns that served the area. The aqueduct was to be some twelve or so miles long and came from the Bethlehem area. Water would flow all the way to Jerusalem and provide the center of the city and the Temple with water for ablutions and other needs.

"Nobody objected to the aqueduct being built, but there had been no cut-and-dried agreement over who was to pay for it. Pilate had asked the Temple authorities to pay their part. Annas hated the Romans and relished an opportunity to embarrass the Governor, so he had the High Priest refuse.

"Pilate was beside himself. Any goodwill he might have had evaporated. Annas had lured him on with general promises to help in financing the supply. When Pilate asked, the promises and offers were summarily taken off the table. Face-to-face meetings with the Roman staff were through junior members of the Temple entourage. Finally, Pilate lost his cool, raided the Temple treasury, and took the money.

"Days of rioting followed. They protested Pilate's desecration of the Temple and seizure of sacred monies derived from the Temple tax people paid. Annas raised that rabble. He had his own retainers promote the riots by invoking the crowd's outrage, claiming that Pilate had taken the Temple money for his own use. That it was for the aqueduct and that various promises had been made was conveniently forgotten. Crowds took to the streets, violence broke out, and people died as Pilate put down the riots forcefully. When the dust settled, complaints were drawn up and sent to Rome.

"I tell you, Annas set Pilate up. So, for the second time, he wrote to Rome. You know that when Pilate first arrived he created riots and mayhem by parading those Standards through the city, and after we had expressed our outrage, he set them up in the Temple Precincts at night. Pilate had to back down then and made Rome look foolish. The business with the aqueduct gave Annas another opportunity to make trouble for Pilate.

"So, since Pilate can't afford too many more major complaints from our so-called authorities, Annas has Pilate just where he wants him."

Jonathon paused, and added quietly, "Shall I tell you why I am here? I am supposed to listen to John's preaching and assess its potential effect on our income stream. Let me tell you, Annas maintains a constant watch over the Temple returns, and he swore he could see a downturn in receipts as a result of John's ministry. I was there, and he asked me for back years of receipts. He went back ten years and traced how Temple business has trended.

"I tell you, that man examined every year and for every downward tick, he found corresponding events that explained it. When he began looking at these last three years, he thought he could see a downturn that could only be explained by the disaffection of the public with the operation of the Temple. He blames John the Baptist for that. He thinks John is reaching people now and that it is beginning to effect how people are responding to what the Temple offers. There is a small drop in receipts for sacrifices, especially the small offerings. Cleanliness rites are way down for local people. We still get a lot of business from abroad, especially at festival times, and that has not decreased. That imbalance has given Annas reason to suspect John as the local cause for the lower receipts."

Jonathon glanced around. When he saw no one near, he said, "Personally I don't think receipts are down that much, but he sees a trend."

I said, "Has he said anything to threaten John? Could he make trouble for us here?"

"He has sent agents to provoke John into indiscretions and to pick up anything they could use against him. I am here as part of that investigation. I am supposed to take careful note of everything he says and who is party to his movement," replied Jonathon.

He looked up, and squinting at the failing light to the west he said thoughtfully, "Annas is very clear about the threat John poses. The Essenes have always objected to the Temple and have purification rites of their own. That has been fine until John came along. Annas, of course, hates all of them, but they have not been a threat until now. So long as they stayed down there by the Salt Sea, Annas has been happy. Now John is becoming mainstream. The Essenic doctrines are leaking out into the national consciousness. The Baptist's words are heard everywhere and by everyone, even if it is second or third hand. The very thing Annas feared is beginning to happen."

Jonathon leaned closer to me, and his voice dropped lower. "There was one occasion when I overheard Annas and Caiaphas talking about the possibility of getting rid of the Baptist. Caiaphas was worried about the Baptist's popularity. The possibility of a backlash was a threat to any such plot working. Annas told Caiaphas the best thing would be to set John up and get either Pilate or King Herod to arrest him. That way, there could be no backlash."

He stared at me, trying to make out my face in the dim light. Was he gauging my reaction? His next words indicated regret, yet commitment to his beliefs. "Jonathon, you and I have known each other for some years now, and I know you cannot be happy serving against the interests of our people, but let us think for a moment." Yes, I needed to tell him what was on my mind, and I gained confidence as I heard my own words and watched him listen closely to me. "Right now you are the only person in a position to help us make a difference. Would you be willing to stay where you are so you can alert us to any moves against the Baptist? You might be able to head off something worse than the usual corruption. When the Messiah appears, you may be able to protect him from the machinations of that crew in Jerusalem."

Jonathon stared at me for a long minute, then shifted his gaze to study the sand at his feet. Finally, he said, "I don't mind giving you fair warning of any threat, but I will not take their money and then betray them. I will not betray even Annas. Scurrilous though he might be, I will not be party to deceit."

I thought again about what I was asking and again stressed, "I am not suggesting you betray the confidence of your masters, but only warn us of those things which are contrary to the interests of our nation."

Jonathon leaned closer to me, and his voice dropped lower. "There was one occasion when I overheard Annas and Caiaphas talking about the possibility of getting rid of the Baptist. The possibility of a backlash was a threat to national life, is being sold to the highest bidder. Bribes, corruption and manipulation are rife." Jonathon picked up a stick and poked at the fire's remains. "I have thought about looking for another job."

I thought for a moment about his position, the risks he took and the valuable information he had just shared. Hesitantly, I expressed my thoughts. "Jonathon, you and I have known each other for some years now, and I know you cannot be happy serving against the interests of our people, but let us think for a moment."

Jonathon rose stiffly to his feet. "I will think about it. You have given me the only reason to continue work under Annas. I will think about staying. If John is right and the Messiah is on his way, then maybe I should stay. I have a place to stay with the rest of the delegation so I should be getting back. I don't need them to begin asking questions about where I have been and to whom I've been talking. Your name does not need to be on their list."

With that, Jonathon moved off taking the left hand path that would lead him up into the town of Jericho. By then it was almost dark, the fire had died down and I thought about following his example and rejoining my friends. However I sat back down on the rock I had occupied for the last hour or so and considered my own position.

I was totally beguiled with the hope of saving and recreating Israel. After listening to Jonathon and putting together what I already knew and what the Baptist preached, it was clear to me our main enemy was not the Romans, but the Sadducees who were spiritually sucking on our people. They had to be the real target. John the Baptist was right. What I had viewed as a simple manifesto now took on the sinister proportions of a civil war with all the implications and consequences. None of us there had thought through what such a course would mean. Would our God indeed accomplish victory for us? Would the Messiah fulfill our agendas, hopes, and plans? Were we just whistling in the wind? I shook my head, unable to answer my own questions.

I, too, rose, stretched and moved off towards the river to wash the dust of the day from my feet and hands. As I stared at the ancient river and watched the water swirl past, I thought of all the blood and history that water had washed down into the Salt Sea. What we envisaged was more of the same. There would be suffering and death for many. We were not playing games any more.

Suddenly I was confronted with the real issues of power and knew my naiveté for what it was—a childish dream and adolescent mischief-making. We could get the Baptist killed just by enthusiastically boosting him and proclaiming him our prophet.

This was, after all, the real world we were playing in.

JESUS

The day after that conversation with Jonathon, Jesus came down to the river. The Baptist saw him first. Standing still as stone, and then with very uncharacteristic excitement, John went and greeted Jesus.

The newcomer didn't look like much to us; just a tall man in his thirties, wearing a rough woolen over-garment.

Later that day, John told us what he had seen. "One evening more than a year ago, shortly after I began to speak out publicly, I was meditating and the Spirit of God spoke to me of this day. I remember quite clearly the Spirit's instruction: that the man on whom I saw the Spirit descend was destined to be the Messiah. That is exactly what I saw today. I tried to point him out to some of you, but he disappeared into the crowd. He will be back tomorrow, no doubt, and then I will introduce you to him."

Eleazor asked, "Have you known him before?"

The Baptist nodded, "Yes, I've known him for years; in fact, we are relatives of a sort. We studied together and spent many nights in conversation, but I was surprised when the Spirit marked him as Messiah. I thought it would be someone bold and powerful, a man who would take on the powers of this world and break them in pieces."

Michael from Beersheba asked, "Are you saying this man is not strong enough? We all know what we are up against. So far there has been no opposition to speak of, but that could change. I've been with you and preparing for this person's coming for almost two years. If he is not going to do much but some more preparing, then I'm not sure I can sit still for another couple of years."

John hurried to reply. "No, this man is very thoughtful. He sees and understands others so much better than anybody else I know. He appears to know what is going on in a person by simply listening to him for ten minutes. He is very intelligent and asks the worst sort of questions. Nothing is obvious to him. As a friend I could ask for none better, but I wonder at him being the chosen Servant of God, the Holy One.

"The last I heard of him he was studying in Egypt and was supposed to be there for at least another couple of years. Here he is, and the Spirit certainly fell on him, almost like a dove alighting on its perch. The Spirit just became part of him."

The next day the man in the raw woolen over-garment came through the crowd to speak with John. They stood and talked for at least half an hour, then the stranger moved off, exchanged a word or two with a few other people and made his way through the crowd.

The Baptist came over to several of us, and exclaimed, "That's him. I mentioned you to him as wanting to talk. Just follow him. He is expecting you."

It didn't take us long to make up our minds. We hurried in the direction he had been heading, and we walked quickly to catch up with him. Before we had gone ten steps, he spun around and looked at us. His first words to us were a question. "What are you looking for?"

We didn't know what to say, so an awkward silence fell on us. Andrew finally said, "Where are you staying?"

Jesus didn't answer the question but said, "Come and see!"

That was typical of Jesus. He always wanted to know what you wanted or what you thought. Jesus would push people until they declared what they wanted and where they stood. Another aspect of Jesus was how he left everything open. "Come and see" was an invitation, which was never rescinded for any of us, right down to this day.

Here I am now, many years after that fateful day. I am old. All of those other men have died: Peter, Andrew, Matthew, Paul, Thomas and a whole lot of others, and only I am left. Those first words of Jesus still ring in my ears—*come and see!*

I glance at my tired, worn-out body. Soon, I will again be going to see where Jesus lives. His words were like that. He could say, "Let's eat," and you would find yourself thinking of his words as they referred to other things or other situations.

"Come and see," he had said, and so we did.

We followed him and introduced ourselves, and we were still there late into the evening. He probed a bit, questioned us about conditions at home, what the people wanted, and so on.

What was remarkable about that day was how he listened to us. I felt that when I spoke, Jesus thought my opinions or comments were the most important things in the universe at that moment. He had all the time in the world for me, and he wanted me to talk until I was empty. He did not critique what I said or what the others said, but you could see he was taking it in.

Jesus was not like the Baptist, who was full of certainty and moral uprightness. Rather, he came from a viewpoint far removed, and his horizon was growing as a result of listening to you. That was the difference. What I said or what the others said was important, and though we were young, hot-headed, and, as I realize now, dead wrong, Jesus did not argue, criticize our points of view, or dismiss us.

There we were, young men eager to bring change and rebellion to the country, and yet he never once put us down or denied our vision. It took us years to see beyond the horizons of this world to the horizons of the next. Jesus saw, but he was patient.

After spending a little time with Jesus, I went back to Jerusalem. A month later I again hiked the twenty miles down to the Jordan and was surprised to find a few of John's disciples from Galilee still there. Jesus had disappeared, and they were hanging around hoping he would return.

Just when I was thinking of returning to Jerusalem to get on with my life, Jesus returned. The measure of my relief indicated how much I needed a leader, or at least someone to whom I could give my allegiance. John's vision attracted so many of us, like moths to a flame. Jesus was very different. He invited us and welcomed all of us who took him seriously.

During the month I had spent back in Jerusalem I had gone over and over in my mind all the questions Jesus had asked. I wanted to go back and amplify my answers. I wanted to explain myself to him. Above all I wanted to tell him what we all needed. It never occurred to me to want to ask him what he thought needed to be done. What we all wanted was someone to lead us in accomplishing our objectives. We had become part of the problem, for we had forgotten it was the

Kingdom of God we sought and not our own ideas of a Kingdom made in our image.

I look back now, from the perspective of an old man, and everything is clear. I understand about Jesus' idea of a Kingdom, his idea of a new Israel and his idea of a revolution, but back then I felt an impatience with his searching questions and thoughtful silences. He raised questions about our assumptions and wondered about the impact of our intended actions. We tried hard to win him over to our viewpoint.

We were blind to everything but our own enthusiastic desire for radical change. We didn't call it civil war, or open revolution, but that is what it would have meant. Naïve and hot-headed, like hunting dogs that have the scent of game, we were impatient to be off.

Forty years later we saw the results of such a revolt against the temporal powers that ruled our nation. Israel ceased to exist and Jerusalem was no more.

CONVERSATIONS ON THE ROAD TO GALILEE

The men from Galilee decided they needed to go back home. Some of them had already gone, but a few had held on, hoping Jesus would return. Simon, Andrew, and Philip had been there with John the Baptist when Jesus returned, so they stayed for a few more days.

Over breakfast the next morning, Jesus joined us. I think he had been outside by himself for some hours before we ever got up. He looked across to Simon and Andrew. "Would you object if I came along with you to Galilee?" They were stunned. They looked at each other and then Simon, having gathered nods from the others, said, "Wonderful, of course, please join us. We will be delighted."

Jesus turned to me and asked, "Are you able to come with us? I know you have many things to do in Jerusalem, but I would value your company."

I thought for a moment, calculating that a message to my manager Aholiab and a word of explanation to a couple of friends would look after most contingencies. I replied, "Yes, I can take another couple of weeks off; everything is slow at this time. Shipping is mostly over for the year. So, yes, I can come."

We had been the ones to look for Jesus, to seek him out, and go over to stay with him. We hung on his words and wrestled with the questions he put to us, but none of us had considered we were anything to him. Yes, he was glad to see us. He made us welcome, and he shared a lot of his thoughts and ideas with us, but never had it crossed our minds that he wanted us around.

Were we with him, or was he with us? I think he was seeking our companionship and really wanted to be with us. The journey was four days of solid walking, and we were a close group by the time we arrived. Later, I wondered what he saw in any of us. There were all kinds of sharp people down by the river with John; why us over all of them?

In any case, we left soon after breakfast and made our way up the Jordan Valley towards the Sea of Galilee. Nobody knew Jesus then, so we slipped along without much hindrance. As we walked we walked through time. We passed where the people of Israel crossed the Jordan when they first entered their new home, and we saw where David camped. We were walking through the history of our people: the place where Elijah crossed the river, the place where Elisha fished for his axe head, where the Syrian general washed, and much more.

Here I am now on Patmos, a refugee from my own land and my own people. I miss the land of Israel so much. How we loved the very earth, rocks, trees, and rivers. Every one of them had a story to tell.

We had no idea at the time that there would be a new chapter added each time Jesus stopped, or when he had healed someone, or when he fed more than 5,000 people. Neither did we think of the Roman legions that would march that road on their way to destroy the towns of Galilee forty years later.

When I think of the pain of my people, I am saddened beyond belief, and I think afresh of my own people's deaths.

Those four days, though, were all laughter and thoughtful discussion. At one point, he asked me, "What did you think when John pointed me out as the Lamb of God, or as the one he was speaking about?"

The question took me by surprise. "What do you mean?"

Jesus again asked me, "What do you expect of the Messiah?"

"I have not thought beyond the obvious. I expect him to raise up the people, take back the country from the Romans, and reduce the crushing taxation. Above all I want to see a new and Holy Israel. In other words, I expect to see him usher in a new Israel that sees our God as the center of all life. I would especially like to see the present people who are running things at the Temple kicked out and then everything cleansed and made Holy. Another thing, I would like to see the sacrifices made available to more people and for all the extra service charges to be dropped for sacrifices of all kinds.

"And yet another thing," I went on, warming to the theme, "I want to see all our mercenaries come back. I don't want to see any more of our young men fighting battles for pagans. I would also like to see business opportunities opened up to all. Right now we who try to sell goods to the Temple authorities face price-fixing and other unfair practices. People have to be able to make a living."

"John was clear he thought you were the Messiah. I heard him myself on two occasions. You were the one he had been expecting. He had been told to expect a sign that would identify the right person when he appeared. The sign was some dove or pigeon was going to land on you or maybe anoint you." I laughed at that thought. "I did not see any funny-looking bird, but John was adamant. He saw the spirit landing on you quite clearly. That was the sign he had been waiting for."

Jesus smiled. "No, I was not anointed by a pigeon or any other kind of bird. However the spirit certainly made itself known to me the moment I came down towards John at the river. You really haven't thought too much about it, have you? I suspect you have listened to John and got ideas from other hotheads. Examine everything afresh. First of all, am I the Messiah just because John said so? What if John the Baptist is just another crazy nut? I know he is not a nut, but he could still be wrong. What makes me or anyone else a Messiah?

"You want your Messiah to save you from the Romans, save you from your rulers, and save you from yourselves. The Messiah is the Servant of God, not your servant.

"You know I disappeared for a while after I first met you. Do you know where I went and why? No? Well, I took off into the desert beyond the River Jordan. I needed to be alone with God, because I had to sort out my thoughts. Have you any idea what it was like to be told you were the Messiah? Just imagine for yourself what it was like! For years, I've had crazy ideas like that, but I've mistrusted them. In the desert, I came face to face with that question—was I indeed the Messiah? There had been plenty of crazies who thought they were, but could I possibly be the Messiah?

"For a week, I wrestled with that one question over and over again until I felt I was going mad. Do you know what finally happened? I decided to prove myself to be the Messiah, or to prove I was not. Either way, I would know.

"I said to myself, turn some of these rocks into bread, then you will know for sure. What a diabolic temptation! If I had done so, that would have been the end of me. Finally, I understood the insidious nature of the temptation. I had to utterly trust my God, my father. If he made me the Messiah, that was that!

"Remember that line in Scripture, 'Man is not to live on bread alone, but on every word that comes from the mouth of God'? Can you see how insidious that temptation is? The Baptist recognizes me, so what? I only want to be what my Father in heaven is calling me to be. If I am His Messiah, fine! The Messiah is not a title or an honor, but a horrendous role. That is what came through. I began to glimpse the enormous job to be done.

"As soon as I saw that temptation for what it was, I simply knew that my Father has called me. That was only the beginning.

"Not long after, the old devil was back with more temptations. So I was the Messiah and, yes, I was certainly a good choice, perhaps kingly material. Always distrust Satan when he agrees with you. Watch for the trap he is busy setting."

Jesus unhooked his flask and took a drink from the leather water bottle. He wiped it with his hand and offered it to me.

"What was I to do? Here I was, the Messiah, but to what end? Do you realize there is no job description in all of Scripture? There are just generalities."

He took back the flask and hung it back on its strap. "Where am I to start? My first thought was for all the poor, the troubled, or the sick. They are but a tiny part of the problem, but, as Messiah, look how much good I could do: spread the tax burden, curb crime, improve roads, and all the other issues I could solve.

"The whole moral foundation of our society needs revamping, and the spirit of those old covenants with God acclaimed afresh. Just think of what Israel would be like if the rich and powerful shared what they had with the poor. Think of what our nation would be like if the big estates were either broken up and returned to our people, or those running them did so to employ, house, and protect those who needed to work and belong.

"Roman occupation is not all bad. Their system of roads, justice, and central authority is not bad when you consider how we have suffered under people like Herod, Agrippa and a host of other tyrants whose only interest is to keep all the power and wealth for themselves.

"Look at how people are impoverished by taxes, ripped off by the moneylenders they have to go to for money to buy the next year's seed, and the land speculators who snatch up property when the small farmer can't meet all his obligations. Our people are being used, exploited, and then discarded.

"Yes, if I were King, sitting on David's throne, there is much I would change. As for Rome, we may be safer within her Empire than outside. All those hotheads who want to throw the Romans out never look down the road to see who would take their place, or what would eventually happen. No, if we were to play our cards right, we could become an example of social stability at the same time as developing our economic resources, Rome would back us."

Jesus nodded at his own words. "Now that is a thought: if I were indeed sitting on David's throne, I would offer Rome help in educating the countries under their Empire. We could make the whole Mediterranean basin one of peace, co-operation, and social responsibility. Think what that would mean for our own Jewish people living in those cities.

They would, through my direction, become respected consultants to their governments, courts, and social development committees. We would have so many people wanting to trade with us, work with us, even work for us, that Israel would be so affluent we could forgo taxes. Our own people would become moral leaders and enlightened teachers in a world fraught with gross hatred, greed, and fear."

I was taken aback for a moment and then I could see the huge potential Jesus was outlining. I said, "Yes, what a vision!" I waved my staff at the distant horizon across the Jordan Valley and went on in my excitement, "Kings and princes would come and all the peoples of the world would see Jerusalem as the source of their hope.

"Jesus, you must see these visions you have are what God wants you to do. Take power and use it. Become what you've just described. Take power and wealth so you can do all these wonderful things. If all the power resided in your hands, then you can indeed make happen just what you've described."

Jesus looked at me in silence for a long moment and then stalked on, his eyes tracing the soaring flight of a hawk off to our right. Finally, he spoke again. "In the desert, the Tempter said exactly the same thing. I needed to take power into my own hands. I had to own the means of power, and above all I had to control people, especially the ones who mattered. 'In fact,' the Tempter said, 'people who were the makers and shakers would line up behind me' if I would declare myself."

"The Tempter?" said I. "You mean all this is only a temptation?"

"Yes," said Jesus. "What the Tempter was saying was, 'Do it my way, be my Messiah, play the game like it has always been played. Dominate and subjugate people to my views and high-minded agendas and hand the whole thing over to me.'" Jesus shook his head. "Falling down and worshipping Satan would be less of a betrayal than this ransoming of God's will to the highest bidder."

"But Jesus," I said, "maybe God, may he be blessed forever, wants you to do exactly this. Why not look at it as religious reform? Take over the Temple, assume the spiritual authority over the nation, and thus make this a religious reformation. If you directed your efforts through the religious machine, the whole thing would be a Holy endeavor. The worship of our God could spread throughout the world, and you would thus create a firm basis for all the social reform you want to make."

Jesus stopped walking and stared at me, his dark eyes thoughtful and his brow furrowed. "You don't understand at all, do you? How long would it take for such a perfect system to be corrupted? One year, two years, maybe, before the natural urges of people would begin to wake up again. Greed, arrogance, fear, jealousy and remembered slights, and half-remembered hatreds would tear the fabric of the dream apart. People would fight for power; people would defend their nests and rip off those who cannot defend themselves. Who would do this? The very people we would put in power.

"No, John, there is a more profound revolution to accomplish beyond any of you young hotheads' understanding. The Messiahship is about taking the heart of stone out of people and putting in a new heart of flesh. It is nothing short of redeeming people from the inside out. I've listened to John the Baptist, and I've also heard your friends' hopes, but the Kingdom of God has got to be a whole lot more than that."

I was devastated by Jesus' words. "Do you mean that the Messiah isn't going to do any of what John the Baptist talked about? All that talk down by the river was a fire built of wet wood, all smoke and no flame? You never said you thought we were wrong. Why didn't you tell us what you were thinking?"

We had crested a hill and began the long downhill stretch to the river. As we lengthened our stride, Jesus smiled and looked at me so warmly that I felt all my anger and puzzlement dissolve.

"John," Jesus said, "don't you think I need to listen, think and then pray a great deal before ever I launch my ministry? Right there is the crux of the matter—not my ministry, but my Father's will. His program must run. Our first commandment applies to me, do you remember? 'You shall love the Lord your God with all your heart, with all your soul and with all your mind, and Him only shall you serve!'"

I looked up at Jesus and I saw on his face such a great certainty that, for a moment, I forgot there was no real answer to the questions asked. Yet, as we continued on our journey, I felt so much lighter. My mind was full of thoughts as we traveled in silence. How right he was!

Of course people would fail. Of course the next group of people with power would, after a short time, be no better than those we had. What a nightmare! But a new heart? How on earth were we going to do that and for whom? There was no way we were going to turn everyone around.

Then what was the answer? Jesus did not know! He hadn't said so, but he did not know. I was not sure whether I was disappointed or moved that he had let me share his thoughts. Finally, I smiled across at him as we walked. "You don't know what to do, do you?"

He raised his face to the sky and said, "No, not at all, and you know what? That is good enough for me right now. It's not my time yet; I'm not ready. Be patient and stick with me—you will see."

We walked another mile in silence. It was late morning and the heat was beginning to get to me. I motioned to a shady rock, well polished by previous travelers, and suggested we take a break.

As we sat there, Jesus reflected aloud, "You know, John, there is another problem I face. Whatever God's will is, whatever my Father has in mind, is going to require me conveying the idea to a whole lot of people. I will have to obtain buy-in. Imagine for a moment I am the Messiah. How do I tell other people? Do I walk up to them and say, 'Hi, I am glad to meet you. I am the Messiah'? Think, for a moment, how on earth you would tell them!

"One of the afternoons out there in the wilderness, I imagined being up on the parapet of the Temple, the platform where the trumpet is blown from. I imagined launching myself out and miraculously dropping down safely into the crowd below. After all, do you remember the text? 'Angels would bear me up lest I dash my foot against a stone.' Even Caiaphas and the rest of his cronies couldn't question my authority then.

"I knew the thought was absurd, but nevertheless, just how am I to convey to people who I am?"

I rummaged in my satchel for some raisins, found them and offered some to Jesus. I sat back, munching on the dried fruit, took a swig from my water bottle and looked across at Jesus, who sat frowning at the ground.

He continued, "After all, there have been a number of self-styled messiahs. Do you remember Simon, who led a bunch of people into the desert? Then, there was Thaddeus. Some of them were crazy, while others have been hucksters out to bamboozle the weak-hearted. So, no, I have to separate myself from that crowd."

"And you seriously thought of taking a header off the Temple parapet?" I asked.

Jesus thought for a moment and a grin broke across his face. With a short laugh, he shook his head. "No, I just thought up the most outrageous publicity stunt I could. Imagine it: I would have a few of you out in the crowd give advance notice and allow enough time for everyone in Jerusalem to be on hand to watch. I bet even Caiaphas would turn out. He would, of course, be delighted to see me spread all over the courtyard."

"I'm glad you were not serious about the jumping. I'm beginning to understand the problem. You can't really advertise that you're the Messiah because if you have to prove it to people, you've erected a barrier between them and you. They will not necessarily share your vision."

Jesus replied, "Yes, you've got it! I can't buy men's souls with trickery or manipulate them into acquiescence by force. That is not God's way, my Father forces no one to believe in Him, but He knows when people are ready to respond or understand. My Father is neither arbitrary nor manipulative, so no PR stunts, no advance publicity, no public canvassing committees."

Jesus rose and nodded down the path. "Let's try to catch up with the others. They will be wondering what has happened to us."

With that, he set off and I followed him along the path close to the riverbank. He adjusted his bag a little and continued his thought. "Of course, there is more to this question than not wowing people with mighty miracles. Everyone assumes they know what the Messiah is and is supposed to do, but even I don't know. Setting myself up as the Messiah would mean being inundated with people who wanted to control, direct, and channel my ministry along the lines of their agendas. The Tempter would love that. He would effectively hijack my ministry and force me into the hands of his own people. My answer had to be a resounding *No!* To go along with that suggestion would be tantamount to tempting God, and there is a commandment about that."

I nodded. He was correct.

We walked in silence for a while. After we'd covered almost another mile, I asked, "Then what? If you can't announce your Messiahship, and you can't seize power by force, just how do you expect to proceed?"

"Good question, John. Right now, the fewer people who know about me, the better. So, please, no talk about Messiahs or Kings even among yourselves. I believe people will recognize me for what I am in time. Remember, those who listen, hear."

A couple of other travelers caught up with us, so that was the end of the conversation. Soon, Jesus was walking with the newcomers, asking them questions and listening intently, not just to their answers, but to them.

For my part, I walked on, thinking of what Jesus had said. For the first time, I saw how difficult the situation was, and I began to get a glimpse, as if a curtain had been twitched aside, of God moving in our midst.

All around me, the heat of the Jordan Valley beat at me, but for a moment, my body was chilled and goose bumps covered my arms and legs.

GALILEE AND NAZARETH

We arrived in Capernaum in the early evening on the fourth day, and everyone gave us a great welcome. Simon, who had traveled with us, was glad to see his wife, and other members of our group returned to their households.

Jesus stayed with a local family. They introduced him to everyone in town, for by evening the word had gotten around that the men were back.

Jesus was strangely silent and withdrawn for the next few days. He was listening and pondering not only other people's comments but also his own thoughts. I had watched him enough to know how well he absorbed what was around him and mixed this new information with what he'd already known. Eventually, I knew, he would formulate an opinion and share it with us, or explain a revelation he'd had during one of the times he spent alone in prayer.

Jesus was adamant that we not mention what John had said of him, or even talk too much about his ideas. "My time has not yet come, so for the moment, put the whole thing aside."

On the third day after our arrival, rested and ready to move on, we left the rest of the group in Capernaum. He and I and two others, who were journeying to the coast, began the ascent into the hills around Nazareth. I had never been there, and when I arrived I realized why. It was a small collection of houses, a few stores in the front rooms of some, and a village well. There were the usual assorted clutter of rough shelters for various uses, but it was like a hundred other small villages throughout the Galilee. Nestled in a little V-shaped valley in the limestone hills, it was the place Jesus had grown up, and where his family still dwelled.

As we entered the village, the few people who were in the dusty street eyed us with curiosity. I was surprised that nobody greeted Jesus. The two traveling with us made their way over to the well. We turned a corner and made for a house not far from the middle of the group of houses beyond the well. Jesus led the way.

When he came to the door, I saw him pause and open the door a few inches to stick his head in the doorway. There was silence for a moment, followed by a whirl of motion inside. The door flew open, and Jesus was embraced and drawn into the house.

I decided maybe I should wait, so I sauntered over to the well and explained to my fellow travelers, "I guess he wasn't expected. I will wait a few minutes."

I looked around the village and felt my curiosity grow. Nobody had waved at us when we came into town. Nobody called out, "Hi, Jesus." I wondered how long it had been since he was here. Where had he been since he left? After a few minutes I picked up my satchel and went back to the house.

Jesus' mother was the first of the family I met. She was alone when we arrived, but the rest of the family was not far away and word spread to them fast. Soon I was introduced to his sisters, and finally his three brothers. I don't know what I had imagined, but I was surprised by how normal and ordinary they were. These folk worked. Their hands were rough, their bodies thin and hard. They were no different from any of the laborers and craftsmen seen all over Galilee.

From their conversation, things had improved economically. Sepphoris, the town five miles north of Nazareth, had developed into the governing city of the area. Consequently, building programs and hard cash infused the local economy. At least two of Jesus' brothers had found work there, and were still finishing out a large construction project at a Roman villa there. They described a whole host of non-Jewish items: hot and cold baths that had been built and mosaic work and sculptures. This was the first time they had seen images of people and living things. I should remind you that no Jew may make any carved or molded image of any living thing, and to do so was to break one of the commandments. I remember how torn the brothers were between condemning the mosaics and sculptures and really admiring the skill it took to create them. Their world was meeting another, and it created conflict.

Jesus' mother was just plain wonderful. Since I first met her that day, I have gotten to know her, and I looked after her following Jesus' death. On the day we arrived in Nazareth, she had already been a widow for more than five years. Without doubt, Mary had found her feet. She never tired of helping out, organizing things, and sometimes confronting people whom she thought needed it. However, she did it so beautifully that no one objected. Mary could get away with anything, and her sons just ate out of her hand. Even Jesus could never say no to her. Her secret was she loved everyone. When I met her, I recognized in her what had impressed me about Jesus. He really respected and loved the individuals he met.

Jesus was finally recognized and welcomed back by the entire village. While we were travelling Jesus had mentioned far away places he had visited, yet I had not realized this was the first time he had been back to his home for some years. Nobody asked where he had been, for these people knew nothing beyond their world. The conversation was of people they knew, funny situations that had occurred, or pieces of local news. Jesus joined right in, and everyone was delighted to bring him up to date.

Jesus melted back into his family as if he had not been gone. There was no mention of John the Baptist's characterization of Jesus, nor any discussion of the matters that Jesus and I had talked about. Instead, Jesus wanted to know what had been happening in his hometown and what had happened to the various people with whom he had grown up. The brothers reminisced about times past and who had married whom. His interest was more than casual. More than once I saw a shadow, as if of regret, cross his face.

I was treated well as a guest. The brothers wanted to know what I did, and when I told them I was in business in Jerusalem, they pumped me for information about what was happening there. They told me more about their work in Sephoris, and saw me as a denizen of that greater world they'd encountered.

In James I saw the beginnings of a profound curiosity about the outside world. He asked me searching questions about the prevalence of baths, of villas and what decorations were now acceptable to the inhabitants of Jerusalem. I described to him some of the latest fashions in home decorations and design, as well as explained about the confines of the city. He was very interested in the renovation of older buildings because it was just this kind of work he had been doing in Sephoris. He added that as people became more affluent they asked for enlarged and redesigned homes, especially in Sephoris.

Three days later we left Nazareth and began our return journey to Jerusalem. I was relieved to be on the road again because I was unaccustomed to the close proximity of so many. The house had been no bigger than my apartment in Jerusalem. There had been a constant coming and going as people barged in and had tête-a-têtes with Mary over anything and everything going on in the town. My head was full of questions and I couldn't wait to get to open country, away from Jesus' family and friends.

Going south, we descended from the hilly country around Nazareth and made for Caesarea and the coast road.

"Jesus," I began, "you have not been back here for years. The people of the village hardly knew you. Have you been studying, or working elsewhere?"

Jesus turned to me with a quizzical smile on his face. "I wondered when you were going to ask me about what I have been doing for the last fifteen years. It is the past fifteen years you want to know about, isn't it?"

My face blushed at being caught so blatantly. I said, carefully, "Well, you had to have been somewhere. You've been studying with someone. You've had to live somehow. You don't look as if you begged your way through life. Do you mind me asking if you were a part of that community down by the Salt Sea? I assume you were, because you seemed to know those visitors quite well. They also knew you. The other question I have is, did you know John the Baptist before? In all our conversations you have never referred to other teachers or rabbis who taught you."

"Does it matter where I have been or what I have done?" Jesus replied. "The present is where the Kingdom of God is making itself known. Yes, there were teachers, there were fellow students and John was one of them for a time. I must leave them all behind for I am not a product of their making, nor am I to be what they expect. The thing that exercises my mind day and night is what I am to do. I think I am ready to begin a teaching ministry making myself available to those who seek me out. I am thinking of following John's example and moving down by the river, away from Jerusalem. What do you think?"

"Well, I imagine you can control what happens better if you are a good day's distance from Jerusalem. I don't know how the authorities would react to you setting up shop in Jerusalem. What form do you think your ministry will take?"

Jesus looked at the ochre-colored hills surrounding us and the small farms rapidly receding from our view. "I want to reach the lost sheep of the house of Israel. How about that as a mission statement?"

"Well, that is a tall order. Several writers in scripture lament those of our people who no longer care about our nation and live like Gentiles. Who are the lost sheep in your eyes? Is it fair to ask what you hope to do for these lost sheep? What if they are happy being lost? What have you got to offer them? I don't mean to be awkward, but many of those

I have met in Jerusalem are quite happy the way things are. They are mostly estranged from our national institutions and culture. They want little or nothing to do with any of that."

Jesus nodded at that. "Yes, that is precisely the issue. The way things are right now does nothing for the person who has a token of common sense. Look at the rules, look at the requirements. Once you have played the establishment's game are you any better off? No! Are you anymore respected or accepted by the clergy? No! Do you feel better? No! So what do people get out of their subservience? Nothing! That is precisely my point. The people the present system disenfranchises are the very ones who find themselves on the outside and have little or no desire to be on the inside or, in other words, part of Israel. These are they who have no respect for the establishment and find they can do very well without it.

"That does not mean they live without God, or not find Him in their own way. Some even desire to find a way into His presence. Most of them assume they are not wanted, and therefore no point in them seeking the Lord.

"But there is a place for them. These are sought by God, and they are my objective. Do you know that merchants who are not approved by the authorities are condemned by the religious crowd as sinners, and they are put into the same class as tax collectors and other people who help make our world go round? Yet the Temple's own people are up to their elbows in trade and they are held to be holy, clean and wholesome. So what is my mission? I want to seek out those who have been told there is no place for them, and give them the good news that there is, indeed, a place for them and that it is all prepared, and their seat warmed."

As we talked I could feel the pent-up passion in Jesus. There was a deep well of righteousness that I had tapped into by my questions. Everything in me wanted to respond with a mighty affirmative, but all I could say was, "I see."

Jesus replied, "Yes, you do see, and you may not have much to say about it now, but stick with me and one day you will be telling others about just what you have seen. Meanwhile there are a lot of people who don't want to see. Nobody is as blind as those who have eyes but refuse to use them. You know, John, those too are the lost sheep of Israel. One of my favorite verses from Isaiah is that one about opening the eyes of the blind. Imagine being able to get to Caiaphas, for example, and open his eyes. I tell you, he is a lost sheep just as much as the most materialistic merchant."

"I can't imagine you getting very far with him though," I glibly laughed.

Jesus halted in full stride and I swung round to face him. He said, "But John, Caiaphas too is a child of God. Can you imagine the cost to our heavenly Father at the prospect of losing Caiaphas forever? Think of the hope he had for him when he was a child and when he was a young man. Do you think our Father has changed his mind about Caiaphas, or does He grieve over his destruction?"

We walked on in silence. I was ashamed at my shallow views, but to tell you the truth, I had sympathy for the most materialistic merchant but none for Caiaphas. He reminded me of a mule's backend.

Yet what Jesus said had to be right. God called each of us into existence with hope and expectation, so why would he not despair even over Caiaphas and continue to hope that he would make it back? I thought of a verse from one of the psalms, "Search me out, O God, and know my heart: try me and know my thoughts. See if there be any wickedness in me and lead me in the way everlasting." I saw what Jesus was talking about. All Caiaphas had to do was to earnestly pray that prayer, and that would, in effect, begin his return.

In a part of my mind I hoped Caiaphas wouldn't do this because I loved to hate him. I comforted myself with the assurance that he wouldn't even consider such an act of humility.

Jesus broke in on my thoughts. "You don't know though. Can you pray that he might, or do you, also, need to pray that prayer, 'look well if there be any wickedness in me?"

"How did you know what I was thinking? All right, I admit it. I was indulging in my personal opinion and somehow assuming God must think the same. His way is not our way, is it? I have a long way to go, don't I?"

"Don't try too hard or take it too seriously for the moment," he said, "because you have yet to see the Kingdom unfold. When you do, you will be more able to pray that prayer and many others. There is time.

"I see a town ahead. That must be Simonias. We'll take a break there. I would like to make Gabata by nightfall. The heat is not too bad this early in the year, so we can walk this afternoon."

The Return Journey

Coming down out of the hills, we walked through the fields already green with the young crops. We saw people at work, hoeing and weeding. The earth here looked fertile and deep, quite different from the stony soil we had seen in the hills.

We walked into the middle of town and made our way towards the well where a number of people congregated as usual. One woman broke away from the knot of women standing by the well and greeted us.

"Welcome! Let me draw you some water. You must be dry as a bone after walking in this heat. Where have you come from?"

Jesus smiled back at her. "Nazareth." The other people eyed us with faint curiosity and asked a couple of questions about where we were headed. The woman retrieved her water vessel and poured water into a couple of rough carved wooden cups. She handed them to us.

"Why not rest over by the fig tree there and I will bring you some bread. You look as if you could use something to eat." We sat down on a stone bench obviously placed there for just this purpose. The woman came back with a plate of dates and a hunk of coarse bread. Her daughter clung to her skirts, ogling us, staring at us with one eye and turning her face to look with the other eye. Two of the women standing nearby murmured something and one shook her head slightly as she looked at the young child.

The woman apologized for how the young girl stared at us. "Little Marion can't see very well; we don't know why. She chatters away, or she asks a string of never-ending questions, but I have to keep her with me. Here, Marion, take this plate and offer the gentlemen more dates."

Marion carefully took the plate and brought it to each of us, but with a curiously studied attention to the ground and to us. Jesus stretched out his hands to steady the plate.

"May I have some dates?" he asked her.

The little girl immediately replied. "Yes. My brother picked them." He climbed the tree. They are our best dates."

Jesus asked how many brothers she had.

"Oh, I have three brothers, and they're all working. My sister is married, so she isn't with us anymore. My favorite brother is Michael. He takes me with him wherever he goes when he's not working. He doesn't let me bang into things. I just love it when he takes my hand and lets me run with him. I really am a good runner."

Jesus surreptitiously studied the little girl and very carefully placed his hand over her eyes for just a moment. He withdrew his hand, frowned, and sat in silence for a moment, gazing out over the countryside.

The little girl inquired, "Are you going to Jerusalem? I love Jerusalem! My daddy takes us there every year. He always takes me to the Temple, and he makes a special prayer for me. Do you ever go to the Temple?"

I told her I lived in Jerusalem, and she immediately wanted to know everything about what I did and about the High Priest. Her mother came bustling back, and Jesus got to his feet.

"We must be on our way," he said. "Thank you for your bread, and may our God bless you and all your household."

I could hear the voice of little Marion. "Mommy, let me carry the pitcher. I won't drop it. I can see easily. There's no more mist; it just went away."

Jesus headed down the road, and I followed. For a time, we walked in silence. Then, half apologizing, he said, "Little Marion, can you imagine what her future would have been with poor eyesight? Who would want her? How would she earn a living? Our nation can barely care for those who can hear, see, run, and work. What hope would there have been for her?"

I stopped walking for a moment, looked at Jesus, and asked, "What do you mean, 'What hope would there have been?' Did something happen that I missed?"

"Oh, come on," Jesus shrugged, "sometimes I just can't help myself."

"What do you mean, 'help yourself'? What did you do? What happened?"

"I didn't do anything except my blessing, but I felt it happen. Just as I touched her, I felt a surge go through me. I wanted it to happen, but it wasn't me. The surge came through me. Well, I'm glad it did, but let's push on. I don't want a fuss. Maybe her mother won't notice right away."

"Do you mean you just healed little Marion?" I asked.

"Well, no, just a little adjustment. Her eyes are perfectly fine, but they needed a little help. That is all," he said.

"A little bit of help came through you. Is that what you're saying?"

"Oh, yes. That's another problem. The whole power of God is available, and sometimes there is a connection to me and things happen. The first time it happened, it scared me to death, but now I understand it is our Father's power, just waiting to be released into the world. It doesn't take much to let it happen."

"So, why not make that your ministry? You could go out and heal everyone. Goodness knows, so many need it. That would have your name on everyone's lips," I said.

"No, that takes us back to the original problem. I may not captivate people with tricks, or buy them with miracles. If I were to heal a person, then in one way, it is a sign that the Kingdom of Heaven has happened to him, our Heavenly Father has drawn near, the Spirit has moved. In other words, the healing has a radical meaning for his life. The healing is only for so long as the man lives, but the sign or meaning behind the healing is forever. Just going around healing people isn't my primary purpose."

"So, with little Marion, where's the sign for her? You didn't say anything. She can only be five years of age, so she certainly will not understand. Why, in her case, did you heal?"

"Why? Well, sometimes, I can't help it. It's a long story." At that, Jesus turned and grinned at me, "What do you think her father was praying for when he took her to the Temple? Maybe I am the answer to his prayer."

"I don't understand why you can't use the power you have for good. After all, there is that bit in Isaiah about the blind seeing, the lame walking, and the deaf hearing."

"Ah, yes, I was afraid you might mention that. Frankly, I do not yet see how this power may be used. Listen to that: 'how the power may be used.' I don't think it may be used, but it will make itself known. I have no power to turn it on, but only to deny it. That I can't do, any more than I could turn my back on Marion. Who has free will before those beautiful eyes trying so hard to see?"

With that, Jesus picked up the pace. "Come on. Let's get down out of these hills. I want to be at Caesarea by tomorrow night."

On the way over to the coast we left Mt. Carmel on our right, crossing the Kishon River. Even I could tell this area was richer and the earth more productive. Jesus was curious about everything, and he especially wanted to know firsthand about conditions in his beloved Israel. Every village or inn we came to was another scroll for him to open. People's lives, and the history of their families, were all information he craved. Therefore, as we made our way to Caesarea, Jesus took special note of the building activities; the villas going up in the foothills and the aqueduct built to supply water for the Roman cities on the coast. He made little comment about the changes, but was most interested in how the people were affected.

As we left the Galilee and entered the Roman administrative area, the Roman presence was much greater. I wasn't sure what the difference was at first, but back in the Galilee, Herod ruled or at least appeared to be in charge. The few soldiers we had seen were a scruffy lot and looked more dangerous to the average citizen than any wrong-doers. I remembered the almost furtive looks we got when we entered villages in the Galilee, as if people expected the worst.

Here in the lowlands, spread out before Caesarea, there was order. We saw one squad of Roman soldiers marching in towards the city, escorting a supply wagon, but no others until we got to the city. Yet the countryside felt secure, and people were going about their business. That third day of the journey, we met many more people along the road. We had been walking in silence for half an hour, enjoying the relative cool of the early morning and the land emerging from a light mist.

Finally, I asked Jesus, "You said earlier, on the way up to Capernaum, that our idea of the Kingdom was all wrong. You were not a little scornful of the idea of revolt and ushering in a new era for Israel, but I notice you haven't told me what your idea of the Kingdom is."

"Hmm," ruminated Jesus, "good question. First of all, it is the Kingdom of God. As such, its inception and conception belong to God. Although I understand your question, I really cannot answer it. I have a prayer I use when I meditate on the coming Kingdom. I say, 'O, Father in heaven, glorious God and Father of Israel, thy Kingdom come, thy will be done on earth like it is in heaven.' Right now, I am concentrating on listening to the Father and being instructed by His Spirit, so that I am one with God, and I merge my will in His. So, yes, I am beginning to know a little of God's will, but only as far as I discern my own notions and ideas."

"Look, I realize you don't have everything planned out, but can't you tell me a little more about your idea, or rather your Father's idea, of the Kingdom of God?" I asked.

"First of all," Jesus began," is 'when.' How about now, right now, and not in the future, but already happening now? Maybe the Kingdom is always right now. 'Where' is, of course, the next thing. Where will the Kingdom of God appear?

"How about the Kingdom of God happening right here? We can step over the threshold of the Kingdom, right here and right now."

"You mean the Kingdom is something I can make happen right here?" I said.

"No, John, you don't make it happen. Rather, you open your eyes and see, open your ears and listen, and you will realize the Kingdom of God is happening all around you now," said he.

I was stunned. "But surely," I said, "We can't just sit on our hands and do nothing. Nor can we expect change to happen unless we help the process a little."

Jesus smiled. "First, you have to learn to sit still. Next, you have to finally learn how to let go of all your own agendas and wait. Yes, *wait*, to be filled with your Father's agendas."

"'My Father's agendas'...that is something I've heard from you a lot. Why 'my father'? I am confused."

Jesus walked on for a few yards. "Don't you remember the psalmist saying, 'For it was you who formed my inward parts, you who knit me together in my mother's womb'?"

"Yes, but…"

Jesus held up his hand. "No 'yes, buts.' Just think about your origins for a moment. If God did as that psalmist said, what does it make God to you? So, no more 'yes, buts.'

"The problem we face is that, just as you don't see yourself as belonging to God, so the population in general feels the same way. If you allowed yourself to believe you were a child of God, and beloved of your father, would not you have stepped right into the Kingdom of Heaven?"

"Yes, if I can believe that, I suppose you are right; I would be there. In a way, there would be nowhere else to go."

"Good," said Jesus. "Now you understand the issue. Ushering in the Kingdom of God starts with everyone being invited to the party. The revolution is in your own heart. It's not out there, but in you."

At this, he stabbed his finger at my chest. For a moment, I got a glimpse of what he meant, but I quickly lost it. "I can't do it! I just cannot believe God knows me, takes any interest in me or, for that matter, gives much attention to my life. I can't do it! I can't make myself over."

"That is the point. That is the first part of my job, to see the stumbling block removed from your path, and to see you embrace your Heavenly Father. You appreciate how problematic it is for you, so now consider the problem of doing that for all our people. Can you see what I'm driving at?"

For a moment, I saw the vision he was describing. I looked out over the plain, with the Kishon River running through it, and I saw—melding with the beauty of the morning in that place—another beauty of the people who belonged there. Jesus smiled at me. "Now that you have caught a glimpse of the Kingdom of God, do you want to exchange it for another revolution, another bloody war in the vain hope of peace?"

I looked at him, wondering but not surprised that he knew my thoughts. In a quiet but matter-of-fact voice, he went on. "That is the Kingdom of God. I am beginning to see parts of it, but there still eludes me any idea of how this vision can become real for our people. It is God's will, Our Father's hope.

"Where to start? What are the steps by which this vision may take on sinew and flesh?" ruminated Jesus.

"Do you remember the words of Isaiah? 'Ho, everyone, come to the waters, and you that have no money, come buy and eat.' We have sold righteousness for profit, withheld forgiveness, and doled out holiness with the stinginess of moneylenders, when all the time they are free."

I paused for a moment, unslung my satchel and moved it to the other shoulder. I looked out at the horizon and could see the Great Sea way off in the distance, glinting in the sun and reflecting silver shafts of light here and there. I shook my head and walked on in thoughtful silence. Everything in me objected to the idea of forgiveness being free.

Finally I protested. "I don't see how you can change the way things are. People need to work hard at righteousness, or they won't think it worth having. People have to sacrifice to have a sense of forgiveness. If forgiveness comes too easy, then it has no value. When I sacrifice, my sense of well-being is in direct proportion to how big the sacrifice is. A couple of pigeons are good for a monthly cleansing, but at least a couple of times a year I feel it necessary to pay for a lamb. Purification can't come cheap."

Jesus smiled back at me. "Just listen to yourself. An animal has to die just so you can feel clean? Why don't you clean up your act? Then nothing has to die! Look over there. See those sheep with their lambs. Why do you need to take one of those lambs from its mother just so you can feel better?"

I looked where he was pointing. The newborn lambs were chasing each other and presented us with a spectacle of innocence. It was that innocence that made them candidates for sacrifice. That was the innocence the sinner wanted for himself. "But…" I began.

"No buts," he retorted. "You can't buy innocence."

"Okay, what about cleanliness?" I said. "You can go into Jerusalem, rub shoulders with who knows who and, by the time you come home, you could be unclean from their touch."

"Good," said Jesus. "Now we are getting somewhere. Go home, wash, change your clothes for something comfortable, and that's an end to being unclean. Don't confuse dirt and dust with sin. Cleaning up the outside is not the same as purifying the inside."

"I don't understand how you are going to get people to believe their sins are forgiven if they don't have to pay. Look at all the sacrifices the laws require every day," I replied.

"Have you ever heard these words of the Psalmist? 'If I were hungry, I would not tell you, for the world and all that is in it is mine.' Do I eat the flesh of bulls or drink the blood of goats? Offer to God a sacrifice of thanksgiving and pay your vows to the Most High.

"What do you think God wants from you? How about these words: 'Create in me a clean heart, O God, and put a new and right spirit within me?' No, it's time we abandoned this confusion of righteousness and cleanliness, of dirt and sin. Grace is free."

Jesus fell silent, and we walked on down to the plain and towards the river. He was lost in thought, as if pondering his own last question. For the life of me, I couldn't see how grace could be given away. I can remember thinking, "Grace, now that is a new idea. What does he mean by grace?"

That afternoon, we rested until the heat of midday dropped some, then we continued.

Jesus shared more of his thoughts. "The time has come for me to begin teaching what I see and know. The Baptist has part of the answer. He is calling people to repent and provides them with a ritual of cleansing. So far so good, but we have to take it one more step, namely to give people a way of understanding that they are forgiven, whole, with a new heart within them."

"How will you do that?" I asked.

"I like John's use of ablutions; people understand water, washing, and being clean. It's just that we have to take the whole idea a step further."

"How would your baptism be different? John baptized me, but it didn't do much for me. Where would you do this?"

"I would prefer to be within reach of Jerusalem. I want people to be able to find me." So Jesus sketched out his plan to begin a ministry of baptism, but a baptism of forgiveness rather than repentance. I thought that was splitting hairs, but I didn't say so.

Caesarea was our last coastal city, and on the fifth day we headed east, away from the coast and began the ascent to Jerusalem. In the distance, the Mediterranean Sea shimmered and sparkled in the sun. Vineyards cloaked the lower slopes of the mountains among which Jerusalem nestled. Fig trees and pomegranates hung in the middle of sculpted branches. Hedgerows were turning brown as summer approached.

We were taking a break on the first day after we left Caesarea and looking out to the west, where we could see the city laid out in the distance. There was the aqueduct snaking down from the north, bringing water for the whole city, and there were the harbor walls and moles embracing ships from all over the Mediterranean. We could see them loading and unloading at the wharves. As we watched, a boat rowing from the harbor passed and the next minute its sails were set, and, like a bird, the boat glided across the shimmering blue-green sea.

I wondered aloud where the boat was going and who was on board. Jesus stared at it and eventually answered, "That boat will be touching land here and there, but its real home is the sea. Sailors on it were at home and only visitors to the land. Everywhere the boat touches, there will be our people. Those boats have taken our people and spread them throughout the lands of the Mediterranean."

I asked Jesus, "Are all of our people everywhere to be part of the Kingdom of God?"

Jesus nodded his head. "Oh, yes, they are children of God and part of Israel."

"But how will we reach them, how can we include them?"

Jesus nodded at the boat now well out from the shore. "In one of those."

Then he studied Caesarea for a while and asked me, "John, can you see the theatre over there, that circular building with rows of seating? Have you ever been to a play in one of their theaters?"

Of course I had not. For us Jews, anything Greek or Roman was suspect, and we generally avoided contact with the Greek culture, which tended to corrupt our national cultural heritage.

Jesus ignored my lack of response. "There are people there who pretend to be other people, then discourse on ideas and even act out fights and passions in front of everyone. None of it is real, but like good stories everywhere, you are left wondering."

"Do you mean to say you have been to one of those plays?" I asked, surprised.

"Oh yes," said Jesus, "and I've been on one of those boats. You've no idea how big the world is physically and how broad the universe of man's thoughts."

"But Jesus, if we allow ourselves to embrace all of that," and I waved wildly at the world at my feet, "we will lose our sense of belonging to Israel. People will wander off and become like everyone else."

Jesus stood staring out towards the city fringed to the east with the deep blue of the Great Sea. "John, can you imagine your Father in Heaven making room for Gentiles? I met one or two really first-rate people, and they were not Jews. Will they be left outside the Kingdom?" could he think such things? Where had he been: Alexandria in Egypt, or Antioch in Syria? Surely he hadn't gone to Rome or to that sinkhole of iniquity, Athens?

I came over to stand beside him. We had gained a little altitude and vineyards terraced the slopes beneath us. Their brilliant new growth made the region look as if it was bursting with life. I waited beside him but said nothing. I was dumbfounded by the question. How

"You know, John, it's our Father's world and those too are his children. Yes, we are His chosen people, but we have been chosen for a purpose. Do you remember the promise to Abraham? That by his seed all the nations on earth would be blessed, or bless themselves. We may be required to hold ourselves apart from the world, and for good reason. We as a nation have been forged like an iron tool is heated, hammered and cooled by the metal worker, but to what end? Here we are at this new moment when our relationship with that world out there changes." Jesus stabbed his finger at the white city laid out in the distance.

"I told you of the temptations I experienced. Those temptations were part of this same question. In Isaiah, there is a servant of God who suffers all kinds of ill treatment and is even killed but rises again and again like Israel has. Why should Israel have to suffer? Why can't we be like every other nation and have a country without everyone trampling back and forth in it? I am beginning to think we are not supposed to have a country separated off from others.

"We as a people are called to be separate. I have met many of our people who live out there in the world and they are still children of Abraham. I see in them a bridge for a different world, but I don't see that world clearly. I feel this moment is like the time before an egg hatches and a bird is born. Will the little bird be able to break out of the hard shell? Will it survive? We are on the cusp of a massive change but I have not got a clear view of what lies ahead. Like that little bird inside the shell we are pecking away at the inside, but we have no idea of what the world outside is like because we have never seen it. I think we as a nation are going to find out."

"Surely," I began, and let my voice trail off. There was nothing to say in response to such a crazy idea. Israel was Israel, and we were not Jews by choice so why were we supposed to do anything? Jesus went on, apparently not noticing my total lack of understanding.

"I have already told you what I think about the prospects of war and believing God will come to our aid. I don't think that is on God's agenda at all. There is no future in war or in revolting and pursuing the dream of an independent nation, as our brothers the Essenes hope. They are wrong in hoping for cataclysm and judgment for the rest of the world. Israel has something to offer, but I have no idea how, or in what form we can offer what we have and have it be heard out there. How all the peoples of the world could possibly be included escapes me. I must remember to pray about it again tonight."

I asked him where he had been but he was immersed in his own thoughts and did not reply. He sat for almost an hour looking into the distance, as if trying to look beyond the horizon.

Finally he rose, dusted himself off, picked up his satchel and declared, "Time we pushed on. This is the time we scatter questions like seeds, and we have to wait for the answers to germinate and bring forth their harvest. Now let's walk and leave the questions to germinate and sprout so that we can enjoy their harvest by and by."

We made our way east, up over the golden hills toward Jerusalem. Four hours later I parted from Jesus by the city gates. He moved off, walking along the road outside the walls, where he would pick up the main path towards Jericho. I turned in through the city gates and made my way through the crush of people. After the days in the open country the crowds felt oppressive to me, and the noise was a cacophony of sounds from every direction.

I made my way back to my little apartment, squeezed between two other houses. I had been gone so long that I was surprised by how indifferent I was to its embrace. For the first time I wished I was somewhere else. I had begun to belong elsewhere.

I dropped my bag, took my stone water jug, and stepped down to the well around the corner. I washed off the dust, found a relatively clean robe, and changed out of the dust-laden clothes I had walked in for five days. I went out and picked up some bread and olives from a vendor two streets down the hill. As I sat eating by myself, I felt the lurch of loneliness. My thoughts went to Jesus, the companionship of the man, and I began to wrestle with what he had shared with me.

His ideas were not mainstream. He clearly had no plan to pursue, and of course he had never said for sure that he was the Messiah. I found myself hoping he was not. Maybe John was wrong. Jesus had little else but questions at the moment, and wouldn't the Messiah know what he was supposed to do?

I realized why I no longer felt at home in my own room. I had grown accustomed to his presence and for a moment I felt jealous of the people he would soon be sitting down to dinner with. Next week, I vowed to go see him. Who knew what would happen from there.

THE BEGINNING OF JESUS' MINISTRY

That evening I went through the days of thought and questioning I had experienced on the road. At first I was just working through my impressions of Jesus the man, but a thought occurred to me. Maybe the Baptist's disclosure had not gone unreported. Jesus may not see himself as a threat, but others might. How could I check out what was happening without raising suspicions and making things worse?

I decided to look up my friend Jonathon and sound him out on whether there was any official interest in Jesus. I was beginning to realize the enormity of Jesus' endeavor, for the world of Messiahs and Kings was not a world to play hapless games in. The players were serious heavyweights, with long memories who played by their own rules. Jesus' ideas and questioning cut right across all of their agendas and all of their assumptions. Jesus' point of view was not going to be appreciated by the powers reigning in Jerusalem, Caesarea, and Rome.

I went round the back of Annas' house and asked one of the maids to tell Jonathon I was there. She came back and reported that he couldn't remember who I was and was in any case too busy to meet with people looking for job openings.

The maid was young, and so I asked her what was going on that everyone was so uptight. She shrugged her shoulders. "Meetings. First, there was one with Caiaphas; next, with some envoys from King Herod; and then there were other comings and goings. That was all last week. Food for this lot, wine for those. Things are okay now. Would you like me to fix you a snack? I'm off duty in a few minutes."

I followed her into the servants' room beyond the kitchen. It opened onto a courtyard where a couple of servants were cleaning silver containers. They were rubbing lemon on them and polishing them with rags. The maid, whose name was Hanna, brought some wine, well-watered-down, of course, and bread, with some of the best olives I had ever tasted.

She asked me what I wanted to talk to Jonathon about. I told her I needed a job, and I thought Jonathon might know if something were coming up. I told her I could write and I knew figures and even had experience with administration of households. Hanna asked me where I met Jonathon. At that point, I decided to play it safe and downplayed our meeting as if it happened merely by chance. "I just thought he might remember me and give me a moment."

Hanna nodded and looked down at her hands. I quickly thanked her, got up, and said goodbye.

It appeared Jonathon chose not to know me anymore. Why would he do that? I could not believe he was dusting me off, but I was beginning to think there were reasons he might not want to admit knowing me. Could something have happened?

I knew where his parents lived, and I also knew he spent the Sabbath with them. When I visited them that evening, they welcomed me as one of Jonathon's friends. I explained that I wanted to see Jonathon but really didn't want to upset his schedule at work, and just as I expected, his mother immediately invited me to supper on the Sabbath.

Friday evening, I was there an hour early. Jonathon was already there. I had been fearful that perhaps I was an inconvenience for him, maybe he would give me a cool reception and even express exasperation at my appearance. Instead, he greeted me with open arms. Relief was in his voice when he said my name.

His first question was, "How is Jesus?" Followed by, "Where is he?" I filled him in with the physical details of our trip. Then, over an appetizer his mother produced for us, he started to quiz me further on what Jesus had said.

"Is he the Messiah? What do you think?"

I was wary. I remembered what Jesus had said on the way to Capernaum: "Please don't discuss messiahs among yourselves, and certainly not with others." I replied very noncommittally, "Jesus has not said he is anything of the sort, but then, he hasn't claimed to be anything at all. Why do you ask?"

Jonathon bit his nails reflectively for a moment. Yes, he was a nail biter. He very quietly told me a little of what had been going on recently.

"As you know Annas has had me compiling records of Temple receipts for this last three years and comparing them with earlier years. At first, I could see little change, but there is a small negative trend. I did not think this was anything, and in my report I downplayed the fall-off, calling it insignificant.

"Annas had me in his office and skewered me with his sarcasm. Then, he went through my figures. I was glad I had done a thorough job of collating them, or otherwise he would have had my head."

Jonathon paused, so I asked him what significance Annas ascribed to the data.

His response was cautious, as if choosing his words with care. "First, he saw the drop-off as the early indication of a trend. Next, he asked me a couple of questions about the time he sent me down to check out John the Baptist. What he wanted to know was whether John was in fact convincing people to accept his version of purification instead of that offered by the Temple, or was John merely advertising his own brand of general religious observance."

I shook my head in amusement. "That old goat doesn't know the half of it. You should hear what Jesus is thinking. Annas would have a coronary if he knew."

"John, Annas doesn't know about Jesus, but he sees the Baptist as a threat. After he had gone through my figures, he had me check through the previous two years, then another year before that. He was right; there is a trend. There has been a miniscule drop-off over the last two years, with a definite acceleration in the last six months, and it does coincide with the Baptist's appearance. Quite frankly, though, I don't see why Annas is upset because the drop is miniscule. He had Caiaphas in there for a couple of hours. Then Annas had several meetings with Mordecai, the head of Temple Intelligence.

"I heard Mordecai grumble to his second in command, 'Maybe Annas is past it, or maybe he doesn't have enough to do anymore.' Nobody is taking Annas too seriously, but Annas has quizzed most of his staff about what they know about the Baptist. You know what he found? Even some of the help had been down there to the River Jordan, and they knew about him and his message.

"Annas had a private talk with a couple of envoys from King Herod. They had been visiting with Caiaphas on the issue of Temple tax collection. As usual, I was at my desk when they came out. I heard one say to Annas, 'Herod will want to investigate this Baptist fellow. We really don't want any more crazies leading people out into the desert or causing trouble.' I saw Annas rubbing his hands together as he always does when he thinks he has done something clever. I have an idea Annas intends to use Herod against John the Baptist.

"When you turned up at Annas' house, John, I thought it best for you and me not to take chances with Annas. If he suspected I was sympathetic to the Baptist's message, he would kick me out, or worse. I doubt whether he knows you have been a disciple of John, but you could be on an old list."

I pondered what I had just heard, and replied, "When you sent back that message, Jonathon, about there being no positions open,

I realized you were warning me off. I thought something must have happened or worse still some action had already been taken. At first we thought the whole thing was a lark, but now I'm thinking we're in the middle of something serious, something very big. There are going to be repercussions. The Baptizer could be in real danger, though from what you have said the authorities are only now waking up to what is happening. I don't like the thought of Annas alerting Herod. The enemies of that fox have a habit of disappearing."

"Look," said Jonathon, "I'm concerned about John the Baptist, but I do not think Annas has heard of Jesus, or if he has, he has not heard about what John said of him. I can only think that those sent down there to report on John had not got up that early. After all it was barely mid morning when Jesus arrived. You spent the rest of the day with him, but things went on as usual by the river. John went on to say there was one among us whose sandals he was not worthy to untie, and that though he, John baptized with water, this other one would do it with fire. There was no attempt to identify Jesus directly with that statement."

I thought through what Jonathon had said, and I felt somewhat relieved. I had to add though, "Personally, if I were Annas, I would let John the Baptist alone and stay clear of Jesus. Something is coming down that goes beyond the kind of revolution we've talked about so often. I can't tell you what that is, because I don't know, but Jesus is at its center. You and I and the others must keep our mouths shut. Annas is quite capable of having Jesus disappear or meet with an accident. His reaction to John the Baptist shows he knows something is up."

Jonathon nodded in reply and I went on, "Annas is no slouch. He has been around too long to be taken unawares. For your sake, for Jesus' sake, and for your parents' sake, I would suggest you be careful about visiting with Jesus, or even mentioning him. I would imagine there will be a couple of informers hanging around Jesus' camp just as soon as he begins to open up. Everyone will be on a list. What I will do is keep you up-to-date on Jesus' activities. We need a safe place to meet."

Jonathon immediately said, "How about here. You do know that my father has already met Jesus? Some months ago, he heard him talking to a group of young seminarians. He was impressed. Look, just come by here any day at suppertime. I eat with them most nights."

I left their house later that evening full of appreciation for his family's simple faithful lives. The ritual of the Sabbath meal and following prayers soothed me. All over Israel, people like his parents were sharing their food, listening to the stories of our nation and hearing the words God has spoken to us through his chosen ones.

Why should he not do so again? Maybe? Then, I thought of Jesus and I was filled with a sense of concern for him.

I appointed myself Jesus' chief watchdog.

Decades later, as I sat on Patmos and recalled this long-ago decision, I chuckled at the thought of my efforts to protect Jesus. Thinking of what happened in the end, I said aloud to a small brown lizard crawling on the wall near my desk, "Little good did it do."

His Ministry by the Jordan

For generations we had been beaten down, our country trampled, exploited and robbed. We had been promised by all kinds of religious people that our God would step in and save us. Our enemies would be finally destroyed and God's own special agent would lead the fight and ensure victory.

Face it, we would all like to see ourselves vindicated, and our enemies thoroughly punished. Privation, famine and loss of our children, our brothers and our parents have left all of us relishing a violent solution.

Over the next three years, Jesus drew for us a picture of a very different Kingdom without the Temple and sacrifice at its center. To replace sacrifice, he gradually evolved a new path to holiness that came to be known as 'The Way.'

Before he embarked on that program, he made as public a statement of his intentions as he possibly could and all before consulting us or giving us any warning.

Not a month after we got back from our trip through Galilee and the western part of the country, he invited us to join him in Jerusalem for the feast of unleavened bread. If I had known what he intended to do, I would not have gone. He didn't exactly throw himself off the parapet of the Temple as he said when describing his temptations, but it was the next best thing.

When I joined him in Jerusalem, Jesus at first roamed through the crowd, milling around the merchants, money changers and vendors of animals for the sacrifices. I saw him gazing up at the Temple structure that housed the Holy of Holies, the very center, or navel, of our life as a nation.

From casually walking through the people, he changed to a whirl of activity. Jesus picked up some old camel reins, tied them together, and headed toward the money changers and those who sold doves. He kicked over tables, lashed the merchants with his makeshift whip, and released all the animals that had been brought there to be sold as sacrifices.

Pandemonium set in. Animals ran loose, people screamed, and the Temple guards didn't know whether to arrest Jesus, drag him off, or round up the animals! In the end, they didn't touch him, but in swept Temple Officials.

Jesus rounded on them and attacked them verbally and directly. "You have made the Temple a den of thieves, instead of a house of prayer!"

The senior member of the Temple Clergy thrust his face at Jesus and ground out, "How dare you disrupt the operation of the Temple and disrupt the chain of sacrifices for today?" He turned on his attendants and screamed, "Get those animals rounded up, set up the stalls again. Go out and reassure the people they will be able to purchase their sacrifices in a few minutes." He addressed Jesus again and snarled, "By whose authority do you dare to intervene in this way?"

Jesus stood ominously still and silent before him and quietly asserted, "I don't need any authority to stop this abominable waste of life for no good reason. Enough, no more sacrifices. This is a house of prayer, not a place of blood and death."

The Temple Official drew himself up and looked around for support. Three of his attendants had returned from rounding up animals, and they pushed closer to him. As if reassured by their presence, he spun back to Jesus. "Ha! Give us a sign that you have such authority. Let us see what authority you really have."

Jesus shook his head. "I tell you what, tear this place down and in three days I will build a new one."

"You are mad," said the official. "You are out of your mind! It has taken forty-six years to build this Temple, and you think you would build another one in three days?"

Jesus looked at the steps leading down to the lower courtyard and the city beyond. Three sheep made a sudden bolt, and down and away they went. He smiled and returned his gaze to the official. "You see," he said, shaking his head, "they are not willing sacrifices. Just give them half a chance and they know not to stay around here. What do you think all this blood and suffering achieves? None of it achieves anything."

Looking up at a row of pigeons perched on a ledge well out of reach, he shouted to the birds, "Fly! This is a place of death. Go." He clapped his hands at them, and they took off as one, wheeling away from us in the courtyard and heading east.

Jesus looked long and hard at the stunned official and slowly turned his back on him. Walking towards the steps that led us in the direction of the sheep, Jesus strolled down and away from the Temple market. No longer rooted in place by the surprising scene, I hurried after him.

"Jesus," I began, "do you realize that by now the High Priest will be fully informed of what you did, and within a few minutes he will issue orders to bring you in. Nobody talks to those people like that, especially on their home turf."

"I know, I know. If you want to break into a strong man's house, you have to tie him up first or you're in trouble. Well, just think of this as my way of starting to hobble those murderers." He sighed and walked taller as he thought of something. "Do you know why Gatus removed Annas from the post of High Priest? He was illegally killing off people who opposed him. That was too much even for the Romans. They are all men of blood and it's not animal blood either. I tell you, that place will be destroyed, along with everything that goes on there. It is only a matter of time before their violent stupidity breaks out and brings down the whole edifice."

In silence I guided Jesus down the narrow streets away from the Temple and out towards Bethany. What a day. I was very glad to go back to our camp by the Jordan.

I think Jesus may have been aware that he had gone too far, for the moment. At least, we all hoped that is what he thought, for the rest of us were scared. We were under no illusion as to what lengths the authorities would go if they felt threatened. He had challenged the whole establishment and described their operation as a pointless waste, achieving nothing.

The effect of this outburst, we realized later, was to establish Jesus as an old-style prophetic character. With this one act, his name became known to everyone who had interest in and concerns about Jerusalem and, in particular, the Temple monopoly.

This event determined for Jesus his mission statement and published it to all those who wanted to hear it.

Over the course of the next few years, influential men sought him quietly. They listened, questioned and went away to puzzle out just what he intended. Some of these were powerful financial brokers who sensed blood in the water or change in the air.

The sheets from Annas' Diary during this time period mirror this scenario, but for Annas, those observations awakened suspicion and eventually a deadly enmity. Financiers, merchants, lawyers, members of the Sanhedrin and other influential people over a three-year period gravitated towards Jesus.

Annas' concerns are best expressed in his own words.

What an outrage! Some upstart attacked us right in the Temple courtyard!

What is Caiaphas about? He had this fake prophet in his hands and he let him go!

The man has declared himself, whoever he is. I am of two minds whether to haul him in or wait. If I act precipitously, any political connections he may have will go underground. There has to be more to it than this. Why did the fellow go off the deep end and attack our merchants in the Courtyard? There is no follow-up. No other protests. He was all by himself. There were some hangers-on with him, but they did not participate. It was almost a non-event. Was it just bad planning or did he do it on the spur of the moment?

Everyone was talking about it for all of a day. This report suggests the people in the marketplace mostly didn't get it and shrugged the whole thing off. Fine.

No, we will leave him for the moment. After all, what would we charge him with? And if we got to court, he would have the chance of addressing everyone. Maybe that is what he wants, a platform. No, we will not give him a platform.

Letting the animals go like that worries me. First we had the Baptist attack our cleansing rituals and now this fellow could be attacking the sacrifices themselves. I wonder whether they are coordinating these events. Certainly, we must investigate him.

I've had no report of him before. Where is he from? Does he have followers and where is his base of operations? He is most likely another one of the crazies this place attracts. I would be inclined to forget the whole thing, but for that bit about letting the sacrificial animals go. What connection, if any, does he have with that Baptizer down by the Jordan? We need to know that.

I remember very clearly my own panic at the time, but as the days went by and there was no reaction from the authorities, I relaxed. I had no idea the event not only gave Jesus a degree of notoriety but was the first stone falling that eventually became an avalanche. Annas' suspicions would, over the years, develop into full-fledged murderous opposition to Jesus and all he stood for.

After his proclamation, Jesus settled down to proclaiming an alternative to what the Temple offered and to describing a Kingdom of God very different from that hoped for by most of us. During those early years Jesus mostly talked about what the Kingdom of God was not. He evolved his own ideas of a Kingdom of God that were not based on vindication, revenge and a repressive religious regime. Jesus' ideas were not what we as a people wanted. Some of us never got that old expectation out of our heads, and many of our brothers and sisters continue to this day, decades later, believing in a localized Kingdom set up for vindication and vengeance over those who oppressed them.

In these modern times, in light of the recent persecutions and the horrors we've been through, perpetuated first by Nero and followed by other Roman Emperors, including this last persecution by Domitian, there has been a resurgence of this way of thinking among Christians. I find myself wallowing in these same thoughts. I, and many others, wanted Jesus to return and utterly destroy our enemies. Yet that was not the message Jesus left with us. He had no vision of an earthly kingdom with all our enemies destroyed or groveling at his feet. Today, I know it will never happen.

If I am to be healed of these memories of my friends' torture and death in Ephesus, I have to give those sick hopes up. When I let myself wallow in those expectations, those scenes in the square in Ephesus still parade themselves behind my eyes day and night.

In contrast, I remember those early days when he began to teach. He gentled the people like we calm a fretful animal. He talked little about the future and never mentioned judgment to come or retribution and vengeance on our enemies. Instead he was concerned about the individual's needs. Time after time he took a person through their own experience and he helped them look at everything in an alternate way. There was no negativity or judgment but rather he evoked hope and possibility.

This is what he is doing again with me now, as I work through the horrors of these last months and write about my experiences with him in an attempt to heal myself on the Island of Patmos. Deep within me I feel connected with him still and, like a vine rooted in the earth, I feel myself rooted and drawing sustenance from the divine.

I have here the diary entry in which Annas first knows of Jesus' name and activities specifically attributed to him. Keep in mind, this was still relatively early on in Jesus' ministry, yet he had purposefully attracted the attention of the authorities. Jesus' 'in your face attitude' was intentional and from then on I always tensed against the next outbreak of his confrontational style.

Jesus of Nazareth. So, we have a name for that upstart who created all that fuss. Nazareth? That's up by Sephoris. Being from Nazareth is a lousy start for any successful career.

Here is a list of followers as far as my sources can tell. Hmm. Nobodies, all of them. Probably young men who want to spit at the world. There is nothing here to worry about except that he is friends with the Baptist. I knew it! So we have a brace of would-be prophets. God help us! We will keep our eye on him. Maybe I should send an agent down there to report back regularly.

Back then, all kinds of people came to visit with Jesus, so it was easy for Annas to have someone infiltrate our little group. After the first week or so following the Jerusalem incident, we never gave our security another thought.

I was always amazed at who sought Jesus, especially the rough customers, such as soldiers, and other hard men. I wasn't at all surprised by the good number of merchants and business people. We never knew the names of all those who came. Men occasionally brought their wives who, of course, remained at a respectful distance and took no part in the discussions. I think Jesus was especially attentive to the women who came by themselves, for they braved the social restrictions of the day. Little groups of them came together and the men clustered around Jesus looked askance at these women, for we all assumed they were prostitutes from Jerusalem who had no men to bring them or protect them. First one would come closer and listen, then others would approach. I would see the men nudged each other, but Jesus treated these women like everyone else. Some of the women did nothing more than bawl their eyes out. I fear they were not used to being treated with respect.

I was always thrilled to see the unexpected happen for people, and it did, over and over again. One day I thought to myself, John, you are seeing God move. He is doing something.

I spent as much time down by the Jordan as I could, while still keeping my business going. People came and went regularly, some staying for a couple of days, and others coming for a day and staying for a week. There were not huge crowds, but a steady stream of searchers and those who were looking for something they could ill define. Others came in hope of help with their lives. Most often these were the sick.

About eighteen months after he had started working there by the Jordan, a deputation turned up from the Essene monastery about six or seven miles south along the Salt Sea shoreline. Two of the brothers approached, and, from the time he saw them coming up the road, Jesus became quiet and wary. He greeted them, however, and went on with his teaching. After he finished, he went into the back area of the cave in which we had made our camp.

He told me afterwards that they were a deputation from the council of the Essene community and wanted to verify John's opinion that he, Jesus, was the Holy One of Israel.

"What do I say?" said Jesus. "The problem is that what they think the Messiah is, and what he should do, are not in line with what I know of God and how I understand his will. I am certainly not the Messiah they are looking for. They are going to stay the night and go back tomorrow. Why don't you sit in and listen?"

He paced. "I don't like the implications of what they are suggesting. Essentially, they want to adopt me as their Messiah and begin to promote me. They certainly have members all through Judea and especially around Jerusalem. I don't want to be owned or promoted by them. Oh, I trust them in one way, but not in another. They are earnest holy men who have longed to see the Promised of Israel. Unfortunately, I think they are wrong."

I wanted to hear more of Jesus' thoughts on this. "How are they wrong?"

It took Jesus several minutes to respond, although he ceased his pacing and eventually settled in a chair. "There will be no trumpet blast, no battles with legions of angels. There will be no victory with the eventual creation of a Kingdom like that of David.

"Would you look after those people from Hebron? There is another bunch that cannot see beyond an improved Kingdom of David. Look after them. There is food, and a little wine that Jorial left yesterday. The apricots are especially good. I need to be alone for a few hours."

With that, Jesus left, climbed up the wadi, and disappeared among the rocks and scrub that littered the area. Doing his bidding, I took food to the men from Hebron and sat with them for a while.

Simeon was the head of the Essene delegation, and he had grown restless as the day wore on without having time with Jesus. I tried engaging him in conversation, but he held himself aloof and would not respond to my advances. I could do little more than give them lunch and later some of what remained of our bread and cheese. Our stock was getting low, but this did not faze Simeon, and he went on waiting. Then in the evening, he too left the camp and wandered back into the scrub.

Night fell, and I sat waiting for Jesus to come back. When it was fully dark, the youngest member of the deputation approached us. He asked if he could come in and wait so I invited him to sit down by the fire. He looked around intently, and finally asked, "Jesus back yet?"

"No," I replied. "He is out there." I nodded towards the dark hulk of the hill behind us. "And he will be some time yet tonight. Can I get you some wine? We had a visit from a friend in Jerusalem who kindly left us a whole skin."

"No. Thank you, though. We do not use strong drink. We abstain from wine."

"Of course. I am sorry. I forgot. You Essenes mostly follow the ways of the Nazirites. I admire your dedication. I couldn't do what you do."

The young man said, "I am Tobiah and I came with the others because I wanted to see the Messiah. Now, I am confused. Is he the Messiah or not? We've not had a straight answer."

"I don't know for sure, but I would imagine that question is not as simple as you imagine. Just what kind of Messiah do you have in mind?"

Tobiah didn't reply and asked another question instead. "But if he is the Messiah, surely he would know? When Simeon asked him whether John the Baptist was right, Jesus didn't respond. He just sat there drawing in the sand. Why wouldn't he answer?"

"You don't get it, do you? Whose Messiah is he? Is he the Messiah of your people? Is that the Messiah you are asking about? Or are you asking whether he is the chosen servant of our God, one who will do the will of our Father?"

"But that is just the point. The God of Israel will appoint a Messiah who will accomplish just what you have described. We have suffered enough. We have been exploited too long. We have to throw off the shackles of imperialism, and the exploitation by greedy, power hungry and unholy clergy, and usher in a new era. It is time we saw the nations come to Jerusalem in humility and bow to the House in which the name of the Divine dwells."

I remembered the conversation between Jesus and I as we walked north towards Galilee. Jesus had described the temptations he had to work through. Here they were again, in the mouth of a young zealot who wanted so fervently to see vindication.

I saw the terrible weakness of the hope, for here before me was the flawed human into whose hands we would entrust the new Kingdom. There would be hundreds like him, struggling for power, influence and advantage. Jesus was right. What a mess.

I found myself parroting Jesus own words to me on earlier occasions. "I believe he is not concerned with whether or not he is the Messiah, but what Our Father in Heaven is calling him to do. He does not see the Messiah as a title, but as a task or job to be done. I don't think he is clear about the nature of that role or task. If he says to you, 'Yes, I am the Messiah,' you will assume he means the kind of Messiah you believe in. His task is not to listen to any of us, but to Our Father, the God of Israel. That means all our assumptions are likely to be wrong. God does not think the way we think."

"Yes," he quietly responded. "I had not thought of that. But we have studied and prayed for decades about this very subject and we are sure of the vision of the Messiah."

Two figures picked their way down the path. Simeon and Jesus came into the firelight, nodded to both of us sitting there and found seats close to the fire.

Simeon rocked back and forward as if trying to bring himself to say something. "Jesus, I just have to know. Yes, I have to take an answer back to those who sent me, but I want to know. Can't you understand how much I and others have looked forward to the moment we see the Messiah stand before us and claim his throne?"

Jesus didn't answer for the longest time. Finally Simeon said, "Why can't you answer?"

"The question is too simple," said Jesus. "The issue is more complicated than just yes or no."

Then, Simeon began to tell him what the council had said when they heard John the Baptist had recognized him as the Messiah. "The prevailing view is that John was wrong to declare you the Messiah. Many of the senior members remembered the struggle they had with you as a novice and even more so later. You constantly challenged their views and their authority as they exercised it. Jesus, you made enemies among some of the other men, and you even questioned some of the Community's rules."

Simeon paused a moment and, with a slight smile, said to me, "Did you know they finally sent him off to Egypt to study with the Therapeutae Brothers? Then he went to Damascus. The real problem arose on the way from Egypt to Damascus. He went up the coast road through Joppa, up though Caesarea to Tyre, then over through Galilee."

I broke in. "What's wrong with that?"

"Jesus didn't just travel through those places. He stayed in Alexandria; he stayed in Caesarea. There is a rumor that he went to the theater there. He sat among Gentiles; he listened to their entertainment. He defiled himself, not only by their touch, but also by listening to their words. We have reports he spent days in taverns by the docks in Caesarea and Tyre. He talked with their seamen and even went on board one of their boats."

Simeon glanced around the group and settled his gaze on Jesus. "No wonder the council doubts John the Baptist's opinion. This is not the way the Lord's Messiah should behave."

Jesus simply smiled. "You really do have a problem, don't you?" He dropped his eyes to the fire, a faint smile on his face. Was he, perhaps, recalling memories that had been stirred by Simeon's disclosures of his past?

Shrugging his shoulders, Jesus once again focused on us. "Those were not rumors; they were reports of just a few adventures I had. There is so much to know about the world. One of the most important things I discovered was that I was not defiled by anything going on around me, wherever I was. No, don't look aghast, it is true. Have you thought that we who are dedicated to our Father, the Holy One, take with us holiness and it is we that contaminate evil with good?"

I looked up sharply, for the idea was new to me.

Jesus knew he had our full attention. "I found that wherever I went, people were just the same. Their children were just as beautiful and innocent as any Jewish child of the strictest observer of our faith. It was true of Gentiles as well as our brothers who appear to us to have exiled themselves from the Covenant. I do not know what this means, and I refuse to speculate or speak of this among the people. This is a question I must ask, and I don't blame you for being alarmed at it. However, it is a relevant question when considering the role of the Messiah."

Silence gathered around us as we each considered the implications of what Jesus had just said. I debated about putting more wood on the fire, but remembered we would likely need some for breakfast, and decided to save what little wood we had left. A slight breeze from the canyon behind us brightened the fire for a moment.

As if the fire had prompted him, Simeon looked at Jesus and commented on Jesus' most recent opinion on the role of the Messiah. "The problem, as I see it, is that you and John are operating on your own. The council doesn't think you are the Messiah, which means only John the Baptist thinks you are. The general opinion of John is that he is a little crazy, and I agree. He has lived a solitary life for too long. When we thrust him out of the community he took to the dessert. We heard he was living off the land, roaming the wadis and avoiding human contact. The next thing we heard was that eighteen months ago he began to attract people to himself. He was preaching and exhorting them to prepare for the Day of the Lord. He was doing exactly what we were doing in our community, but the people he was inviting were any who would listen. He used our lustrations of purity and our words of cleansing for all kinds of people. There was no period of preparation, no years of study. He invited all those unclean, compromised, and decadent people to repent? The view of the brotherhood is we've got to clean house, not clutter it up with people like that. I saw women down there. They had no husbands, if you get my meaning. John even talked with them. He baptized them! I shouldn't wonder if the water that ran off of them didn't contaminate the whole of the Jordan. So are we going to take John's word? Not likely. That brings me back to you. The reports we had of your adventures cause us to seriously doubt you have any future place or role in the coming Kingdom, let alone be its prime mover."

Simeon didn't stop there and was warming to his unvarnished comments. "Let me give you an example." He looked over to me and said, "You should know that we don't drink wine or other alcoholic drinks, but we had reports of Jesus in those taverns." He again addressed himself to Jesus and continued, "When you were in those taverns, or with people like merchants, you were seen to drink wine. We don't have reports of just one occasion but four or five times, and each time we have two or more witnesses. Worse still, you have showed no shame or regret, nor do you deny it. I tell you, we just cannot have a wine imbiber as the Messiah."

During Simeon's diatribe, Jesus sat still, his face inscrutable. He let Simeon's words settle before he spoke. "As you say, I am a wine drinker, I mingle with the crowds, and I do not protect myself from the unclean or even the diseased. I have even been known to dance."

Simeon jumped up and shook his finger at Jesus. "Will you take this seriously? Okay, maybe you are and maybe you are not. Please, let's be serious for a moment. Personally, I think John the Baptist has been out in the sun too much, and you've become another opportunist. No, I don't think you are crazy, but I think you're beginning to like the idea of being the Messiah and you are playing hard to get. Jesus, I always thought a lot of you. I thought you had so much potential, but now I am beginning to doubt my judgment. Help me, say something to refute our objections, deny our allegations."

Jesus stared at Simeon and I swear he was reading Simeon just as you would a scroll. He finally smiled. I tell you, that smile said more than words, for it also contained affection for Simeon.

All the tension was gone. Simeon kind of collapsed and sat back down, all of his official displeasure leaking out and blowing away on the evening breeze.

Calmer now, Simeon still had something to say. "Look, Jesus, you need to know for sure. If word gets around that John the Baptist has proclaimed you Messiah, and it will, you will be in danger. There are people in Jerusalem who don't like self-styled Messiahs. They play rough. Let me suggest something. Just between you and us, why not do a little test. Moses, Elijah, and the other leaders were able to do signs. Moses beat water out of a rock; Elijah pulled some amazing things. How about you? Some of the reports we got from the Therapeutae were very positive. You have a gift for healing."

"You want me to run a test? Prove to myself and to you whether I am the Messiah or not?"

"Right! How did you guess? Just something minor will do. If you have the power then okay, we can talk about the next steps, but if nothing happens, you pack up and go home. How about it?"

"No!"

"No!"

"No?" said Simeon. "You need confirmation that you are the Messiah. Look, the Messiah is going to need legions of angels—where are yours? You're going to have to fight battles—what experience do you have? There is a world out there that has to be overcome!"

"Ah, yes," said Jesus, "legions of angels! I don't think I am going to need them."

Simeon tried again. "Jesus, the issue is you still need to know for sure if you are the Messiah. Try a little test."

"Absolutely not!" Jesus cried. "Simeon, you are wrong. There will be no test. I've been through this already. There was an occasion several months ago when I was wrestling with this very question and I thought, why not turn a couple of rocks into bread? I could feed a lot of people that way, and as you may know there are a lot of hungry people out there and the one thing Israel has a lot of is rocks. But I told myself no. Do you remember the words, 'Man cannot live by bread alone…'?"

Simeon filled in the rest. "But by every word that proceeds out of the mouth of God.'"

"Yes, you see, Simeon," Jesus continued, "that is the point. It doesn't matter what you think, or what I think, about this issue. I find it important not to know, but rather to have to trust God, and serve Him. In other words, I am satisfied to do the work He wants and walk one step at a time."

Simeon stared at the ground for a while. "All right, I see what you mean. No tests then, but will you tell me when you know?"

Jesus frowned. Looking at Simeon with that concentration he reserved for certain situations or people, he said very quietly, "Simeon, let everything drop. Let it go. You cannot carry the world on your shoulders. Join me, work with me, and let's watch God at work."

He continued, knowing Simeon was listening closely. "Sometimes, I feel like a very small child with God and that I want to imitate Him, just as a little child imitates his parents, but now he is calling me to stand with Him like a grown son. I would like to say to my Father in Heaven, 'I'm not ready,' but no son is ever ready to stand beside his father as a grown man. This is my issue, to take on myself the authority our Father alone can give. He gives it to him whom he calls—no other. Once I say yes to that authority, there can be no turning back and nothing held back. No one plows a furrow and keeps looking back."

Simeon and I sat there for a while, both of us quiet while we pondered Jesus' dilemma. Then Simeon stood up. "I think I understand. You have to make perfect your own will to present yourself to our Father in Heaven as a perfect and pure gift, even a sacrifice, as it were. I can see," he went on, "that to do so is not to be confused with outward compliance, the adoption of a job description, or even agreeing on a mission statement. It doesn't have anything to do with whether you drank wine or with whom you rubbed shoulders. I am sorry I brought that up. How insignificant."

Simeon drew a deep breath and continued in a subdued tone. "I don't know how to put this, but maybe I have to do the same. I am all wrapped up in our common objectives, goals, and behavioral norms, and I have taken back what I thought I had given to my God. I've fallen away; I have been all wrapped up in my own thoughts, dazzled by my own expectations, and I've put them all into the mouth of our God then pretended they came from Him."

None of us said anything, and Simeon shrugged. "So, what do I tell the brothers? 'Maybe he is the Messiah, or maybe not?'" Simeone shook his head, not at all satisfied. "Jesus, leave us out of the equation, for now. Don't count us out, but give us time. Meanwhile, what if you make contact with our community in Jerusalem? They are good men and closer to the world to which you are sent. Oh, yes, I believe you are sent to the world, all right; I just don't see the way you must take."

Jesus thanked him. "Simeon, when you walked in today, I knew why you had come. I did not want to answer you. Little by little, I am coming to that crucial moment of decision. I know what it will be, but, as I said, it has to be total and perfect.

"Now I have a thought for you. It's a gift, as it were, something for you to unpack when you are ready. Does our Father in Heaven want to save Israel, his people, or does he want to save the world, His world that he created?"

Simeon embraced Jesus. "Shalom."

Tobiah, the young man from Bet Yahud, had politely remained apart from the discussion. I knew he must have overheard it all, but I could not tell what was going on in his mind.

After Simeon left, Tobiah told me, "Now I'm even more confused."

He held himself rigidly away from Jesus as he went to embrace him. "I am sorry, I apologize, I came here thinking one thing, and now I don't know where I am or what to believe. I had hoped, but now I am bewildered. I don't know what to do."

Jesus said, "Shalom, my friend. Go back, and do not try to find an answer to your question. If you can just wait in patience, the answer will find you but in God's time."

With that, Tobiah went to the doorway. He lingered for a moment, then, with considerable sadness, said, "Thank you. I will wait, and maybe I will come back." With one last glance at Jesus, he said, "Shalom," and ducked out into the gathering dusk.

Jesus looked across the fire at me. "I was not ready to talk to Simeon tonight because, although he means well, he would misunderstand what I intend to do. You've seen enough of the operations of the Temple to know that mess has got to be rooted out of the midst of the nation. While that is there, people will turn to it and everything that goes on there, to satisfy their superstition.

"I also recognize I have a lot of teaching to do. There are many who are disenfranchised or disgusted with what goes on, and I have something very positive to offer them in response to their questing. If we take down the Temple operation, and we deny the efficacy of sacrifice, for example, we have to offer them something else. There are curious ideas about God that wash around Jerusalem. I have to give the people an alternative glimpse of the real nature of the God of Israel.

"That brings me to the next point. I have to create among the people a sense of belonging with each other, and without any organization, give them a sense of their freedom to think and decide for themselves. When we can bring these objectives together, people will be able to choose for themselves and no longer give allegiance out of fear and superstition. At the heart of all of us is the spirit that our Father placed there at creation, and I must clear away the nonsense, so that spirit can be let loose.

"All this has to be done before we ever talk of the Kingdom of God. There is a lot of ground preparation necessary."

I sat back against the rock wall and thought about everything we'd discussed tonight. I could see things falling in place for Jesus, but I could not see how he was going to achieve his goals. The Temple wasn't going to blow away in the wind, nor were people likely to change because he said they should. "How are you going to do this? Do you have any specific plans?"

"I must spend more time in Jerusalem. I can't hide out here. These last few months have been useful, and they've given me introductions to some interesting people. I'm now known in Jerusalem, and so I can build on that."

I asked the obvious question. "Have you considered the danger? If they are thinking of arresting John, how much more easy will it be for them to take you?"

"This has to be done in the open. No secret meetings or organizations. The authorities can hear everything and engage me if they choose."

I nodded my head as if I agreed but secretly I was alarmed at the thought of Jesus walking right into the Temple square and saying out loud what he had said to me. I also knew it was no good for me to express my alarm. He would reassure me against my better judgment, then persuade me to go with him, and that was exactly what happened.

NICODEMUS

After Simeon's visit, Jesus seemed freed from constraints. Over the next year he occasionally visited Jerusalem and stayed with Lazarus, a young man who lived outside the city in the village of Bethany. Mary and Martha, his sisters, were great women and made us welcome from the start. Lazarus was one of the up-and-coming movers and shakers. I knew he was well connected to members of the government and, as I realized later, knew and was known by a lot of the right people there in Jerusalem.

Jesus did not spend all his time by the Jordan but moved about, visiting other cities and communities. He visited as far north as Galilee and went to visit his family in Nazareth. Basically, he walked the length of the country, meeting and teaching people on the way. Sometimes I went along, but at other times he went alone.

Later, the people he met on those journeys looked him up in Jerusalem when they attended the festivals. After three years or so Jesus had laid down a network of people who sought him and addressed him as Master or Rabbi. Respect for him as a teacher grew. He prepared many to look forward to a new way, or path, to righteousness. Many of these people were so receptive to the teachings that we disciples offered years later.

In Jerusalem he was not only known among the influential members of the community, but was frequently a guest of the Essene community in Jerusalem. They welcomed him as a fellow brother, and accorded him hospitality and spiritual companionship.

During the next three years, Jesus discreetly formed friendships with many throughout Jerusalem. Pharisees, members of the Sanhedrin, officials who worked at the Temple and other governmental offices, and those who brokered power all found their way to Lazarus' house and sat with Jesus for long hours over meals. There were merchants, lawyers and students from the Temple schools.

One night, a member of the Sanhedrin came to talk with Jesus. We were again staying with Lazarus and his sisters. His name was Nicodemus. He started out reasonably, admitting Jesus' authority, and you could see he was trying his best. Jesus just waded right in.

Instead of replying to Nicodemus, Jesus said, "You have to be born anew." What on earth did he mean? Nicodemus was so puzzled he blabbered on about going back into the mother's womb and being born all over again. The poor guy couldn't get it right. I think the obtuseness of Nicodemus surprised Jesus.

"What? You are a leader of the people, and you don't get it?" said he. "If you can't understand this, how are you going to understand the rest of what you need to know?"

Nicodemus left, and Jesus was kind of quiet for a while. I was a little upset by the way Jesus set the bar so high for Nicodemus. After all, he was a member of the Sanhedrin and he had shown courage and goodwill in coming to see Jesus.

These were early days. Already, the Temple intelligence services were beginning to take notice. "The Temple Intelligence Commission"... that's an oxymoron if ever there was one. They were a nasty bunch. I got to see them up close later on, and, of course, Annas used them to pull Jesus in.

At the time, I didn't realize the impact Annas would have on all of us. Years later, as I read excerpts from his diary, I uncover more examples of his greed and power-hungry scheming. In this excerpt, and from this point forward, Jesus was firmly on Annas' watch list.

Tuesday, late in the evening

I see here in this report Jesus of Nazareth is developing good connections. He's close to Lazarus and his sisters. Nicodemus of the Sanhedrin and Matthias the banker are mentioned.

Here's one I am surprised to see. He is crooked as a camel's hind leg. And look at these last ones. All of them are merchants but none of them are part of our Temple operations. Is that significant?

This Jesus must know what kind of people they are. So why does he humor them? I must look into this. Tomorrow I will review whatever additional information we have at hand. I think I would like to take a look at the political background of some of these people.

Wednesday

My secretary has just brought in the documents I asked for on that list of names in the report on Jesus. I see that he has been courted by a number of people I would have thought would be the last people on earth to want to listen to a prophet or whatever he is.

Here is another, he would sell his own mother if there was a buyer. Knowing her though, there will never be a buyer. Spare me from such people.

I don't get it. Who is courting who? Are they courting Jesus, hoping he'll turn out to have some serious clout, or is he courting them?

Maybe he's just glad to have a full meal and a cup of wine.

Now that is an interesting question. Who does this fellow get his food from? The Baptizer apparently ate anything he could catch, but I see this man likes real food and not a little wine. He is no Essene for sure, they are an abstemious bunch of killjoys. No wine, no sex, just study, write and not much else. I see he has gathered a regular coterie of disciples.

I must ask for a full list of his followers. His disciples are probably misguided young men who will not amount to much on their own, but his other supporters are investing in him. What do they hope to gain?

Monday, four weeks later

A month ago I asked for a list of the Nazarene's supporters. Here it is, and I don't like what I see. There are more here than I expected. I should have paid attention to those early reports.

So, if he is no Essene, likes his food and drink, doesn't fast much, and generally acts authoritatively around anyone who will listen to him, what is his intention?

So what is he teaching that these people want to support him? There are amounts against most of these names and they are significant amounts of cash, though not enough to suggest any kind of preparation for uprising or anything like that. Donations are regular, as if for running expenses. So, he has substantial support on the one hand, but he is not looking for large scale investment on the other.

In comparing the new report with this three month old report and the one from last month, I see that the numbers of people seeking him out are not huge but constant. He has been at it for three years and the stream of people has not dried up. What is it they are hearing? Why do they go back to him?

He has kept a low profile in Jerusalem, but I see here there have been a number of visits, particularly at festival times. I suppose while he stays on the periphery we can leave him alone. His operation seems to be the other side of the Jordan just like the Baptizer. Miracles seem to be his big draw. That may explain a lot of the regular stream of people seeing him over a long period of time. I wonder if he is any good. My sciatica could do with a little help.

Miracles mean he is a fake, he has something to hide, and that means he is on the make somehow. At present he is useful, for the crowd needs someone to look to and follow. They'll be happy with him for a while and move on, especially if he's full of promises he can't fulfill or miracles that don't last.

No, we'll watch him, check out his contacts and look for the real threat to come from there. The more I think of it, the more I am concerned about a cabal, a secret group of men on the make who have found themselves a figure head to rally the people around.

I wonder how best to deal with this. If there is some secret conspiracy developing, the Nazarene might lead me to it. I must get Jonathon to send my agents a directive with new instructions.

Shall I tell Caiaphas and have him bring it up at the Sanhedrin? No! Better to limit the exposure for the time being. There may even be Sanhedrin members who are part of any such cabal and I would give them warning. I don't want to do that. I think the next thing to do is look for any evidence that a political power group is forming around him. I need to hear more about what he is teaching. Those two things are enough for now.

This has just come in. It's a report of a dinner meeting last night between the Nazarene and a group of business people. An old friend of mine was there as an influential Pharisee. The guest list reads like a who's who of old family businesses in town. What is the head tax farmer doing hosting such a dinner meeting? He has nothing in common with any religious person, prophet or no prophet. I am surprised those Pharisees went, but I guess they are like anyone else, the thought of a good meal salves anyone's conscience. I wonder what they talked about. Maybe I should ask Elias to stop by.

The night Nicodemus came to us was definitely a turning point. Up to that moment, Jesus had been content to teach, heal and baptize. I think maybe, after Nicodemus, Jesus realized he had to become more proactive in his teaching. He already knew that offering an alternative to the sacrificial system would take a lot of patience and widespread, long-term teaching on a new set of fundamentals.

Annas had still more to say about Jesus during this time period.

Well, this Jesus has been a fixture for three years now, but mostly keeping to himself down by the Jordan. People continue to seek him out, but he is not aggressively recruiting followers. Unlike John the Baptist he has not sought to develop a following. Also unlike the Baptist, he collects makers and shakers as if he were one of them. I see his social activity has increased this last twelve months. Maybe he is ready to make his move and now has or soon will have the backing he needs.

The other possibility is merchants who are not licensed for the Temple Courtyard are backing him. His opposition to our operations is well known now and he would make a natural partner for them. Could this be the start of a planned campaign against our businesses? I got no word from my agent observing that group. I will send word to him to penetrate the group more fully. I need him to forewarn me of the next planned attack. If we knew when, we could be ready for him and take him.

Now what? I think it time to tighten up on the licensing for merchants operating in the precincts of the Temple. I think an increase is called for. It's almost four years since we had any increase.

I've got to talk to Caiaphas about all this.

Next day

Caiaphas was no use at all.

What worries me is who is behind this Jesus. This doesn't feel right. He is going after the power brokers. Why? What kind of promises is he making? Those people don't do anything for nothing, but they always have their noses to the wind scenting out trouble or prey. Do they think we here at the Temple are vulnerable? What do they know and we don't know?

Here is another report of an innocent dinner party. These people don't know innocence. Their interest may be procuring entry into the Temple markets.

Should we open the licensing process to all and invite bidding for contracts and licensing? I really don't want to do that, but would it bring those people into our circle? That is an option. I will have to see how things develop.

12

MAKERS AND SHAKERS

Reading that entry from Annas' diary has brought back the whole thing to me. How long ago that event was, yet my memories of it now are clear as a bell.

I was at that dinner. We were invited to the house of one of the head banking families. He also invited six other businessmen and five or so Pharisees. Thomas, Nathaniel, Judas and of course Jesus filled out the guest list around the table that night.

I remember the house with sumptuous floor and wall coverings littering the place. Wine was poured, plates of tasty morsels were circulated as we mingled with each other. Finally we were all there and we were seated at one of the most beautiful dinner tables I have ever seen. It must have been imported from Africa for it was not a wood from Judea. It was a high polished dark brown heavily grained wood. We drank from silver cups and washed our fingers in bowls of scented water beside each plate.

Judas bent over to me and whispered, "Why am I always in the wrong business?"

They drew Jesus into their conversation, treating him with warmth and an easy familiarity. He responded in kind. He was not put off by their business stories or their attitudes. He was relaxed and enjoying the humor and debate that ran round the room.

Just when everything was going well, the Pharisees, who were sitting in a group by themselves, began to snipe at what they saw as failings in Jesus. "He eats with tax collectors and merchants." "I cannot understand what Jesus sees in these men. They are tradesmen. Their whole life is buying, selling, and lending."

Jesus rounded on them. "These also are sons of Israel and therefore part of the Kingdom of God." With that he had the attention of the whole room. "The way you look down on your brothers is not good, but there is more to this than you might think. Imagine a shepherd who found one of his sheep had strayed. He left the flock and hunted all over for the lost sheep, and when he found it he came down from the hills and that night invited all his neighbors in to celebrate his finding the sheep.

"Lighten up, let loose, be glad these people are showing an interest, for heaven's sake," Jesus told them, and launched into another parable that advanced his teaching another step. "There was a woman who lost one of her dowry coins. The woman turned out her whole house and searched until she found it. Then, like the shepherd, she said to her friends, 'Come on over and rejoice with me; I have found the coin I had lost.'"

Jesus leaned in, capturing everyone's attention. "Just as the woman lost part of her history, her dowry, this part of herself, so God has lost part of Himself in losing these sons of Israel and He delights in their return."

Silence fell on everyone. The clink of the servants setting down the dishes for the next course was the only sound.

Jesus began another story. "A rich man had two sons and the younger son demanded money from his father, left home, travelling to distant places and living a riotous life wherever he found himself. He bought friends and companionship by lavishing gifts and entertainment on those he attracted. When his money gave out nobody returned his generosity, and his so-called friends dropped him. He got a job feeding pigs. Then one day when he was so low he had to look up to see bottom, he said to himself, 'What am I doing here? My father has servants better off than me. Enough! I will go home. I will tell Father just what a fool I have been and ask to be taken on as one of the hired help.'"

"His father had never given up hope he would come back and one day he saw him. Though still almost half a mile away he knew it was him. He ran out to meet him, threw his arms round him, dragged him into the house and dressed him up and put the family ring on his finger, gave orders for the fatted calf to be butchered and a feast to be prepared. The young man never got a chance to say anything."

I saw one of the guests pause with his cup to his lips, then, without drinking, set it down. He wiped a hand over his face and stared at the table.

Jesus went on, "Meanwhile, the older son was as usual working out in the fields, and when he heard what was happening, he was mad. When his father came out to him, he ground out, 'You've never given me so much as a baby goat to have a party with my friends, but this son of yours drags his sorry self home after going through your money with a bunch of worthless people and you are celebrating with a whole calf? It's not fair!'

"Then his father said, 'But son, this brother of yours was lost and is found. It is a great occasion and we have to celebrate it. Relax, everything I have is yours; you are always with me. Come on in and enjoy the party.'"

Relax, everything I have is yours; you are always with me. Join the party. I still hear those words and remember the faces of the self-righteous clergy sitting there isolated and stuck in their ugliness. Jesus looked over at them and I saw three of them nod ever so slightly at him, and they waited for him to go on.

After a minute of collecting his thoughts, Jesus looked at us four disciples and began a companion parable to the earlier one. "A rich man had a steward who had been effectively destroying his business. He called the steward to him and warned him, 'I am auditing the accounts, and if what I hear is true, you are out of here.'"

I saw the businessmen prick up their ears, and one nodded his head in deprecating agreement. "Yep, I have one of those."

Jesus smiled over at him and went on. "But this one knew the game was up and he would therefore be out on the street. Faced with that prospect, he came up with a scheme he thought might net him another job. He called all those who owed money to the business and promptly went about currying favor with the debtors by giving them huge discounts for cash. His intent was to tap them for a position later on. The first one came in and the steward asked, 'How much do you owe?' The man replied, 'A hundred gallons of olive oil.' I tell you what, give me cash for fifty gallons and we will call it paid.' The next man came in and when asked how much do you owe said, "A hundred bushels of wheat.' Again the steward said, 'Okay, we will call it paid in full if you can give me cash for eighty bushels.' Customers were only too glad to take advantage of the deals he was offering them and all the others who owed large amounts were happy to settle up."

There was a general shaking of heads at the other end of the table at this point, and one man said, "I would take the deal, but, no, I wouldn't hire him. Who would want such a weasel?"

Jesus nodded in agreement, and went on. "In came the owner of the wholesale business and began his audit. He saw from the accounts and the cash in the drawer exactly what the steward had done, but did not know the steward's reasoning. In consequence, he said, 'Well done!' The steward had, in the first place, created a cash flow crisis by offering or allowing extended lines of credit to people who shouldn't have them. The business stalled and without cash flow was in danger of serious failure."

He addressed the businessmen. "Am I right?" They nodded. "When the steward offered his special deal, he was in effect applying the one solution to getting things going. He effectively discounted the amounts owed, collected what he could get, and that returned the business to a viable state. He was doing the right thing for the wrong reason." Laughter erupted from the businessmen, but they sobered as the full meaning hit them.

His audacity! I saw that Jesus was holding the businessman up as an example, using him to illustrate God's attitude to sin. I took a couple of minutes to work it out, but Jesus was saying, "God is like a business-man who is not interested in what cannot be collected but only in what can be collected so that he can get on with business. God is not in the business of debt collection but making life happen."

He looked at Judas, Thomas and me. "You can learn a lesson from these people. They know more about human nature than a raft of reli-gious people, so listen to them."

Jesus took his wine cup and drank from it, then lowering it, fixed his attention on the businessmen. "Your wealth gives you power," he began, "but you may not misuse either to victimize others. Divorce for your own convenience and other easy outs are not acceptable. That is an abuse of your power and position. There is something else, you have responsibilities beyond your own interests. Let me put it this way: There was a rich man who had everything he ever wanted and saw no reason to take others into his consideration. He especially ignored the unpleasant realities of the world around him.

"Every day he left his house and he never noticed a beggar who was to be seen daily, right outside his gate. The beggar—let's call him Lazarus—died and was received by Abraham as one of his own. The rich man died, and he found himself in torment. From a long way off, the rich man could see Abraham, who was attended by the beggar the rich man had finally recognized. The rich man said, 'Father Abraham, please send Lazarus down to just cool my tongue with a little water. I am burning up in this heat.'

"Old Father Abraham shook his head. 'You had your good life and Lazarus his hell. Now you have to make up for it. Anyway, you can't get there from here.' The rich man begged, 'Father Abraham, please send someone to my family, to warn my brothers so they don't end up here.' Abraham said, 'No. They have the law and the prophets, so they should know by now what their responsibilities are.'"

I saw Jesus plunk his hands flat on the table and look at the businessmen and taking them in one at a time, said, "It is not enough for you to not misuse your power to oppress others, but you have to accept responsibility for those less fortunate or capable than yourselves. You all know this deep in your hearts. So use your great gifts and skill to help others. They too are children of Abraham, and without them, you cannot participate in eternal life. We belong together."

Conversation erupted all around the table as men checked with their neighbors about what Jesus had meant. Jesus took a sip of wine and looked around at the hubbub of conversation. With a small nod, he bent to his plate and began to eat. Thomas gave me a surreptitious thumbs-up. Nobody had escaped unscathed.

On another occasion, we were staying with Lazarus and his sisters, Martha and Mary, when we were visited by three Pharisees, Annanias, Martheus and Janus. They were treated with familiarity by Lazarus and welcomed to partake of a meal that Martha expertly threw together as if she had known there would be guests. During the meal the three felt Jesus out with very general questions, and Jesus waited for their real concerns to emerge. I sipped slowly from my wine, waited and watched. I had seen this skirmishing before, as people came to argue about prepared positions or to challenge Jesus with test questions.

Finally Janus asked, "Why do bad things happen to good people? And what is the point of observance of the law if it provides no protection from the vagaries of nature?" Jesus refused to be drawn out immediately. He sat looking from one to the other inviting them to enlarge on the issue. Martha came in just then, cleared the last of the dishes from the table, and placed two lamps in the darkening room.

Comments flew back and forth. Martheus said, "I believe we must apply our minds to understand God. There is no such thing as Fate. Everything depends on us doing the right thing. If a person is struck by lightning then it is because of sin. If we could know all the details then we would see that the cause was either his sin, the sins of his parents or maybe even grandparents."

I thought that was nonsense and I waited anxiously for Jesus to squash them. They had come hoping to trap him. Jesus still did nothing, forcing the others to dig themselves in deeper.

Janus picked up the point and between mouthfuls, continued, "I must add, too, that if all the people become obedient to the Law, then we would not see such accidents and the suffering of the people would be greatly diminished. We would in effect see the dawning of the promised Kingdom."

Martheus continued, "You have to realize all actions bring their consequences, and a person has, therefore, to obey the Law in all its minutiae, each detail, in order to have a seamless moral life. You have to practice the law until its observance is part of you. You do not have to think about it."

I looked over at Jesus again expecting him to tell them what nonsense this all was, but he sat intently listening to them make their points.

In his desire to soften the harshness of his companions' perspective, Annanias explained, "If people do not abide by the law and make it their way of life, then they are open to all the consequences. Things just don't go right for them. They make bad decisions, these are followed by reactive practices, and finally desperate actions. Regret and excuses follow, but there has been set in motion an inevitable train of consequences."

I had to admit Annanias had a point. I very much wanted to jump in and say, "Yes, but…!" However, being in the company of Jesus had cured me of that habit. Instead I accepted some more wine and waited.

Martheus waving his cup back and forth, jumped in again, "And when things go wrong in a person's life, obviously as a result of that person breaking the Law, or his or her parents, then you have fulfilled what the prophet Ezekiel said. The sins are visited upon the heads of the children and the children's children, until the third or fourth generation." He set his cup down with a triumphant thump.

"Are you saying that your Father in heaven, the God of Israel, keeps score of all our sins and punishes us for them, and even punishes our children for those same sins?" Jesus asked. He shook his head. "You are just plain wrong."

Annanias licked his fingers clean, then wiped his fingers on a cloth he produced from his belt, and reflected quietly, "A child may have a willful, disobedient bent. Where does that come from? Even with parents who do their best to correct him, he may still become violent, a thief or worse. Such a boy refuses to learn. Where does such a spirit of obstinate willfulness come from?

Martheus was still working on his dish of lamb, soaking up the juices with a morsel of bread, and added without looking up, "Good point. His parents may have done their best, but that defective spirit may come from the sins of past generations. Even more important than that is when the sins of generations add up, in that case, the child is born with them in some form or another. He may be born lame, blind, or maybe deaf. How else can you explain why these things happen?

Jesus said, "Ezekiel wrote, 'And no more shall it be said that the sins of the parents be visited upon the children.' No, no, no! All of us are *becoming*. We are all learning. You see no hope for people, but our Father needs from each of you with eternal hope. All our Father needs from any of you is one small yes. He never loses faith in you. He believes in you and that part of Him that dwells within you."

Annanias leaned forward. "You say our Father believes in me? But…" He paused and looked around desperately.

Jesus smiled at him. "You're stuck aren't you? There is no need for judgment, no place for punishment is there? Your nightmare is that the Father believes in you.

Janus broke in, saying, "No! He knows all the sin I am made of. He knows all the sins that down the years have gone to make me who I am. Nobody can escape the consequences of his past generations. That is why we believe if everyone obeys the Law, then there is no sin to pass on. That is why we say if everyone were to obey the law in all its details for just a day, you would see the Kingdom of God dawning." With a flourish he downed the last of his wine and set it out to be refilled, looking around at the rest of us with a look of triumph on his face.

Jesus shook his head and quietly added, "That is never going to happen, and no amount of exhortation or threats will make it work. What if we could do as the prophets said and swapped the heart of stone in each of us, for a heart of flesh?"

Annanias thoughtfully replied, "That sounds nice, but how do we do that? Sacrifice doesn't help."

Jesus said, "You've got to want it and accept it on the Father's terms. Maybe accidents and disasters that we ascribe to the sin of people are accidents of the earth. Lightning strikes on the hilltops and the top of trees. Most lightning touches no one. Does that mean God wastes a lot of perfectly good lightning? Think of how silly that sounds."

Martheus, now setting his polished plate aside and wiping one hand against the other, exclaimed, "When you put it like that, it does sound absurd, but I suspect you are being cynical. As Janus said, 'Then what?' Are we to believe the person was just unfortunate? Then why does God, our Heavenly Father, who, according to you, loves his people, let it happen?"

Jesus said, "Well, I suppose I was a little cynical. That kind of thinking leads you into a blind dry wadi, in which there is little but a few pools of slimy water, and you can't drink the little there is."

Jesus lowered his head in thought, as he wrestled with the question. Finally, he looked up. "Our Father in Heaven did not only create the world, but He is still creating it. The suffering of everything in his creation is born by him as the cost of the process of creating. Do you not think the frightened bull that is sacrificed is not His, and its pain is not His pain? A bird does not fall to earth but He knows it.

"The suffering of the world is the price the Father willingly pays for us all to be part of creation, from the beetle I crush under my sandal to the person who dies in a flood. There is no veil drawn over the eyes of God so that He might not see the suffering. He does not have to punish. Try that on for size, God does not punish."

I rolled the idea around in my head and found I couldn't let go of the idea that God punished. Since then I have been able to do so, but at that time I was still mired in the thinking of leaders like those who sat there that night.

Annanias quietly added, "Ah, I've always been struck by God's love for us. I've never understood why He bothers. You say He is still working on His creation? He is not finished with it yet?"

Jesus said, "Finished? He has barely started. You Pharisees believe in the resurrection of everyone. Well, does that mean that at the resurrection you are frozen the way you are? I think it means you get to go on learning and growing in wisdom and understanding. This life is just the beginning of the beginning."

Martheus folded his arms across his ample stomach and broke in, "You mean eternal life. I've heard that phrase. I don't like it. That means there would be no judgment of the sinful and no rewarding the righteous. That can't be right."

Annanias said, "The idea of God's love for the whole world is surely wrong, although if it is so it can be nothing else but the strong bond that is the force of creation in Genesis. Was love the language God spoke in the beginning when he said, 'let there be light'? What about obedience and the punishment of Adam and Eve? They were kicked out of the garden don't forget."

Jesus nodded, "Was that a necessary step for them to become fully human and not just lay-abouts in a garden they didn't make? I have always wanted to object to their existence being ideal. Look at us here thinking, questioning and pondering these things. If we were still in the garden we would have nothing to ask and maybe nothing to think with."

Janus, who had been watching the others argue back and forth said, "That is going too far. We are still paying for their disobedience. Adam's sin has been passed on to us, that is why we have to observe the law exactly and show we are obedient, unlike Adam. Of course God punishes the wicked and rewards the righteous. You cannot believe we will not be rewarded for all our hard work? You are also suggesting that this world is God's world and it is the way he expects it to be. What happens to the idea your friends the Essenes have, that the world is evil, and His chosen ones are responsible for the prosecution of the conflict between good and evil in the world?

Our job is to be pure, and therefore on God's side! I think we've gotten off the point. Bad things happen to good people. You've got to explain that, and the answer has got to be the person's guilt. Why it happens that way is not for us to know."

As I listened to them I thought what nasty people they were. However cleverly they argued, what they wanted was to deny others anything good. Their self righteousness was odious.

Jesus looked across to Annanias, "Are we unworthy servants always falling short of His expectations, or did He create us in His image so that like children trying to help their parents we join him in the continuing act of creation? Does he not rejoice like a parent when we get it right and with love and patience like a good parent encourage and lead us when we don't? When we destroy and lay waste to everything around us, does not our Father mourn as a parent mourns when he sees his child destroying himself?"

Silence fell in the room. Oil lamps had been lit, and one smoked badly, as if it was empty.

"Oh, my God, the heart of God must constantly break," groaned Annanias.

Jesus said, "Yes, but also His heart is renewed by every moment of new birth. Maybe the love is there to help that happen."

Martheus shook his head, "It's late; I can't follow you. There is too much to deal with here. God's concern is for us to obey the Law, all of the Law. I can't get beyond that. God has to punish us, look at all the threats in the books of the law, and the threats in the books of the prophets." He bowed to Lazarus, and thanked him for the excellent supper, saying, "Perhaps you will congratulate Martha on the lamb. It was the best I've had for a long time."

He got up, covered his head with his shawl, bowed gently to the rest of us, then to Jesus, and made to go. Janus heaved himself up, swigged the last of his wine, and said it was time for him to go also. Janus said, "Very interesting, speculative but interesting. You know we cannot go down that road. People need discipline and the threat of punishment if they do disobey. People are like horses, you have to put a bit and bridle on them to get anywhere. That last idea of yours won't work at all. But, good night, Jesus, be careful. Your thoughts are dangerous, but I don't need to tell you that."

We sat in silence again. Annanias made no move to go. Jesus watched him with an intensity that grew into prayer. I saw him close his eyes, and his lips moved in prayer.

Annanias said, "Punishment of the guilty for punishment's sake never made sense to me. You are right. That whole argument for God exacting every last ounce of what we owe is a dead end. Maybe the Law is to help redress the balance in the cost of creation to God. If I do a work of generosity, do you think it eases God's pain? Does it add to His sense of His creation being worthwhile? What a thought! How I would like that to be true."

Silence fell again, and Jesus, still as a statue, would not disturb the gathering moment that brimmed full for Annanias. The smoking oil lamp finally went out. The other one seemed to brighten as its importance rose as the only light left to us.

Annanias nodded to the lamp, "You see, one goes out, and it is left to the other to light the whole room. Thank you for your thoughts. I must go now, but may I come back? There is so much. If even half of what you say is true, there is so much."

For a while we sat there in the light of the one lamp. Martha had cleared away the last of the dishes. I sat there relieved that the others had gone. I found myself utterly repelled by what drove their thinking. Those clergy wanted people punished, they wanted people to suffer. Lazarus broke the silence finally. "I have never thought that God did or didn't punish. I just assumed that we got what we deserved somehow. If He does not punish then a lot of things change. Does anything really matter to Him or is He above all our petty nonsense?"

Jesus looked across at Lazarus for a long moment and answered, "No, he is not above all our nonsense, and what happens matters. Creation is a party He is throwing. Your response needs to be like being invited to a wedding feast. You get excited at the prospects of the party, you get all dressed up and everyone else is there. Soon you are all singing and dancing and having a great time. All you have to do is say yes, let's go to the party, and the rest begins to follow. However, if you say no, I don't enjoy parties, I don't like so and so, or I can't stand spending the day hanging around a bunch of people making fools of themselves, then you miss out. You are left unmarked, unchanged, even left alone. When you make a habit of missing out, it is not long before people stop inviting you. Then what happens?"

Lazarus thought for a moment, and responded, "So you are saying Our Father is inviting us to life, and it is like a party, full of dancing and singing with those we share life with? Then, of course, it would be me who punishes myself when I refuse His invitation. He doesn't have to punish me, I can do it all myself."

"But what about the rest of the things that go wrong? You really think that being struck by lightning is just being in the wrong place at the wrong time?"

Jesus nodded. "That's about it. No, there is no correlation between sin and misfortune, although sometimes what we do brings upon us misfortune as a natural consequence. That though, is most often stupidity, and of course stupidity is not sin and is not forgivable. You are supposed to learn from it."

I had been listening to all of this conversation, and I could contain myself no longer, "But the Essenes talk about everything being fate. Everything is foretold, and the future is set. They teach how to prophesy about what is coming down, and there are stories about those prophecies being visited upon the heads of not a few criminal types."

Jesus looked up and searched my face. After a moment's thought he quietly said, "Maybe there is no such thing as the future."

"What do you mean no future? I cried, "God has to know everything. He has to know what is going to happen."

"Let me explain it like this. Imagine a potter who decides to make a complicated pot. He has in his head a picture of what he wants to make, but the clay has something to say about what it finally looks like. Maybe the clay is rough, is full of impurities, or the glaze does not fire as expected. Anyway, between the potter, the clay and the fire, a pot is made, and what comes out is not quite what the potter had in mind, instead it is full of interesting little compromises. Think of the future as being filled with lots of little compromises. Jeremiah said, 'God is the potter and we the clay.' I think he had a powerful insight there."

Everything in me objected to the idea of there being no future. "No," I said. "God must have established the future, if not, anything could happen."

Jesus laughed lightly. "You mean everything might get out of control? Well, what do you think, can God handle the present? Look, you have to think of the present and the future, like a tapestry. The weaver weaves into his cloth all kinds of different wools and makes patterns with what he has. The back of the cloth is a mess, full of ends and knots, and there does not appear to be a pattern and it is the back of the pattern most people see. When you look at the other side, there is the pattern in all its detail and complexity. The more you look at it the more there is there. That is how I see God weaving tomorrow out of today. God makes tomorrow out of what we do today."

"You mean that what I do is that important?" I replied.

"Yes," he said, "and what is more, you can either be just another part of the pattern, or you can join the Father and add your little pattern to the whole. So, no, there is no set future, but, yes, God knows where He is going. I call that the will of God. Why do you think I spend so much time in prayer? It is not so I may know the future, but that I might understand the will of my Father. Then set about fitting myself to it, and acting out his will?"

I felt a movement behind me so I turned round. There was Mary, Lazarus' sister. I realized she had been there all along. I looked up at Lazarus, who just smiled and shook his head slightly with a little smile towards his sister. Yes, he knew she had been listening and pretending not to, but once the Pharisees left, she had been waiting for the opportunity to say something. Now she put down the knitting she had been doing. "We women know there is no tomorrow unless we make it. No child unless we bear it, no hope unless we will it. So yes, I know that what the master is saying has to be so. All women know there is no meal to set before you men unless we make it. Maybe we have deprived you of the opportunity to understand this by doing everything."

"Mary," said Lazarus, "You are too much. Please excuse her."

Jesus held up his hand as if to cut him off. "No, she is right, she understands, and yes, women would understand what I have said more easily than men." Looking at Mary, he asked, "What did you think of our earlier conversation?"

Mary hesitated for a moment, looked at Lazarus as if to ask permission to speak, then, as if daring him to say no, went on in a rush, "Well, for us, punishment is something we do not administer. We all too often bear it in one form or another. You are talking about a God I would like to know, rather than one I have always feared and written off as having it in for us women especially. You see, if He is the way He has always been portrayed by you men then I cannot ever know such a God. I can only fear him like some dark threat at night. I cannot identify with Him or know Him. For the first time I am really beginning to see the possibility of doing just that, of knowing God all by myself, with no help from anyone else."

With that we sat back and fell into silence which was finally broken by Lazarus getting up, and, as if we were all waiting for that signal, we arose from our cushions and I took my leave of the others.

As I walked down the road the two miles back to Jerusalem, I thought over the evening. What to make of Jesus' words? I felt the fears of the darkness pressing about me, and I started at a noise in the grass close by. It was as if all my fears came back to mock such hopefulness and that talk of grace. It was as if the fears in my own head gabbled like demons in denial of everything I had heard.

Yet did I detect behind those fears the fear of fears threatened with a light that would put them out of business? Fears cast into their own darkness.

ANNAS' DIARY

These next sheets of Annas' diary tell me that I was not the only one having nightmares. If nightmares are—as most people think—evidence of upheaval in the spiritual realm, then there swirled around Jesus a most virulent reaction to his presence.

Thursday, late evening

I see here miracles have been reported. The crowd loves that kind of entertainment and I suspect contribute heavily to their own deception. (I must ask the students in our seminary to discuss just how much people want to be deceived? That would be a good topic for the final year students.)

Back to this Nazarene. We've tracked him thoroughly now. We know his major donors, as well as his organizational set up. There's remarkably little of the latter for the length of time he has been around. I see a long list of contacts, but no evidence of any contracts or agreements that we've heard about. With what we pay out to informers I am sure we would have heard something if it was out there.

This man is a serious threat. I just know it. What is it that is setting off alarm bells in me? Why do I feel him to be a threat? When I look at his file, and consider all the reports objectively, there is still no evidence of a political angle. There is no cabal. I've looked into that. I've had summaries of what he has been teaching the people in these gatherings of his, but again there is nothing truly politically subversive. Much of it is popular pap at best and dead wrong at worst.

He demonstrates a broad knowledge of the law. He says he is not here to overthrow the law. That's good of him. I have that quote here somewhere. Ah, yes..."But I am here to fulfill the law." That is double talk. Nobody can fulfill the law, what does he mean?

Also I note here he is very free with the "Fatherhood of God." Talks about our God as if he has had a personal introduction. 'Father' of us all. That takes us into realms of unjustified individualism. 'Father of Israel,' yes, but not of every individual. Maybe that is what I see that is wrong with him. If everyone were His child, may His name be blessed for evermore, and as children each had access to their Father then what would be the place of the Temple or our priesthood for that matter?

The other troubling issue is his attitude towards sacrifice. Here he quotes psalms and passages from the prophets. "Do I eat the flesh of bulls or drink the blood of he-goats? Offer God a sacrifice of thanksgiving and fulfill your vows to the most High."

Well, I can't see a problem with that. I am all for them fulfilling and paying their vows.

Here is a passage from Amos that he quotes, "I loathe your pilgrim feasts. I take no pleasure in your whole offerings. I shall not accept them." Well, Amos doesn't count because he was talking about Samaria.

He is definitely questioning sacrifice as having any place in our national devotions, but he is going to have an uphill struggle in convincing people of that. What's he going to replace it with? People need to feel as if they have made expiation, paid for their sin or bought God's favor. That's why sacrifice works. It may have nothing to do with God, and everything to do with people's fears. The reality is that as far as the people are concerned, blood, has to be shed, and they don't feel right if blood is not shed. He can't change human nature.

That riot he caused when he first started has always worried me. He stormed into the Temple precincts and released all the animals. That was a statement. I've always thought it was more than objection to our commercial enterprises. Looking at all of these comments about sacrifice I believe the freeing of the animals that day was intended by him to be a major statement of his position like one of the old prophets acting out his point of view. Maybe he is trying to be a prophet. It's a long time since we had one of those.

At first I thought his objection to our operation of the Temple came straight out of those Essenes. They just hate us and think they could do better, but I see from all these references his objection to us is more profound. What he is saying is sacrifice achieves nothing, but gives people a false sense of righteousness and therefore a false sense of security before God.

That is nonsense. There has always been sacrifice. Every man knows he needs to make sacrifice. How about Abraham? The Baptizer was bad enough with his cleansing rituals and call to repentance. A lot of people took him seriously, but this Nazarene's point of view goes way beyond that of John the Baptizer.

What if he hopes to weaken people's opinion of the efficacy of our services and lead a revolt to unseat us? He would have the people behind him and he could supplant us with their general approval. Even the Romans are realists and wouldn't care if that happened, so long as there was not too much bloodshed. Pilate hates me, I know. Would he turn a blind eye to this fellow or even give him covert support? I have had no rumors of any interest from that quarter.

So how might this Nazarene be planning this? He has lots of contacts, lots of powerful friends, but no overt organization. I see nothing here. What am I missing?

Friday morning, early

I had a lousy night. Dreams of animals, sheep, oxen and goats all massing and advancing on me. They wouldn't take their eyes off of me. When I went back to sleep there they were again, but now coming from far away. There were flocks and herds of them slowly walking towards me. I awoke again and for the third time there were the animals, but this time there were young children and even youths slowly walking towards me. The fourth time though was even worse. I dreamed there was a figure like a man, stood behind all those flocks and herds and thundered at me, "Why?"

He reminded me of that scroll by the supposed prophet Daniel. I wonder if we have a copy, and if not I will send Jonathon out to find one.

"Why?"
"Why?"
"Why?" That is not a question.

Sunday afternoon

This prophet Daniel sounds like those crazies down by the Salt Sea. This is why we Sadducees don't put much stock in the writings of the prophets. This book of Daniel reads like a history book. Look here, "And he will set up the abominable thing that causes desolation." Well we all know when that was to the very day. All these references to kingdoms rising and falling are history, not prophecy, so what's the point of it? I don't think this was written with foresight, but with hindsight. You don't need to be a prophet to tell what happened in the past.

Here is the passage, "And when I looked up I saw a man robed in linen with a belt of gold of Ophir around his waist. His body glowed like topaz, his face shone like lightning, his eyes flamed like torches and his feet and arms like bronze." No, that is not it. Okay. Here is the part that I am looking for, "And his voice sounded like the voice of a multitude." That's what I heard, a voice like a multitude.

What am I doing? It was a dream, nothing more. Reading this stuff makes anyone crazy. If I start to take notice of this kind of prognostication I might as well join the crazies down there in their monastery.

"Why?" Why, what? Enough of this, nobody has a voice like the sound of a multitude. Maybe I will ask Caiaphas to stop over. There's nothing like listening to that buffoon to bring me back to earth.

14

DREAMS AND TERRORS

After the dinner party with Lazarus and the Pharisees I spent the next week going about my own business. My father imported foods and marketable items from up north and from the seaports of the West and had made it into a respectable operation. I had the job of overseeing the accounts. The only way I could stop the questioning in my head was to bury myself in the work. I was way behind, so there was plenty to occupy myself with.

The questions came back night after night. I awoke in the very early hours of the second morning and began to visit again all that had been said. If there was no punishment, if there was no future already determined, then what of sin, what of judgment? Was there no evil in the world? Satan, the great tempter, certainly afflicted us all. No, we were so capable of not just breaking the law but real evil, of destructive thoughts and acts. I must go back and ask Jesus as soon as I could break free again. Meanwhile I would go and visit Jonathon. I wanted to share with him some of these amazing ideas.

With that course of action planned, I was able to sleep. My dreams were confused, and I can still remember the broiling tumultuous thoughts that pursued each other through my mind as I slept. Finally, I had a terrifying dream. I saw a monstrous figure emerge from below the floor, and surrounded by flames and smoke, armed and wearing a horned helmet on his head, a giant figure loomed over me. I knew he intended nothing less than my destruction. If he were to but touch me I knew I would be no more. Fear and horror swept over me like a flood. Rooted to the spot, I realized if I turned and ran, he would catch me. If I but moved he would seize me. For some reason I called out Jesus' name. Behind me as I faced that figure in all its terrible threatening roaring, I heard his voice, "Stand, he cannot touch you! He has no power but the power of your fear!"

The tide of terror in me began to ebb away, and though the monstrous apparition still threatened me, a peace came flooding into me, and then I saw it. I saw the diabolic monster could not touch me and that it had no power of its own. As I watched I fancied I detected uncertainty in it. I was no longer overwhelmed with terror, but instead profoundly curious, as if the figure was a thing to be studied or observed. Then unbidden, a laugh broke from my lips and the figure looked disconcerted, and I felt laughter welling up in waves. The figure faltered, tried to roar more convincingly, but its outline seemed to be blowing away like mist. Gradually its form thinned, and, as if claimed by its own insubstantial gravity, began to slowly descend back in the middle of the now guttering flames, until, despairing, he was swallowed up in the welter of fire below.

I woke from the dream with the memory still clinging to my mind. The words of Jesus in the dream hung there in the air like words of cold fire, "Stand, he cannot touch you, he has no power but the power of your fear."

What had happened? Was that the evil one? Was that Satan come to seize me as I dared to raise doubts about his domain? Jesus' words still rang in my head. I did not know how, but that figure had no power. Was Satan ultimately without power? Was it true that he only had the power we gave him? How could Jesus know this? What did it say about him? Who could know such a thing? Who was he?

I went about my chores with little enthusiasm that day. It was Friday and I could hardly wait until evening when I made my way to Jonathon's parents' house.

With relief I entered the cool, orderly routine of the Sabbath preparations. Jonathon was not there yet, so I had a few moments with his parents. Inevitably they asked about Jesus, and for the life of me I could tell them little of all that had happened since I last saw them. I had no words to describe what I had begun to perceive.

Jonathon came in before the Sabbath began, and we were enveloped by the age-old customs and familiar words. During the meal, I felt lulled by the gentle actions and affirmation of our life together as God's people. For a moment I could travel in the footsteps of so many, and I did not have to make my own path.

After dinner Jonathon and I sat outside under a fig tree, its figs just beginning to ripen. Jonathon could hardly contain himself. "I am so glad you came tonight. There is something very serious beginning to happen. Annas has had three conferences with envoys from Herod, and Herod has agreed to move against John the Baptist. I don't know what Annas offered him, but he has agreed to arrest John, and take him north to his capital. Annas is obsessed by John; he had Caiaphas in his office for two hours, ranting and raving about the danger John represented. Caiaphas came out of there looking grim, but it is Annas driving the action against John. Can you get word to John? This was last Monday, so we have maybe a week before Herod's people will make a move. They will find some excuse to take him and, knowing John, there will be a bag full of things they can choose from."

I would have to go down there, but first I would tell Jesus. Suddenly I felt as if everything was getting way out of hand. The conversation yesterday, that dream and now this. It's all beginning to go too fast.

On the first day of the week I hiked over to where Jesus was teaching and baptizing. I arrived late evening, just in time to catch him before he took his customary solitary vigil. I told him about Herod's intention to take John the Baptist. Strangely enough he was unmoved by the news.

He finally said, "Annas is going after the wrong person. John is no threat. He doesn't realize where the threat is truly coming from, but that wily old goat can smell danger. Herod will arrest John, he will not run away, and he will stare the soldiers down, scare the pants off them, but finally they will take him into custody. Now that I think about it, I can just see John the Baptist going willingly, and savoring the chance to harangue Herod, berating him in front of all his courtiers. I even feel sympathy for Herod. No, I think we can do little to move John to hide or run away. We will send a messenger and warn him. Thank Jonathon for me. This is the first move of Annas, and now we have to be very careful. I must pray, thank you for the information. Maybe we can talk in the morning, I can see there is more." He lightly gripped my shoulder and gave it a gentle squeeze. "We will talk tomorrow."

With that he turned and disappeared in the gathering darkness. Above, the stars were coming out; a slight warm air moved down the wadi. Everything was so normal, so quiet. His words came to mind, "Stand, he has no power except what you give him." My concern for John the Baptist evaporated so I looked for a place to make a bed and sleep. There were no dreams that night.

I awoke cramped and cold under the thin blanket that was available at Jesus' camp by the Jordan. The fire was going, and I went over to it to warm myself. The heat on my back felt good. Then I went down to the river to rinse my face, arms and hands. I sat down with my back against a rock and let my mind drift back over the last few days.

I wondered what was happening to John the Baptist. His response to our warning was just as Jesus had expected. He expressed hope that Herod would come and take him to his court. John had a few things he wanted to say to him.

Jesus shook his head over the message and said, "John is like the rest of the nation. He does not understand the evil that he is up against, and the gathering forces have no investment in either listening to criticism or pleas for understanding. The people do not have long before the culmination of their own anger, hatred and despair will make them vulnerable to the temptation to take matters into their own hands. That intractable attitude and self-righteousness will bring down upon them the irresistible forces of the Empire. That will be the end of Israel. Can't you feel it?"

My thoughts went to Jesus' teachings on the Kingdom. After my dream about the giant demonic being, I was aware there were levels of our spiritual lives involved that belied the simplistic notions expressed by others. There were questions I still had to ask Jesus, but here, he was so often surrounded by hordes of others, and I really didn't want to talk about my dream in front of them.

Not ten minutes later Jesus settled beside me. I hadn't heard him approach. He gestured to the river. "What would Israel be without the Jordan? It defines us and is a symbol of our enduring among the hostilities of a world that has no thought for us. The Jordan runs between banks that border desert or semi-desert, and to the banks it touches it brings life. Its waters begin in the cold, snow covered mountains, and it is fed from springs and sudden floods. How like Israel."

I had been only half listening to Jesus' words, but the next ones caught my attention. "John, you have something on your mind. I believe you want to ask me a question or two."

I was taken aback by this sudden breaking in on my thoughts, so I told him my dream of the demonic figure although I stopped before I told him of hearing his voice behind me.

He sat there for a good while, grim-faced and thoughtful. Finally he raised his eyes to mine. "Yes, that discussion with Ananias and the others would no doubt cause the demonic to panic. You realize that to believe utterly in the Father, and to join so whole-heartedly with him in His will, is to deny any place for the demonic. You must have taken our discussion most seriously.

"Don't ever take the force of evil for granted. The more we move towards the divine, the more reactive are the forces of evil. What is your question? I can see you have churned it round and around until it is almost butter."

I smiled at his likening my thinking process to making butter. "You said in my dream, 'Stand, he has no power except what you give him.' At least that was the meaning of your words. I realized that to be true, but I do not know how. Your words made it true. Does the demonic have power or not? I have thought the evil one is very much to be feared. Are we not to fear him? Was this dream just my imagination?"

Jesus smiled to himself and said, "The first thing you have to know about the Satan is that he is the father of lies. Nothing, I mean nothing he says is to be trusted, especially when he tells the truth. Even then there is a lie hidden in the truth, like a fish hook hidden in bait. But he is useful to us because he gives us the rational and emotional reason why we should follow our own inclinations. He poses as our friend and gives us assurance that our needs are justified and our reasons correct. You will, like everyone, not recognize the evil around you, and by your quiescence, even give grudging support to activities that appear necessary."

I nodded as if I understood, but that was a little beyond me. I asked, "But the evil I do, isn't that caused by him?"

"You don't do evil, but the no-no's you pull are sometimes sin. Sin is not evil. A person is not evil. He is a sinner. Even that snake Annas is only a sinner; he is not evil. He is forgivable if he would turn to his God and surrender his pride, his thirst for power and his overwhelming fear that he has used to make walls around himself. However, look who he has surrounded himself with. When like minded people come together, and act out of their sin, in this case out of their fear, greed and arrogance, then evil is born in their midst and takes on a life of its own.

"Evil corrupts. It sucks in even the well-intentioned, until respectability covers it from view. However, its monstrous power grows. For example, the merchants and money people do not see what their greed does to the small farmer. They do not appreciate the despair they cause by their heartless use of the law. They support the law and use their influence to increase the severity of its effects, all in the name of order, but they are driven by their greed. The result is an evil that presses the people like olives, or stamps on them like grapes trodden at harvest time. One man is sinful in his greed, but evil exists and requires the loyalty of each sinner. The individual is thus seconded to its dark forces. Do not underestimate evil."

"So what you are saying is I should be more afraid of the evil in this city than that apparition in my dream?"

"That's right. That form you saw in your dream was drawn from your very spirit. Two things can be said of the devil; that he exists and that he doesn't exist. They are both equally true. As you saw in your dream, he was a very real threatening figure, and apparently very substantial. That is the lie made out of your fears, stitched together out of ideas and pictures fed you by parents and others. I told you he is the father of lies, and the first lie you must remember is that he has substance. He has no substance until you give it to him out of your own fears."

Jesus could see I was having trouble following him so he explained further.

"Let me ask you, do you believe in God? Of course. Well, if you believe in God you cannot believe in Satan. Your faith in your Father precludes any belief in the devil. My words in your dream were true, the evil one cannot touch you. He can only exist by the energy you give him. When you felt my presence in the dream, you stood your ground, you felt the fear drain out of you, and as you gazed at the evil one he became less and less substantial. In your words he began to blow away in the wind, until in despair he subsided into the earth.

"Thus he is born out of people's fear, feeds on their sin, and grows in power and influence. So, you can see, there is no Evil One unless you give him form."

I sat there for a moment. The sun had gained strength, and I was warmed through with its light. I looked out at the world of river and desert and felt the solidity of it all. There was no place for the evil one to lurk, because even the darkest night was but a place for the Spirit of God to roam.

Yet, at Jesus' words, I could feel in myself the place where fear could grow and faith burn dim. I felt the darkness crouched, waiting for me to turn and run. I heard Jesus' words from my dream— "Stand!" —and I felt that strange confidence and the darkness within my fear began to recede, thin and blow away.

I said, "I can't understand all that you have explained, but I can see how it is so. Your presence was vital to what happened. If you had not appeared in my dream what would have happened? Were you a dream or were you there? Where did those words come from?"

Jesus bowed his head. "I was there, one way or another, I was there. Yes, those words are mine, but don't ask me to tell you how it is so. At least, not yet, for I am only beginning to understand these things myself."

After several moments, he continued. "It's not only evil that you have to worry about, but the suffering that results. Pray to be delivered from evil, but also pray not to be overwhelmed by the results of that evil. War is an example. The victors go home, the losers bury their dead, but the people starve. The fields are unplanted, the herds depleted, and hatred and resentment are multiplied. Pray not to be led into such a time of suffering. That is what is concerning me about all the misguided talk about the coming Kingdom. The Kingdom of God cannot be founded on the hatred and violence we see all around us. The conflagration that must result from such evil will bring upon the people a time of suffering not experienced since our exile to Babylon. Pray to be spared that time of tribulation."

I had felt warmed by the rays of the morning sun, but at his words I felt a chill settle on me. There was dread in his voice, as if he were already mourning the suffering of the land.

He spun 'round and cried, "John, we have work to do. Yes, you as well. Come, it is time for me to return to Jerusalem. We will go up to the festival. You go ahead and ask Lazarus if he would let us stay with them. There will be six or so."

I was surprised and my face must have shown it, because Jesus said, "It's okay. I will behave myself. I promise there will be no more riots. I will not interfere with the Temple business this time. Though I can promise you, ultimately I intend to bring down that whole rotten mess we are all enslaved to.

"Not this time, though, because we must start to build a strategy that will accomplish our Father's will rather than become tainted and overwhelmed by the evil squatting there. I need to be there and experience it all firsthand again. I need to listen and consider carefully what the real battle is that must be fought."

Return to Jerusalem and the Pool of Bethesda

On my return to my apartment I found a message from Jonathon. That evening I turned up at his parents' house before dinner time and, of course, was welcomed in as if I were one of the family. I had begun to think of myself as just that, and as I sat down I allowed myself to be enwrapped in the warmth of this ordinary, devout family. Here was both sanctity and sanctuary.

I heard the noise of Jonathon's arrival in the hallway. My mind returned to those present, to the warm room, and the joy in Jonathon's face as he welcomed me. We caught up with the general news, and I told him what was new on our end and tried to explain some of the discussions we had had. Unfortunately, I was not very good at explaining some of the more profound issues Jesus had spoken of. Jonathon understood though and pumped me dry of what little I could offer him. I also talked about some of the people who were now seeking Jesus, including not a few teachers and scribes.

He finally said, "Yes, I have heard he is attracting some very interesting people. There are a few Pharisees who go down there I believe, as well as groups of merchants and business people."

"How did you know?" I asked.

"Annas got a report from one of his spies. I don't know which one, but I think a part of the regular group who hang around Jesus."

"What did the report have to say?" I asked, "Was there anything important in it?"

"Well, the reason I left you that note was I think Jesus needs to understand Annas has transferred his concern from John to him. The report, which I heard read out to Annas, was quite specific about who had visited him, the core teachings and what appears to be Jesus' political objectives. What he does not like is the company Jesus keeps. He had me research the list of those merchants and business people who have spent time with him. You are aware the people on that list are outside the Temple monopoly and have been trying for years to break into the money exchange, animal and produce markets. Those people have power, and they are close to the Roman authorities. Annas sees a plot to attack his authority by those who have greatest cause to hate him."

"Did the report mention Lazarus? Who else is on the list?" I said.

"Yes, Lazarus is there, Nicodemus, Ananias, Mordecai, the banker, a couple of tax farmers, and above all, James the aide to Pilate. The Romans are also keeping their eye on Jesus?"

"I have so much to tell you," I said. "Yes, Jesus does talk about the Kingdom of God, but not in the terms Annas would, or maybe even could think. Annas is right about Jesus' opposition to the Temple, but again, not the way he is thinking. I don't know the whole picture, and I don't think Jesus sees it all clearly, but in these last weeks the outline of his ministry has become clearer. He is coming to the Festival. You will have a chance to meet him."

Jonathon's eyes lit up, but he was very concerned. "Annas has told Caiaphas to have him taken if he shows his face around the Temple. He had Caiaphas in his office for over an hour yesterday and told him to be prepared for trouble. On the one hand, I think he expects some protests when John the Baptist is arrested, but he also talked about a more general threat and that Jesus seemed to be the focus. Please tell Jesus to watch out and not to take risks."

"Trying to tell Jesus not to take risks is like trying to tell the waves not to beat on the shore too hard. They have their own rhythm, and that is that. Jesus is coming with the intention of being at the festival. I think he wants to be part of his nation as they celebrate their freedom once again. What I can do is have a few of the others keep a look out and try to head off any trouble. From what he said, he does not want this to be a public event. He has a lot to think about, and it is his people he wants to see, hear and consider."

Jonathon shook his head. "I would like to come to him, but I think it best if I stay back. Maybe this weekend I can be part of the crowd and just happen into him. Is he going to be in the Temple at all, or will he just be in Jerusalem? I really meant what I said about Caiaphas having his orders to arrest him if he comes near the Temple."

"What would they arrest him for?" I asked.

"Annas told Caiaphas to charge him with desecrating the Temple property and anything else they could think of that came out of that last episode when he let all the animals loose and upset the tables."

"That was years ago," I said. "I think he needed to make a statement that what was demonstrated there in the Temple precincts—that was the heart of the issue for him. Letting the animals go was definitive, as if he was saying to himself, no more sacrifices. One day early on when I had first met him, he asked me why an animal had to die for me to feel cleansed. He told me to clean up my act, then nothing would have to die. I still think about that, and if that is true for me, how much more true is it for the nation?"

Jonathon looked incredulous. "I thought he was just mad at the commercialization of the process. We cannot do without the essential sacrifices. What would happen?"

"See what I mean," I replied. "The issues are not what we think. They are much bigger. Why should any animal have to die for the nation? He says, let the nation start acting like the people of God, and sacrifices are a way for us to avoid responsibility. Why should anything have to suffer for our lack of understanding or willful ignorance? Whoa, listen to me. I never said anything like that before, but that is what I am beginning to see and understand.

"The stakes are different, and from what you tell me, Annas has caught the scent of something and can feel rather than see the possible threat. Let me say one more thing, then I will shut up. He knows the Father. There is a lot he is unsure of, but he is without any doubt about our Father, about our God. He knows Him. I mentioned the power of healing that seems to flow through him, well it is from God, but it does not come from very far away. I think the Father is present when he is around. At least that is what it feels like to me."

I left Jonathon's parents house and returned to my own apartment. I had talked to Lazarus on the way here, so that was done. I wondered what else I should do. I thought of the work I had let go for the last week and thought about the people who were waiting for me to contact them. I realized that, rather than be an inconvenience, they were an opportunity. Maybe some of them had questions about Jesus, or would like to meet him. I hadn't thought of it before, but now I began to understand what Jesus had said that morning down by the Jordan, namely that I too had work to do.

Two days later Jesus entered Jerusalem quietly in mid morning. He had stayed the night in Bethany with Lazarus and his sisters. We met just outside the Pool of Bethesda as we had arranged. Rather than wander about the streets and draw attention to ourselves we ducked into the porticos surrounding the pool. It was a bad idea.

Shielded from the sun we watched the people crowding the pool area. The sick and crippled lay around in various attitudes of dejection. Most of them had attendants who helped them move about. I supposed they were family members. Here was the story of every city. There were always a group of chronically ill people unable to do much, and gathering in hopeless crowds. Some had had accidents that had left them paralyzed or broken, some were crippled from birth, while others had diseases which deprived them of their strength. Jesus and I walked among those by the edge of the portico in which we had taken shelter from the sun.

Jesus bent over one man who was propped against the stonework and asked him how long he had been there. I was surprised when he said that he had been coming to that pool for years and that he had been crippled from birth. Jesus squatted down beside him and asked why he still came there.

The man gazed around the pool and explained himself: "I want to be healed, and they say that every now and again an angel comes and stirs up the pool and when that happens the first person in the pool is cured. I keep hoping maybe it could be me, but I don't have anyone to help me so I never make it down there in time."

Jesus looked at everyone praying by the pool. I'm sure he saw what I did: when you looked at it from the vantage point of those there, the slim hope of an answer to their prayers was better than the nothing they lived with daily.

Jesus muttered, "Waiting for an angel. How like mankind. Waiting for an angel to do something because we cannot do anything ourselves. There is a very real parallel between what we see here and what is true out there," and he nodded towards the street outside, "people are waiting to be healed, waiting for someone to change their lives, waiting for the Messiah to come, waiting for an angel to stir the waters, waiting to be saved from themselves and each other."

He asked the man, "Do you want to walk? Do you want to be healed?"

I caught his arm. "No, Jesus, not here. We should not draw attention to ourselves." But it was too late.

The man stared at Jesus. "Yes, you bet I do. Yes, I would do anything to be healed."

Jesus commanded, "Get up, pick up your pallet and go home."

For a long moment the man looked at Jesus searching his face then as if galvanized by determination tried to struggle to his feet. At first he could barely move. He got up on one knee, then, with mounting surprise on his face, he struggled but succeeded in getting the other knee beneath him. With a hand from Jesus, the man finally stood, weaving and tottering on his own legs. He looked down at his pallet and tried to bend towards it but he almost fell. Carefully, with his back against the stonework, he bent down and struggled to pick up his mattress of straw.

A man next to him, who was obviously the relative of a wreck of a person lying next to us, rushed over and said, "Here let me help you." With his assistance, our new friend gathered his pallet in his arms, looked at Jesus again, and turned and made his way step by halting step towards the entrance to the pool.

I caught Jesus' arm again. "Come on, let's go, please. We don't want to create a scene. There will be uproar in a minute."

Finally Jesus headed out, with me cutting our way through the crowd. The cry was already taken up. "Did you see that? Benni just walked out of here! How did it happen?"

The shouting was getting louder and attracted the attention of people in the street. Soon we were going against an increasing stream of people who were inevitably attracted to the uproar.

I led Jesus to my apartment, and we went in and washed our hands and feet as was customary. I stood there with the water dripping off my arms and thinking, "Now what? How can we go anywhere? It is going to be like trying to hide a camel at a dinner party."

Jesus looked at me and smiled, then broke into a loud laugh. "If you could only see yourself, you, too, would break up laughing. I do believe you are scared to death of Caiaphas and his people. Don't worry about him. No, I do not want to have an encounter with the authorities right now. It will come, but at my choosing."

He paused. Lowering his head to the bowl, he splashed water over his face and it ran down his beard. He dried himself with the sleeve of his outer garment, grinned at me, and walked out towards the little patio.

DISTURBING THE PEACE

Before following Jesus into my little courtyard, I opened my cupboard and took out what was left of the Sabbath bread Jonathon's parents had given me, along with the cucumber-and-yogurt spread I had purchased the day before. I set water to heat on the hot embers of that morning's cooking fire before joining Jesus.

We sat outside in the courtyard to enjoy the shade of my one lemon tree. I wanted to confront him about what he had just allowed to happen, but I didn't know how. Stalling, I broke off some of the bread and slathered the yogurt mixture on it. We both ate with relish. I went back inside and returned with two cups of warm mint tea. I sipped at mine, and peered at Jesus over the rim of my cup.

He was sitting back, looking up at the patch of sky enclosed by the buildings around us, his bread nearly eaten.

I asked, "How come you cannot walk through Jerusalem without getting involved with someone?" I shook my head. "No, don't answer that. This is why you've come, isn't it?"

Jesus licked his fingers one at a time. "Well, now that you mention it, yes, I've come to interfere and to be involved with people." He reached for more bread. "Like one of our dances, the tempo starts slowly. Today's event was that first drum beat. Tomorrow or next week there will be other events, and the tempo will quicken. I will increase the tempo until the people of the city, and especially the officialdom that dominates this place, will have to react."

Jesus looked up when we heard a loud rap at the front door. I went back in the house and opened the door to Jonathon, who I invited to join us in the courtyard.

I introduced them to each other. Jonathon looked surprised to find Jesus there, so he addressed himself to me. "I thought you should know: the lame man who was healed earlier this morning is now in trouble. He was caught carrying his mattress in the street on the Sabbath. Apparently he was on his way to the Temple with a mattress!"

Jonathon's gaze found Jesus. "He told them that the man who had healed him ordered him to pick his mattress up and take it way. When I heard the report, I knew it must be you. Am I right?"

Jesus shrugged his shoulders. "Yes, I did help a lame man get up. I did not intend to upset anyone, but tell me more."

Jonathon continued. "Well, the clergy are upset. The man told them what happened loudly enough for other people to hear. You can bet the story is all over the city by now." He shook his head in amazement. "The man stood his ground and refused to be silenced. He told the clergy and the people exactly what happened."

My first reaction was disbelief. Jesus saw my expression. "You see, John, the man had the guts to stand up against those characters once he had his prayers heard. That's what a miracle is for. All he needed was a little help, and now he has shown us the way. As I was saying before Jonathon arrived, we must begin to make ourselves felt here. This event is the first step. Our friend is a sign to all of us, a sign to this city, to the authorities and to us. It is time for us to be seen, be heard and for us to be about the work of our Father."

As Jonathon and I sat and pondered what we were about to undertake, Jesus took a long drink of his tea. When he finished, he looked up at Jonathon. "Thank you, Jonathon, for bringing us this news. But I suspect that is not the only reason you came."

Jonathon paused for a moment, as if carefully wording what he wanted to say. "The report was sent immediately to the High Priest's house. Caiaphas will know by now and if he knows, then so does Annas. You are in danger of being taken."

I interrupted, "Jesus' name was not mentioned by that cripple. Besides, we have just returned to the city. No one will think of us."

"If I can make the connection to you, you bet others will! Annas, especially, remembers the last time you were here, and this will bring you to mind. He knows you are here!" Jonathon's fear seemed to overwhelm him. "This will only help him find you. He has already ordered you to be arrested because of your attack on the business in the Temple courtyard. He has not forgotten you." Jonathon softened his harsh words. "He has given orders to find whoever was responsible for the healing."

"Jesus, Jonathon is right. If Annas thinks you are responsible, he will stop at nothing to find you. We must hide. You must not be seen."

Jesus shook his head, unafraid. "He will not make a move during the day, even if he believes I am the one he is looking for. His time is the night. People are already agitated, and Annas' police will be careful not to create a riot that the Romans could notice. Did you hear me a moment ago? It is time! So, let us go out into the streets. I need to see and hear people. I want to understand the people who live in this city, and all the currents of violence and hate that seem to flow just under the surface."

I tried to interrupt, but Jesus stopped me. "This city is like a well-laid fire, awaiting a spark. Or maybe below it lives a horrendous beast of old, waiting to break out from the ruins on which this city is built and devour and destroy everything in its path. Such is the tension I feel when I walk through the gates of the city."

I knew it was no good arguing with him when he had made up his mind. I picked up the remains of the food and took it back into the food preparation area. Reluctantly, I pulled on my light cloak, "Okay, let's go."

As we walked through the gates that led to the street, Jesus spoke quietly. "John, do you remember our discussion on evil? Well, here we see how the violence, greed and enmity of individuals have bred an evil which will soon be full grown. Then you will see the tribulations and suffering that comes from that evil. I cannot urge you enough to pray to be delivered from that time, or you will be sucked in and destroyed.

"That goes for you too, Jonathon. Such powerful and diabolic enmities must eventually explode. Like storm clouds building over the mountains, they can only go so high, store so much water in their folds and concentrate so much lightning in their base before they burst, lashing the earth below, bringing floods, torrents and death. But unlike a storm, there will be nowhere to hide when the evil here breaks forth."

This heavy thought was enough to silence our small group for several minutes. We were all lost in our own thoughts when Jonathon suddenly asked, "Jesus, where are we going?"

Jesus looked up. "I think I would like to visit the Temple. It is almost time for prayer." He grinned, his smile breaking through our somber mood. "I promise you I will not make trouble."

"You don't have to *make* trouble. I think from now on trouble will be out looking for *you*," I said lightly. I tried to joke, but the reality of the statement made it hard to laugh.

We had not gone far when Tobias and Jared, two of our supporters, joined us. I was glad to see them, since Jesus was now less exposed with four of us around him. Jonathon quietly excused himself after their arrival to return to his office quarters.

Our group of four, including Jesus, continued walking along roads filled with people. We moved with the crowd up towards the Temple, which shone in the light of midday.

My old love and pride returned; love for my God and my people, and pride that the very Name of God Himself dwelt there in that edifice.

I was proud that we, his people, bore the name Israel—a name he had given us, to Jacob, meaning *One Who Strives with God.*

But as we ascended the steps of that great building, jostling with the crowd, I asked myself whether we now wrestled with each other rather than the Divine.

Instead of focusing our efforts on defeating evil, we spent time and effort fighting each other. The Essenes, the Pharisees, and the Sadducees bickered and quarreled among themselves over questions concerning observance and worship of God. Violence erupted as a result of the profound disagreement on such matters. Divine worship should bring peace and unity, I thought bitterly, not fighting and violence.

As I looked at the soaring walls of the Temple, now bathed in the full afternoon light, I thought of how contrary the quiet presence of God dwelling in the incensed air of the Holy of Holies was to the heated passions of the people with their turbulent attitudes. How wrong they all were. They did not deserve the name of Israel.

I glanced at Jesus as we walked, ready to share my insight with him, and he caught my eye. Nodding at the Temple walls, he said, "That place should be a house of prayer set in our midst. How often has our Father sought to gather us to Him? His name dwells in our midst, and calls us to prayer. We fulfill our devotions and obligations, leave His presence, and we fill ourselves with antagonism and violence. There is something very wrong at the heart of Israel when we no longer come together in unity."

I nodded enthusiastically, thrilled that Jesus shared my feelings.

He continued. "Look even at the Essenes, those models of dedication and asceticism. They have gone into the desert to prepare a way for our God, yet their writings and their words are full of thoughts of war, of crushing victories. They think the nature of God is displayed in that violence."

His sadness and despair deepened his voice. "They are so wrong. Such hatred and violence come out of the souls of men, not out of the heart of God! There will always be wars, but God doesn't need to help us start them. Mankind does it all by itself."

I interjected, "Perhaps it is all part of that animal spirit which is inside man."

Jesus smiled. "You do animals a disservice, for no other animal wars among themselves as men do. Only we are condemned to maim and kill each other. The lion kills to eat, the tiger stalks her prey and guards her den, but we hunt each other down and exhibit our violence as virtue. We take pride in it. There is a need for redemption of the heart of mankind. All mankind must be redeemed, not just a few of us."

The whole of mankind? How on earth could we, or anyone else, bring that kind of profound change to these people, and to people everywhere? The question haunted me as we climbed uphill.

Finally, we reached the base of stairs leading to the main square of the Temple. We were about to start up when the man Jesus had healed came down the stairs, still carrying his bag of straw. He used the wall for stability, as if his legs were stiff after sleep, and he looked intently at each step.

He paused when he sensed our group standing in his way. He peered at Jesus' face for several seconds, and suddenly his face broke into a huge smile of delight.

"Master, thank you, thank you! See, I am truly walking. I haven't gotten used to it yet, but I'm getting the hang of it. I have given thanks to God for what you did. He has answered my prayers! Thank you, Master, thank you." He was crying and laughing at the same time.

Jesus invited him to come with us back up to the Temple, but the man shook his head and looked anxiously over his shoulder. "No, they threw me out. I was carrying my mattress as you told me to do, and those priests caught me and bawled me out for carrying it. It's the Sabbath. I suppose I was wrong to be carrying it, but I didn't think in the excitement of the moment."

"You did nothing wrong," said Jesus. "You needed to get that bag of straw back to your home. Giving thanks to God for your healing was the right thing to do. You are on the right path. Don't let them tell you differently."

"Did you tell the clergy who had healed you?" I asked anxiously.

The man hung his head. "No. I am sorry, but in the excitement of what you did for me, I never asked your name. Oh, Master, I could not tell them who you were."

Jesus glanced quickly at me, returned his gaze to the older man and clapped him on the shoulder with a laugh. "I think my young friend is glad you did not tell the clergy who I am." He gently put his hand on the man's shoulder, and smiled kindly. "Go on home. Your legs will grow stronger and your confidence will increase. Take it slowly; you have a whole new life to put together. Remember, the healing was only the beginning—a sign the rest of you needs to follow."

With that, Jesus continued his climb up the steps. Tobias and Jared followed him. The healed man, whose name we still did not know, called after Jesus, "And thank you again, Master!" He smiled at me. "Perhaps tomorrow I will try jumping, a little, as I've seen children do."

He returned to the task of going down the steps, carefully negotiating each one with a little flourish as if every step were a particular triumph. I watched him until he entered the swirling crowd of people on the street below and was finally lost to my sight. I made my way up the rest of the steps.

Inside the courtyard, we ran into a flock of Pharisees. When they saw us, they paused and looked at each other as if to confirm their suspicions. Undoubtedly, these were the clergy from whom the lame man had escaped.

Now, they drew themselves up like a wall before us. My heart sank; this was what I had feared. There was going to be a confrontation. The Pharisee in the middle of the front rank called out to Jesus, "Are you responsible for this outrage on the Sabbath day?"

Jesus ignored the challenge, and continued to walk towards them at a normal pace, as if he were greeting a friend. "Which outrage has been committed now?" he asked lightly. "Has someone's anger and self-righteousness disturbed the true observance of the Sabbath? Or has some fellow been guilty of impropriety by denying God's goodness even on the Sabbath?"

For a moment there was silence at his challenge, and a little runt of a man poked his head round the edge of the front rank. He yelled, "Don't deny it! You healed that man down by the pool of Bethesda, you caused him to go through the streets carrying his bedroll, and you dared to give him dispensation from the fate God had placed on him. Crippled for his sins, you released him from the consequences of his sins and defied the judgment of God."

"Ah, yes, that was me. Our Father has listened to his prayers for thirty-eight years, and during all that time this man never complained about his lot, but simply prayed to be able to walk. He never gave up believing in God, and today he has my Father's answer. Don't you think that is wonderful? After all these years, God responded to the prayers of that faithful son of Israel."

"That is monstrous," snarled the tall Pharisee in the middle. "Do you imagine you are doing the will of God by thwarting his demands for holiness and purity? Do you not know that to encourage such a man as that to flout the requirements of the law is to put him in jeopardy all over again? There he was, walking through the streets with his bedroll for everyone to see, on the Sabbath, even! You not only caused him to sin, but everyone who saw him will now be tempted to hold a lesser regard for the Sabbath laws."

Jesus held up his hand. "Stop. This man has been healed. His prayers were heard by our Father in Heaven and I carried out my Father's answer to all those prayers. This is a son of Israel made whole, brought back into the fold once more. He asked, God answered, and I acted. Do you have a problem with that?"

The lead Pharisee was so angry he could barely speak. "What are you saying? Are you claiming to know God? Your familiarity with the Father seems to know no bounds. Your overwhelming and insufferable self-promotion amounts to blasphemy. You claim to know about the prayers of that sinful wretch, and that the Father heard them. What makes you think that is not just your arrogant imagination?"

Jesus suddenly let his anger break through his normally composed attitude. "Did you notice the man's legs? Did you see him walk? The deal is done. You are too late. Your contempt for God's word—by which this man stands healed—is noted, but what the Father purposed is already accomplished." He raised his voice loud enough so the people around him could hear. "Beware, for His word is abroad, it is at work, and is even now revealing itself in the world."

Silence fell on the group before us. They looked rooted to the spot. After what seemed an eternity, the tall Pharisee who appeared to be their leader made several indistinct noises, glared at Jesus and finally walked back through his supporters. The rest of the group followed him, and many of its members casting frightened glances at Jesus.

Jesus watched them go. He glanced around for me and, when he apparently noticed the crowd for the first time, said to them, "No one can do very much by themselves, and I can do nothing except that which proceeds from the will of my Father. Moses and the prophets knew that all they said and did proceeded from the mouth of God."

Many of the crowd looked uneasy with talk of God active in their lives. Whispers came from the corners of his audience, but Jesus continued, undaunted. "Hear what I said to those clergy, that the word of God is out, it is in the world and it is at work. Look around you and see the signs. This city has one slim chance for peace. Therefore, be about the work of our Father in Heaven, recognize His actions for what they are, and give glory to Him in Heaven."

I saw some from the crowd shrug and move off, but others pressed around Jesus, asking questions and begging him to tell them more. I knew what was going to happen. I could feel the eyes of the watching guards on the back of my neck. It would only be minutes before they would break up the knot of men, recognize Jesus and arrest him.

I quickly slipped towards the center of the crowd and took Jesus' arm. Tobias and his friend helped me steer Jesus back towards the stairs. I looked back and saw three guards moving towards us, and another two who looked as if they might cut us off at the top of the stairs. Fortunately, the sheer number of people in the crowd slowed down the guards' progress.

After a moment I realized what was happening. The delay was intentional. People were impeding the guards by simply getting in their way!

Smiling, Jesus nodded in understanding at the crowd's actions and accepted them for what they were. He allowed us to hurry him down the stairs, out into the street, and away into the labyrinth of alleyways that was the city.

I remember thinking at the time that this was no way to start a ministry to that city. Back then, I still suffered from the unconscious fear that Jerusalem engendered. Scratch the surface of the Temple organization anywhere and just below the surface was that inscrutable corruption, backed by unfettered violence. There was no negotiating with it, and there was no possible dialogue. Any opposition was systematically crushed. Back then I was still haunted by the vision of Jesus turning over the exchange tables and letting the animals out. I even imagined Jesus would have been tolerated, maybe even listened to, if he had not been so confrontational. What a vain hope.

7

Tensions and Reflections

"We need to be gone now. We'll take the east gate and get onto the open road. You've poked enough at the hornets' nest for today," I said.

Jesus made no comment but allowed us to lead him through the gate and out into the bright sunlight beyond the massive archways. As we slowed our pace, he said, "Did you notice the crowd? The people in that square understood what I was saying, and they were willing to act on our behalf. I tell you, it is time for harvest. The fields are white. The time is very soon. We have to get more laborers to help with it.

I looked around at the people pushing and shoving their way through the crowded streets. "I don't see many of these ready to help, but right now we need to get out of the city. If you go on stirring up trouble here, you will not see any harvest time. Those Pharisees were really upset at you."

We made for Bethany and the safety of Lazerus' household. After taking some refreshment in the form of some fresh figs and lemon flavored water, I walked back to the city. By the time I walked in through the gate, dusk was falling and the city was noisy with people taking their leave of others. Nothing seemed amiss. It was as if the event at the Temple hadn't happened. I angled off towards Jonathon's parents' house. Though it was late I found he had just arrived, and bade me follow him through into the little patio beyond the house.

Before I could sit down, he whirled to face me. "Annas had a full report of Jesus' actions today. Annas has put his agents on full alert and he wants every scrap of information about Jesus. He wants to know his friends, his opinions, his teachings and his past history. Jesus must be very careful. Jerusalem is no place for him. Too many accidents can happen here. Too many people disappear in the city, and there are spies everywhere. Believe me, the Pharisees have spies, the Romans have spies, the revolutionaries have spies, even the Essenes have their lines of communication, but they are nothing compared with those of Annas. I tell you he sits in his office and broods and plans. He loves intrigue."

As I listened to Jonathon I felt a deep frustration at Jesus' own indifference to questions of his safety. I took some comfort from the way the crowd responded to him that afternoon and told Jonathon the whole story of what happened. I added, "Maybe it is the common people who are his real hope. I don't see what his game plan is. He definitely has one, but he has not shared it with us.

"But what nags at me are his conversations about the real struggle underlying everything; the struggle with evil. These are not directed against Annas or even the power blocks represented by the Romans and the Herodians, but at something else more sinister, more profound that is universal to human experience and endeavor."

I remembered my dream again, and shivered as I felt again the overpowering confidence of that horrific image as it bore down upon me, and I thought of its powerlessness when I, strengthened by Jesus' quiet voice, stood against its approach and laughed in its face.

Jonathon was looking at me curiously. "What was that about? You looked like you'd left and gone elsewhere for a few moments. What's going on with you, John?"

I debated about telling him, but replied, "Jonathon, I am sure Jesus is not concerned with political power or simply teaching our people a new way to handle their lives. There is something more. All Jesus' conversations have as a theme the lie that is being told about God's nature, and the stark truth of his true nature that stands in contrast to it. War as a goal, political power as a necessary evil, and the ever-escalating demand for purity are alien to that nature. Jesus has a direct experience and knowledge of the divine.

"Jonathon, as one person knows another, and recognizes them without a second thought, so Jesus knows the Divine. Just as I am beginning to know Jesus, so he knows The Father. He knows God."

Jonathon stared at me wordlessly. The idea flew against all we—as Jews—knew and thought about our God, that unknowable and ineffable author of our existence.

Later, after Jonathon had gone, and I sat there in my house, beside the slight light of an oil lamp squatting on the table, I could not get the thought out of my mind that Jesus knew God. My final thought before I blew out the candle and the darkness rushed in from the four corners of my room was, "Oh, no, what have I gotten myself into?"

I was overcome by the enormity of what I had glimpsed, and chilled to the bone. I did not know whether it was fear or excitement. I finally had to laugh; the issue was far too big to be taken seriously.

That night I dreamed of mountains tottering on their foundations and puffed-up nations blowing away and loudmouthed orators blabbing undecipherable nonsense, and all the while, there was that insistent presence that denied their veracity.

I awoke with a sense of loneliness and I thought about going 'round to Jonathon's place and catching him before he went off to Annas' palace. I looked at where the sun was and decided it was too late—Jonathon would have left for the day.

Instead I applied myself to my business which, by the look of the pile of invoices left by my head man, was going to take me the rest of the day. Soon the thoughts that had possessed my mind retreated in the face of normalcy and good ol' business issues.

I picked up the first invoice.

THE SAMARITAN WOMAN

Three days later I hiked down toward where Jesus had made his camp by the Jordan. As I walked into the camp there were new faces among those I had come to expect around him. There were quite a few who harked back to John the Baptist but I heard much more laughter and none of the dour seriousness John's message encouraged. Jesus' teaching was taking hold, but not as beliefs, which were the hallmark of most instructional teaching, but rather as concepts. What did it mean to be a Jew? What was holiness? Was it more than cleanliness? Just what did sacrifice achieve and who really benefited from it?

The rest of that day I sat in on several conversations of this kind. That night by a fire made out of flood born wood collected beside the river, people sang and some danced to the music on a stretch of sand cleared of stones. There was a little wine and that got shared around, passed from hand to hand. At first Jesus was there laughing and challenging. Then he was gone. Nobody noticed and nobody thought anything of it, but I knew the signs, he was out there in prayer. I gave up thinking about him, and fell in with the good humor of the occasion.

I heard again the story of the man Jesus had healed in Jerusalem, although the narrator hadn't been a witness. Nothing was said about the crippled man, nothing about his struggle to stand and his courage as he faced a new life, but everyone wanted to hear of Jesus' facing down the Pharisees and doing so right there in the Temple Square.

As the fire burned down and people dozed, I looked about me and saw again that heedless hope of young men who were ready to spit into the eye of authority. Many of those there I never saw again, but others followed Jesus throughout the next two years and were with us in Jerusalem at the end. Judas Iscariot was there that night, and I think one of the more thoughtful. He listened more than the others, and paid attention to each of those present, calling them all by name by the end of the evening.

Thomas too was there. A thoughtful, quiet and insightful person, he said little. But when he did say something, it was profound. Jesus was important to him in a very deep way. I think Jesus gave Thomas hope for himself and for his world, and somewhere along the line, Jesus had brought him out of absolute and black despair.

I looked at the rest, and wondered whether Annas' agents had infiltrated the group. There would be nothing to stop them. Surely there was one here, but which? I looked around again but the innocence of the faces blinked back at me. No, there was no one. I looked out into the darkness afraid for Jesus out there by himself. In prayer, oblivious to everything around him, he was an easy target for a sicarii. Those terrorists were the perfect tool for someone like Annas. I counted the men. I thought they were all there. I was just imagining things but the next morning when Jesus appeared by the fire I felt a surge of relief.

Jesus looked across the smoldering remnants of the fire that someone had raked together and stoked with a few pieces of wood that had escaped the flames the night before. "Would you come with me back to Nazareth? I have been invited to a wedding there and I think I will go. Can you take time away? Some of these," and he indicated the sleeping forms of his followers, "will come along so don't feel obliged to come. I will be all right without you."

"Of course," I replied instantly. "When do you want to leave? I tidied up a lot of stuff before I left yesterday and at this time of year there will be no big shipments coming in for at least two weeks." There was no condemnation in his eyes, no shadow of disapproval as I mentioned business concerns, just a nod of comprehension.

"Right, let's leave by midmorning. I want to head inland and take the mountain road up through Samaria."

"Samaria!" I said in surprise. "Why there? We will not find the hospitality that we would if we went up the Jordan. That way is also a whole lot harder on the feet, and there are serious dangers from groups of robbers."

"Yes, you are right, but all the same I want to go back through that area. As for robbers, I think there will be enough of us, and we are poor enough that no respectable robber band is going to bother us. They would probably take pity on us and give us something instead," said Jesus.

I smiled and got to my feet. "I am ready when you are. Are you going to invite everyone or choose those you want to come along?"

"No, it's not time for me to choose my particular disciples. I will let them all know and those who want to come along can. I'll be back in a couple of weeks. Maybe some of them are ready to continue receiving people who come to see me, and they can baptize them for me. Several of them have really got a grasp on the essentials. If I am not here they will do even better. Maybe I will ask one or two to stay here and carry on with things. After all it's not magic. That way our visitors will not be entirely disappointed."

By noon as the sun beat down out of a perfect fall sky, we trudged up towards the high road that ran through the hills that bisected our land of Israel. We camped that night in a wadi that ran down from the hills towards the Jordan, now far below us and off to the East. The locusts clicked away in the brush and there was the warm smell of oils from the desert plants that hemmed us in.

We set a guard. I took the middle watch. I think Jesus suggested the watch just to placate my worries. As I ended my watch an hour before sunup, I looked again toward where he was sleeping and realized he was gone. Jesus was at prayer, and knew what he was doing. I did not have to look after him. Evil did not threaten him, but rather he threatened evil.

I sat musing in the darkness, and had to admit I was hard put to find a way to express all my regard for him. I imagined I could feel him out there in the darkness. I could sense his existence firming up in my consciousness, like a rock or a tree takes on shape as the morning light grays out the night. He was back amongst us as the others awoke.

The next day we were up on the road, heading towards Samaria. Late in the year the mornings were cool especially up in the hills. As we trekked along we walked in twos and threes. Sometimes I walked with Jesus, and at other times I chatted with one of the others.

Judas Iscariot was one of us, and in the late morning he joined me and another man as we walked. Our conversation was desultory at first, but Judas asked me about my business, about how I had met Jesus, and how long I had known him. My ingrained suspicious nature impelled me to answer cautiously, and in very general terms. I wondered if he was a spy, but I had wondered about each of them in turn.

Judas told me why he was there. He had been on the edge of a revolutionary group, and had come to listen to Jesus because someone had said he was a rabble-rouser. He had spent three days there at first, and went away confused. As he allowed what Jesus had said to percolate, he realized that his own anger and violence were counterproductive. "I swear I didn't mean to change my attitude, but in spite of myself I let go of those thoughts of revolt and instead, looked at the world around me from a fresh place. It was as if what Jesus had said burrowed into me and took root, and started to grow all by itself. Now I'm back and I think I've found what I have been looking for. The only thing is I still don't know what that 'it' is. All I know is that I have stopped looking."

I was somewhat mollified by this disclosure. How like my own experience. Jesus had never convinced me by argument, but rather what he said had simply taken root and become my own thinking and gave birth to all kinds of other insights. That is what excited me.

Late afternoon we dragged into Sychar. The afternoon had been hot and dry and we were ready for a stop. We would stay the night in Sychar if we could and if not, we would go on a little and camp. Jesus told us to go on and leave him by the well. We needed supplies so we walked into town, leaving Jesus by Jacob's well. It was a real well and had been dug by Jacob's men over 1500 years before. At least that was the story. Our land is full of history. Every stream, every crag or every valley had its history and as we walked someone would be bound to call out what he had heard from father or uncle or if he was lucky, his grandfather.

On our return to the well with food and a couple of other items, we found there was unfolding another of those anomalous events that were common when you traveled with Jesus. He was talking to a Samaritan woman. She was in her forties and an unusually attractive person, full of animation and not at all overcome by being in the presence of us all. Other women, with their jugs and water containers at their feet, stood watching. They had come to draw water for the evening's ablutions and other household uses but now were enjoying whatever had been going on in our absence.

We came in on the tail end of what had clearly been a serious conversation, for we heard Jesus say, "I, who now speak to you, am he."

The woman moved over to the other women and exclaimed, "He told me everything I have ever done. He must be a prophet." With which she spun on her heel and almost ran off towards the town. We accepted some water from a woman who had just hauled up her container, and we moved off to sit in the shade of trees, uphill from the well. We all looked at Jesus expecting him to explain what had happened.

He said nothing and as we unpacked the food we had bought, he continued to sit in silence wrapped in thought. He looked up as I offered him some bread, cheese and dates, but he waved the food aside. "Not right now, thank you. I'm chewing on something else."

I asked if anyone else had given him food, but there were only blank responses to my question.

Not an hour after that there came a whole host of men from the little town of Sychar. They were led by the woman to whom Jesus had been talking when we arrived. We all rose, expecting trouble. One did not talk and hold long conversations with women you did not know, especially in a strange location. A town or village's menfolk often viewed with intense suspicion any such exchange and would respond violently to any intrusion into their perceived area of privilege.

Jesus did not rise, but sat quietly, as if he was receiving a deputation. As the woman approached she slowed, and as she came before Jesus, said to the men following her, "This is the man. He is a prophet, or maybe even the Messiah. He told me all about my five husbands, and he knew about you and me, Thomas. I had come to draw water, and he asked me for some."

"He can't be a prophet. He would have known not to ask you," said a squat young man on the fringe of the twenty or so men who had now assembled in front of us. There was a titter from the rest.

The woman raised her hand as if to strike the man and he ducked away in humor. There was a story here, and we were going to hear it. So some of us sat back down, while the rest of us relaxed. Jesus was content to say nothing but watched the scene and especially the woman with a frank sense of appreciation on his face.

She picked up where she left off. "Well, yes, I did ask him what he thought he was doing asking a woman for a drink, and him being a Jew, and all. He said the oddest thing, that if I knew who he was I would have asked him for water and he would have given me running water. That didn't make sense to me because the well was deep and he had no container so how was he going to get water. Anyhow, he was thirsty himself and so why say such a thing? I thought he was just being arrogant like any Jew. I said 'What, do you think yourself greater than our own Jacob who gave us the well in the first place?'

"He said, 'Drink this water and you will be thirsty again, but drink the water I will give you and you will never be thirsty again.' Well, I didn't know what he meant, but the thought of not having to drag myself down here every day to fetch water sounded too good to be true so I said, 'Hey, give me some of that, I will take a bucketful. I'll not have to traipse down here twice a day.' I was trying to push his buttons, but instead of getting hot under the collar as any of you would have done, he just said, 'Go call your husband and come back here.'

"When I told him I had no husband, it was then he told me everything about my life."

"Not everything, I hope," said a voice from the press of men.

"No, I didn't tell him about you, you little toad," she said, and went on, "but he knew about my five husbands and about you and me, Thomas. Now how could he know that if he wasn't a prophet?"

By this time the crowd was thoroughly enjoying the story, clearly she was a character they all appreciated and had come to tolerate. Later we were to hear how every one of them had felt the bite of her tongue and the sharp lash of her wit. There was an air of expectation about those village men, as if they had turned out to watch her take on someone else for a change. This time it was a stranger who had run into her scorn and waspish humor. They were all behind her to a man; she was their own, and giving a good account of herself.

I noticed them looking over to Jesus and watching to see how he was taking it. He, on his part, looked as if he appreciated her forthrightness, and smiled faintly when she repeated his words.

A nod accompanied her description of her claim that their ancestors had worshipped on the mountain there forever, and that they went all the way back to Jacob. She continued with his assertion that the time was coming when everyone would worship in spirit and in truth and not go either to Jerusalem or the mountain.

At that, Jesus got up, and smiling at the woman, said, "Yes, the time is coming when we will not be worshipping in Jerusalem or for that matter here on this mountain. Worship is to be in spirit and in truth."

After he had received a drink from a bowl of water handed around, he explained. "The moment has come when a new relationship with God is to be launched. Instead of priests who take your sacrifices and perform the rites for you, each of you will be responsible for your life before God. You will each have to cultivate your own spiritual selves, and regulate the demands of your souls, your emotional selves, so that you are no longer ruled by your passions but welcome the Spirit of God welling up in you. That spirit will become like a well of water bubbling up in you, constantly irrigating your lives and bringing new life and growth. Welcome that spirit, invite it to overwhelm your souls and bodies, you will grow as you were meant. Think of it as like a grain of wheat that begins to root and shoot. All you have to do is keep it damp and it will do the growing itself."

Very quickly the conversation became two-way, and questions flew. Jesus, listening intently, answered each with humor and incisive comment. I looked around and saw how the men were enjoying this stranger for they were all around him, sitting at his feet, and thinking along with him.

One of them said, "Look, the time! It's getting late. Don't try to get to Samaria tonight. Stay with us." There was a chorus of invitations and Jesus nodded his compliance, looked at us, and on our behalf accepted the hospitality. We all got up and, dusting ourselves off, moved off in one solid group towards Sychar, which was less than half a mile up the valley.

The woman walked beside Jesus, and everyone was content to surround them in a throng of good humor and friendliness. One of them said, as we moved along, "Well, when Jas came back with that story we were skeptical. We thought she was pulling one of her jokes on us all, but now I apologize for doubting you, Jas, because you, Sir, are making sense. I've had private thoughts of my own but I never dared open my mouth about such things but you have said openly what I have thought. God doesn't belong in the pocket of some priest, He is here," and he thumped his chest, "and he is even in you." And he pushed the shoulder of a young, tousled, dirty-faced young man who was galumphing along beside him. "Well, maybe there are some exceptions," he grinned.

There followed a couple of days when Jesus spent time with the people of Sychar. Joanna, or Jas, as she was affectionately referred to by everyone in the village, entered into the conversations vociferously. In contrast, the other women of the town gathered round the periphery, and watched.

The rabbi, or rather, the leader of their synagogue, was a thoughtful person and he sifted through Jesus' words carefully. The subject of the Kingdom of heaven came up, and he asked point blank whether Jesus included them in it.

For a full minute, Jesus thought about the question, and looked around the hushed and serious faces before he spoke. Being born a Jew does not ensure it, neither does being a Samaritan exclude you. Maybe the invitation is made, and each person gets to reply for himself. Like a wedding party, the friends are invited and there are those who wouldn't miss it for the world. There are others who have what they consider more important things to do and so they refuse the invitation, and there are people who would not be seen dead at the wedding. What is your reply to the invitation?"

At this, Jesus continued to study the faces about him. "There is one more thing, though. It is the bridegroom who invites you to the wedding, no one else. The bridegroom gets to decide who is invited. Nobody gets to deny others his or her invitation, and nobody gets to decide who should accept, but each person invited."

For us men with him, this was a surprise. He had never talked like this before. We looked at each other as if to confirm what we were hearing. Quite honestly we couldn't wait to get him on the road and challenge him on this one. From the moment Jesus encountered that woman, there was a change in him.

As the next day wore on, he relaxed even more, and for a while seemed free of the shadow that had been creeping over him as the months went by. With these strangers, these Samaritans, it was as if he could set aside the calculating and speculating, and simply enjoy the people around him.

By that second day there was a warmth and openness in Jesus we had not encountered even down by the Jordan. That last evening the wine came out, and the women had baked some special treats for everyone and there was quite a party. The men danced and sang. We Jews joined in one by one until we were all dancing, even Jesus.

At one point early in the evening a woman approached Jesus with a platter of freshly baked bread and, kneeling before him, asked him to bless it. What should have been a perfunctory ritual became a moment of great solemnity. Jesus took the bread and blessed it, but instead of handing it back to the woman to be served, he passed it directly to everyone. I took my share, of course, but as I ate it, I fancied I was eating his blessing. Smiles ran through the crowd. Yes, we were all in. In spite of myself I saw the rest of the crowd as my brothers and sisters, or rather, as my family.

Of course that was only for as long as the party went on. Later, I wondered what had come over me and I couldn't wait to get on the road.

The next day, we were up early. If we were to get to Cana in time for the wedding we had to push on fast. A few people were up. They gave us bread, fruit and goat's cheese to help us along, and we were off.

We were hardly out of earshot of the town when Judas Iscariot moved alongside Jesus and asked him about the evening before. Did he really mean that Samaritans were to be part of the Kingdom of Heaven or just those few people whom we had met? He said, "You never discussed that with us or mentioned it before. I think we were put on the spot."

I drew closer to hear Jesus' answer because I was intending to ask the same question. Jesus responded after a moment's thought. "You were willing to accept their hospitality, but you are not willing to receive them as equal in the sight of God?"

"No, I liked them well enough, they were kind to us, and goodness knows you spent a lot of time with them, but they are not Jews, they are not part of any Jewish Kingdom," said Judas.

"That is what the Essenes, the Sadducees, the Pharisees and the Herodians all think. They see the Kingdom of God to be a Jewish kingdom, but it is not. It is God's Kingdom and, as I said last night, the Bridegroom and nobody else gets to decide who is invited to a wedding. Salvation comes from us, but tell me, who does it not include? I am asking myself that question too. Where do we stop?

"We have been taught to believe we are the chosen ones, and so we are, but chosen for what? Are we called to privilege or is it responsibility? Do we share our blessing or do we keep it for ourselves? In what container are you going to keep that blessing, how will you preserve it? Have you known anyone who has been able to preserve the blessing of God without sharing it with everyone around? God's blessing runs through your fingers if you try to keep it. Well, where does that stop being true? At the borders of our nation or do we include the Samaritans, and if the Samaritans then what? No, I do not see where the line is drawn, but don't be upset; it is not for you to decide, or even approve or disapprove."

We walked on in silence. Both Judas and I studied the ground on which we walked with unaccustomed interest. Later, Judas murmured, "I wish I hadn't asked the question. So we've got to include the Samaritans now. I thought the job was hard enough. Where do we stop? Jesus needs to narrow his goals, not increase them."

I agreed with him, but walked on in silence. I felt the tension in myself between the new attitudes I had learned from Jesus, and the old hatreds and assumptions I had learned as a Jew. Samaritans were to be included? Now that was a stretch.

The Wedding at Cana

We went on in silence for a while. Samaria lay just ahead, and the hour was early. We decided not to stop but to pass through as quickly as possible. We filled our water flasks at the well and went on unnoticed. There were others on the road now. We were seven in number, and so as we walked we split up, and as was customary joined the other travelers on our way North.

We camped out that night, and the next morning we were off early. With only ten miles to go we were still fresh, and approached Nazareth just after noon. We walked up the hill and dropped down into the little hamlet.

The houses were clumped together close to the well. The surrounding hills were dried out, and covered with the brown, whispering grass of fall. Once the rain fell in a month, there would be new green grass mantling even the high ground. Some farmers had plowed their little plots in the valley bottom where the soil was deeper and most likely more fertile.

I saw a herd of goats, or were they sheep, working their way along the skyline, their heads down, foraging among the rough grasses for a mouthful of nourishing fodder. The figure of a young boy followed the sheep, swinging his stick at goodness knows what, maybe thistles with their bursting seed pods, their seeds floating away on the slight breeze coming up the valley.

This time, as we walked down the central street between houses, the few people outside in the heat of the day acknowledged Jesus and at least one stopped to greet him. This was an improvement since our first visit.

Jesus' family was assembled in their best clothes, their washed and shining faces looked unlike the young men I had met on my first trip. Here they were, all ready to go to a party, and all they were waiting for was Jesus. We, by contrast, were dusty and sweaty from the journey. We washed in water from the stone pots set out for that purpose, and sat for a while eating bread and some olives and dried figs, which we washed down with wine very much diluted with water as was the custom, especially in poorer areas.

We learned the wedding was due to start that afternoon, and by the anticipation of the brothers they were ready to be off. Jesus did not explain why we were later than he had planned, neither did they ask. They fell to talking about the wedding: who was getting married, and who else were going to be participants.

Mary, Jesus' mother had packed up utensils and panniers of food. The young ones finally couldn't wait, and hoisted these on their backs and went on ahead of us. Mary and Jesus exchanged some quiet words, and smiling with pleasure at his company, she allowed him to lead her out of the house onto the path to Cana. The six of us followed on.

Judas fell in beside me and was full of questions. "So, that's his family? They all look as if they are rubbed raw and worn down by the earth. You will not find hands like theirs in Jerusalem. What happened to his father?"

"He died about ten years ago. The family has had a tough time, or so it appeared last time I was here. I don't know how he died, but I fancy it was one more misfortune that they have faced together. Did you notice Mary? She has the strength of will to harness those boys of hers to put food on the table and clothes on their backs. When I was here before, the villagers had a profound appreciation for Mary. Amongst other things, she makes sure those in the village who have little still get enough. One story I heard was of her shaming one tight wad to unbend and help another bad luck case. Not only did the person let down and give, but now Mary and he are best friends. Guess who she goes to when she needs help with something? Anyway, that was the story. I don't know who it was, but no doubt he will be there this afternoon."

I said to Judas, "If you wonder at all where Jesus gets his care for others you need only look at his mother. Did you notice how they had those few quiet words before they set out. They haven't seen each other for months and those few words were all they needed to say to each other. I doubt she knows just what kind of trouble he could get himself into. I wonder if she worries about him, it doesn't look like it, but is it ignorance or is it confidence in him?"

"She looks to me like she is in on some secret they have together. You were right about the greeting. Just a couple of questions, short answers and they were ready to be with the rest of us. I would say she is not afraid for him, but looking at her I think she knows—or at least is expecting—something more than we see. I feel as if I just walked into a family secret. Whatever questions we have, the answers can be traced to this house. She knows more than you think."

The hour's walk to Cana was mostly in silence, as Judas and I walking side-by-side considered the questions we had given voice to. Once we were there, we were soon lost in the crowds of arriving people. They were all intent on catching up with the news from the other towns and communities around. We made our way through the hubbub of people's greetings, to the courtyard behind the building

I noticed Jesus' brothers off to one corner. They already had started their partying, and were greeting friends from the area as each new-comer entered the garden. Soon a gaggle of young men stood chatting, joking and laughing with each other and casting surreptitious glances at a group of demur young ladies who were greeting long-lost friends as they arrived.

Soon the party was in full swing. Food was laid out, musicians began playing, and we awaited the arrival of the groom with his entourage. Much later, after the ceremonies had been completed, the party settled down to a boisterous roar, as everyone from Cana and a fair number from each of the other hamlets arrived and piled into the general reception.

Jesus' brothers were full of the party spirit and contributed their fair share to the crisis that occurred on the second day. We were going to be reduced to bringing our own bottles of wine, and that was something the bridegroom would never live down. His supply of wine was running out and this would mean a premature end to the festivities. There was quite a little bustle in and out of the kitchen, as messages were passed to the head of the feast, and a lot of head shaking. Finally I saw the people from the kitchen walk, dejected, back towards the food preparation areas and the courtyard beyond.

Not long after that Mary came through to the area in which we were all partying, looking for someone—Jesus, undoubtedly. He was watching the festivities, and talking to friends from Nazareth. I had watched the little drama unfold so I went over and joined them just in time to hear Mary ask Jesus to give her a hand with something in the kitchen. He moved off after her, and I followed at a discreet distance.

Mary noticed me and waited for me to catch up before she told us what the problem was. "We are down to the last few skins of wine and there is no more to be had in the village." She looked directly at Jesus. "Would you help, please? This is a disaster for them. It is no way to begin a life together. I am sure you can think of something. Please."

I've never seen Jesus put out, before or since. He normally had a good grasp of the issues and came up with solutions easily enough. Now, though, he looked at his mother with exasperation etching his features. Finally he shook his head. "What am I going to do with you, Mom? I am not ready. It's not time."

Mary placed her hand on his arm. "I know, dear, but what can we do?" Mary instructed a couple of servants nearby to do what Jesus told them. "It will be all right," she confided.

Jesus caught my eye, grimaced and, with a sigh of resignation, told the kitchen staff to fill the stone jars they used for water purification. In the Jewish manner, these had to be stone, or the water couldn't be used for washing. Water was dipped out of them for use in purification rituals. They were at least thirty gallons each and very heavy.

The servants filled them back up with water that, as part of the purification process, had to come from the well or from a running stream. Jesus told them to draw off the water and let the master of the feast taste it.

The kitchen staff looked at each other and stared down into the water. One of them shrugged, took a dipper, drew some of the liquid off, and, lo and behold, it was wine. The water, or rather wine, was good stuff, too, as we soon found out.

Jesus shushed up all of us, and told the servants not to say anything. Needless to say, they couldn't keep their mouths shut, but nobody really noticed. The party went on, and in the hubbub it was all forgotten, but not by me.

This event was a kind of sign to me. Jesus didn't do it for himself, or to show off his skills. He tried hard not to draw attention to himself, but I had to agree with Judas: his mother Mary knew a lot more than she let on. She knew what he meant when he said, "It's not time yet." She also knew he could do something, and would. Maybe he couldn't help himself, or maybe he couldn't deny her.

For myself, this awed me in a way the future miracles in Jerusalem would not. I found myself wondering, not for the first time, just who Jesus really was, and what was his "time." Somehow the idea of him being the Messiah as John the Baptist had declared had not translated into much more than a title in my head.

Now, as if I were peering behind a heavy curtain I was seeing the real person, and the raw power and passion of the man. There was more to him than we knew. How would he use his power? What was he waiting for?

After the wedding we relaxed for a day or two, and decided to stroll over to Sephoris to visit friends and see what was happening there. I watched as Jesus moved among the people, and occasionally saluted someone he remembered. His curiosity was insatiable, and he asked questions of everyone he encountered.

He was relaxed, and enjoyed the camaraderie of the place—he even took the trouble to engage some of the soldiers in conversation. They were from Syria and had signed on for duty because there was nothing for them at home. Within minutes Jesus had them talking about their families and friends they had left behind. Their stories of sadness and loneliness poured out.

Judas kept back, but Thomas and I pressed in, as a ring of soldiers stood around us. The transformation I had seen so often, happened here, and soon laughter and shared memories flew around the group. After awhile we took our leave of them, and Judas rejoined us as we walked on. By late afternoon we slipped out of town and were back in Nazareth by the time the sun went down.

20
ARREST OF THE BAPTIST AND MOVES AGAINST JESUS

Four days later we were back in Jerusalem. Jesus left me there and continued on to Bethany. Anxious to get the news of the latest developments I met Jonathon at his parents' house. He was beside himself.

"Where have you been? It has started. Herod has taken John the Baptist. He was arrested three days ago. Annas had me send a letter to Herod congratulating him on his scrupulosity over the law in removing John. Then, he asked me for the file on Jesus. He spent an hour reading all the reports. He sent for Caiaphas, and the two of them were in there for at least an hour. Please, warn Jesus. Tell him to hide somewhere safe for the moment. I tell you, Annas has marked him down for removal."

My first reaction was to shout out in denial, but I remembered the warnings we had passed on to John. Why hadn't he listened!? Finally, I let myself imagine John locked away in darkness, most likely in a dungeon, amidst rats and worse scurrying about.

I felt sick with dread at what I knew must follow. Forgotten and abandoned, people rotted away once they were imprisoned at the King's pleasure. There would be no trial, no one to speak for him—just never-ending night with the occasional visit of a guard who would throw some food on the floor.

A flood of deep regret passed over me, for John had been the beginning of everything for me. When I was floundering around, he gave me something to believe in. He baptized me and set me on my road. Tears prickled behind my eyelids. I blinked them away and sought a place to slump down on.

So, it has started! My fears were not ridiculous, but very real. What was Jesus' present location? I calculated that Lazarus would know about John by now, and Jesus would know he was next. I decided he would be safe for the moment because Annas would not know he was back in town, but would Jesus stay away? I realized I had to be careful how I phrased my concerns and warnings. Jesus might just choose to challenge Annas right there in Jerusalem. He might attack the merchants in the Temple again. I went to bed but not to sleep, and finally at sun rise, I left my house for Bethany. Jesus was there. He was grim faced, and he had obviously heard the news. Now what?

Jesus greeted me. "You have heard the news? It was as I expected, though Herod has taken his time about it. I expect our friends in Jerusalem had to remind him a couple of times before he plucked up courage to face John the Baptist. John was intimidating when he wanted to be. I heard the soldiers who arrested him were relieved when he went with them quietly. I bet they thought he would call down fire on them or turn them into some animal." Jesus laughed at the thought and continued, "By now, Herod will have had his first tongue-lashing and may be regretting getting in bed with Annas."

He frowned, and sighed. "John has done his job; now it is my time. I've sent a message to him, and I know his disciples will see he gets looked after. I don't see how Herod can let him go. He doesn't even know why he had him arrested. John was my cousin, you know."

"Can we talk about you for a moment?" I asked. "Jonathon told me last night that Annas is focusing his attention on you. I think you should leave and retire to the desert somewhere. Here you are but two or three miles from the Temple and Annas could have you picked up any time."

Jesus smiled for a moment at the urgency in my voice, but ignored my request. "I am glad you arrived early. I want to go back into Jerusalem, and maybe even visit the Temple. Will you come with me?"

I couldn't believe he would disregard his own safety to this extent, and felt a moment of acute anxiety. Jesus stared at me, awaiting my answer, and I knew I would not change his mind. I shrugged, "Of course I will come. Somebody has to carry the news of your arrest to your friends." Jesus simply quirked an eyebrow at me, which irritated me all the more. "Did you not hear me a moment ago? Annas spent hours reviewing your file and conferred with Caiaphas for another hour or so. You can bet they have laid plans to take you the next time you raise your head there."

Jesus shook his head. "No, not yet. They are interested in me, yes, and Annas senses me as a threat, but what has he got? A crippled man healed, some basic teaching in the Temple square for a few hours, and little else. Granted he will have reports of our work down by the Jordan, and certainly accounts of our evening conversations with our friends but all in all I don't think he knows what I am. John did not openly divulge my secret. No one is talking Messiah. Some may have questions about me. I know a few like Nicodemus and his friends are very interested in what I am going to do next. Annas can feel my presence I think. I can certainly feel his scrutiny, but he is puzzled. He does not know. He has questions, and he is wondering just who and what I am and what I intend to do. He knows I am coming after him, and all he stands for, but he doesn't know how. He will not make his move until he knows more."

"Jesus, in Cana you told your mother, 'It wasn't time yet.' And I have a feeling that all you've done so far is scouting the battlefield. You go to Jerusalem, you test and probe, and you withdraw. You are teaching and baptizing a few people, but that doesn't appear to be your main objective. It is as if you are offering people what they expect, yet there is something else you have up your sleeve. What is your objective? Where are we going with this?"

Jesus looked at me a long time. "Are you still with me, even if you don't know?"

"Of course I am," I said with a trace of frustration in my voice, "but I would like to know what we are doing. John the Baptist fingered you as the 'Lamb of God' and you have spoken of God in different terms than any of the other voices we hear about the place, but you have attacked the Temple operations, you have seen fit to make a stir on the Sabbath and have gone out of your way to make yourself felt. Next, you leave so that everyone is left wondering. Judas and the others were asking the same questions on the way back from Nazareth. You have a timetable. You have an objective. You have said to me that you did not know, and that you were still working it out in your head, but I think you now know. John's arrest is a signal to you. Tell us what has changed, and where are you going with this?"

Jesus motioned for me to sit down. I looked for a seat and found one on a bench by the wall in the shade of a fig tree planted close to the wall. Slowly he began. "Yes, I do know what I am to do. Yes, John's arrest is a signal. Now I must carry out my part. As for the objective, I plan to destroy the Temple and all it stands for. You heard me say that to Caiaphas. At least they cannot complain that I didn't give them fair warning."

"Destroy the Temple?' I thought you were not serious when you said that. That building has taken years and years to build and you cannot just push it over. Do you mean figuratively you will destroy the workings of the Temple, or overthrow the organization of the Sadducees?"

Jesus shook his head. "No. More than just figuratively, but to destroy, wipe out, eradicate the Temple as the center of our nation."

"How?" I asked. "The Temple is not going to go away, the High Priest and all his family will not just blow away. You have not formed alliances, you have turned your back on force, and decried the efforts of the Essenes and others who want the same but are bent on doing it by revolution. What is your plan?"

He was silent for a moment, marshalling his thoughts, before he replied, "I don't know how, but I am sure that the Temple and especially what it stands for has to go. The sacrifices, the assumptions behind them and the power of those who have a death grip on our people have to be broken down. The building itself is the least important, but that too will eventually go. I am the weapon chosen by our Father to bring all this about. I don't know how, but I see my next step is to close with the authorities there in Jerusalem and make them sweat.

"Tomorrow, the Festival begins, and I will be there in Jerusalem. I will walk in the Temple, and I will disturb Annas and his bully-boys. They will notice me, and wonder. They will finally come to understand the threat, but not yet. I need to poke their nest some more. So will you come with me tomorrow? You realize they will be starting a file on you soon."

"Of course I will be with you." I replied, "but what are you going to do? You are not going to attack the clergy or make a scene? You are not going to cause a riot? Don't forget the Romans also are watching for troublemakers, I bet they have a file on you."

Jesus grinned, "No, I promise I will not cause a riot or attack those puffed-up lumps of pomposity. I will just be myself, doing what is asked of me. I'll do nothing that you will not approve of. How about that?"

"Not good enough, Jesus," I replied. "You said something about poking their nest. I don't like the sound of that. It is inconsistent with just being yourself, and doing only what I would approve of." I added, "Maybe I'm wrong there—you being yourself might just cause a riot." I laughed at the idea. "Let's not prod their nest. If you must go into Jerusalem tomorrow, of course I will be there. Are you going to stay here tonight?"

Jesus replied, "Yes, I believe we are invited to dinner with some of the Pharisees. Lazarus will be going, and he has asked me specifically to be with him. You are invited, but I would also prefer to have a couple of the others with me. Maybe Judas and Matthias. Would you look after that?"

"I replied, "Of course. I'll go find them now. I thought I saw Judas in the village. He is always chatting with someone. I bet he knows all their names, has already worked out who is who, and who thinks what. If we get to the point of having a large following, he is going to be very useful." With a nod to Jesus, I went in search of the others.

I had expected to go home that evening and have dinner with Jonathon and his parents. I wanted to glean any other information he might have on what was going on behind the scenes. I weighed Jesus' assessment of the situation against the dire warnings of Jonathon and wondered again at what strategy Jesus might have. He was not making any alliances, he was not organizing a counter force or even speaking of the need to oppose the high priest and his family. What was he doing? Just being himself! I had laughed at the thought before, but now I regarded it with a grim sense of helplessness. He was a force, just his presence was a challenge, his words so reasonable were in themselves a confrontation.

I thought back to the dream of my encounter with the evil one, and remembered Jesus' words from behind me. *Stand. He cannot touch you.* Somehow that obduracy in the face of evil was beginning to be felt by others, and they were disturbed by it.

I shook my head, hoping to dislodge my feeling of dread. Jesus' words about our Father in Heaven accomplishing His will in this matter were no comfort. I wondered if John being thrown in prison was our Father's way of rewarding John for his efforts. I shut my mind to that line of thought. No, we were most definitely in some kind of battle, and there would be casualties.

For a moment I thought about Jonathon at home with his parents as they prepared for the Festival. Given our conversation during the last hour I knew I could hardly sit there with Jonathon and pretend Jesus was taking Jonathon's warnings seriously. No, I had to stay the night and go in with Jesus in the morning.

Instead, tonight I would enjoy Lazarus' sister Mary's presence. I had come to appreciate her spirited way of inserting herself into the conversations. Too bad she would not be with us at dinner. Neither she nor Martha was invited, as was the custom in Jewish circles of the day. Simon, a Pharisee, had invited a select group of his friends. Judas, Matthias and I were there, but very much in the background. Jesus was the guest of honor.

This was a meeting of power brokers. These were very sensible people, and they had questions of Jesus that clearly indicated their willingness to ally themselves with him. The probing was not overt, but they wanted to know what his objectives were. Discussion on the direction of the nation, the policies of Caiaphas and even the office of Pilate the Roman Governor were all points of conversation. They led inexorably to the question of who Jesus was, and what were his objectives. These were politicians, not bad people, just wanting the best for themselves and for the nation. They were testing the wind like animals scenting the smell of a predator.

They did not find themselves at variance with Jesus' objections to the whole political status quo, especially the way the Temple was used to empower one family, who plundered the people and gave little in exchange. I think Jesus' raw spiritual power and authority both attracted them and gave them pause. The Pharisaic approach to the relationship between God and men assumed we were responsible for carrying out His will, and afterwards we claimed we were responsible for carrying out expected God to do much at all. The sight of Jesus healing people did not fit with their expectations. Holiness, for example, was a remote standard, and it was something you had to achieve by yourself. God's pleasure was reserved for you when you did achieve it.

After the meal, as we lay reclining at the table and the conversation was turning to this real gulf between Jesus and his hosts, there was a disturbance at the door.

A woman burst into the room.

Seeing Jesus, she came around the table and approached him from behind her. Judas, sitting next to me, gave me a knowing nudge. Simon, our host, was flustered by this intrusion and embarrassed for his guests. Two of them further down the table exchanged appalled glances and muttered to each other.

The reaction at the table was immediate. It was as if we all shrank from her. Judas, sitting next to me, gave me a knowing nudge. Simon, our host, was flustered by this intrusion and embarrassed for his guests. Two of them further down the table exchanged appalled glances and muttered to each other.

Simon heard what they had said and nodded his head, agreeing with them. Judas indicated another couple of men who sat tense and still. I wondered what their problem was, for they both looked as if they had one.

Jesus allowed the woman to complete her act of devotion, placed his hand on her head as if to still her agitation. She sat back on her heels and dropped her head in quiet surrender. Jesus looked down on her for a few moments, and unhurriedly said, "Simon, I have something to say to you. May I?"

Simon and the rest of the table were released from their paralysis.

"Of course," he answered. "Go on, please." He sounded relieved of the responsibility for this embarrassment to his guests, and looked to Jesus to explain and remove the problem. Little did he know it was going to get a lot worse.

Jesus reflected for another couple of moments before he slowly spoke. "Simon, tell me. If two men owed debts to a third, one of which owed a thousand dollars and the other owed fifty, and the third person forgave both debts. Now which of the two would love him the most?"

Simon hesitated, knowing a gulf opened before him, but was unable to stop stepping into it. He finally replied, "The one that had owed the most and who was forgiven the most."

Jesus dipped his head in agreement. "When I came in this evening, you gave me no water to wash my feet, but just an ablution for my hands. There was no kiss of greeting, no expression of pleasure for my presence. But see this woman, she has not stopped bathing my feet with her tears and wiping them with her hair. Her sins are many and some of you know that from personal experience." At this, he glanced down the table at the two men whom I had noticed earlier, and who now stared transfixed at the woman kneeling before Jesus, who added, "but her sins are forgiven, and hence this display of appreciation."

He extended his hand to the woman and helped her up. "Go on home, your sins are forgiven. Start over." Glancing at his feet and back to her bowed head, he added, "Thank you."

His glance encompassed everyone at the table, finally resting on Simon. "You asked for my credentials this evening, you asked for my game plan and you wanted to know my mission. Now you have answers to all your questions if you care to think about them. All the evidence is before you. I cannot make it more clear than what your eyes tell you and your ears confirm."

The party broke up amid a buzz of speculative talk, with much shaking of the heads and puzzled looks at Jesus. He smiled at them. "I came here tonight for your sake, not mine. Look at the obstacles you put in everyone's way. Think of what little hope that woman had before she heard me this afternoon. Yes, I know what kind of woman she has been. Yes, I know what our scriptures say, but how would you restore her? If we are agreed no sacrifice is going to wipe her clean, then what? You remember the prophet Jeremiah spoke of a new heart. How do you propose to give her a new heart?

"Now you know why I am here: for those who have sinned much and those who have sinned little. It's not the well person who needs a doctor, but the sick. Think it through! None of you are far from the Kingdom of God."

The company broke up and people took their leave. We did also, and went out into the velvet night. As we stepped outside I felt a palpable caress of the cool dry air dropping off the higher ground of the Temple mount. The city was quiet and benign. Odd sounds echoed on the night air. Stars tracked across the sky and for a moment I felt the years of our presence there in Jerusalem. I thought of David storming the heights, I thought of Abraham and Melchizedec, the line of prisoners being led off to Babylon, the return of their descendants, and all the passion and suffering that this square mile had seen.

There was a secondary mission going on here. One that had a beginning, long, long ago. It was still running. While other new agendas ruled the day, in the evening you could feel the older, primitive will of the divine, unhurriedly bringing about its inscrutable purpose. This darkness was not the darkness of the cloud that obscured the light and which dragged behind the purposes of men, but the soft, velvety touch of mystery, which welcomed us and sought an opportunity to reveal itself to us.

As I looked at the stars so cold and glittering in the sky, I felt them call out to me as if in invitation to explore heaven itself. Nothing was denied me, nothing was denied any of us if only we would open our eyes and see, or listen with our ears and understand.

I paused in thought for a moment. Not for us to believe, but for us to understand. That was the distinction that had escaped me. That evening Jesus asked the guests to consider what they had seen, not so they could believe but that they would understand. Believing would not make them part of the Kingdom of God, but understanding brought with it participation, consent and acceptance of being part of it all. I finally got it.

We all were invited, but we all had to be willing to participate in the dances, the songs, the rituals of the wedding feast. It was like the wedding at Cana, all the people from miles around came. They did not just accept the invitation, but joined in the dancing, the singing, the stories, the laughter and the wine. Yet, it took Jesus to supply the wine, in order for the party to go beyond the expected limits of the ordinary. I smiled at the memory of Jesus flummoxed by his mother's demand for him to do something. Like the wedding, the Kingdom of Heaven goes on beyond the limits of the ordinary and did I dare think that Jesus would provide the wine to fuel the party beyond our expectations? I grew excited by my speculation and impressed with my insights.

As I gazed out into the night I thought, yes, of course, that was Jesus' intent. Common sense asserted itself, however, and my next thought was, "But how could one man do any such thing?"

Reality intruded. I couldn't see a thing and I had to feel my way down that first narrow street. My soaring thoughts crashed to earth in the face of the chilly evening and a toe-stubbing darkness. I looked for the moon to light my way, but there was none. Along with the other guests, I had to feel my way back to the house of Lazarus.

Jesus ranged alongside me, and matched my thought exactly. "See, you have to walk in the light when you can, for the darkness comes and no one can see."

Just those words out of the darkness lit my mind again and called me back to my own thoughts of him supplying the wine for the Kingdom, the light to lighten our darkness, his words to strengthen us to stand.

Jesus' voice came to me again from the darkness. "There is a small window of opportunity. If they do not seize it, darkness will fall and they, like us right now, will be unable to find their way. John, they are all close, but I fear for them because from where they stand they can only see how far it is across the gulf that separates them from the Kingdom of Heaven."

Decades later, I sit on Patmos in the dark, looking out towards the mainland. I remember how sad Jesus was when he couldn't quite reach someone. As we walked home that night, he had been sad. Not for that woman, but for those men. He so wanted them with him, but only for their sake. He never sought to make use of anyone. He wanted us for our own sake. I can't think of anyone else for whom that is true.

21
CONFRONTATION

The next morning Jesus was ready to move into the city and begin his nest poking. I was under no illusion about his intentions. Jesus' words to Simon, his host of the night before, still rang in my ears: "Simon, I have something to say to you."

No, I knew today was not going to be easy. I could imagine Jesus saying the same thing, but to our enemy: "Caiaphas, I have something to say to you." But Caiaphas was far, far from the Kingdom of God, and didn't know it. Poor Caiaphas!

We met Jonathon as we'd arranged at my little house, tucked down an alley and out of the main throng. His face was drawn, and he looked about him with an urgency that he had not had before. When he saw us, he greeted me with his customary warmth but he greeted Jesus in an almost stiff and formal way. "Master, John has talked about you so often that I feel as if I know you as well as he does. I regret I have not been able to listen to you as so many have done. I am, though, a follower. I, too, am a disciple in my own way."

Jesus greeted him and put him at his ease. "Jonathon, your friendship with John is one of the good things John has shared with me. You are a person who loves strongly and you seek truth. I see you, but I see your fear for us all. Will you come with us now or do you prefer to maintain your cover? I think you would be better off doing what you have been doing. After all, no doubt you will hear all about what we do."

Jonathon was disconcerted for a moment. He realized Jesus had seen his discomfort, weighed all the issues and let him off the hook. "Master, everyone is talking about you. The ordinary people are full of speculation about you, and some are already talking about you as the Messiah. They are creating a situation which may become dangerous for you. The Temple authorities have given instructions for you to be brought before the High Priest. They have no real reason for your arrest, but you would be held at the pleasure of the High Priest."

"I doubt they will attempt to do it during daylight because the crowds are waiting to see you, to hear you and watch your performance. I have no doubt that just your presence in the Temple precincts will be enough to spark the crowd's enthusiasm. Please be careful. Caiaphas has had instructions from Annas, and I know contingency plans have been drafted. Orders have been passed out."

Jesus smiled at Jonathon's earnest demeanor. "Thank you for your concern. Yes, you are right, the people do expect me, and in one way I am loathe to play to their desire to be entertained. They want to see wonders and healings but do they even know what I am talking about? As for the High Priest and his men, I doubt they have the guts to interfere. I do not need to be circumspect at this stage."

I felt a surge of hope and relief as I heard him express his need for caution.

We went inside, and in the shade of the little courtyard behind my home, we sat and listened to Jonathon. I produced a few figs I had bought three days ago before I had left to see Jesus, and which were now almost too ripe. Jonathon filled us in on the news from Herod's court.

John the Baptist was apparently still being held, and would be indefinitely. Concern over that last appearance of Jesus had prompted some questioning among the various groups but nothing more. Apart from the time Jesus had thrown out the animal sellers and money changers from the Temple precincts, there was nothing they could point to as actionable. There was a genuine fear amongst those in authority that if there was a riot, the Romans would clamp down hard on the city. One little riot and the guards would be out in the streets beating heads and arresting ringleaders. Pilate had no trouble acting with speed and dispatch.

After Jonathon had gone, we left my apartment and walked up towards the Temple mount. We came to the flights of stairs that led through a massive archway and there the Temple lay before us. Like every other time I had seen the Temple from this angle, I caught my breath. As a Jew I was looking at the heart of my country, ethereal and lofty. I called to mind the words of some of the writers of the Essenes who saw Jerusalem as the center of a Kingdom that would last a thousand years and the Temple as the center of that Kingdom.

I contrasted that with the reality; the bickering, in fighting and outright violence of our leaders. There would be no thousand-year kingdom, there never had been, there was no hope we could all live together in that kind of peace. Intrigue, the selling of political favors and brokering of power would corrupt the kingdom before it was even a reality.

Jesus was right. There could be no earthly kingdom. The prophets had to be talking about something else entirely.

As I mounted the last steps I saw the crowds milling on the pavement. Our presence went unnoticed for a few moments as we advanced, but soon enough men recognized Jesus and pulled back from us as we advanced. I saw two men duck away and hurry off. I thought grimly that Caiaphas and even Annas would be alerted to our presence in the next few minutes. Jesus took no notice of any of this but proceeded towards the courtyard of the Temple as if to go about his own business, which, of course, was true.

From the crowd someone called out, "Jesus, they are waiting for you. Don't go in there."

Another voice called, "They've got your number. You're just another trickster with your so-called miracles."

"What do you want with us," another cried. "We don't need any more Messiahs around here confusing the people."

Others joined in and soon there were cries of "No, he is a prophet! Jesus, speak to us, what must we do? What is this new way you are talking about?"

Soon questions were flying from both sides, and Jesus slowed his steps. He faced them. There were a few hostile faces, but most were curious and others plainly much more than curious.

He looked around, trying to make eye contact with all of them who would meet his gaze. "I am not here on my own account. I have been sent to you to call you back to the purpose of your God, your Father and my Father. As the prophet Isaiah said, I have come to make the lame walk, the blind see, and preach good news to the poor. What I do is not my own will but the will of my God and your God, my Father and your Father.

"John the Baptist called to you all to repent, and prepare for this day. I am here to announce to you forgiveness of your sins. Put away the works of darkness, the violence, revenge, the buying of favors and the struggle for power. If a man hits you on one side of your face to insult you and to provoke you, turn to him your other cheek. Renounce violence. Since the days of Isaac you have been taught to exact revenge from those who attack you, to hate those who hate you, to oppose those who disagree with you and in all ways maintain your honor in the face of other's opinions. I say to you, pray for those who hate you. If someone takes your shirt, give him your coat also.

"What does it matter what the next man thinks of you, when your Father in Heaven sees the inside of you? Honor comes from God, not from the people around you. Put away violence from this city and make this place holy, dedicated to our God. You think sacrifices will gain you a place in God's favor? Never, but a broken and contrite heart God never despises. Read what the prophets have to say, do you think God stopped speaking to you when Moses died?"

A shout came from the back of the crowd. "How do we know what you are saying is true? You might want us to become passive and compliant so you and those behind you can take advantage of us. Do you think we are stupid?"

"Listen to yourself," said Jesus. "As I have said, this teaching is not mine but from Him who sent me. You find the same words in the prophets. Don't take my word for it, but try it for yourselves. Anyone who resolves in his heart to do the will of God will know whether this teaching is from God or whether I have my own agendas as you suggest."

An aging man voiced his concern. "You are asking the impossible. It is our right, no, it is our responsibility to avenge insults and injuries others do to us and our families. Shall I not do anything to preserve the good name of my father? Do I not have the responsibility to wipe out him who dishonors my sister or my daughter?"

"Yes," shouted another, "Moses said an eye for an eye, tooth for a tooth. Are you changing what Moses told us?"

Jesus smiled at the man, and held his hand up for a moment to command a silence so he could be heard in the growing hubbub. "Yes, I am changing what Moses said. I'm telling you to turn the other cheek, if someone forces you to go a mile out of your way, go with him twice that. Moses was faced with a people who were broken into tribes and warring families. Blood feuds went on for generations. He established a law that only permitted you to take a very limited revenge.

"Before Moses, violent men like you would kill whole families, follow old hatred for generations and exact horrific penalties for the least injury. In turn they were killed by the remnants of families left. So feuds went on generation after generation, all for some point of honor long forgotten. Moses stopped all that, and established the limitations of revenge you could take.

"That law still stands, but I am saying to you that to do the will of our Father, to be the people of our God, to be children of God we must renounce even the desire for revenge. I say to you love those who hate you, pray for those who despitefully use you, and do not return evil for evil. Let hate, hurt and all evil die with you. Don't pass it on, turn from sin and bring it before your God. Confess the evil done to you and don't stretch your hand out to take that evil and make it your own."

The man who had asked if Jesus was changing what Moses had said spoke again, but this time quietly. "You are asking too much. I cannot ignore insults or intended injuries. Yet as I look at this city I see it's full of violence just as you said. We are a violent people, part of a violent family of peoples. Everywhere you turn others force themselves on you, and if you let them, they will take delight in trampling on you."

Addressing those around him, he gestured to the city, the Temple and the distant hills. "But if we don't give up the violence, what is going to happen to all of this? We have to come together if we are to have any hope for a peaceful life for our children and our grand children." He walked away, shaking his head, and pushed his way back through the crowd. The silence grew as others contemplated the reality that was their daily experience of the city of God.

A flock of Pharisees bustled up. The one in the lead came to a halt before Jesus and glared at the quiet crowd; the man obviously wanted to ask what was going on, for a silent, thoughtful crowd was no common experience in Jerusalem. Finally he snarled, "Now what are you trying to tell the people? You do not have the authority to teach here in the Temple precincts. You are a disturbing influence and we must ask you to desist."

Jesus looked the spokesman up and down and replied, "Moses gave you the law, and still, after all this time, none of you keep it. You cannot teach the people to keep it, and you can't help yourselves, and you call yourselves teachers. You would muzzle me yet not be able to offer these people anything except very conditional promises."

The Pharisee tossed his head and snorted, "You cannot observe even the most basic rules of the Sabbath; you've run roughshod over the fundamental requirements of our laws. Therefore you are not a creditable teacher of anything. We have evidence of your indulging the whims of people on the Sabbath when they could well come to you later. We've warned you several times about meddling in the affairs of the nation and you have taken no notice. You still act as if you were some prophet or someone sent directly from the presence of God."

At this, the man drew himself up to his full height and announced to the people gathered there, "We have to inform you, we are sure this man is an imposter and should not be listened to. We suspect these miracles he is purported to have done are prearranged tricks and no healings have taken place." He paused dramatically and imperiously pointed towards the entrance to the courtyard, glaring at the crowd. "Leave! Pay no more attention to this imposter."

From the back of the crowd came a voice. "Get lost, you old windbag. We will listen to whomever we please. You've never taken any notice of us until someone else starts teaching us."

Another voice chimed in. "He makes more sense than all the rest of you put together. We're for you, Jesus. Don't let them run you off."

Shouts from the crowd grew in volume as they took delight in the discomfort of the five representatives of the Pharisees. Jesus held up his hand and the crowd fell silent.

Jesus addressed the Pharisee but everyone quieted so they could hear what he said. "You are angry at me because I healed a lame man on the Sabbath day. I know what you teach as well as you, but let me just say this; you are wrong. You, yourselves circumcise on the Sabbath so that the law of Moses can be applied, how much more should we heal a man's whole body on the Sabbath if we can. You have strayed from the central requirement of our Father, that we should prefer mercy to sacrifice. Therefore I ask you to not judge by surface appearance but by right judgment. Your way is not God's way."

"You have a demon," screamed the Pharisee. "Beware, all of you. He will bewitch you with his fine words. The authorities are investigating him. They will know what to do with him if he continues this course." To Jesus, he ground out, "Continue and you will be disposed of. Unlike John the Baptist you will not be held at the pleasure of King Herod but put away permanently."

On hearing this threat, the crowd moved threateningly in towards the small party of Pharisees, and a buzz of speculation went up. "Then it is true. The Temple clergy do want to kill him." "Do you think they know more than they are letting on?" "Maybe he is the Messiah and they don't want it known yet."

This was what I feared most. Once the guards got involved and the people pushed back, there could be ignited one of those incidents that might grow into full-fledged rioting. Jesus would be accused of instigating it, and that would be the end of him.

At this point a section of guards pushed through the ranks of the crowds and took up station between the people and the Pharisees.

Jesus spoke once more. "You know me, and you know where I am from. I am not here of my own accord. The one who sent me is true, and you don't know Him at all. You should be very afraid."

At this the Pharisee, who was obviously the leader, screamed at the guards to arrest Jesus.

With one glance at the Pharisee's spokesman, Jesus dismissed him with a motion of his hand. Calmly facing the crowd, he paused, smiled at them and slipped between them. The crowd opened before Jesus and closed behind him as the soldiers moved in. I saw the individuals intentionally jostling the guards who finally extricated themselves from the melee and went off to report. I wiped my face with my sleeve, and with considerable relief went after Jesus.

Meanwhile the crowd was very pleased with themselves and excitedly speculated about Jesus. The last I heard, as I hurried out of the Temple precincts, was, "Maybe he is the Messiah. After all, he stood up to those Pharisees."

"No, I doubt it, he is from Galilee. The Messiah will come down from heaven or just appear."

"I loved it, that Pharisee guy was huffing and puffing like a camel."

"The best part was when Jesus just told them they were plain wrong. Nobody dares ever to stand up and tell them that."

"Do you think the Messiah, when he comes, could do any better?"

I ran down the steps and caught up with Jesus further down the street. I couldn't keep from scolding him. "That is just what I was concerned about. All you have to do is show yourself and trouble finds you. Those guards were not sure what to do, but next time they will know exactly what to do. Let's call it a day. I think we should go on down to the Jordan and give things time to cool down."

Jesus refrained from answering, and we made our way back to my place. We sat in silence for a while. Jesus said to me, "Do you know what happened back there?"

"You nearly got yourself arrested, you came close to starting a riot and you insulted one of the powers that be in the Pharisaic camp. You accomplished all that within thirty minutes. Don't you think you are a little abrasive? Maybe just a little hard on those men? They take themselves very seriously."

"John, get this into your head: it is not the Pharisees we have to watch for, but the Temple people. The Pharisees will huff and puff but never take decisive action. They will debate it, communicate their displeasure to the High Priest and . . . nothing. The Sanhedrin will not take it up or even discuss it. No, that was all smoke and no flame. I think tomorrow we can do better?"

"Tomorrow?" I croaked. "You can't . . ." My voice trailed off as Jesus smiled over at me.

"For a moment, John, you sounded like a frog. The people are beginning to take sides. Those people declared themselves today. You will see, we will own that place during the day. At night, without the people's protection, it is a different matter. Ultimately we have to trust the people."

Later that afternoon, Jonathon slipped in and filled in the rest of the picture. "Caiaphas ordered guards to arrest you on sight. He has also alerted the members of the Sanhedrin who are most sympathetic to him, so that they will have you before a panel immediately so they can get rid of you right away. Their excuse will be that Roman concerns at the unrest you are creating will result in repressive tactics by the Romans. Caiaphas intends to act to head off any such hardship for the people of Jerusalem. At least that will be the story."

Jesus explained, "You see, we are forcing the Temple to reveal itself. Caiaphas will not go out on a limb himself, and he will avoid confronting me personally. I intend to make arresting me and trying me far too risky for our friend. I think tomorrow we will be very moderate, and very sensible of the people's concerns. Let's be clear about one thing, I have no interest in promoting strife and violence among the people. The Romans have no part in this struggle.

"My intent is to destroy the Temple as a center of power and tyranny. The Temple sacrifices shall cease, and we will worship in spirit and in truth. You remember the words I spoke to that woman we met at the well in Samaria. That discussion helped me put several pieces together, and gave me this new direction. I now see more clearly what has to happen. We must all learn to worship in spirit and in truth and no longer expect animals and birds to take responsibility for our shortcomings. There must be no more using a goat to carry away the sins of the nation. We all have to be responsible to the Lord for our sins and the sins of our nation. So there will be no buying Him off, no bribery with burning meat, or worse still, no more selling His favor to the highest bidder."

I looked over to Jonathon and wanted to say, "See what I mean?" But before I could, Jonathon objected. "But the clergy will have no jobs, no support, no food for their families. There will be no industry in knick knacks and stuff that people buy to remind them of their pilgrimage to Jerusalem. This is not going to be just between you and Caiaphas, this is going to be devastating. The clergy will not take this lying down. You are likely to finish up as one of the sacrifices."

Jesus stared at Jonathon for a moment. "What did you say? That I would become one of the sacrifices?"

Jonathon shrugged. "I meant that these men are, by their office, butchers. They kill as part of their work. If you try to take away their livelihood, you could be a casualty, especially if you were arrested and imprisoned. Don't let it happen!"

Jesus sat back, raised his steepled fingers to his face and thoughtfully tapped his chin. "Jonathon," he began, but let the words trail off. Suddenly, he stood up. "Come, it's getting late we should leave for Bethany. Thank you, Jonathon. Knowing what is going on in the minds of those people is helpful." I picked up my satchel, and we all left my apartment.

The following day we accompanied Jesus into the Temple porticos. There, sitting in the shade with his back to the wall, Jesus quickly attracted a small throng whom he proceeded to teach. He asked them about how the Lord punished sinners.

One and all agreed that the Lord caused bad things to happen to them. If not to them, then to their children. One angry older man said, "Ezekiel said that the sins of the parents will be visited upon the heads of their children and their children's children until the fourth and fifth generation. What do you think of that?"

Jesus looked out over the crowd, asked if everyone had heard the question and continued, "Ezekiel said, 'No more shall it be said that the sins of the parents will be visited upon the heads of the children.' No more. We have to learn to take responsibility for our own sins. Let them die with us, and not pass on the suffering we have inherited. You, sir," and he looked directly at the man who had spoken, "imagine you are righteous, and you are even more sure you are right. Look into the face of the Lord, and imagine trying to justify yourself. Look at how you have snarled your way through family life, look at how insensitive you are to other's opinions. Yet with all your boiling rage and potential violence not far away, you too are sought by the Lord. If you will take responsibility and if you will give up your self-righteousness, your Father in Heaven will renew your life. You will have a new innocence, and with new eyes you will see the world the way the Lord sees it."

The man puffed and huffed, and tried to maintain eye contact with Jesus, but finally broke away, pushing roughly through the crowd. Jesus looked after him, A shadow of regret passed across his face. "He will be back. It is not too late for him. It is not too late for any of you."

A man at the back of the crowd called out, "Why does our Father in Heaven cause people to catch leprosy? Why do people die young like my little Shasa? You say our Father in Heaven loves us and wants good for us, but why so much suffering?"

Jesus held up his hand to stem the murmuring of agreement that rippled through them. "Do you not think the Lord feels even more acutely than you the pain of your daughter, her fear, and her love for you as she faded away? Look beyond her disease to its causes. You had found no work for a year. You were all having to eat what you could beg, and your little Shasa gave her piece of bread to your young son more often than not. Weak, she contracted an illness and fever that burned her up.

"Your child died because of the evil that stalks our nation. The farmer loses his farm, the moneylenders demand more interest on their loans, and finally the family has to eat the seed corn they were saving for the next sowing time. What you suffer from is the evil that is abroad in the world, and that is going to require something a lot more powerful that the sacrifice of a goat or even a bull.

"Don't blame the Lord for the suffering you have to bear because of the greed, injustice and insensitivity that is found everywhere throughout our land. Yes, the Lord has heard your prayers and the prayers of your daughter as she lay dying and He has sent me."

I had heard some of the same points before, so I let my attention wander around the courtyard. I noticed two Pharisees standing off by themselves. One looked at the other, gave a nod, and whispered in the second man's ear. The next moment one of them headed out into the sunshine and purposefully headed down some steps towards the city below. For a moment I thought he had gone for the guard, and Jesus' words about the starving people and the greed of the merchants might have been seen as incendiary, but he had gone the other way, away from where the Temple Guards were.

Jesus went on with his teaching. He had a very different idea about what our God, the Lord and the Father of our nation was like. He seemed to speak to their particular needs as if he knew their special circumstances. He spoke gently to them, spoke of the Lord's love for them and His will for the whole nation. He spoke about the sin of the world, not in phrases of anger, but in deep regret and sorrow. He talked of the results of that sin, starvation, families being broken up and people having to beg for food to keep themselves alive.

There were not a few in the crowd who had come to the city from the countryside looking for work and found less on the streets of Jerusalem than in the places they had left. Now in cramped quarters and crowded squalor they lived a precarious life.

To these Jesus spoke with a gentle compassion, never inciting them to anger, but encouraging them to see what the causes of their poverty were, and the changes that needed to happen. He got up, and walked among them, one man he paused before, and took his hand in his and straightened the hand. The man looked astonished, flexed his hand as if for the first time and sobbed, "Thank you," and dropped to his knees.

So it continued: Jesus moved among the people, and there was a touch here, or his hand rested on someone there. The people quieted like a wild animal gentled out of its fear by kindness. I looked up and noticed the portico was ringed by guards. They had assembled quietly and now watched as Jesus moved among the people. He returned to where he had been sitting and sat down.

I kept an eye on the guards. They were not moving, but just watching us. For a moment there was silence in the square. From the back of the crowd one man called out, "What shall we do? What do you want us to do?"

Jesus looked out over the heads of the people to the man who had spoken. "Love your neighbor; you are in it together. Don't let the other sink. Care for each other and bear each other's burden. Your lives are hard, but with each other's help you can see each other through."

The people looked at each other, and here and there individuals bowed their heads. I thought in shame maybe, but I realized they were praying.

This sacred moment was abruptly interrupted. Another crowd broke into the square. This group, in contrast to those sitting around Jesus in silence, was animated with hostility and triumph. The man who I had seen slip off into town was at their head, and as they entered the area, he indicated Jesus.

I got up hastily, thinking there was going to be violence, but Jesus held up his hand. Others who had been listening stood, and I could feel their power as they rose to protect Jesus. They remained silent, watchful and obviously suspicious of the small group of Pharisees that now crowded into the space.

From behind them, two men brought forward a struggling, frightened woman, whom they threw to the ground in front of Jesus. The chief Pharisee there said, "This woman was caught in the very act of adultery. There is no doubt she is guilty. Now the law of Moses dictates that such a woman must be stoned. What do you say? Do you agree with Moses in this or are you trying to overthrow all our traditions along with the very law itself?"

Jesus, who was still sitting by the wall on the low bench, bent down to trace some letters or shapes in the dust. There was silence, and only their looks of smug certainty marred the moment, as if they had finally cornered Jesus. I didn't know what Jesus would come up with, but I knew it was going to be good so I relaxed and waited. I glanced once more at the guards, but they were watching the proceedings as avidly as all the rest.

Jesus looked up and announced, "Whichever one of you who is without sin, you begin, and throw the first stone."

As he said this he straightened up and, one after another, looked each of the Pharisees in the eyes until they flinched away from his gaze. The eldest of the Pharisees was the first to turn away. The rest followed him out into the sun without looking at each other, but tried to show a studied nonchalance, as if nothing had happened. They disappeared down the steps.

The woman sat up in the dust from where she'd fallen when they released her. Jesus said, "Did no one condemn you?"

"No one," said the woman. For a moment she gathered herself in order to steel herself against the next onslaught.

Jesus said, "Neither do I. But go, clean yourself up, and clean up your act. No more adultery. Sin no more; be something else." He stood, reached forward with his hand and helped her up. She looked back and forth between him and the men ringing her.

Jesus looked at several partly veiled women—as propriety required—standing together as they looked on from the edge of the crowd. "Make a place for her. Take her in. Look after her."

They looked uncertain, as if they had been caught in a place they shouldn't have been and listening when they should have ignored this meeting of men. One dropped her hand from her veil and let it fall away, took a step forward and beckoned the woman.

The woman, with bent head, allowed herself to be taken into the group of women who had at first hesitated. They looked back at Jesus, understood what he expected of them, finally forsook their reserve and embraced her. They led her to a shaded place where they sat her down between them. I could see she was weeping and shaking violently.

Jesus nodded to the little group of women. "That is how it works. That is how you do mercy. On the other hand, you all saw how thin a blanket righteousness is. Don't trust in it, but mercy on the other hand is a tough act for sin to follow."

At this there was a general hubbub. I noticed the officer in charge of the guards who had been witness to all of this catch the eyes of his men. He gave a little shake of his head and nodded back to the guardhouse whence they had come. One by one they filed slowly and almost reluctantly out. People got up from the stones and soft voices were raised in wonderment. "Is he the prophet Elijah do you think? Could this be the Messiah?"

We left, and the warmth of the people wafted after us. Not a few men joined us as we walked down into the city. We hung around with them, chatting and going over the encounter. Jesus was asked into a house for refreshment and we all barged in. The man's wife brought in cool water flavored with a lemon juice and some little honey cakes. The room was bare, and Jesus ate sparingly of one little cake as if he understood how little there was for the family. I could see though that he was moved by the warmth of the people. Those inside the house and those hanging in the door and the windows all wanted a look at him and to hear accounts of what had happened.

Out of the city, down through the Kedron Valley and up to Bethany we went. That night we heard from Nicodemus how the guards had come back empty-handed and Caiaphas had berated them when the Captain and his second-in-command reported in that they had not arrested Jesus. The Captain as good as told Caiaphas to go and do his own dirty work. "I, for one, am having nothing to do with arresting that man. Nobody speaks like him and there was no harm in anything he said. No, there was no inciting to violence, no contravention of the law, and, in fact, he upheld the law." Nicodemus beamed his approval.

I felt better than the day before. At least in the opinions among the people in the square, the guards and now with Nicodemus' report, I could see a swing in Jesus' favor. Jesus had been right. He needed to trust the ordinary people of Jerusalem.

So, Caiaphas has failed again. He came 'round an hour ago full of excuses and whining about how hard it is to pin this Nazarene down. Apparently he is not actively fomenting revolt. Caiaphas thinks perhaps he should be left alone until he can be discredited in some way. "Never has anyone spoken like this," Caiaphas told me the guard captain said, "so why should we arrest him?" If the fool really said that, he should be demoted. Who is he to judge?

There are otherways to deal with him. What is obvious is he is firming up popular support among the ordinary people. Where were his backers this morning? I didn't hear of anyone of importance being there, just whoever happened to be in the Temple square. Maybe Caiaphas has a point, let him go on until he gives us a better idea what he is up to. Maybe a campaign to discredit him would be a more efficient way to deal with him.

As someone from Nazareth, he falls under Herod's jurisdiction, but I don't see him being of any use. When

Herod is next in town maybe I could talk to him. On second thought, maybe not. Herod might swallow the line this Jesus fellow is selling.

I think we should keep the guards away. We don't want him turning their heads. If we decide to pick him up it can be at night but I think there are other solutions we could use.

I must ask young Jonathon to write to Herod and have him check out Jesus' family, friends and connections. There is a lot we don't know about this man.

22
HEALING THE BLIND MAN

That night Jesus, Judas, Thomas, Nicodemus and I went for a late-night stroll down onto the Mount of Olives. There was an olive press there, which, at that time of night, was not in operation, but we could smell the rich aroma of the crushed olives.

Jesus asked us to wait for him and went off to pray. We settled down, making ourselves comfortable sitting on the low wall which ran around the olive press. We talked about the day. Judas had not been there and wanted to know every detail, as usual, so we told him.

Judas responded, "The question in everybody's mind: who is he? Is he the Messiah? There are some odd things I don't understand. He seems to know a lot about people's lives, for example, that man yesterday whose daughter died. He talked to the guy as if he knew all about it. It is not as if he goes around collecting information on people."

Thomas replied with a shrug, "Maybe it was a good guess."

So the conversation went on. The question of who Jesus was went unanswered. We speculated on Jesus' next moves and wondered what his ultimate goal was. None of the others had any better idea than I did.

"Do you think Jesus knows?" I wondered aloud. "Maybe he hasn't told us because he doesn't know and is feeling his way along." Before anyone could reply, Jesus returned, and we took the trail up over the ridge back to Bethany and Lazarus' home.

The next day saw us back in Jerusalem. It was the Sabbath so people were milling about. We were in discussion over some of the things Jesus had been saying. None of us wanted to give up the notion that a thoroughly bad person should have bad things happen to him, and therefore disaster was the result of wrong doing somehow.

Jesus kept quiet and let us work it out for ourselves. Finally, though, Judas pointed to a beggar and asked, "Jesus, this blind man, who sinned in his case? Did he sin or was it his parents? To have been born blind surely could not have been his fault?"

Jesus stopped by the beggar and told Judas, "Neither he nor his parents sinned. Justice, fairness or punishment had nothing to do with his blindness, though you could say he is blind so you can see the power of God at work." With that he lifted the man to his feet and asked him, "How long have you been blind?"

"Me, Master?" The middle-aged man tried to look towards where Jesus' voice had come from. "Me, I've never been able to see. I have a couple of friends, and they bring me each day to the Temple steps, and I sit here until they come and get me in the evening.

"I can't see nobody but I hear them. I heard you go by yesterday. You went by mid-morning, and not an hour or so later you came back. and there were a whole lot of others with you. I recognize voices. I know many of them that go in and out and know those who give and those who never see me. When you cannot see you hear more than people like you to know."

Jesus spat on the ground and made a little blob of mud. He took it and smeared it on the man's eyes. "Now go and wash in the pool of Siloam. You can find your way there?"

The blind man touched the mud on his eyelids and repeated Jesus' directions. "Pool of Siloam. Yes, I can get there, but why? Someone else might take my spot." He stopped and listened to Jesus silently waiting for him to make up his mind. "Okay, I will go if you say so. I can get someone to help me if I need to. No, it doesn't matter if someone takes my place just today."

The man took off, feeling his way down the street towards the pool. I watched him go with a mixture of alarm and admiration at how Jesus had arranged the matter. I looked across at Jesus as we mounted the steps, and he shrugged his shoulders. I said, "You sent him off to the Pool of Siloam to buy time, didn't you? He will find he can see, start making a noise about it, and we will be long gone."

Jesus grinned at me. "See how I take your concerns seriously? You are right, I could have looked after him right there, but it was also better for him to take an active part in what was to happen."

"Okay, so this time, this person did not ask you for help. Judas brought him to your attention. So, why him, this time?"

Jesus thought for a moment. "There we were talking about him as if he didn't matter, but he heard everything. You were asking about who sinned. What do you think he thought about that? Here he has sat in darkness for all his life, and you want to blame him for it, or worse still, you want to blame his mother and father from whom he has received the only love and care he has ever known. What do you think he thought about your question?

Judas and I exchanged guilty glances. Jesus was right. Neither of us gave a second thought to the man or even considered what it felt to be abstractly discussed like that.

Jesus went on, "He listens to that pity and judgment all day as people drop coins in his basket, and most of them not only pity him but judge him as being responsible for the way he is. People think that just because he is blind he is stupid, but he is not. His hearing is acute, and he hears what's in the hearts of people. You heard him. He recognizes everyone by their voices and knows those who give and those who don't. So what was different about us?

"In his hearing you asked the question about who was responsible. Do you think I could leave him there sitting in his darkness after we had passed? Like so many he is stuck in his own place not by his own volition but the nonsense we spout."

"Jesus, we were only trying to follow through with what we had been discussing. Now you are mad at us."

"No, I am not mad at you but at the gross stupidity of clergy and well-meaning religious folk who stand in judgment of such people. That certainly stirs me up. Just think of what nonsense that man has had to sit and listen to year in and year out. So, yes, I am angry, and that is why I healed him. He needs a little of what he has never dared hope for. Today he will see what he has only heard of." Jesus stomped off in the direction of the bench by the wall we used the day before. Sheepishly, we followed him at a distance.

Jesus led us to the shaded bench and within a few minutes some of those I recognized from the day before came and sat with us, greeting Jesus as *Rabbi* and *Master*. Jesus made himself comfortable and began his customary teaching.

That morning it was all about the conditions we bring upon ourselves and those conditions we are not responsible for. A rich man is no more blessed than a poor man, and as he stated emphatically just because a man was lucky didn't mean he was favored by the Lord or that he had an advantage when it came to the spiritual life. "It is harder for a rope to go through the eye of a needle, than it is for such a person to enter the Kingdom of Heaven."

That caused a stir. "Do you mean the rich are not part of the Kingdom?" asked a prosperous looking person on the edge of the little crowd Jesus had attracted.

Jesus responded, "No, I said it is more difficult. Everything you own, owns you. You have many obligations. You are so self-sufficient, what need have you of the Almighty? Again, you no doubt find it hard to be generous especially to those much less successful than yourself. You give dinner parties to those of your own status or those above, hoping to attract their good will, but if you are to enter the Kingdom, you will need to give dinner parties for those who are starving or are without influence."

Jesus paused but the man waited as if he was willing to hear more. Jesus continued, "Can you see how you are isolated by your riches and protected from the vagaries of life? Your empathy for others is affected, and you have become insensitive. So yes, it is harder for you, a rich man to enter the Kingdom of Heaven. Take heart though, for it is by no means impossible. You can be patron to the poor, you can be their protector. I can see this presents some problems for you. Come, sit here with us. Make room for him, John."

The man hesitated, and deliberately made his way into the group and took his place amid the growing number of regular listeners. A crowd broke into the Temple square at the far end. There was shouting and cries of jubilation.

Judas caught my eye and, in a low voice, asked, "Now what? Looks like someone has been crowned king for the day." The crowd milled around someone in the center, and they moved towards the sanctuary.

Quickly guards barred the way, but the crowd was not subdued, and became even more emphatic about whatever had stirred it up. The guards wavered, and clergy came bustling up. Three of them waded into the middle of the fray and were obviously debating with someone there. Their shouts reached us in the darkened corner. I looked at Jesus and was about to ask him what he thought was going on, when I saw the amusement in his eyes.

He smiled at me. "See, riots happen without me. I promised you I would not get involved today. You can't blame me for that riot."

There was something in his eyes, though, that made me turn to take another look at the crowd. What was going on? At the center, clergy were talking to someone whom I could not see for he was somewhat short. Finally the clergy seemed to give way, and they led him towards the Temple offices. They were not arresting him, and the crowd followed on after them.

I looked back at Jesus, who by this time looked as if he was inordinately pleased with himself. It was the blind man. Jesus did set up the disturbance. He had loosed the blind man like an arrow right at the heart of the clergy. How were they going to explain this one away? They could not even blame Jesus because the blind man didn't know who he was and had never seen him, but they would know. Maybe not right away, but they would soon find out.

Jesus went on with his teaching but I can't remember what it was about. My mind was on the blind man. Finally I got up and left Jesus sitting there and made my way after the rabble who were no longer boisterous, but anxious observers as if watching a camel race they had bet on.

I came up to them and asked a man (who, by the smell of him and the stains of saffron and other spices, worked in one of the spice stalls down in the city) what the noise was all about. He replied, "A blind man has just been healed. We all know him, and he's always been blind and now he can see. He is on his way to show the clergy."

"Who did the healing?"

"The man doesn't know because he couldn't see who it was. Some are saying it might be the Messiah. I heard someone say it was one of the brothers from the Essenes, some said it could have been that Jesus who has been here for the last week. Nobody knows but we're going to find out. The clergy will figure it out."

I pushed on through the crowd, until I was inside the entryway of the staff offices. One of the senior staff had come down and wanted to know what was happening. One of the young Pharisees explained that the man had been healed and had come to give thanks for the miracle. "Then what's all the noise about? Let him go into the Temple court, give thanks and clear out with all the other ruffians. Get this riff-raff out of here."

"But, sir, you do not understand. He claims he was born blind, and has been one of the beggars at the Temple gate for twenty years, and a man healed him. He can now see. Everyone knows him throughout Jerusalem. Every man has seen him as they have gone up into the Temple enclosure. I thought perhaps the High Priest should know about this. We are, after all, on full alert for anything abnormal."

The senior staffer thought for a moment and, to the man who had been healed, asked not unkindly, "Is this true? Were you born blind?"

The man somewhat awed by the company, nodded soberly, "I do not know who he was. I couldn't see him but he made a little mud from spit and plastered it on my eyes. He said, 'Go wash it off in the pool of Siloam.' I had heard him go by before, and I knew his voice, but I never saw him. I got myself down to the pool and washed as he had told me, and I could see."

"Hmn. Then why all this noise and excitement? Can't you just go home?"

"I am sorry, sir, but I have never seen anything before. I could only hear the voices of people, and now I see you all. The beauty of these buildings, the trees! I did not know what a tree looked like. What a beautiful world you live in. I have never seen it before."

With this he again turned to the people who followed him, and they in turn laughed and clapped him on the back. The considerable crowd moved restlessly. One man shouted, "Have you ever heard of a man born blind being healed?"

Another took up the cry, shouting, "What are you going to do about the man who healed him? He has got to be a prophet at least."

"Yes," shouted another, "you are not going to get any better than that."

At this the staffer gave an order to someone behind him. I heard him order the young staff member to find the blind man's relatives and check out the story. He asked the man that had been blind, "You say you don't know who this man was? He is not likely to be a prophet or a Holy Man, but is likely one of the cheap fakers that this place attracts. We have seen this kind of hysteria before. You will most likely wake up tomorrow and be back begging on the steps again. You cannot think this is for real."

The man stood rooted to the spot and stared in astonishment at the Priest. With a muted roar said, "No! Tomorrow I will wake up, and I will watch the sun rise out of the East. This is a true miracle and no cheap fakery. Whoever heard anyone heal a man blind from birth? I tell you this man is truly a Holy Person. I know he is. I heard it in his voice. He ordered me to wash, he wanted me to see. Everyday, you all have passed by me, and some of you have given me a few coins. I know each of you by your voice, but this man's voice is different. He told me what to do, and it was done. Just like that, my blindness was gone. It was in his voice. That's why I will see the sunrise tomorrow. The healing power was in his words. This is not going to go away."

The Priest pompously drew himself up and stared with disbelief at the man. Finally with a hiss he said, "Who do you think you are? Who are you to question my opinion? We know who this man is, and we know there is no good in him. He is trouble. Don't you dare question our judgment!"

I felt a wave of alarm go through me as I expected to see the man cave in under the onslaught. Instead he took a miniscule step forward.

"Whoever heard of a sinner being able to heal a person who was blind? He has to be a holy man; he has to be a prophet at least."

The Priest gave ground for a moment. "We shall see. I have sent for your parents," they will confirm whether you were born blind or whether you have been pretending all these years and defrauding the good-hearted and generous people entering the Temple. Maybe you are the fraud. Maybe you are now seeking a way to capitalize on the religious fervor released around here during this festival."

The blind man looked as if he had been struck. Gazing at those who had pressed into the passageway with him, said, "Who is blind? I thought I was blind, but my darkness was nothing compared to this. How can an honest man answer such an accusation? All I have ever wanted was to see, and now that I do, you are turning my blessing into something mean and nasty. Is this what you priests do?"

Incredulous now, he continued. "You don't want this to be true. You hope you can make all this blow away. I don't think you believe the Lord does anything. Maybe you are jealous because the Lord, may His Name be praised, does not work through you. The thought He might be working through someone else is just too much for you. When you are blind, you cannot see anyone, but only hear the voice. You learn to discern what a person is by his voice, and I hear your voice and it is without good in it. I came here to give thanks, to share my blessing and I thought you would be glad, but you are not. Grace is a stranger to you."

The young priest who had hurried out when we first arrived came back in and spoke quietly to the senior Priest. I did not hear it all, but he had talked to the parents who he had met hurrying to the Temple because they had heard their son was in trouble. The young priest had asked them directly if their son was indeed blind. He had even told them that the man could see and therefore may have been pretending all these years in order to beg on the steps of the Temple.

The parents were, of course, scared by this interest shown by the authorities and apparently replied that they knew nothing about how he could see now, but that all they knew was that he was born blind. He had never been able to see at all, and just this morning he left the house as usual and was still blind.

The older priest asked a couple of other questions, and the young man shook his head. To another question he nodded his head towards the inner chambers of the offices and muttered something in a low voice. The older priest dismissed him and stood glowering at everyone.

Advancing towards the blind man again, he reluctantly admitted, "Well, your parents say you were born blind and that you have always been blind. We are going to have to look into this, because we have a good idea who did this. Tell me again just what happened."

"Sir, I've already told you once. This man was talking to some other people, and one of them pointed me out, and the man stopped right by me and as he was still talking to the others, he spat. The next thing I knew he was pasting stuff all over my eye lids and around my eyes. He told me to go wash it off at the pool of Siloam. I did, and I could see, only light at first, but after a few minutes I did see things clearly. I've told you all this already, so why do you want me to keep repeating it? Maybe you want to become one of his disciples and learn how to do the same."

At this the staff person exploded. "You, who were obviously born in sin, have lived in sin, now try to instruct us. We know who this man is that did this. We know he is a sinner, a charlatan, an upstart from up north. We are disciples of Moses, we know God spoke to Moses, but as for this man, we don't know where he is from or what he is up to."

Scornfully, the man who could now see replied to the other man's arrogance. "You mean that a man heals someone born blind, and you don't know where he is from. How could he do such a thing unless he was from the Lord? Whoever he is, he knows the Lord. He prays and must do what he hears the Lord tell him, or otherwise he couldn't do anything like this. No one opens the eyes of someone born blind. When you are blind from birth you don't know what it is to see. You don't know whether you have eyes. When a person loses their sight they still see what they remember. I had nothing to remember. How he did it or what he did I do not know, only that he did, and he has to be something more than your average sinner as you suggest."

"Get out," roared the Priest. "You were conceived in sin and born in sin. Why else do you think you were born blind? Now you are trying to teach us?"

The people who had come in with the blind man inched forward, and angry comments were hurled from deep inside the group. At this the guards jumped in front of the people and pushed them out of the building, back into the sunlit square.

They surrounded the man who had been blind and patted him on the back. From their puddle of indignation, they looked back at the doorway through which they had been ejected and muttered ribald comments.

I was not surprised at the callous reception given our friend. The fresh air and sunlight of the courtyard were a relief after the gloom of the building's interior and the oppressive ugliness of our friend's reception. I thought, yes, this is exactly what Jesus has been trying to tell us.

By this time I had gotten clear of the crowd and walked back to the opposite end of the square where I could see the squatting people around Jesus. When I arrived, Jesus, with a slight inclination of his head towards the melee, gave me an inquiring look. I nodded and shrugged. A brief smile passed between us.

I sat back down with my back against the wall and thought over the episode. Just who was Jesus? The clergy ought to be scared. I measured the priest against Jesus' world, and there was no point at which they could agree. I thought forward to try and see what was going to happen in the future, and I came up empty. Nothing good would come out of this. Maybe the blind man was right: the clergy are the blind ones, and they are more blind because they don't know they can't see.

The morning wore on, and the square filled with people. I sat in the sun and let the enthusiastic group talk over another point Jesus had made. I heard Jesus say to the merchant whom Jesus had invited to join us earlier, "You have two coats, and you see someone with nothing but a few rags keeping him warm. Have you ever thought about giving that man one of your coats?"

The man shifted awkwardly and admitted he had. Jesus went on, "That was the voice of the Lord. Now if you had given him the coat, would you now be glad or sorry you thought of it?"

Again the man nodded and sheepishly admitted he would be glad he had done it.

"Having two coats is fine," continued Jesus. "You give one away, so go buy another, and you will have one to give away the next day. Maybe giving away your coat could become a habit." The man looked around him and saw everyone else smiling at the idea of giving your coat away becoming a habit and laughed outright. I had seen Jesus work this kind of miracle before, but today there was outright laughter at the idea. They were all waiting for more.

Jesus continued. "When it becomes a habit, you will know freedom, and you will know others and see them as your brothers, for are we not all children of Abraham? What does it mean to be a Jew? Are we not called to be the Kingdom of God? Give, you'll never regret giving, but you always regret not giving. So open your hands everyone, let the world slip through your fingers and you will find you will be glad, because everything will be returned to you somehow, and the same measure you used will be used to return it to you except that the measuring cup will be pressed down, filled again and heaped up so it overflows."

I had been keeping half an eye on the other end of the square, and now I saw that the crowd had dispersed except for a knot of supporters for the ex-blind man. They were walking towards us. I felt alarm at the possibility of Jesus being positively identified as the culprit in the healing. I caught Jesus' eye and nodded down the square towards the approaching group. Silence fell on those gathered around Jesus as the other men approached.

Jesus stood and greeted the man. When the man heard Jesus' voice, he exclaimed, "You are him!" Turning to the rest of those with him, he said excitedly, "This is the man who did it!" He came forward and fell at Jesus' feet, weeping with joy.

Jesus bent down and pulled him to his feet, confidentially muttering, "I hear the clergy kicked you out. They didn't want to know, did they?"

The ex-blind man laughed aloud, "No, they did not want to believe me."

"What about you?" said Jesus. "Do you believe? Do you believe in the grace you've received, do you believe in the Son of Man?

The man hesitated and asked, "Who is he? If you tell me, I will believe in him."

"You've met him already. In fact, it is I who speaks to you."

The man stepped forward and embraced Jesus. "Believe in what you can do? I do. How can I not?"

Over the man's hunched shoulders Jesus addressed the people around him, "I have come into the world to open the eyes of everyone so all of you can see and understand these things. For many it will mean judgment because there are those who think they see and they don't. They can't be helped. Their blindness is complete."

Next to me two young men I identified as Pharisees from their dress leaned in to each other. "Is he calling us blind?" I heard one say.

Jesus, catching their conversation, said to them, "No, you are not blind. You really want to know, and you are asking good questions. You also know there is a lot wrong with how things are. You can see the sin, you know so much has to be changed, but you don't know how. Blind? No! But yet you are with so many others unwillingly part of the problem.

"The people recognize the voice of God, He calls them by name, and they know it when they hear it. Those clergy, who this man ran into today, cared nothing for him. They were not shepherds to him. The people know it. They are not deceived. They can smell a phony a mile off."

I watched the faces of the young Pharisees relax. With these few deft words he invited them to be part of the solution, to be of those who saw. He stepped over towards the rest of us sitting there and stood beside us.

Jesus spoke directly to them, "Loving the people is the only way. You clergy must learn to respect these people and nurture them. Think of yourselves as the doorway to a sheepfold. It is how the sheep come and go, and you, similarly, are the entrance for people to understanding and the Kingdom. Others who try to enter by another way are like thieves and rustlers wanting to take advantage of the people. Well, the people will not follow leaders like that. Sooner or later they will say, 'No.'

"Right now, the people look up and are not fed. That is where I come in. I am like that door to a sheepfold I described."

Jesus looked away from the young Pharisees, and he addressed those near him. "You have been used, constrained, controlled and treated with disdain for too long. So, just like sheep in a sheepfold, in the Kingdom of God you will be able to go in and out without interference. There will be nobody to push you around and you will have authority in yourselves to seek your salvation in the presence of the Lord, all for free. This is why I have come, that you may have life, and have it abundantly. Yes, that includes you, clergy." He looked over to the two Pharisees again, "You, especially, because you have wound the law around yourselves so tightly that you can't help yourselves. You are stuck. So I am here to cut you free."

Jesus looked out over those gathered around him and, with a solemnity I had not seen before, shared with them his thoughts. "I cannot pull back. You know what kind of power squats over there. What do you think will happen? I do not doubt that to bring about the Kingdom of God for you who seek it will cost me my life. That sacrifice is nothing compared with purchasing your salvation for our Father in Heaven. I am committed to you all, I have measured the cost, I am ready to pay it, and I know it is the Father's will. You are all his chosen people and He, through me, will draw you to Himself."

At this, the whole group mumbled among themselves. I heard one of the older clergy say openly so others could hear, "He has a demon. He is out of his mind."

Others shook their heads. "No, he is right. We are shorn like sheep and booted out of the Temple as if it was not ours. We are bound with so much law that we cannot move. Anyway, a demon can't open the eyes of a blind person."

Jesus looked at the dismayed faces around him. "It is in the Father's hands. Not mine and not yours."

He walked away, but a group of Pharisees that had assembled on the fringes of those listening stopped him. "Are you the Messiah? Don't keep us in suspense. Tell us clearly. Just yes or no."

Jesus promptly shook his head. "I've already told you. Think it through. Whose works have I been doing? Where does the power come from? Look at the evidence. However, nothing is quite as you understand it, for the objective is to give you all eternal life, and that is going to take more than a few miracles. No new dynasty, no kingdom of this world, but the Kingdom of God, and as part of that Kingdom you are called to eternal life."

Jesus walked among the people and exchanged words and comments with them. Finally he headed for the steps down into the city. I followed, but as I did I heard one of the Pharisees on the periphery say, "Still no answer." I was out of earshot to hear the rest and hurried to catch up with Jesus as he made his way through the crowd.

The Sabbath was a good time for people, and they were out in the streets talking, laughing and seemingly without a care in the world. I relaxed as we put more distance between us and the Temple. Jesus avoided making eye contact with anyone and forged ahead until we were back to my apartment. He went in, paused long enough to remove his sandals, perfunctorily washed his feet, splashed water on his face from the stone vessel before the door, and entered. For a long while we sat in silence. He raised his head and looked at me, shook it sadly, and looked down at his hands clasped in his lap. "Do you know what happened out there?"

After reviewing the events of the afternoon in my head I replied, "Up until the last questions by the Pharisees, I thought things had gone well. I do not understand why you cannot just admit you are indeed the Messiah, and leave it at that. At the end you talked about the necessity of dying in order to procure eternal life for everyone. I have had no problem giving up the idea of an earthly kingdom and a return to the old glory days of David, but I can't see what your dying has got to do with the Kingdom of God."

Jesus leaned back and rested his head against the wall. He admitted in a tired voice, "I don't know either, but as I go further down this road, I begin to glimpse what our Father is about. Yes, I admit I intended to cause trouble for the authorities today. They will have gotten the message loud and clear.

"Annas will even now be listening to reports from whoever received that young blind man, and he will be disturbed. Tomorrow he will have Caiaphas arrest me. He knows the people are beginning to ask too many questions about his whole operation, and today he had a blind man stand up to his people and tell them they were dead wrong. This is what he fears most. John the Baptist began it, and offered free cleansing from their sins. Next, for the last few years I have been preaching the forgiveness of sins for free, and in addition I've been offering people an alternative source of spiritual power. I am making the Temple irrelevant. Annas knows that, Caiaphas hasn't a clue but knows he is losing some kind of battle he did not know he was fighting. I told everyone when we first started, my objective was to destroy the Temple and build a new one not built with hands. All the teaching and miracles are part of the process, they are a means to an end not the end itself.

"Let's have something to eat, rest a little and after sunset, when the Sabbath is over, I want to go back to Bethany. Early tomorrow morning we will quietly leave for the Jordan. I would like to push Annas over the edge. He is about ready to make open moves against me, but I am not ready for that confrontation. That will happen but on my terms. For the moment we will retreat, but I would dearly like to give him one final push to send him into meltdown like a lump of ice on a sunny day."

I nodded. "You know what I think about you staying in Jerusalem; I will be only too glad to get you out of the city." I quickly pulled together my few things I needed for traveling and threw them in my satchel. "Let's go. Let's get you out of here before you change your mind."

As we left my apartment and I closed the door behind me, I had the impression of finality. The thought crossed my mind that I would not be back. I had no clue where we were going, but with Jesus as companion I felt no concern.

I followed him down the alley, feeling light-hearted and carefree. If I had stopped to think for a moment I would have recognized the warning signs. Jesus was not finished with Jerusalem. He had hardly begun. Things were going to get a lot worse.

26 RAISING OF LAZARUS AND THE WAY NORTH

That night we arrived in Bethany. We ate with Mary and Martha because Lazarus had gone to bed by the time we arrived. Over the supper Martha had quickly assembled, I told Mary of some of the events in Jerusalem and confided to her my relief we were leaving. Jesus smiled at my descriptions of his encounters and commented on how dramatic I made everything sound.

Martha looked over at Jesus and asked how long he intended to be gone. Jesus shook his head. "I think we will not be back until next year. I have a lot to do in Galilee before I come south again. Do try to keep contact with all our friends. Remember what I have taught you and exchange ideas with each other."

Jesus asked us to be ready for an early start, so we retired soon after supper. Early the next morning, we took our leave of Martha and asked her to say goodbye to Lazarus, whom we had not seen. Mary said he had been out in the sun all the previous day and had one of his headaches.

When Jesus asked if he could help, Mary shook her head. "It is nothing. He will be fine by the time he wakes up this morning." Jesus looked thoughtful for a moment, started to say something, but thought better of it.

He led us out onto the path down to the road to Jericho. I waved goodbye to the two sisters. We had stayed with them many times over the last year, and their home had become a safe place for us. There existed a sense of family between us. With an acute sense of regret, I followed the others down the road.

Judas, Thomas and two brothers from the Jerusalem community of Essenes made up our party. Soon we were in open country with the rock-strewn topography of that area on either side of us. The steep descent took us six hours at least.

Down by the Jordan we met up with the rest of the brothers who had been assisting those who came to them for help. Some they had baptized, others they had prayed with, while still others they fed, talked with and sent them on their way.

One of the traders in fruit and dried condiments from the valley came bustling in. We knew him as a frequent traveler on the road up to Jerusalem, and we had met him at Bethany more than once. He kept Lazarus' business supplied with fresh fruit, especially dates.

As he approached he looked around urgently. "Is Jesus here? I have a message from Mary."

I nodded my head towards the temporary hut Jesus was using and followed the man over there. "Mary said for me to give you a message. Her brother is really sick. They think he is dying. He is unconscious. I think they need you."

"Thank you," said Jesus and as the man left, went back to his own thoughts. I stayed and waited.

Finally Jesus lifted his head. "This illness isn't going to kill him. He will recover in a day or two, in fact he is probably on the mend by now. I have come to the conclusion it is time for us to retreat to the North. As I said at dinner last night, I think Galilee is the right place for us right now. There I will prepare myself for the final conflict and raise enough support for the authorities to have to take me seriously."

We talked on about the men we had already met from that region, and we laid out a provisional campaign that would start in Capernaum and extend around the Sea of Galilee and back inland as far as Nazareth. Over the last three years we had been there more than once and many of the men from there had been to visit us down by the Jordan. I felt immediate relief at the thought of being out from under the brooding presence of Annas and his far-flung secret service.

Jesus went on to say, "We will take just a few of the brothers with us. Ask Judas to choose three to come with us and be prepared to start in a couple of days. The rest can stay here and watch what is happening in Jerusalem. This is a good listening post, and I would like to keep myself informed about what is happening up there." He nodded towards Jerusalem some twenty miles away.

That was not to happen, though, for early on the third day, when we were ready to begin our journey north, a messenger from Mary in Bethany stumbled into camp. He had traveled down from Jerusalem the previous day, but, arriving late, could not find us in the dark. Lazarus was dead. He had died early on Monday morning. As was customary, he had been buried the same day.

Jesus looked stricken. He asked a couple of questions of the messenger, but the messenger had little to add to what he had said already. There were at least thirty of us standing around Jesus waiting for him to tell us what he wanted us to do.

"I must go back to Jerusalem," he told us. "John, Thomas and Judas can come with me, but the rest of you wait here for us. When we come back, be ready to leave right away. We might be in a hurry, so stay close to the camp and have your things packed."

With this we retraced our steps up the long steep road to Jerusalem. Normally we walked at a good mile-consuming pace, but that day Jesus set a blistering pace full of urgency.

After a long silence as we followed him up the roadway, I asked why the speed. We would normally arrive late in the afternoon, and surely that would be time enough.

"John, I may have made a huge mistake. I was sure that Lazarus was not in danger and that he would not die. I think I told you that when we got that first message. I may be wrong, but I am afraid a terrible mistake has been made. If so, every hour counts. I want to be in Bethany as soon as we can get there."

With that an uneasy silence fell on us all, for we neither understood nor did he say anything more, but strode on ahead and left us to keep up.

Early afternoon we arrived and were met with the news that Lazarus was indeed dead and had been in the tomb four days. There was a house full of people who had come from Jerusalem and the suburbs, all there honoring Lazarus and of course consoling the sisters.

Martha, who was as usual preparing the food for everyone and organizing its distribution among the guests, came bustling up. "Oh, Master, if only you had been here, my brother would not have died."

With that she burst into tears and clung to Jesus. I had never seen her lose that aura of control before, and now within the safety of Jesus' presence her grief came pouring out.

Jesus put a protective arm round her. "Martha, your brother will live. Take heart."

Martha swallowed a sob. "I know he will at the resurrection on the last day, but I can't bear it. I wish you had been here. I know you loved him like a brother, and if you had been here you would have healed him. I know you would have."

Jesus said, "We must hurry. Do you believe there is life and power in me?"

"Yes, you are the Messiah," she whispered. "Let me go and tell Mary. She will want to greet you."

She hurried back to the house and returned with Mary at her side. When Mary saw Jesus, she fell at his feet. Jesus helped her stand up and drew her to him. The people who had been in the house came and stood around them.

Jesus raised his eyes to the sky, and I could see he was crying for his friend. I also thought he was appealing to the heavens as if to ask why. Recollecting himself, he asked urgently, "Where have you laid him? I must see him."

They led him through the property to a rock outcrop behind the house and there showed him the tomb. Tears ran down his cheeks into his beard. He hurried forward, and the rest of us bustled up behind him. We were ten feet from the tomb when he stopped and ordered the stone to be rolled away. At this Martha objected, "He has been dead four days and by now there will be a terrible smell."

Jesus said, "Did I not tell you, you would see the glory of God?"

As the attendants moved the stone, he looked up to heaven and I heard him pray very quietly. "Thank you, Father. I was not wrong. Thank you, thank you."

Gazing into the tomb, he cried, "Lazarus, come out!"

Silence fell on the mass of people who now stared towards the tomb with fear and dread. Nothing moved until after several minutes a shadow shifted deep in the darkness of the cave tomb. To everyone's horror there appeared a shrouded figure stumbling towards the light.

People gasped. Some covered their eyes and others muttered incantations. Jesus stood there, a look of great relief on his face. "Let him loose, give him a hand. Don't be afraid. He is alive."

At Jesus' words, people drew away from him, fear and amazement clearly written on their faces. These were some of the movers and shakers of the city and not easily surprised, moved or swayed. Still, they were totally overcome with a mixture of terror and awe. As I watched, I realized they were all close to panic. I saw several turn and bolt for the village.

By now, Lazarus was being helped to a sitting position on a bench placed in the garden for mourners. He looked terribly pale and could hardly keep himself upright. Two attendants brought a litter and carried him into the house.

Martha brought a plate of food and a cup with watered wine to him. He drank thirstily and took one of the little cakes from the plate. Martha and Mary stood by. He looked up at them, gave them a slight smile and a huge grimace of affection. He shook his head and, unable to find words, extended his arms to embrace them. Several long moments later, Lazarus released them and looked toward the figure of Jesus entering the room.

The crowd in Lazarus' home made way for Jesus. Lazarus reached out his hand, and Jesus came and took it gently.

Lazarus managed to croak, "Thank you. I heard your voice. I dreamed you would come. I had a sense of waiting for you. I knew it was you. Thank you."

He asked his sisters, "How long have I been gone?"

The crush of people in the room grew larger, and outside I could hear others asking about what was happening. Inside, people were recovering from the shock of seeing Lazarus walk out of that tomb, but they maintained a respectful silence. Only when Martha brought a cloak and draped it over him, covering the grave clothes, did people relax. Lazarus waved at them and tried to say something but couldn't manage much more than, "I am surprised to see you all here."

We all laughed with relief. Soon everyone was talking, and the hubbub of conversation filled the room. I heard Martha say, "Oh, Lazarus, I can't believe you are here. I thought you had gone." Tears flowed down her cheeks, and she sobbed and sobbed. Dabbing at her eyes with a napkin, she tried to get control of herself but gave way to another wave of sobbing. She rose and escaped to the kitchen from which she emerged after a few minutes her usual calm, controlled self. Mary, looking pale and horrified, said, "Oh, Lazarus, how terrible for you. Lost in the darkness and waking up in the tomb!"

Lazarus put his hand out and hugged Mary to him. "It is okay. No, it was not terrible. I remember very little. Only a great light and a sense I had to come back here. What I remember now is the pain in my head, the darkness filling me, and then that light. I wanted to stay there, but I was told I had to go back. It was then I heard your voice," and he nodded to Jesus, "and there was light in the tomb, and I found myself in this." He waved at his grave clothes.

Two attendants helped him walk the few steps to his room. Jesus went in to him and stayed with him for an hour. The rest of us waited. Nobody wanted to leave, but outside in the sunshine where we now assembled the speculation began. Judas, Thomas and I stood together in silence. Men looked over to us, but did not approach us. Events had set us apart. I felt their fear and puzzlement directed towards us.

Uncomfortable there, I returned to the cool darkness of the house. When Jesus emerged from Lazarus' room, he quietly reassured the sisters about Lazarus' condition. He gave them some advice about Lazarus' immediate needs for rest and quiet and suggested one of them should always sit with him for the next two days. "Be sure to keep a lamp burning in the room and allow only his closest friends in to see him," Jesus advised. "He doesn't need everyone staring at him as if he is a freak."

Martha asked Jesus to stay but he took her hands and shook his head. "No, we must be on our way. We cannot get to Jericho tonight but after what has happened we must get as far as we can. We are on our way to Galilee. Look after Lazarus. Don't let him do too much. He has been very sick." He hugged her. "Don't let him go out alone. In fact, make sure there are at least a couple of guards with him. Above all don't let him go into Jerusalem. When I think about how the authorities will take this I am concerned for his safety. He could be an embarrassment for them."

I summoned Judas and Thomas from the garden. Martha led us through the house and let us out a side door. We slipped out, avoiding the growing crowd of people in the garden. I thought of how the story would spread like wildfire, and everyone from Bethany would be out in front of the house by now. I dreaded getting entangled with them and having Jesus mobbed.

We were soon on the road and walked until the sun set, when we found a place to camp. There were four of us, so not a good target for thieves. I had a suspicion Jesus was not worried about thieves or bandits, but others. We camped well off the road with our backs to rock walls. The tiny fire we made was not visible from the road. We were well-hidden, but we could see down onto the road—an ideal location. We all understood the liability we had incurred with that afternoon's work so we took turns keeping an eye on the road.

In silence, we ate the food Martha had packed for us. All three of us avoided Jesus' eyes because none of us were able to digest what we had seen. My head was full of questions, but I did not know how to ask them. Finally, I looked across at Jesus and felt an awe overshadowing the warmth of friendship I had felt until now.

The events of the day had set him apart from us.

One by one, we huddled under our cloaks and tried to sleep. Nobody wanted to ask Jesus anything, and we could see Jesus was far from being ready to talk about what had happened.

Judas volunteered, "I think we should keep watch on the road. It might be better if we know who is ahead of us. I will take the first watch since I'm not sure I can sleep yet. I'll wake you next, John. Tomorrow will be a long day."

Dawn had barely touched the hills behind us as we broke camp and started down towards Jericho. We bypassed the town and continued on our way north along the Jordan road. At the fork in the road for Ephraim we made the ascent into the hill country surrounding Ephraim, which nestled in its sharp water cut wadi. There, the disciples Jesus had sent on ahead were waiting for us.

Thomas, Judas and I told the rest of them what had happened. Jesus had withdrawn from our group to be alone and no doubt would be gone until late evening. We set some food aside for him, but none of us had much of an appetite. Instead we sat around rehashing what we had seen over the last months.

It was Thomas who asked, "Just what does this all mean? Where are we to go now? Clearly there is no going back. Jerusalem is off limits."

Judas broke in. "The roads will be watched, and we will be wanted men. The Temple authorities can't ignore Jesus now. They will have to respond. I think there will be an order out for Jesus' arrest by morning. Healing that blind man was bad enough, but what could the Temple clergy do? This raising of Lazarus is unambiguous. They have to react?"

After the others had settled down I stayed up with Judas. We sat by the fire with our arms round our knees. I now realized what Jesus' intent had been over the last few weeks. He had carefully orchestrated a series of blows against the Temple staff: the lame man, the woman taken in adultery, the blind man, and, as a coup de grâce, the raising of Lazarus from the dead. If I had not seen it with my own eyes I would not have believed it.

I shuddered at the memory of the figure, sheathed in a fine linen shroud, barely standing upright at the entrance of the tomb and holding onto the rock wall beside him for support. I was one of the first to reach him. I had helped untie the headband from his face, and Judas had untied the bandage that hobbled him like a mule.

As I went over the scene in my mind, I wondered why there was no smell of decomposition. There was the smell of the spices the sisters had used and the smell of the earth, as well as a lingering smell from the bones of dead long deposited there, but there was no sickly smell of present-day decomposition.

I asked Judas, "When we freed Lazarus from his shroud, did you smell anything strange?"

Judas thought for a moment. "Not really. There were the spices, of course, but nothing much else. The cave was certainly musty, but I didn't notice it particularly. Why?"

"Well, isn't it strange when you think about it? Lazarus did not smell the way you would expect him to smell if he had been dead four days. There was no smell of decay. Even in the cool of the tomb his body would have leaked all its bodily fluids. His brain would have turned to liquid. There were no leaks—a few stains, yes—but I can't remember any signs of the decay you would expect. He was whole."

Judas reflected for a minute and finally asked, "You don't think it was a set-up do you? It couldn't have been a plot between Lazarus and Jesus could it?"

I thought about it for a while as Judas continued talking. "If so, maybe the sisters were in on it. After all, they were the ones who buried him. There is no way they could not have known because of the work they did on him. He could not have faked being dead and have his sisters wash him and prepare his body. They would have felt him respond in some way. It's hard to think those two would be in on anything so risky, I don't see it."

"Martha and Mary? No. Neither of them is capable of that kind of trickery," I replied.

Judas tossed out another thought. "I guess the real question is if Jesus knew about this ahead of time, and planned it—or at least agreed to it."

I remembered the shock Jesus exhibited when he heard Lazarus was dead and the top-speed journey back to Bethany. I thought again of the sorrow and shock in the eyes of the sisters and was sure they were not part of it. "No it was not a set up."

"Okay," Judas continued, "but could Lazarus have used some drug or other? There are substances that can put you to sleep, but too much and you sleep forever. There is the juice from the poppy for example. Could he have taken too much of a drug he used when he was under the weather, let us say, and was all but gone?"

"Judas, I have no idea." Tired of talking about it with him, I pulled my cloak over my shoulders, made myself comfortable on the ground and at least pretended I was going to sleep.

Instead, my thoughts tumbled over themselves. I went over everything of the last few days, time after time. I remembered Jesus saying Lazarus was ill but it would not kill him and also that conversation about him sleeping and going to wake him. I was convinced Lazarus had indeed been sick, but Jesus thought there was neither reason for concern nor the need to backtrack to Bethany.

Once we had returned to Bethany, Jesus soon lost that look of dread that had overcome him as we hiked toward Bethany. After we arrived, Jesus had taken command of the strange situation in his inimitable way,.

No, it was not a set-up. In retrospect, I wondered if Jesus had thought he had miscalculated and lost his friend. Those tears he shed as he came to the tomb were real, but were they tears of relief or tears of guilt at the pain he had caused his friends? No, I thought, they were tears of relief and almost a savage joy in awaking Lazarus.

This was not the first time someone had come to after being buried, but being unconscious for four days was a long time. I considered other possibilities. Being unconscious, hardly breathing, and with an undetectable heartbeat meant he was all but dead, and left there in the dark for four days meant that he would have been dead but for the intervention. Was that the reason for the urgency on our return trip to Bethany? For most people in that condition, there was no way back, anyhow. So, yes, Lazarus was raised from the dead.

This was like spilled wine: we were not going to get it back in the wine skin. There was no turning back.

24

THE OFFICIAL RESPONSE

Unbeknownst to us, but not surprisingly, there was an uproar in Jerusalem. The story of Lazarus' being raised from the dead went through the city like wildfire. There was no stopping it, and, though it was denied, everyone wanted to believe it so the story circulated quickly. Annas heard about it within an hour.

We later heard the story of Annas' tirade from both Jonathon, who witnessed it, and from Nicodemus, who, as a member of the Sanhedrin, had to endure the trial-in-absentia that was held. Nicodemus even supplied us with the official language of the verdict.

According to Jonathon, Annas exploded when he heard about Jesus' latest miracle. "I knew it," he yelled, and he banged his fist on the table. "I could tell he was leading up to something. Call Caiaphas and send out notices to all the members of the Sanhedrin that we must have a meeting first thing in the morning."

Caiaphas was ushered in fifteen minutes later. He was uneasy at the sight of his father-in-law sitting grim and silent behind his desk. Annas let Caiaphas sweat for a while before he finally asked, "Have you heard?"

Caiaphas nodded.

"What are you going to do about it?"

Caiaphas shook his head. "There is nothing we can do about it now. From the accounts I have heard, Lazarus had been in the tomb for four days, and Jesus called him forth. He was still wrapped in his grave clothes. Witnesses saw it all happen, and these were not just ten hand-picked witnesses, but over a hundred men from all over Jerusalem and beyond. There is not much we can do. There is no point in sending a squad of men up there to arrest him. I doubt if the men would do it. They are spooked by him. They are all thinking if he can raise someone from the dead, what could he do if he got mad at them?"

Annas pounded on his desk. "All along I have been urging you to build a case against him, arrest him, harass his disciples and followers, but you have prevaricated on every occasion. Now we have a mess on our hands. If the Nazarene returned right now, every man in this city would be out there to greet him. Tell me, who is supposed to raise the dead? Tell me!"

Caiaphas mumbled, "The Messiah, but you are not seriously suggesting he is the Messiah, are you?"

Annas shook his head. "No, but the crowds are beginning to think he is. This is one of the signs of the Messiah. If he walked down any street in Jerusalem tonight, people would rush together and begin to hail him as the Messiah. Even if he were, we could not afford for him to be declared as such by the crowds tonight. We have got to put this down before it gets out of hand. Can you imagine what the Roman response would be if this Jesus person was declared the Messiah and therefore King of Israel? Do you think they would sit on their hands the way you do? Before nightfall the streets would be cleared, blood would be running in the gutters and we, or rather shall I say you, would be trying to explain yourself to Pilate.

This is just what he has been waiting for. There is nothing Pilate would like better than to cast suspicion on our whole operation here and have an excuse to ransack the treasury like he did before. If he thought you had anything to do with this religious Messiah, what do you think he would do with you? He could make a case of treason against you if he half tried. He could, in letters to Rome, give proof of your support for this Messiah or he might just crucify you and use those letters to justify his decision. Do I have your attention now?"

Caiaphas had blanched under his headdress. He timorously suggested, "Maybe we should alert Pilate. Let him take care of Jesus of Nazareth. That would prove we have no part in any such insurrection."

Annas smiled thinly. "You do not think he would take advantage of the opportunity to discredit us and maybe remove us from contention, do you? We are a thorn in his side. We cause more trouble than any other group in the Empire, so do you not think Pilate would be delighted to have an excuse to do away with all our hard-won privileges?

"No, first I want it circulated that the whole thing was a hoax. Lazarus was not dead, and his apparent death was cooked up by his sisters. Make it an authoritative source of information, maybe some of the men who were there. Get that out as soon as you can. Not too many details. Just get it on the street that it was a hoax.

"The next thing to do is get the Sanhedrin together and debate this. I have already sent out notices in your name to all members of the council. There will be a meeting tomorrow morning. You will, of course, be there with a carefully thought out point of view."

Caiaphas nodded his agreement, then his eyes went wide as he asked, "But what is his crime? That has been the trouble all along. He doesn't say anything or do anything that is illegal. Even healing on the Sabbath is controversial but hardly a crime. Raising the dead is not a crime. Nobody has done it before so there is no such crime on our books or in the scriptures."

Annas raised his eyes to the ceiling as if praying for patience at the machinations of a child. "Precisely. So, therefore, I want you to prepare your case against him on the grounds of necromancy. Certainly he trafficked with the dead, spoke with the dead, I understand. What kind of deal has he made with those who keep the underworld do you suppose? Why not include that with the rumors? People will grab onto that.

"I don't think you have to have an airtight case, but good enough to scare everyone and give them an excuse to condemn Jesus. Tomorrow I want the Sanhedrin to issue a warrant for his arrest, and I want you to have squads of men standing by to pick him up wherever he is. Start at Bethany, go as far as Jericho and down to those Essenes south of there at their settlement. One group should go north up the Jordan Valley. Another squad should search the city. Bring him in. That squad that goes to Bethany, you might have them bring Lazarus in for questioning. On second thought, maybe not. Everyone in the city would want to see him. We may need to deal with him later though. Maybe if he died again very soon the power of the miracle would be mooted somewhat."

Caiaphas shifted uncomfortably and broke in. "You don't suppose it was a miracle, that he did indeed raise Lazarus from death?"

Annas shook his head in disbelief. "I don't understand you. Can you not see that we cannot afford to believe it, even if he raised a hundred Lazaruses. We have to protect the Temple from these people who would dismantle our way of life. Did not this Jesus say he would tear down the Temple and rebuild it? You can't imagine he was talking about the buildings themselves. So what do you think he meant? He has something else in mind, and I cannot see it all yet.

"Ever since that John the Baptist began his preaching down by the Jordan, there has been a growing attrition of respect for this institution. I've tracked some drops in income, the number of sacrifices offered and attendance at the national sacrifices. I think we should remind Herod it's time to get rid of the Baptist. I think Herod has gone soft on the man. I heard he even invited this Baptist fellow up to entertain himself and his court. In fact, now that I think about it, maybe we should talk to Queen Herodias. She hates John the Baptist. He calls her a slut, among other things. I rather think she would be a better instrument than Herod. Yes, it's time we cleaned house.

"Now, another thing, the squad you send to Jericho: get them to check the other side of the Jordan and even further up the Jordan Valley. My source said Jesus and those with him in Bethany left immediately after the Lazarus thing. No, we will not refer to it as being raised. I rather think

Jesus has withdrawn to the wilderness to let things cool down. Well, things are not going to cool down."

Annas paused and watched Caiaphas squirm uncomfortably under his heavy garments and surreptitiously scratch his side.

Annas reflected, "I wonder if this Jesus thinks he has gone too far? It's hard to know what is going on in his mind. I understand his objective is our monopoly on the Temple operations, but he has not put together any political force or any true power base that I can identify. There are a lot of people in this city who support him or at least could be said to follow him, but they are not forming themselves into a coherent force that could do us any harm. The best thing is for us to get rid of him before he can bring some of the troublemakers together and form a power base.

"When he surfaces I want him arrested right away, and that means we have to have the Sanhedrin issue that warrant. That is your job. I have my sources of information of course, but I do not trust them to stay loyal if they get too close to him. He could turn them, so I have to be careful about using them. Jonathon, I want to follow up on that idea of contacting Queen Herodias. Stay behind, and we will draft a letter."

The Sanhedrin met the next morning. Every member who was in town was there. The news of the raising of Lazarus was the sole item on their agenda. The members assembled and most of them were Pharisees, but the Sadducees were well represented, and of course Caiaphas presided as High Priest.

Speculation had been rife about what had actually happened. Rumors were circulated that Jesus had been in touch with the powers of the underworld, that demonic forces were involved, or that the evil one had himself made it possible. Some had been present in Bethany the previous day, but everyone had heard the rumors.

After the session was declared open, Nicodemus stood up to lay out what had happened, for he had been there as a friend of the sisters and Lazarus himself. He witnessed the whole thing, as did about seventy-five others. None of those witnesses saw anything that could cast doubt on what Jesus had done or support the rumors being circulated.

Finally Nicodemus declared, "God had clearly worked through this man, Jesus. By ascribing this to evil spirits and worse, the Sanhedrin would be denying the Lord himself."

Caiaphas rose, pointed at Nicodemus and said, "You are one of his disciples. Your sympathies undermine your judgment. There is no history of anyone being raised from the dead after four days. It is an evil spirit in disguise as Lazarus. We are dealing with the possibility that this Jesus fellow has opened a window into the world of the dead and the evil spirits that inhabit it and will thereby endanger our nation.

"Further, he is leading people astray. A couple of days ago we had the case of a blind man being healed, and inside an hour we nearly had a riot as we tried to verify the truth of what the man was claiming. Jesus is systematically destroying the integrity of our Temple by his teaching. Many of you have heard the slanders against our institutions. The implications behind much of what he says are that there is no need for sacrifices, no need for atonement, but just a life of prayer."

A ripple of assent went round the room, as well as a general shaking of the gray beards as their High Priest referred to how Jesus had challenged the centuries-old traditions they all revered.

Caiaphas continued. "You all remember the riot he caused when he turned over the tables of the merchants and let out all the animals held there for sale. That was a statement denying the efficacy of our sacrifices, and he has not stopped attacking us since then. That was over three years ago, and we have continued to act with restraint and forbearance. We have even been wayward in our responsibilities to protect the people from charlatans, as he most surely is. Now we have to act. We are the fortified position he is trying to undermine, and his intent has to be no less than to bring down the whole infrastructure of our organization so he can supplant us. This latest event is the most serious and indicates he is about to make his move. It cannot be but violent and disastrous for our nation. For this reason we must act, but there is another reason we must bring an end to his activities."

Everyone in the room sat waiting for another revelation, and Caiaphas milked the situation for all he could. He looked around at the faces of those present and, with a dramatic sweep of his hand, said, "He is misleading the people, leading Israel astray and is most likely in touch with the powers of evil. He must be held accountable and answer for the great harm he has done by opening a window into the underworld. Think of what demonic forces could be or even now are released into our world. Clearly he has been guilty of necromancy, for he certainly has been consorting with the dead. You all witnessed him addressing Lazarus. We must rid ourselves of this danger, and we must not shirk our duty. He should be condemned, and the penalty for that is to be stoned. I don't see any way out for us but to draw a line here. He has overstepped that line. His miracles have left many wondering how he performs them, and many have been taken in by the miracles. Well, now we understand where he is getting that power from. The people have to be alerted. We cannot let them be duped. It is our duty to protect them from this rise of the demonic force among us."

A cacophony of voices erupted when Caiaphas finally sat down. The debate went on for some time, but as the rumors were reiterated and the fears magnified, the support for Nicodemus and his friends evaporated.

Caiaphas stood and read aloud the wording of condemnation proceedings against Jesus. It was written into the record, which Nicodemus later shared with us:

"WE, THE MEMBERS OF THE SANHEDRIN, FIND THE PERSON JESUS OF NAZARETH GUILTY OF NECROMANCY, CONSORTING WITH THE EVIL ONE AND LEADING ISRAEL ASTRAY. HE IS HEREBY CONDEMNED TO BE STONED. IF ANYONE KNOWS ANYTHING WHICH MIGHT BE UTTERED IN HIS DEFENSE THEN LET THAT PERSON MAKE HIMSELF KNOWN TO THIS BODY OF THE PEOPLE. IF ANYONE KNOWS WHERE HE IS, LET HIM COME FORWARD AND ALERT THE OFFICERS OF THE SANHEDRIN."

Caiaphas drew himself up and, resplendent in his regalia, proceeded to examine each person there, requiring him to declare his vote on the verdict he had just read. One after the other agreed, until only a group of the younger and more resolute Pharisees remained. These voted no, one after another, but their numbers were not sufficient to carry the day. Nicodemus and those around him sat in silent opposition.

Caiaphas rose to his feet once more, read the statement aloud again and declared it the will of the whole body. "In voting for this measure you have wisely acted, for in this matter we have to be like Solomon. None of us like to condemn a man, especially in his absence, but we have to act. In this case it is better for one man to die for the nation than the whole of Israel to suffer."

The warrant for Jesus' arrest was issued and published. The squads went through the city and proclamations were made in its public places, but nobody came forward. A sullen stillness was observed in those who heard the proclamation, and not a few went away, shaking their heads. Others hurled taunts and insults but at least no stones flew.

Annas heard the reports with grim satisfaction and uncharacteristically congratulated Caiaphas on his part.

Part 2

The Kingdom of God

25
THE WAY NORTH

Two days after we left Bethany, we dragged ourselves into Ephraim where we met the three disciples Jesus had sent on ahead of us. All that happened in Bethany felt to be a thousand years ago. As we climbed up into the hills Jesus walked by himself, hour after hour. He was wrapped in his own thoughts for the whole of that journey, all the way from our camp by Jericho. I hesitated to ask him any questions about Lazarus. I walked with Thomas for a time, then Judas, but neither of them broached the subject.

At Ephraim we ate supper and sat in the gathering dusk with Marcus, Thaddeus and Simon from Beersheba. Naturally they wanted to know the whole story, which we told haltingly, for we were no longer sure about what we had actually seen. The other disciples fell silent, pondering what had occurred. Thaddeus finally asked, "So what does it mean?"

None of us knew, and we sat looking into the fire, which now gave us the only light available.

Jesus' voice came from behind us, "What it means is we cannot go back to Jerusalem for a time. Our work there is not done. When we return, we will be in a great power struggle, a spiritual battle."

We all looked at each other in the flickering firelight. I thought I heard Judas exclaim under his breath, "Finally."

His comment went unnoticed. Jesus went on, "Tomorrow we will go north to Galilee. There we have plenty of friends, and we will be safe from the interference of the Temple police. Word will get out, and I am sure the authorities will learn where we are in no time at all. As far as the authorities are concerned, Galilee is of no importance, and we can do no harm there. Not only that, but we will be in Herod's jurisdiction, and any trespassing on his authority by others will be seriously resented."

Good, we might even be protected, I thought, and remembered John in prison, and wondered how I could get a message to him. I put the thought aside for the moment but promised myself to bring it up later.

Jesus continued, "I suspect there will be searches made for us through the Jordan Valley but nobody will interfere with us if we go west over the mountain road, and north, through Samaritan country."

I asked whether we would visit Sychar, or go around the city. Jesus said, "No, we will stop there." I felt relief, for right now I wanted to be among friends. We had lived on the edge of uncertainty for months; now being around our Samaritan friends felt just what we needed.

Jesus went on, "Get some rest now, for we need to be away from here before the rest of the town is up. I don't want to draw attention to ourselves, and I would rather leave no indication which way we have gone."

That night when the others had turned in I sat with Jesus and listened as he reflected on what had happened at Bethany. "You know, John, I thought for one horrible moment I had made a terrible mistake about Lazarus. I had been so sure Lazarus would recover without me. When I heard he had died and was already buried, I did not understand how that could be. My first thought was I had made a mistake, but at another level I knew I hadn't. However, I realized if I had stayed just that extra hour or so, then Lazarus would have been fine. None of this needed to happen. My one concern as we raced back up the road to Bethany was whether we would be in time. John, I can't tell you how relieved I was when I arrived, and I knew we had made it."

I smiled at him in the dark and said, "I will never forget the moment you called Lazarus out. I still see him in my imagination clutching the wall and struggling with the grave clothes. You certainly gave all of us a scare. Warn us next time you do something like that."

Jesus chuckled. "Sure, I will warn you next time, but John, you can't imagine how relieved I felt when I saw him holding onto the wall there. Only then did I know everything was going to be all right."

"You never thought about the consequences, or what the authorities might make of it?"

I could faintly see Jesus smile in the darkness. "No, I am sorry, John, I never gave those people a thought. You know, everything I do comes from Him who sent me. The works I do are His, not mine. Take this last event, for example. I looked for something which would cause the authorities to overreact, and I thought that healing that blind man was it. We certainly stirred up enough trouble, and I thought it time to begin the last phase of my journey. That is why I was in such a hurry, and we left for Jericho immediately after the Sabbath." Jesus scratched the side of his beard and stared into the dying flames.

"This healing of Lazarus has blown the roof off everything. There is no going back now." He gave a suppressed chuckle, "John, I didn't mean to do it. No, really. Now it is all over, Lazarus is all right, and our friends are safe. I think the situation is hilarious. Caiaphas is going to wet his pants. People in Jerusalem will be talking 'Messiah' for sure, and the Temple clergy will all be in alarm mode by now. This raising of Lazarus is far more effective than I could have hoped for. Don't ever think our God has no sense of humor." I heard Jesus again laugh softly to himself.

I could hardly manage a faint smile, but it was so good to see Jesus his old self again. I asked him, "Now what? You've mentioned Galilee, and from other comments, you have at least a broad outline of what you need to do from here."

Jesus crouched low with his arms pushed forward on his knees, staring into the fire, "I plan to begin the last phase once we get to Galilee. The Kingdom of Heaven is on its way. It's coming, and nothing will stop it. It is upon us. My job now is to train up people to be effective witnesses to the nature of that Kingdom and to redefine the expectations we may have of that new state. You've been with me long enough to know that it is not easy to redirect people's expectations when they have been led to believe something else."

Jesus took a stick and raked the embers of the fire together and threw a few twigs onto the coals. There was a moment of brightness as one caught and flared briefly. "Do you remember the confusion those brothers from the Essene community felt when I tried to explain things to them? And there was Nicodemus, the night when he came to me? The Kingdom of God is in the great tradition of the Prophets, but our religious structure has always been the product of the priestly tradition with its ever greater demand for political control. We are going to change that."

I frowned to myself. "But Galilee is hardly the place to do that." Jesus went on with his thought, "The Temple priests continue the traditions of a thousand years or more, and they think what they are doing makes a difference, but it doesn't. Remember that psalm, 'If I am hungry I will not tell you, I abhor your burnt offerings, I hate your solemn fasts.' The clergy will never take that psalm seriously; they cannot, for if they did, they would lose the rationale for their existence. We've been over this before, now we have to do something."

Jesus took some of the wood we had set aside for a breakfast fire and tossed them on the embers. The red coals brightened again but didn't catch. He continued. "We need a coterie of people who understand the future of the faith of Israel and understand the difference between what has passed as the religion of Israel with all its trappings, and the life of the Spirit to which we, the people of Israel, have been called. That call is almost 2,000 years old, and now we are moving to the fruition of the Divine's plans. Abraham, Moses and the prophets saw this day and, confident of the future they saw, they dared to do and say what they did. What they saw is now upon us."

"But why Galilee? What's in Galilee, for heaven's sake?" I asked. "Is that where everything is going to happen?"

Jesus paused a long time, and said quietly, "No, not in Galilee, not in Jerusalem, not in Rome, but within you, John. Within each who will not only hear my word but will listen, and will welcome my word and let it take root in them. It's been happening for you. I don't doubt your part in this, but now you must take what you have and recognize it for what it is. That which is within you already is the Kingdom of God."

"But," I began.

"No buts, John. Just wait. You will see. Now get some sleep; we have a long day tomorrow." He got up, nodded to me and walked away from the little pool of light thrown by the fire.

I watched his figure fade into the darkness as I huddled over the flames consuming the new fuel. My mind churned with what I had heard about Lazarus, and now these last comments so casually lobbed at me left me wide-eyed. I could no more sleep than fly. I drew my cloak around me and decided to keep watch instead.

We reached Sychar in the afternoon of the second day. It didn't take long for Jesus to be recognized. Word of his arrival immediately got out, and flocks of people came to greet us. Some of those with us were surprised by the welcome.

That evening Marcus, Thaddeus and Simeon heard the stories of our earlier visit. Joanna, the woman we had first seen by the well outside the town, was there along with Thomas, now her husband. Thomas and Judas began telling about the events in Jerusalem. The Samaritans loved the story about the discomfort of the clergy, hung on every word about how Lazarus was raised, and clearly understood the wisdom Jesus showed by shaking the dust of Jerusalem off his feet. I think at that point they wanted to claim him as their own.

The people of Sychar asked him to stay, but he shook his head. "No, I have work to do in Galilee. You already have a grasp of what I am about. Keep your ears open for anyone who comes from me. I would appreciate it if you would take them in. Don't be shy about talking to others about the things we talked about last time."

Thomas, Joanna's husband and no longer the reluctant participant, said, "Last time you were here you mentioned the time would come when we would worship not in Jerusalem or here on the mountain, but in spirit and in truth. Is it time?" Nods all round endorsed the question, and I realized these people had grasped the fundamentals of what Jesus had talked about and wanted more. Like an isolated plant of an exotic species, the ideas Jesus had sown a year ago were now growing up.

Jesus thought for a moment. "When you see clouds filling the sky to the west, and the dark clouds begin to cover the mountain top and fill the valleys up there, you know what is coming; you know a storm is brewing. I've set in motion events which are brewing up a different kind of storm, so you can expect to hear and see things happen in the near term. We've told you of what's been happening in Jerusalem, and you will hear more from Galilee where we go now. My intention is change, and you will be part of it."

"Can we do anything?" asked a man on the edge of the firelight.

Jesus thought for a moment. "Tell about what has happened in your village and the changes that you have noticed, take in anyone who comes from me, and use what you already have. If anyone comes from Jerusalem, or is going to Jerusalem, make them welcome, tell them what you know. It's time we put our lamp on a lamp stand. We've kept our light hidden for long enough."

"What if they are Pharisees or Levites? Those characters are not about to take anything from us, and certainly not listen to us. We give that type no slack at all. They don't expect us to, either," countered a black-bearded older man, whose serious attitude had been noticeable on our earlier visit.

Jesus shook his head decisively. "No. Though they take nothing else from you, there is one thing they will take, and that is water. Your well is deep; give them water, but with it give them your friendliness. Tell them I was here. For you, that old attitude towards us Jews needs to go, but if they associate your attitude with me, they will puzzle over it all the way to Jerusalem. Think of it this way: by treating them as brothers, whether they appreciate that or not, you will alarm them. They will not be able to account for the change."

Laughter broke out among the men of Sychar, and a man wearing the leather apron of a smith said, "If making them welcome makes those characters uncomfortable, we can do a good job at that." Laughter followed, but it was good-natured; the men understood what Jesus was inviting them to do.

The next day we passed through Samaria and walked on towards Nazareth. We stayed several days in Nazareth, but it was not a good experience.

Our second day there was the Sabbath, and we went to the synagogue with the rest of the men of the town. Everyone who was in town seemed to have gotten the word that Jesus would be there. Our little party found seats, but the leader of the synagogue beckoned to Jesus, and asked him to speak to us all.

Jesus asked for something, and the next moment the president of the synagogue turned away and brought to Jesus a scroll that Jesus began to unroll. He was looking for something in it. Finally he straightened up and, looking around at all the familiar faces, began to speak.

From Isaiah, Jesus read, "The Spirit of the Lord is upon me because he has anointed me to preach good news to the poor, he has sent me to proclaim release to the captives and recovering of sight to the blind, to set at liberty those who are oppressed, to proclaim the acceptable year of the Lord."

He looked up, passed the scroll back to the president of the synagogue and sat down. I think he had no intention of speaking to the twenty-seven men present and the group of women behind them.

There was silence, and everyone was looking at Jesus. Finally he got to his feet again and stepped out in front of everyone. I saw him hesitate, as if taking a deep breath before jumping into cold water. He began.

"Today this scripture has been fulfilled in your hearing. It has happened, and I am here to do all and more that Isaiah wrote about four hundred years ago. This is the acceptable time of the Lord, this is the moment Israel has been looking and waiting for." Puzzled and skeptical looks greeted this claim. Several looked at each other with a hint of scorn.

"Yes, to open the eyes of the blind and, even more importantly, to make those who can already see, not only see but perceive what is *spirit* and of God. Yes, the lame shall walk, but how much more shall your souls be healed so that you no longer live as if you were cripples emotionally? You are indeed poor but the time is now when all of Israel shall be released from the restrictions you've lived with for centuries, and you will all be given a way to live according to the will of God."

There were a few nods, but several looked confused, and the rest had looks of blank incomprehension on their faces. I distinctly heard one voice say, "Who does he think he is? He is just one of us. Open the eyes of the blind! This I have to see."

Another voice answered him, "He always thought he was better than the rest of us. His mom and brothers are still here, and now he comes back from where ever he has been and expects us to buy his being something special. He is a carpenter, so what does he know?"

"I could tell you a few things about him if I chose to. He is no Moses. I know; I used to hang out with him as a kid," chimed another.

I heard a voice rasp, "We've heard all about what you have been up to, so show us some things like you did in Jerusalem!"

More people chimed in with comments in the same vein, and it became obvious the people there most wanted to see Jesus demonstrate what he could do. My heart sank because I knew Jesus never accommodated people's need for a show. He just couldn't do it, and others never understood that.

Jesus stopped and stared out at those gathered there and began again, but this time with a touch of frustration in his voice. "When there was a famine over all the land and there were many widows in Israel, Elijah was sent to none of them, but only to Zarephath in Lebanon, of all places. There were many lepers in Israel in the time of Elisha, but none of them were healed of their leprosy except Naaman the Syrian. So though I may be from here, I cannot do much here, for you only see me as the person you all think you knew. Face it, I don't do magic tricks, and you don't want from me what I have to offer. I won't do miracles just so you can be entertained." Jesus reluctantly walked towards his seat, but shouts of protest rang out.

"What do you mean you can't give us what we want? Let's see what you can do. We want you to do some of the miracles we have heard about. If you can do them for those people in Jerusalem, you can do them for us."

I was not surprised when Jesus made to leave, but the men there immediately mobbed him. They were not really hostile but didn't want to take no for an answer nor hear what he had to say. Lead by Judas, our party quickly stepped into the melee. Jesus pushed through them, reached us and, shaking his head, allowed us to lead him out of the assembly.

We went back to his home and were packing our few things when Mary, his mother, came in and asked him if he would see a young woman who had come looking for her. Jesus nodded and beckoned for me to join him.

The woman was carrying a child about eighteen months old and wrapped in her shawl. She was crying and frightened. She couldn't utter a word. Jesus quietly and gently took the flushed, limp child from the mother. Passing his hand over the little boy's head, he murmured, "It is his ears." Gently letting his hand caress the little boy's head, Jesus murmured a prayer.

The boy's whimpering trailed off and the boy began to stir. He found his thumb, stuck it in his mouth and snuggled against Jesus' chest.

Jesus smiled at the woman. "I am glad you came. Your son is going to be fine. No damage has been done, but if you had not come he would have lost at least some of his hearing."

When the woman left, Jesus said to Mary, his mother, "We must be off. We will be down by the lake. There are men there who have been waiting for my call for three years. It's time for me to wake them up."

Mary nodded, and said, "I'll pack some food for you. There is bread, cheese, and strips of dried beef I bought just yesterday." With that she left us, only to return a few minutes later.

"There is a young boy who wants to see you. It will not take a moment. I think he's worried about his dad."

Jesus took Mary's hands in his and kissed her fingertips, and said, "These are your people, this one is for you."

We went back out to the other room and there was a young boy about nine years old, looking scared and hesitant, shifting his weight from one foot to the other.

Jesus went to him and greeted him as if he were a man and not a child. The look on Jesus' face was serious and grave. "What are you worried about, for you look as if there is something really wrong and you can't seem to fix it yourself. Can I help?"

The boy stood up straighter, looked Jesus in the eyes and after a few moments gathered his thoughts and gravely responded, "My father is drunk again. He beat my mom last night. I couldn't stop him. I tried. It was the wine. It always does that to him."

Jesus looked as somber as the boy, "Do you love your father?" At the boy's emphatic nod, Jesus went on, "I am going to cast out of him the demon that is destroying him, but I want you to go to him now. I bet he is sleeping off the wine now, right?"

The boy nodded again.

"When he wakes up, I want you to tell him that you love him, that what he did last night was bad for your mother, bad for you and your sisters and little brother, and bad for him. Can you do that?" The boy nodded his head as if mesmerized, and waited for Jesus to go on. "Now, I am going to give you protection, and protection for your whole family for right now. But your father will in time become the defender of his family as he was meant to be. How about that?"

I watched as the boy struggled to be the man Jesus had invited him to be. He was just a kid, but as Jesus said, his love had made it possible for Jesus to help.

Jesus took both of the boy's hands and said to him gravely, "Go, and if you get scared, think of me here with you and I will be there in spirit to help out."

The boy nodded, and very seriously and quietly thanked Jesus. "My mother said not to bother you. I am sorry if I bothered you. I didn't know what to do. Our neighbor told me to come and see you, but I don't think he meant to be helpful. He was with my dad last night when he got drunk. Everyone knows my dad, and I thought if you didn't know him maybe you would be willing to help. Nobody tries anymore."

"But I do know your dad. You don't have to tell him it was me who put you up to this. Knowing will not help him because we grew up here together. We were friends, or at least kind of friends. Just as your love for your dad is between you and God, so keep this between you and me. You don't need to tell anyone."

When the boy had left, Jesus stared at the floor for a few moments. He said quietly, "Love, the love of that boy has saved his father. He has not judged his father, he has forgiven him over and over; in fact, that forgiveness is what has kept the boy's care for his father at a constant pitch despite everything that man has done." He looked up and said to me directly, "John, love is not enough, but without it the man would now be lost. In spite of our reception at the synagogue this morning, the seed has been sown here, and it will bear fruit. That child will not forget this, and he will tell others by and by. It will come out, but only when the ground here is ready to receive it."

I slung my satchel over my shoulder and said, "Time to go before someone else comes by. After what happened at the synagogue I thought this morning was a waste of time, but maybe not. I love to watch you with someone like that kid. You are always so just right. Now if we don't get moving we will be hiking in the dark."

Jesus nodded his compliance, went through to the other room and spent a moment taking leave of his mother. I heard them laughing over his failure to connect there in Nazareth, and he led me out the door into the dazzling light of the square. The other five members of our party were waiting for us, and we immediately set out for Capernaum.

26

The Call

Our small party dropped down into Capernaum on the shores of Lake Genessaret, or the Sea of Galilee, as we knew of it in Jerusalem. Thomas, Judas and the other three went off to look for lodging. Jesus and I followed the beach north to where boats were drawn up on the stony beach; we could see men working on them. As we got closer we could see there were four fishing boats. They were typical working boats, mostly for fishing and only sometimes for transporting people or cargo up and down the lake. Twenty-four to thirty feet in length, some seven or eight feet in beam, and made of thick two-inch planks dowelled together; these heavy, durable boats set a family who owned one above the rest of the people. A family with a boat had a year-round food source, as well as a cash income that so much of the farming population did not have.

As we drew nearer, we could see that the men working at the most southerly boat were completing their morning's work. They were scrubbing the boat down, washing out the blood and fish parts and throwing the detritus overboard. Birds swooped down on the scraps, carrying them away and fighting over the bodies of the fish the men had discarded.

We recognized one of the men as Andrew. He looked up and noticed us, and stepped overboard onto the hard shore with his hand shielding his eyes from the sun's glare off the water. He said something to the other man, who straightened up and looked down the beach to us. He let out a whoop and took off down the beach towards us in his bare feet, only to come to a quick stop as the stones and sharp rock reduced his progress to a hobble. He turned back, sat down on the side of the boat, pulled on his sandals and waited for us. He was huge with a fierce mop of unruly black hair. I recognized Simon.

When we finally came up to them, the black-bearded giant took a few steps to meet Jesus, and, with almost a sob, he enveloped his friend in a huge hug. "Am I relieved to see you! I thought maybe… well never mind that. You are here, that is what is important. Is anyone else with you?"

Jesus waved across at me and said, "You know John, and there are a few others, but you will meet them later."

Jesus looked over at Andrew. "I am so pleased to see you both. How is everything here? Is there peace, or are you under duress?"

Andrew said, "Funny you should mention that. Yesterday there was someone from Jerusalem asking after you. Simon here sent him packing. Is there a reason why he would be here?"

Jesus shook his head. "There is too much to report right now. We will tell you everything this evening. Things have moved a little faster than I imagined, and so here I am."

"Have you come here to hide?" Simon asked quickly. "Because, if so, you've come to the right place. Not a word from any of us. Nobody will mess with you here."

Jesus smiled. "I rather think I am wanted. I don't think Jerusalem is a good place for me right now, but I have not come here to hide. No, I've come to tell you the time is here." Jesus held out his hands to the two men. "The Kingdom of God is upon you, and its good news must be made real to everyone. This is the moment that I referred to when I said my time had not yet come. Well, now it has."

Simon looked at his boat, then at the town in the distance, shimmering in the heat and asked, "What about the boat, what about fishing? What about our families?"

Jesus glanced back and forth between Andrew and Simon and said, "I will teach you how to catch people instead."

Simon caught Andrew's eye and smiled at Jesus. "I don't know, catching people like fish doesn't sound like you."

Jesus dipped his head in agreement and grinned back. "Good for you. You were always forthright with your response. I was thinking more of the huge net you use to surround a whole school of fish and bring them all into the boat. The time has come to gather everyone together, build a force to be reckoned with. No more hiding; we are going to take the light from under the bushel and stick it on the lamp stand so everyone can see it and not mistake it."

"I want to hear more about it when we get back to town," said Simon. "We are almost done here. Come on Andrew, let's get finished."

Jesus and I sat down on the stony beach and watched the pair of them complete their chores. Simon took the carcasses of several dead fish and threw them out into the water. Instantly birds from far away converged on the scene and fought each other for the carcasses. Simon looked over at us, and explained, "Trash fish, bottom feeders; they're not kosher, there is no market for them."

Andrew was sitting in the boat. He looked up at the noise from the birds and smiled. "The birds don't seem to care what kind of fish they eat. They are Gentile birds from the sea. If they were Jewish birds they would know better." He went on inspecting the wet net inch by inch for tears. Andrew looked up for a moment and caught our attention and said to his brother, "Simon, I think you need to be a little more diplomatic about how you deal with strangers. That guy who came by yesterday could have been any kind of official or spy. The way you turned on him and told him to leave, and then threatened him if he should still be in town when we got there, was not polite, to say the least. These are strange times and you never know who you are talking to. He could have been from Herod, and the next thing we know is a detachment of his lackies would be down here stoving in the boat or slashing our nets."

Simon paused from throwing another bucket of water along the stern decking. "He was not from Herod. I had him pegged right away. He was Jerusalem-born and -bred."

"That was no reason to take the boat hook and offer to part his hair for him if he didn't leave." Jesus laughed and Andrew looked over to us, and back to Simon. "One day you are going to overstep the mark and land yourself in trouble." Then to us he said, "I don't mind him getting in trouble, but I don't want to get roped in with him. He always opens that big mouth first before he has given any thought about what he wants to say."

We sat in the warm sun listening to the banter between the two brothers as they worked. Simon chuckled, "I know, I know. But you must agree, when the guy stepped back and fell over into the pile of fish bits you found it funny. I heard you snigger." Then to us he said, "Anyway, he got the message. When we were finished he was gone. There was no sign of him in town."

Andrew looked over to us, and explained, "If Simon had not driven him off, he might have told us what was happening in Jerusalem and maybe explained why he wanted to know if you had been seen up here."

Simon defended himself. "I was worried about Jesus. When that piece of slime started asking about you," he looked at Jesus, "all I could think of was what those bastards would do with you if they got hold of you. I thought something had happened to you, and they were hunting you. Herod has John cooped up in prison, and my fear is you will be next. They want to shut you up."

Andrew interrupted. "My point is, if he had not flown off the handle, we could have gotten news about what's happening in Jerusalem. Instead, he will go back to whoever sent him and report suspicious activity on our part. Maybe even peg us as secret followers or whatever."

Simon threw the last few drops from his bucket at Andrew. "Andrew, I *am* a follower and not a particularly secret one. Galilee is not Jerusalem, and we don't like being pushed around. That was the message I gave the man. I wanted to make clear he should leave us alone and not mess with us."

"You big lump. I knew it was no good talking to you." Andrew shook his head. "Still, it was amusing when he sat in the fish pile." To us he said, "This was a really prissy person and very concerned about himself, and he stepped back and fell right into the pile of trash fish. He will never get the smell out of his clothes."

I enjoyed this back and forth between the brothers. Lying back and looking up at the blue of the sky, I thought with some degree of satisfaction that we were a long way from Jerusalem. We were amongst friends and for the moment safe as we could be within Israel.

I looked over at Jesus, who sat with his arms around his knees, keenly observing every detail of what the brothers were doing.

Finally Simon and Andrew folded the net, stowing it and coiling down its lines. Andrew explained to us over his shoulder, "Tangled lines and tangled nets are bad enough in daylight, but in the hours before dawn you can waste the best fishing hours if you get things twisted up. Right, that's done." These last words were addressed to his brother as he put away the heavy sack full of net.

Simon walked over to us, "We have finished here, so let's go back to the house and hear the whole story. The Kingdom is finally on its way, it will be established here on earth right now, and we are going to help. We've both been waiting for this."

Jesus peered up the beach, shading his eyes in the shimmering haze. He nodded to the north and said, "That boat at the end of the line…are those men working in that boat the friends you were with when I first met you?"

Simon replied, "That's John and James, and that one in the boat is their father. Come on, let's go and surprise them." He took off up the beach, hailing the distant fishermen as they worked over the final stowing of their gear and tucking their catch away in covered baskets that they dipped in the water to keep them cool before setting off for the town.

John and James both swayed up dripping baskets onto their heads and headed towards us. After greetings were exchanged we followed them into town, and Simon welcomed us to his home.

That evening, Thomas, Judas, Thaddeus, Marcus, and Simeon—all from Jerusalem—joined several friends of Simon and Andrew as we all crushed into Simon's house. More came, and soon our group from Jerusalem was sitting in a ring of listeners as we told of the events that led up to us leaving Jerusalem. Men leaned in the doorways and hung through the windows. There were so many who wanted to know the latest news that we finally moved to the little town square. Once there, most everyone from the little town assembled to hear what was going on. Men, women and even some older children turned out.

At first the questions expressed curiosity, but when Jesus explained why he had come and talked about the coming Kingdom of God, he got a very different reception from what I had grown to expect.

"So you say the Kingdom of Heaven is upon us. Where is it?" croaked a man with a large goiter. "I don't see it. It's all very well for you to announce it, and we would love to believe it is true, but is this more false hope?"

"The people around here are used to disappointment; they are skeptical of anything good happening. Our fathers had it the same and our grandfathers before them. Nothing ever improves. You will need to show the people this Kingdom," said James.

His brother John nodded and added, "Jesus, last week Herod's people were through here looking at the fields and checking that we've got the seed in the ground. Do you think they care? No, they are only concerned for how much they can tax us. That's the kingdom we've got."

Jesus sat back on the raised stone platform, and refrained from commenting on what was being said. Others pressed forward with tales of loss, disenfranchisement and suffering. Stories of what had happened flew thick and fast.

A tall thin man with huge bony hands leaning on a staff said, "My little boy has a weakness. Every two or three weeks he is afflicted with an unclean spirit and spends his time coughing and wheezing. I can't give him enough food to strengthen his body to shake off that sickness. He gets weaker each time. Am I to take the food from my other children to save him while Herod takes from us to build another palace? You talk of a Kingdom, but look at us; don't you think we would have a better life if it were possible?"

Another man shouted, "Herod will have something to say about this Kingdom. He does not allow too much freedom. Any resistance would mean his people would be down here the next week. There would be arrests, penalties and confiscation of property. We would finish worse off!"

The tone of frustration and resentment grew stronger, and I thought the whole evening would finish in acrimony and rejection. Jesus would not be heard. A false start would surely take Jesus weeks to deal with. I heard another complaint, "Right now we are getting by.

Harvests have been good for a couple of years, and we can get by. You have to understand things could be a lot worse, and we don't want to risk messing everything up.

I glanced at Judas and Thomas, looking for a sign they were worried enough for us to intervene, when Jesus stood up and stepped towards those gathered there. He asked, "When have things been different? You said it yourself. Your grandfather had the same kind of life. Nothing has changed. Is Herod any worse than Solomon? Solomon was the first of our Kings to tax you. How do you think he built the first Temple? He not only taxed your ancestors, but after the crops were in he made them work on his projects. If they didn't bend to the work, there was a lash or two. Nothing has changed so far as the rule of kings is concerned."

"At least Solomon built something everyone could be proud of. Herod does not. He sits in his palace entertaining himself with all the latest gossip from Rome, sucking up to the Emperor and wondering what he can steal from us and send to Rome to impress Caesar," shouted a voice from the other side of the crowd.

"Yes, and you get to support both Caesar and Herod," continued Jesus. "In principle nothing has changed, and anyone who becomes king will turn and lord it over you in the same way.

"Which of you would not turn into a tyrant if you found yourself on the throne of Herod? Which of you would not insist and coerce everyone to obey your rules? The rules you would make would be to protect yourself, protect your kingdom and provide for you and your friends who made you king."

Jesus looked out at the crowd meeting the eyes of any who would look into his. Silence fell like a curtain, as the people in the square waited for Jesus to go on.

"Your friends would make up titles for themselves, and they would convince you of the need for strong rules, and only they could supply them. Even if one of you became king tomorrow, and the rest of you his courtiers, by next year you would be no different than all the kings of the earth who expect their people to serve them."

"Then what are we to do?" asked an elderly man with a long gray beard.

Another called out from the back of the crowd, "What are you trying to sell us? Are you suggesting you would be a better king? Would you not turn out to be like the rest of them?"

"Yes, why should this Kingdom you are announcing be any different from all the others?" asked a man with tightly folded arms in the front row.

With that question, I knew Jesus finally had the opening he needed. "The Kingdom I have come to announce is the Kingdom of God. Given the nature of the Kingdoms of this world, and that wherever you go there will be an Emperor, a King, a Lord or local land owner all expecting and demanding your obedience, the Kingdom of God is something else entirely.

"Do you remember the psalm, 'Where can I flee from your presence or where can I hide from your face?' The Kingdom of God operates in a totally different way. The first thing is not to worry about those who have power over you physically, or even who can throw you in jail, but rather fear those who can destroy your soul. As I listen to you I hear your anger and hopelessness. You live in fear for what might happen next. Your sons maybe conscripted to fight in a distant land; your daughters taken from you to serve masters far away. These fears rule your lives."

I noticed some nods of agreement here and there by those listening. Others looked down or away as if not wanting to admit to this stranger that he was right.

"The Kingdom of God exists in the midst of just this despair. There is in you something God placed there in the beginning. It is the Spirit of God dwelling in you. It is the breath of God, breathed into Adam at his creation. It is that Spirit I have come to blow to life and make it flame up in you."

The suspicion and resentment that had been so prevalent amongst the people now gave way to a faint stirring of hope. This was the first time I had encountered these Galilean folk, and I realized how different they were from those that mobbed Jesus in Jerusalem. I heard Jesus say in a lower, more compelling voice, "This is the Kingdom the prophets spoke of. As members of God's Kingdom you can be thrown into the darkest prison, and inside you the presence of God's Spirit will shine. You can and will go through the pains of death or see terrible things, but if you are loyal to that Spirit of God, that breath of the divine living in you, you will not fear those who have power over the body. This is the Kingdom I am announcing."

"But what does that change?" asked a dour farm hand with the stains of his work evident on his short tunic, belted round his waist.

"Everything. As that breath of God brings life to you, eternal life will take hold and your anger will change into resolve, your fear into compassion, and you will see those around you through the eyes of God."

There was silence as his words sunk in. My initial thought was that these ideas would be beyond those listening, but at least some understood. A voice broke the silence. "My Maggie will still die; Mark's son will waste away. Our hearts break when we see this. What of our little ones? My wife and I have already buried one child, and now we watch as our youngest daughter goes the same way."

Jesus sat in silence looking at the dusty ground of the village square we were in. Men waited silently, many with arms crossed, as if waiting to see how Jesus would deal with their real-life problems, and not just offer nice ideas or platitudes.

As I looked from face to face, I saw a complicit unity, even a general satisfaction, that, finally, they had been able to tell someone just how bad things were. The unspeakable had been spoken.

Jesus raised his head and looked out over the little crowd and caught the eye of the man who had spoken of his son. "Go, bring your son." To the man who had spoken of his daughter, he said, "And you, go bring your daughter."

Both men hesitated for a moment, caught each other's eye from across the crowd, shrugged, and made their way out of the press of men. The others made way for them and closed the gap.

Jesus spoke softly, his voice filled with compassion. "You've spoken well. This is why I am here. Look at each other. Every one of you carries his own burden. The load is buried in each of you, and you go through your days in dread by yourselves.

I saw a ripple of satisfaction run through those gathered there. Jesus had heard them, and now they were willing to listen.

"Look at each other now. You are together in this moment of clarity. As you stand together, can you not feel the strength you share? Do you not feel the strength between you? This Kingdom of God I speak of is not only in each of you, it is between you. You can't live undefeated by yourself, but together it is a different matter."

I sat up straighter, for this was a departure from what often followed the point Jesus was trying to make. Where was he going with this?

Just then the man who had talked of his daughter came into the little square, carrying a child who could not have been more than four years old. The mother followed, her face full of anxiety. With her right hand she twitched the blanket over the girl's head as if to protect her from some ill.

I watched as Jesus held his arms up to receive the little girl, and the father gently placed her in his lap. At first Jesus did nothing but uncovered her head and looked at the pinched pale face of the little girl. The mother pressed forward anxiously. I saw Jesus pass his hand over the child's head, as if to smooth her hair away. He paused, and I saw his lips move in a silent prayer. He gently returned her to her father's embrace.

The little girl stirred, woke and flung her little arm out of the covering blanket. Looking around at us all, she turned to her father with a puzzled look. "Daddy?"

The man held the girl to him, murmured something to her, and said dazedly to the crowd, "She has not spoken in three days." He stumbled to his wife and delivered the girl into her arms. He hugged his wife and daughter to him.

I heard a collective sigh from the crowd. They looked from Jesus to the child and back. None of us moved.

Mark came back into the square with his son who must have been eight or nine. The boy was painfully thin, his peaked face pale in the soft glow of the setting sun. His eyes were bright points in his face. He coughed and made an attempt to control it, only to erupt again into coughing and wheezing. He looked up at his father in anguish. His father moved him gently forward with his hand towards where Jesus sat.

Jesus reached out for the boy, and asked his name.

"Philip," replied the father.

Jesus addressed the boy. "Philip, come to me." The boy hesitantly stepped towards him and allowed Jesus to draw him closer. Another fit of coughing left him breathless. A few flecks of bright red dotted his sleeve, at the sight of which I heard an audible gasp from those closest to him. Some drew the sleeve of their garments across their noses as if to protect themselves and moved back a step or two.

Jesus murmured to the little boy, whose chest rose and fell with the effort of trying not to cough in the presence of this stranger. Philip fought for breath and looked to Jesus as if wondering what was expected of him. He looked back at his father as if for instruction and again back to Jesus. I heard his father murmur, "Go on, Philip, I'm here. You are all right."

Philip stood, waiting tensely while the coughing threatened to erupt again and overwhelm him, but eventually it subsided.

Jesus placed one hand behind Philip's shoulders and drew the boy closer. Silence settled over the little square. Little Philip stood stiffly, his little chest rising and falling in shallow gasps as he struggled not to cough.

Under Jesus' hand, he began to relax. He stood there, and his little chest expanded fully, and the boy let out his breath. He looked at his father, surprise and delight across his face. He breathed again and smiled.

Jesus released him, and his father squatted down and took little Philip gently into his arms. The father buried his face in the boy's chest and began to sob. One of the men closest to him moved over and laid his hand on his shoulder. Others moved closer and surrounded the father and son.

Jesus got up and withdrew, leaving the men to attend to Mark and little Philip. People moved aside to let him through and closed in around the father and son. Mark gently led his son away.

Nobody spoke for several minutes, and only after Mark and Philip had left the square did the buzz of conversation pick up. I heard speculation and exclamations as the little crowd began to loosen and drift away. Some stayed, eagerly going over what they had just seen.

I looked over at Judas who was on the far side of our group sitting along the edge of the stone platform in the middle of the square. I caught his eye, and he raised one eyebrow as if in question of what we had seen. He and Thomas got up and moved over to me. Simon and Andrew were close by and the four of us left the square together. Thaddeus and Simeon tagged along behind.

Simon was the first to break the silence with a question. "Were those children healed?" Without breaking stride, Thomas, Judas and I all said *yes!* in unison.

When we were in the alley going towards Simon's house, Andrew said, "How did Jesus bring everyone around? I know those people. They are a hard lot. These are Galileans, and they don't let anyone from the outside talk to them like that and especially someone from Jerusalem."

I said, "Don't forget he is from Nazareth, so he does know what these men are like. What you saw was what I have witnessed often enough. You as fishermen might understand better than most, because you throw a net and encompass the whole shoal of fish. This evening Jesus did the same. Everyone is now part of that experience, and nobody wants to be left behind. This is how he is. Time and time again I have seen him reach into people and evoke in them that kind of response. Over and over again he has said that where we gather together in God's name, there He is in the midst of us all. If you ask him about it, but it was the Spirit of God working between and within all of us there. We were all part of what happened." I went on to describe a couple of other times I had witnessed the same effect. I was impressed with myself, for I was not in the habit of taking the lead.

I noticed the next day word had spread throughout the little community. Men went off to their work as usual, walking in two's and three's, talking quietly.

After the blue haze of the cooking fires had drifted down the beach, and the chores were done, the women came. I was sitting in the square with Thomas, Judas, Thaddeus and a couple of men from last night, when I saw three of the women make their way to what I learned later was little Philip's house on the edge of the village. They lingered around the door, and one entered, only to exit and excitedly immerse herself in the group outside.

Soon several women broke away and came across the little square we had met in the night before and made their way towards a small cluster of buildings just outside the village. I could see others hurrying after them. I wondered what Jesus had planned for today and decided to go in search of him. Judas and I left the square and went back into Simon's house.

Inside, Jesus was just finishing some bread, mopping at the remains of the fish he had obviously had for breakfast. "So it begins. Ahh, here is Mirriam. No doubt she will be able to tell us."

Simon's wife came in and looked at Jesus with a mix of awe and fear. "How are the young children this morning?" he asked.

"Everyone is talking about what you did last night. The children are a lot better. Little Margaret is walking, and both are eating." She set down the basket she had been carrying, hesitated for a moment and went on with a rush. "We were all expecting to have to bury those two soon. You know what that does to the whole village?"

I rose, thinking I ought to do something to comfort her or calm her down. She brushed my gesture aside and took a miniscule step towards Jesus. "Everyone always thinks, when will it be our children's turn? When will God take my child? Tell me! Why does God punish us? Why should our children suffer, why?"

Mirriam's face was flushed with anger, but her eyes were filled with tears. As usual in situations like this I felt useless and dithered between trying to help her or retreating and sitting down. I did nothing. It was Jesus who came to her aid. He said, "When did you lose your child?"

Mirriam stood still, her right hand crept to her throat, and her lips began to quiver, "Two years ago," she whispered. "Our first child, a boy. He died in my arms, unable to breathe and hot to hold. What had I done? What had he done? What had Simon done?" she screamed. "I don't envy Mark and his wife, but where were you two years ago? A woman never, never forgets losing a child. Even the next is no replacement. You men can't understand this. God doesn't seem to understand it."

Mirriam, who had at first been ill at ease in Jesus' presence and overcome with awe, was now before Jesus, her eyes burning and her head thrust forward angrily. Gone were her tears and now all her pent-up anger boiled over in a final outburst.

"We don't want any more suffering, no more Kingdom of God, no more promises. We just want our kids to live. You men talk of revolution, fighting for Israel, building a new city. Well, we women don't want any of that. We don't care about your visions. All we care about is not burying those we love. Don't stir us up with false hopes or visions and take our men away from us."

At this she burst into tears. "Don't take my Simon away. He is all I've got!"

Jesus sat immobile for a long time as Mirriam wept for her child and wept for her husband she knew she would be losing.

Finally, as Mirriam's sobs subsided, Jesus quietly asserted, "No, the Lord did not take your child to punish you. No, He did not seek the boy's death, but He has been waiting these last two years to hear you say what you just said. He is the father of us all, we are all His children and the loss of your little one is no less a loss to our Father in Heaven."

Mirriam slumped onto a bench against the wall, wiping at her eyes with the back of her hand. Jesus continued, "He has been waiting for you to share your sorrow with Him, for He mourns the loss of your boy and all the rest of the children who've died here in Capernaum, and for that matter, in every village and town of Israel."

Jesus took her hands and held them lightly. "Stand with Him in His pain, draw near to Him, for the pain of every mother is the pain He bears as the cost of His creating the world. From the beginning until now He is creating the world, and He is not separate from His creation nor from you, your child, or from Simon." Jesus released her hands. "He is not far from all the others of Capernaum. Your suffering is first of all His suffering, so stand with Him."

Mirriam sat gazing into her hands as they lay in her lap and sniffled. "I have never thought that God might suffer too." She bowed her head and began to sob. At last she raised her head and between sobs said, "Will the Lord, may His name be blessed, remember me? For I have screamed at Him in my heart. I have turned my back on Him. Will He want me back?"

"Want you back? You have never been gone from Him. Your job is to stand with Him and stand with the other mothers, wives and lovers who lose those so important to them. Stand between God and them. You know what losing someone is like. Share that knowledge. Make it bear fruit. I promise you your loss is not the end. Your son's death is not the final event you imagine. Your loss is not the final word of our Father."

Mirriam responded with a slow shaking of her head, "My anger was my only consolation. I don't know if I can give it up. Yet, if what you say is true, maybe, maybe . . . I could try." She got up and removed the wooden platter from the table and repeated to herself, "I could try," and went out to the cooking area behind the house.

Judas, who had been sitting in the shadows by the inner wall, looked from Jesus to me and back again and asked, "So, what now? You've started something here that you can't just walk away from. This is not Jerusalem. There you could teach, everyone would argue and you could just go off to Bethany for dinner. You've promised these people something. They expect you to deliver; how can you possibly give them what you've described? Also, you have led them to believe it is happening now, so you don't have much time left to satisfy them."

Jesus sank back onto the low ledge, which ran along the wall and was covered with a rug of rough woven cloth with a single patten running along its borders. I sat down beside him and gazed through the window opening, which framed a narrow view of the square. The warmth of the sun was already building. The heated air above the houses had begun its dance, shimmering in the bright light. We all sat in the comparative darkness listening to the rising sound of the little township coming to life.

I said, "You know, Jesus, Judas has a point. This is not Jerusalem."

Jesus ignored my remark. "Oh, Judas, Judas, you always have to be realistic and practical. Yes, I've promised something, and I've promised it again now.

"This is why we are here. These people, these ordinary people are key components of the Kingdom of God. Not the Temple, not Jerusalem, but here among these people. We've come to raise a revolution but without a sword in hand. You heard those men last night. Did you hear the hopelessness? Did you hear the despair? Well I am here to change that and give them power to belong with each other in the presence of God."

Judas studied his sandals, frowning at them as if they were too tight or uncomfortable. Without looking up he asked, "But why? There is nothing to be had here. Even if you are successful and create that homogenous sense among these people, then what?"

He raised his head and stared Jesus full in the face. "Is it going to be more pie in the sky? They've said they don't need anymore of that. Even Mirriam was clear on that point. So again, I say, what next?"

Jesus responded with a weary groan. "Here we are working with the township as a unity. The ideals that have always been our nation's core strength need to be brought to life again. Read what Moses laid out as the way we should be together, the way he instructed us to care for each other, for justice to be our standard, and mercy and understanding for each other be the strongest characteristic."

I asked, "Is that what we are about here in Galilee, teaching people to care for each other? There has to be more to it than that."

"Yes, John, there is a lot more to it than teaching. Just telling people what they ought to do isn't going to achieve anything; we have to bring the people together so they are an expression of the grace of God to each other. They will be a holy people, prepared and hidden like an arrow in a quiver, a weapon for righteousness in the hand of God. After all, being born an individual Jew is not enough; it's what we are together that matters."

Judas came right back as if he had not heard Jesus' impassioned response, and asked, "Why here, though? Surely if we are to change the nation, the answer lies in Jerusalem."

Jesus shook his head at Judas, "Right from the start I have said I'm sent to the lost sheep of the House of Israel. Galilee is an area looked down on by the powers that be. These people are like a building stone rejected by the builders, but they will become the chief cornerstone."

"You can't be serious. These are good people, but what do they know of the world? What do they know of the law?"

Jesus patiently came back at him, "You have put your finger on the problem. The worldly religious and the religious worldly of Jerusalem know nothing about the Kingdom of God or of the nature of the Divine. Let me put the problem this way: the Jewish people are the salt for the earth, but when they lose their saltiness as the Sadducees have done, how can they regain their saltiness? What's it going to take?"

Judas nodded his head thoughtfully and reluctantly agreed, "Okay, that is true of Jerusalem. I agree that crowd have lost their saltiness all right, and there is nothing left but salt sludge. But these people? They are so needy. I think you stand in danger of manipulating them. Will you be like all the others and use the people for your own ends?"

In response to this confrontation, Jesus looked Judas in the eye and said, "Why are you with me, Judas? Have I bewitched you? Have I manipulated you? Tell me truly, why are you still with me? For almost two years you've kept company with me, and you've got nothing to show for your efforts, so why?"

I saw Judas hesitate and look momentarily disconcerted. His face cleared as he confessed, "You are why I am here. You have so much potential. I can't bear to see you wasting it. I don't doubt your sincerity, but I just don't see how all this is going to work. You need help—real help—from the right people, and you won't find any of them here."

Jesus got up from the ledge on which he sat and went to the window opening and, looking out at the alley beyond, said over his shoulder, "Judas, four years ago I faced that particular temptation. There was a promise made that if I would play the game the way it's always been played and work with those who had the power, then I would be given all the Kingdoms of the earth. Starting here in Galilee is the antithesis to that. You will see. Just be patient."

I saw Judas look up sharply at Jesus' mention of that old temptation. "Maybe this is a place to start. After last night, word will be out and you'll have no trouble getting people to listen to you. Simon said last night that by this evening everyone from miles around will be here. That reminds me, where are Simon and Andrew? I've not seen either of them," said Judas.

Jesus replied, "They were out fishing very early this morning, even before I was up. They are probably cleaning up by now. Maybe I'll go and meet them."

I got up, and together we stepped out of the cool darkness of the house into the bright light outside and went in search of Andrew and Simon. Jesus said, "Maybe we can help them carry some things back to the house."

I smiled to myself as I thought of Jesus carrying a basket of fish back to town, but I realized though I might have trouble doing that, Jesus wouldn't. He could even make carrying fish look normal.

After the evening meal, people assembled outside the door of Simon's house. Jesus rose from the table and moved to the doorway. He surveyed the faces of those squished into the narrow space. "We are too crowded here. Let us go to the square."

People streamed after him and surrounded him in the square. He took his seat on the low platform of limestone seen in every town and used as a step for mounting a wagon or resting your burden as you went from one town to the next.

Jesus let everyone assemble. Judas, Thomas, Thaddeus, Marcus, Simeon and I followed and found seats off to the side. I was surprised that unlike most small town meetings, there was no banter between anyone. Their attention was fixed on Jesus. He returned their gaze, looking from individual to individual and, as if having noticed everyone, smiled to them all.

One of the men I recognized from the previous evening stepped forward, obviously a spokesman for everyone. "Look, Jesus, last night we didn't mean to insult you, nor were we making light of what you said. It is just that we here in Galilee, and especially here in Capernaum, have a hard time with people wanting to tell us what we should be doing, and what we've got to do, and if only we were different or like some other people. Well, tell you the truth, we thought that's what you were going to say.

"The thing is we don't know what to say now. You helped Mark's boy and little Margaret is doing fine, and we don't know what to say. I think I can say we're all glad you're here. You really surprised us last night."

At this, I heard murmurs of assent ripple though the crowd.

I heard another voice say, "Yes, I asked you some of those questions, and I expected you to ridicule me, but you didn't. I hear you're from Jerusalem, but we don't expect any good to come out of there. I am right glad you're here, and maybe I've got more questions for you."

At this feeble attempt at humor, a little chuckle lightened the mood of everyone.

Jesus smiled with everyone else and waved his hand in acknowledgement. He asked after the two children. Margaret's mother, who had been so anxious the night before, pushed through the crowd, pulling beside her the diminutive form of Margaret. I saw the woman pause, kneel before Jesus, and touch his sandal in respect. She rose and moved away.

Little Margaret, who had been self-consciously covering her lower face with her garment and gazing at everyone, now looked at Jesus. She let the corner of cloth fall from her face and walked into his arms. He held her for a moment or two and patted the stone beside him. The murmur from the crowd was different than before. I think it was from the women in particular, who watched as Margaret inched her little body into a sitting position beside Jesus, gravely looking at the crowd. Jesus motioned the mother to sit beside Margaret, and there they all sat. Margaret straightened her skirt, looked up at Jesus beside her and smiled out at the crowd. Everyone laughed with good humor, and not least because not twenty-four hours before they had all thought they would lose her.

I watched as Jesus scanned the crowd in his customary manner, meeting the eyes of all that sought his. He began, "Last night you told me what your lives here were like. You told me your fears, your resentments and the injustice you live with. That is easy to understand, but you told me about something else: that you really did not expect God to do anything. That you were expected to serve Him in Jerusalem as often as possible, pay tax to the Temple and so on. What showed on your faces and was expressed in your voices was the assumption or even the sure knowledge that our God, the glory of our nation, would do nothing for you.

So silent was the crowd that I became aware of the crickets chirping in their hiding places. He continued, "Last night you saw what can happen when you come together. You came together to confront me, to voice honestly what you all recognized as truth. You have not dared think of these questions as prayers to God, but to me you could voice them and through me, challenge Him who has sent me. The healings of these two children are signs that you were heard. They will live among you as symbols that will remind you that God has not forgotten you, nor ignores you, but is very present with you here in Galilee."

A hand was raised and a voice called out, "We heard you were run out of Jerusalem because of this kind of thing," and he indicated little

Margaret sitting there, "and you are here because it's about as far from Jerusalem as you can get."

Jesus laughed. "That's not too far from the truth. When you go stirring up a bee's nest looking for honey, you know you have little time before the whole hive is out to get you. Well, that is about what happened in Jerusalem. So here we are."

He looked over to where I was sitting. "John over there and I met Simon, Andrew, Philip and Nathaniel several years ago. Since then, every time I've met them I have been impressed by their faithfulness and common sense. They are the qualities I see in you; they are the qualities I am looking for. Last night was real confirmation of the reason why I am here. I am not here to hide, but to light a beacon among you that can be seen far off."

Questions flowed. Most of all, the folk there wanted to know about the healings in Jerusalem and especially about the moments when Jesus had run afoul of the authorities. Jesus introduced Judas and Thomas to the people and asked them to tell the stories of what they had seen. Judas stepped forward and told stories of the encounters he had witnessed. Thomas, being more reflective, shared his insights and thoughts about what he had seen.

I have to admit, Judas did a great job and outlined succinctly the tensions and political conflicts we had aroused. The men in particular loved his descriptions of the clergy's discomfort and laughed loudly as he aped the Temple staffers' haughty outrage. I had seen most of them for myself, but the encounters Thomas talked about were moments when Jesus had introduced radical new ideas to his listeners. These drew questions from the people and discussions broke out.

The late afternoon gave way to evening. It was the eve of the Sabbath, and I saw people begin to drift home for their welcoming of that special day.

Jesus finally arose, gave the sleepy Margaret into her mother's arms and, catching Simon's eye, nodded towards the house. We took out leave amid good-natured comments and laughter. I had the impression they regarded us as belonging there.

"Wow," I thought, "it is only the second day, and we have been accepted. That has to be some kind of record for Galilee."

27

Moving Through Galilee

On the Sabbath we went to the gathering for worship. I think every man in town was there. Word had spread to other villages, and there were many men from outside the town.

As we expected, Jesus was asked to speak. The president of the gathering came to Jesus with the scroll of Isaiah and asked him to read from it. This time, Jesus read the part about Isaiah's vision in the Temple. After reading he sat down, but we all waited for him to speak again.

He rose to his feet and began what I considered a very thoughtful response to Isaiah's writings. He did not talk about the people of unclean lips as most teachers do, but rather spoke about the vision of the glory of God. As we listened he laid out for us a new vision of the glory of God; one that reached into Galilee, into Capernaum and into every person. I had heard a lot of it before, but for those there that morning it was a revelation.

Towards the end when he was talking about the promise of the presence of God in any person, there arose a commotion off to one side.

A voice cried out, "What do you want with us, Jesus of Nazareth? Have you come to destroy us? I know who you are—the Holy One of God."

He continued to rail at Jesus, repeating himself and swearing with convulsive force. The men around him tried to shush him up and forcibly constrain him, but he lashed out at them.

The president of the synagogue turned to Jesus. "I apologize for him. He does this all the time. He goes down the street swearing and cursing everyone while jerking his head and his body in spasms. Nobody has been able to do anything with him. He says the most outrageous things, and embarrasses his parents continually. He must be possessed. His parents are fine people; we don't know why he is like this."

Jesus left the little dais on which he stood and advanced toward the man, who screamed all the louder and shrank from Jesus. He screamed louder still, and everyone looked at each other in alarm and fright. Jesus stood in front of him, held his eyes with his for a moment, and ordered the unclean Spirit to come out of him.

What a commotion!

Finally, as if a tooth had been painfully extracted, the man gave a final scream and slumped into the arms of those beside him. People drew back from Jesus as he returned to the dais. Fear was on the faces of all. It was the same fear that I recognized from other times. I knew what they were struggling with. They had been confronted by the power of this man, and felt his enormous will and certainty to heal. They had no words to describe the questions forming in their minds.

The last I saw of the young man, he was being held by a man who must have been his father. I saw the young man nod as if in reply to a question. The two moved off through the crowd. The young man walked quietly with his father's arm across his narrow shoulders. One pock-faced man who had struggled to restrain him two minutes before now patted him on the shoulder and smiled at those around him, as if assuring them the young man was safe to approach.

That afternoon, people brought their sick to Jesus. He had a word for each, or a touch, and some he laid his hands on. "What is this," the folk exclaimed, "this powerful stuff?"

I heard one man say, "Maybe we really do have a champion."

Another said, "Who would have believed it here in Capernaum?"

Simon and Andrew returned early the next morning from fishing. They carried in the baskets of fish, set some aside in the cool darkness of a small recess in the food preparation area, and covered them with a heavy cloth soaked in the lake water. Simon hefted one of the baskets and disappeared through the doorway, stalking off towards the square.

Andrew turned from stowing equipment and motioned towards the little room available for guests and the storage of odds and ends. "Is Jesus up? Have you seen him yet?"

I shook my head. "Either he is sleeping in after yesterday's efforts, or he was gone early. Knowing him, I expect he was out by sunrise and off in the hills up there. That is what he does often. Sometimes it's for hours; I've even known him to be gone days at a time."

"Really? What's he doing? Is he thinking things through or just hanging out by himself? I can understand him needing some time alone after getting swamped with people yesterday. They were all over him." Andrew twitched the curtain to the guest room aside, and upon seeing the empty room, said, "I guess you're right. So now what do we do? Simon and I hurried so we could help with the people."

"I wouldn't bank on him being back any time soon. He could be gone hours, and the rest of us just have to wait. But he's not thinking things through; he will be praying. These are the times he spends with God. He has invited me along a couple of times, and he is just there in prayer. After thirty minutes I fade, but there he is, still going strong. Each time he took me with him, he caught me napping, slapped me on the shoulder to wake me up and started down the trail expecting me to follow."

Simon came back in, looked inquiringly at Andrew and asked, "Where is he?"

When he learned from Andrew that Jesus was gone, he plunged through the door, calling over his shoulder, "Let's find him. I bet I know the place."

With that we three set off, walking though the village, out the other side and following a trail away from the lake towards higher ground.

I puffed behind Simon and, between breaths, complained, "If we just let him come back when he's ready, we will spare ourselves this climb and not interrupt him in what is so important to him."

Simon said, "There are people coming from all around. By midday there will be dozens waiting for him. I've been thinking we will have to regulate all this somehow."

As we turned a corner in the trail, we saw Jesus coming towards us. He greeted us with, "Let me guess, you are looking for me."

We joined him in his descent. Picking our way down the trail, we tried to avoid letting loose rocks roll under our feet.

Jesus went on in silence for a couple of hundred yards and spoke to us all, "We need to move on to the neighboring towns. I want to spread my message all over Galilee, and I want to start with townships on the lake. In particular, those to the south, down as far as Tiberius."

Simon said, "Well, there are people in town now waiting for you. They've come from down the lake as well as back in the hills. What about them?"

Jesus smiled, "Tell you what, you send them away, and tell them I will be visiting their villages, and I will see them there. I don't want to begin another session here. I have come to teach and lead everyone toward a new understanding of God's Kingdom. I'm not just a wonder worker. I don't want the healing of people to be the main attraction. I'm not here to make things more comfortable for everyone."

Simon nodded, quite obviously disappointed, but agreed. "All right, but if they see you, that will be that. Tell you what, why don't you and John avoid the town, slip up the beach and wait for Andrew and me by the boat. We can use the boat to go wherever you want to go and whenever you want to go, even down as far as Tiberius."

Jesus and I took a fork in the path that took us north of the town, and down to the beach. As we walked I explained, "I've not had much opportunity to talk with you for a while. In fact, ever since before you raised Lazarus, things have been moving very fast. I've been thinking, and there are a number of questions I have. Is this a good time?"

"Sure, John, go ahead. Things have indeed changed radically this last month, and now the next step is clear to me. So ask your questions."

"While you were in Jerusalem, I always thought you would be there for years, steadily developing your ministry and spreading your teaching so that changes you have spoken about would gradually be accepted and be put in place. That's not going to happen, is it?"

Jesus reflected for a few moments as he considered my question and examined what I had not stated. "No, much more is needed to move those power blocks in Jerusalem. Right now we are about raising the awareness of a lot of people here and, with some numerical support, go back to Jerusalem and confront the High Priest."

"When you speak of numerical support, are you considering armed force? I really don't see any of these people being much help in that way. I doubt if we could even get to Jericho before we were stopped."

"No, I've said before, no armed force! The need here is to teach these people to live their salvation, to free themselves from the need for the Temple sacrificial system and to deny the Temple their support. You heard those folk the first night. They believe they are required to pay the Temple tax or bad things will happen to them. They are threatened by superstition, fears and religious requirements that are no longer needed. If we build a broad, far-flung community of people who no longer have a use for that system, we will have power to change it. That will be the beginning, but by no means the end."

"Why could you not do that in Jerusalem?"

"In Jerusalem we've got a good number of friends who understand what I am teaching and follow me. They even call me *Master*. They are a network of individuals sharing the same ideals, but here, as you saw these last three days, there are also people who share each other's lives. Ultimately the Kingdom of God is about a people who share their lives. These folk have been living in isolation from each other and, in consequence, tried to cope with the many systems of oppression by themselves. By supporting each other and helping each other, they can better resist the corrosive effects of hardship. They will find power and dignity in a community which has a different motivating force, namely a community based on God's rule of love."

"I see the difference," I told him, "and I think I am beginning to understand what you want to do here. There is already a sense of hope and of course expectation. The only thing that worries me about it is so much depends on you. What happens when you go back to Jerusalem? You have said a couple of times that is where the final confrontation is to be."

"Ah, now that is a good point. Yes, what happens when I leave? Do you remember my mentioning a temptation I experienced in those early months when you first met me? It was the one about all the Kingdoms of the world, but as I said to you one day, none of those earthly kingdoms or empires last very long, so what is the answer? A Kingdom where God is king, and He is the genius of everyone's thought and actions is my ultimate vision: A Kingdom that goes on forever and spreads not by the power of the sword, but by the power of the spirit which enlivens and lights every person. Such a Kingdom would be self-generating and self-governing because each would be serving the divine in each other. Power would not be power over others, but power to do with others for the benefit of the whole."

I stopped walking so I could better focus on how I could pry an answer from Jesus to the question that kept me awake at night. "That is a tall order. You mean that everyone would live by the law. We've been trying that! The Pharisees are working hard on that very thing, but you have said that is not the answer. So again I ask, this vision of yours is incredible, but don't you think it naïve? I think such a vision is possible among a closed group like the brothers down by the Salt Sea, but there they have strict discipline and coercive practices. How on earth are you going to get everyone to cooperate? Think of those people we met in Jerusalem. They were scurrilous individuals who would do anything to obtain an advantage. What is going to change them enough so they can be part of the Kingdom? You've said it's not domination, nor is it absolute obedience to laws, but then what?"

"You are right on. Not everyone is going to be able to get with the program at any one time. Individuals will come to it gradually over time, or finally see it at the end of their lives. Others may never see the Kingdom, but it will be all about them. Remember Nicodemus and what I said to him: 'He must be born again.' Well, for him, that has been going on ever since that night, and as you know he is very much a part of this embryonic kingdom. We are using the word *Kingdom* because we think we know what we mean by it, but it is not adequate. We have no other word that is.

"God is love, and he has planted that love in every person. Our job is to free the spirit in people, and to identify it, personify it and demonstrate it, so that anyone—rich or poor, educated or uneducated—can act authoritatively in the name of the Father of us all. Did you notice the men assemble round Mark that first night? He went down on his knees before his son, and they all moved round him and laid their hands on him. That spirit of compassion is in each of them and, when expressed communally, will save the individual from the effects of any crushing disaster. The individual's burden is lifted and carried by the many. The many grow in awareness and power to what they are called to be. Get it?"

"Jesus, walking with you, listening to you on this beautiful morning, makes it all perfectly obvious. Yes, you are right, but I can only say that in your presence. When I think of the harsh realities of our lives, what you describe retreats and is swamped by the cares of the world. I tell you, Jesus, you have to stick around. Nothing will happen without your being here."

"There is an answer to your objection, but I don't know what it is. I know I have to return to Jerusalem. I know I have to go head to head with that Temple clique, and there's going to be a struggle, but I don't have a clear knowledge of what form or structure the Kingdom of God will take. I know it is in the mind of God, and everything we've done has been consistent with that divine intention. So we're on track."

"That's why you spend those hours up in the hills? You are trying to figure out that Divine purpose?"

"That's not entirely true." We came up to the boat, and Jesus perched himself on the stern decking with his legs over the side. Jesus said, "Simon and Andrew will be some time yet. I ought to have asked them to bring Judas along. He has our cash. I don't want to sponge off the people where we are going. Well, it's no big deal, but something we should think of in the future. Would you look after that? Keep an eye on what we need and pay for it. I don't want to take anything for what we are offering."

He said, "I didn't answer your question back there. The time I spend in prayer is life to me. Without that time in the Father's presence, I would have nothing to say to anyone. Everything I have—the words, the actions, the healings—are from above. During that time I spend alone in the hills, I spend not alone but in conversation with the Father. I am lifted and transported elsewhere by the experience, and I am shown the purpose, intention and will of the Father. Once that suffuses me, I am able to do what you see me do."

"I can see that. Maybe that is exactly what I have been trying to say. We say our prayers when we can, but we don't have the connection you have to the Father. That is why we need you around. That connection sets you apart, and without you the community's connection gets dropped. I watched you yesterday, and power flowed out from you and affected everyone. That young man felt it and resisted it and started screaming, but the rest of them also felt it. It was only after you took charge and acted to help that poor kid that everyone accepted your power and recognized your authority.

"That's why we all need your presence, not just to protect us from bad things happening, but who else has the authority to call forth the evil that surrounds us and cast it to the ground like you did?"

"Well, John, that sums it up. I've said this before, that what's important here is not what I am or what title I go by, but that relationship with the Father. That is also what those hours up in the hills are all about.

"Here they come. By the look of it, Judas is with them too. There are five of them. Do you recognize the other two? I think they are from the other boat. John and James, perhaps. Well, good. Our little expedition has grown. Seven of us. Maybe we can all still fit in one boat."

We sailed off down the west shore of the lake and put ashore in Genessaret. There, people had already heard of our coming and also what had happened in Capernaum. In the late afternoon people assembled, and Jesus taught them about the Kingdom of God. There was the same puzzlement as in the other cities, but at least here Jesus' reputation helped. What they really wanted to see were miracles. This was to be the ever present problem for Jesus. His ministry was a work of power; the power to heal, but also the power of his word. The people would have been satisfied with just the healings.

What Jesus was trying to convey to them was complex. They had no frame of reference to question the religious practices or the social ills they had to live with. Jesus spent a long time listening to those willing to talk, answering questions as briefly as possible but stimulating the people with questions about their lives. As the evening meal approached, Jesus took his leave of the people. He promised to come back and assured them he would spend more time with them.

As Simon had predicted, the late afternoon breeze blew gently and drove us back towards Capernaum. We sat in the boats and talked about the day. Simon couldn't understand why Jesus hadn't taken more advantage of the opportunity, but Jesus said, "No, we introduced ourselves today;

There were a couple of people who needed our help, and we heard their thoughts. That's enough for now. We were there for their sake, not our own. They are not to be won over to our side, or convinced to buy what we are selling."

In the following days we roved all over Galilee. We visited the lakeside communities, travelling by boat most often; we also walked the tracks that connected to those communities up in the hills. These were narrow, centuries-old roads beaten into the limestone by years of use. They cut through the greening fields of grain, winding back and forth to encompass settlements of sometimes only three or four houses. The familiarity and popularity of Jesus grew. As they got to know him, more of the people trusted him and were ready to listen and be taught. These insular people of Galilee adopted him as their own.

People of all types confronted Jesus every day. Jesus could sit quietly on a rock and somehow a confrontation would be created out of thin air. Folk came to him readily, but often did not know what they wanted or even why they were there. Sometimes, full of anger, they would come to him and complain bitterly about a neighbor or a brother who wouldn't give them what they wanted. But Jesus was an expert at drawing out the poison of fear and resentment, bringing peace to people who sought resolution by violent or damaging means. For example, the paralytic was brought by his friends to meet Jesus. The man was so full of guilt and had become so deeply distressed, that he fancied he could not move. He had created a pathetic excuse for retreating from life.

These situations fascinated me, because Jesus reached beyond their superficial wants or demands to touch the heart of their need. Whatever happened flowed through him to them. The paralytic experienced forgiveness; he looked within himself for his guilt, but it was gone. He got up and started to live again.

This did not happen every time. Sometimes it was as if Jesus had to wrestle with more than the demon of a disease or a vengeful, hurt person. These occasions were rare, but they frightened us as we watched Jesus respond. The mad man across the lake in Gadarrea was an example. We were scared stiff, frozen by the spectacle. I remember we stood rooted to the ground at his approach. Jesus stood in front of the man, and with absolute calm spoke to the evil spirit and evicted him.

There was another time when we first met Mary from Magdala. Magdala was a township further south on the lakeshore. Her friend had brought her all the way to Capernaum. My first impression of her was a woman wasting away, and thought she had the wasting disease—tuberculosis—but I was wrong. As she and her friend approached Jesus, she pulled back on her friend's arm and began urgent protests and denial.

As she came before Jesus and met his gaze, she screamed and started trembling. Her face went pale; she grew rigid as a board and fell backwards.

Her friend caught her and lowered her to the ground. Jesus went unhurriedly to her side and knelt in the dust by her. He asked the friend for her name, and, in a quiet voice called the woman's name. "Mary, Mary," he said, over and over. The woman stirred, and he put his arm under her and helped her to sit up. She looked around in panic at all of us standing around her. That strange rigidity threatened to return, but Jesus called her by name again as if summoning her back to him. She clutched blindly to him and let him hold her close to his chest.

Silence fell on the crowd as they watched the struggle; it was fought on a battlefield they could not see, but they were aware that it was of great importance. Someone asked who she was; a voice across the crowd whispered, "I don't know, maybe she is a prostitute or something." He was shushed by the people behind him.

We waited. Jesus was in no hurry to get out of the dust, but settled himself to cradle the woman's inert form. "Is she dead?" someone asked.

Minutes passed. The woman's eyes flickered open and looked around. She looked briefly at Jesus and struggled to her feet. Jesus also rose, and sat her down on the rock he had been sitting on when she first arrived. Leaning into her he very quietly said, "What was done was wrong, and you did not deserve it. You have never done anything to deserve being treated like that."

The woman looked fearfully at him, and for a moment her face paled again, but Jesus spoke, "You did nothing to cause it. You have never done anything to cause it."

The woman looked down at her hands and twisted them back and forth. Long shuddering sobs echoed from her as she shamelessly wept in front of everyone. Jesus once more called her by name, trying to recall her back to the warmth and light of the village square.

We saw the horror and fear in the woman's gaze as she looked inward to scenes we could not see. Her face contorted in terror, in pain, in sorrow, and, once, in frightening anger. Finally, as the sum of all her inner landscapes came crashing down on her, she wept helplessly.

There were women among us, and I caught them looking at each other as if they knew what she was looking at. Finally one stepped forward and put her arm around Mary, and the friend who had brought her was there, too.

Jesus said, "Mary, don't be afraid. I will let nothing hurt you. Will you take me with you back to where you were a few moments ago? I will walk through it all with you. I'll not leave you."

Mary looked terrified and pallor fringed her face again. She looked at Jesus as if to say no, but instead nodded, and took his fingers in her hand. She bowed her head. We watched as her face registered fear and horror all over again. Jesus stood grimly in front of her, and I became aware of changes in his expression as he looked on things we could not see. This went on for half an hour. People got restless and some drifted away, but many of us stayed. We were witnessing a struggle that was new on earth, but against the oldest enemy of us all.

Eventually, as if she were tired out and ready to rest, the woman's attention returned to us. She opened her eyes to take in our looks of hope, curiosity and expectation.

Jesus took her hands in his and, looking her full in the face, said, "None of all those things were your fault. You never wanted any of it; you never deserved to be treated like that. It was wrong. God heard your prayers, and I am here now. You don't need to hide anymore."

Jesus looked across at Simon. "She should not go back or be alone tonight. Would your wife sit with her?" He looked at the women who had come to Mary's aid. "Would one or two others help? You know what to do."

The women of the town closed in around her, protecting her from the men in the square.

That night James was the first one to raise the subject of what had happened that afternoon. Jesus sat for a long time before he tried to answer. "That woman has been so abused that she found refuge in hiding in a dark place where no one could find her. Pain and blame followed her at all other times, and those around her beat her and treated her shamelessly. None of you know what that is like. When you get in a fight you can fight back, but what if you couldn't? What if when you had been beaten you were then blamed for the fight?"

Philip shook his head. "If that happened to any one of us, we would all have something to say. Nobody treats us like that. Right, Simon?"

Simon nodded thoughtfully. "Yes, but we are all men. Would we believe a woman who protested how she was treated? Would we interfere? I just came back from my house, and I got an earful. The place is full of women. I need to stay elsewhere tonight."

Jesus said, "That goes for me too. It's important we leave her to heal, for she must decide on her own to embrace the here and now as her refuge, and not that dark place by herself.

"What to do for her?" asked Jesus, "She has to be defended, for those who were responsible will seek her out. They always have in the past, and they will be here to collect her before long. They will have the law on their side, and they will demand she be handed over to them. We all know how that works, but this time it must not happen. She cannot afford to lose the grip she now has on this world. Simon, do you know anyone going over to Nazareth? I want her to go and be with my mother; she will know what to do, and no one will bully her. I think this woman should be on her way first thing tomorrow and be in the hills before midmorning. If anyone comes looking for her, give them no information at all."

We looked at each other in surprise and nodded our agreement to Jesus. The next morning, Mary of Magdala, as we now called her, made her way towards Nazareth.

In late afternoon two brothers came into town, making inquiries about her. Word had spread, and we closed ranks. No one admitted anything. The women were watching us, and I think that sealed our lips more than Jesus' request.

Finally, three men from the village surrounded the brothers. With a minimal amount of pushing and shoving, they convinced them to leave. I think the importance of this was that, although Jesus healed

Mary, we all found we had a part to play. The whole town was part of her recovery, so we grew in our experience of what it meant to be the Kingdom of God.

28
Personal Reflections

On the Sabbath we were always with a small assembly of men at the synagogue. Ever respectful of protocol, Jesus would wait to be invited to speak. Sometimes healings or long conversations would follow his reading.

The fields ripened, and we saw harvesters bringing in the crops. Judas and I were always there; Simon, Andrew, John, James were often with us, and several other men attached themselves closely to us.

There were few moments we had to ourselves, and I felt as if the core group, with which we had arrived, was being diluted with so many new disciples. Simon, Andrew and some twenty others were taking on themselves the job of working with the people, maintaining the logistics for our journeys and even planning where we should go next. Jesus was steadily building an organization with its own loci and belief system. Mostly, this new core was dedicated to the intention of forging a community that demonstrated Jesus' teachings in practice.

One early morning, as the others shook themselves awake and got themselves together, Jesus invited me to walk with him into the low hills back of the village we were visiting. We sat there for more than fifteen minutes, looking out towards the lake and the thin line of mountains on the other side. Jesus asked me, "Do you see what we are doing?"

After a moment of thought, I said, "People are trying out your ideas. I think they are excited. I would say, though, that you can't be here forever. How do you expect these folk to carry forward such a profound vision and clear direction without your constant attention?"

"I have not solved that problem yet, but my prayer has gone forth and no echo has come back. It has been heard. I don't know, but what is happening is by the grace of God. I am on target, and my objectives are accurate.

"Still, I can tell something has been bugging you for days now. I've seen you struggle with the idea of balancing this whole question of the Kingdom of Heaven with having a normal life. You've wanted to ask me about how we, as Jews, are expected to marry, have children and bring them up knowing our Lord God, and yet here we are unmarried, childless and without any prospects. Is that it?"

"Exactly!" I exclaimed. "Just where are you going with this? Well I know the brothers at the monastery of Essenes are definitely celibate. I know you were part of that community for a while, but in everything you do and say you have rejected their doctrines and community requirements. You never urge celibacy on any of us, but yet here you are over thirty years old and yet alone. David was married a few times, and Solomon over 900 times, but not you."

"John, you are asking about a very personal issue here. You don't know how much I sometimes yearn for the tender caresses, the murmured words of love and just being wanted for myself, but I know all of that is wrong for me.

"To tell you the truth, when Mary would come and sit at my feet during those dinners at Bethany, I really wanted to caress her hair or her face as she looked up at me, but that cannot be for me."

"Why not? I am sure Lazarus would have been delighted for you to show that kind of interest in his sister."

"That is the point. Behind all the gestures, caresses and moments of endearment lies the ancient and eternal need for us to procreate. How long have generations reared generations of children? Our bodies are made to procreate and be fruitful like the rest of creation. This is not for me.

"Would it be fair for me to encourage Mary or any other woman? If I did I would be indicating to her my interest in cohabiting with her, her bearing my children and together bringing them up. The truth is, my job is to usher in the Kingdom of God. I cannot lose my sense of self and divide it between my roles as the Holy One of God and a husband and father. Both those roles are in themselves vital.

"The job of many people in the Kingdom here on earth will be to have a spouse and children. I decided over ten years ago that I had to take part in no banter with women, no unspoken promises, no ambiguity. Among the fellowship of the Children of Light we were all dedicated to celibacy. We were schooled in all kinds of abstinence, fasting, and self denial, so that self discipline and inner direction comes easily to me.

"I move among many people, I see the stories of their lives, the disease, trauma, fears and hopelessness, and this knowledge is not for my profit or benefit. I have been given this understanding for their sake, and for their sake I will remain who I am to them, and take nothing, expect nothing or even hope for anything in return. I am there to be a conduit for God's love for them. Like an irrigation channel with no weeds, no blockages and no debris, I must keep the flow of the Spirit of our Father in Heaven flowing without hindrance."

I hesitated to ask the question that came to my mind, but with Jesus questions were always what he respected most. I asked, "Do you have a choice? Could you decide not to do this work?"

Jesus shook his head. "No. Four years ago I could have turned aside. Do you remember when we first met, I told you of those temptations? Well, there followed a period of wrestling with accepting the responsibility. Finally, I gave my whole self up to Yahweh's invitation. That 'yes' was my complete surrender, and I now have no other life but the one I chose. All else has dropped away, and now I see people through the eyes of God. I see the world the way God sees it."

"Is that hard to maintain? Don't you ever wonder what you are missing?"

"I used to marvel at how easy life was, having renounced so much. That was a huge problem for me. I was proof against temptation, unmoved by people's blandishments and without fear in the face of opposition. I did not have to feel anything, but walk around filled with the certainty of God. I tell you, the Tempter patted me on the back and assured me I was doing beautifully. One day in the early days of my ministry by the Jordan an aging prostitute came, along with a number of other people. The finger of God rested on her. She expected nothing from me. She had come along with the others, but had no hope of benefit for herself.

I don't know her name or what happened to her, but I knew the prayer she had for those others with her. She was full of care, full of wanting for others near her, even though she had no future, no hope for herself. I knew what kind of life she had led. I knew what kind of business she was in, but I heard the Spirit within me say, 'Her soul is mine too.'

"That moment went eternal on me. It spread out in all directions, and I saw the love of the Divine all over, flooding, running and tumbling among us all. That day I was given the gift of loving, or maybe the task of loving as God loves. All the denial, all the self-discipline and rejection of this world was gone. I was instead filled with the delight for all aspects of this world, with delight in people, with pleasure at them. The condition of this great gift I received is that I possess none of them.

"So, going back to your question about marriage and relationships, the answer is no, I don't want or need either, but I revel in the experience for others. I no longer bother to visit the issue, for the love of God fills me so there is no reason to ask the question."

I couldn't help myself. I asked, "But what happened to the woman?"

"I never saw her again, and I don't know who she was. She left with her companions that afternoon, and I prayed for her, I gave thanks for her, and I praised God for her."

"But are you not curious about what happened to her?"

"No, she was the Father's messenger to me. Good happened to her, that I know for sure. What it was I don't know, but letting go of that curiosity is just another side of what I've been describing. I was content to leave her in the hands of the Father, her Father and my Father, her God and my God. The Spirit kindled the fire of God's love in me that day, and a part of loving another is to be able to entrust them entirely to the Father's love. I've thought of her often since then, and I intercede for her sometimes. Are my prayers heard? Yes. How are they answered? I don't need to know. As a part of my faith in my Father, I don't want to know."

By the time we returned to Capernaum, the word had spread to everyone in Galilee. Stories were told in those places we had not visited, and in those we had, Jesus' face was known, his presence and power felt.

Speculation began, and each time another instance occurred, a new wave of interest washed through the region.

When we were on the road between Magdala and Arbela, a leper stood in the middle of the road. There was space to go around him, but none of those in the forefront of our group were willing to try. Sometimes these pathetic creatures would shake down travelers by threatening to embrace them. In this case Judas stepped forward and raised his staff as if to protect us from any threat from him. Jesus stepped around Judas and put his hand on the staff, urging Judas to drop his guard.

Jesus approached the man. "What can I do for you? What do you want?"

The leper sank slowly to his knees, not in obsequious petition but in an agony of relief. Jesus stepped towards him and stood there as the leper regained some control. Raising his hand in a helpless gesture he finally said, "I can't go on. Everything is gone, my family, my friends. I don't know what to do any more. I heard of you. I have prayed to the God of Israel that I might meet you. I have not known until now, but I realize why I prayed what I did. If you wish, if you want to, you can clean me of this filthy disease. If it is too much trouble, please excuse my asking. My prayer has already been answered. I have looked on you, and I now know what hope is. I'm not just thinking of myself, but for us all."

With this he fell silent as if exhausted by his speech. He hung his head and waited.

Jesus drew himself up; I could see him pondering the situation. Finally he spoke, "Yes, I do want you to be healed, to be clean." Jesus stepped closer, reached out his hand and put it on the leper's shoulder, held it there and gently commanded, "Be clean. Now go and do everything according to what Moses laid out for us to do." He told Judas, "Give him enough money that he can make an offering." He addressed the leper who was rising to his feet. "Don't go telling everyone about this."

The man got up, looked at his arms, and in surprise and mounting excitement exclaimed, "My arms are tingling. I can feel it in my hands too. It's happening!"

Jesus said, "Right. Go to the priest in Magdala and show him. By the time you get there the leprosy will be all gone. Don't forget what I said: don't go telling everyone about this."

The man couldn't keep quiet, and the story ran like wildfire throughout the region. In people's minds healing a leper was very different from what they had observed so far. This was a victory over a terrible evil that invaded and destroyed the person before their eyes. The leper was a walking horror and everyone's nightmare. Before long, the whole area was stirred up, and we couldn't go anywhere without being mobbed. We were exhausted, not from the walking, but from the demands of the crowds and their growing insistence for attention. Jesus needed to regroup. I could see this huge popularity was worrying him, and I asked him, "What did you expect? You heal a leper, and there is no way he is going to keep his mouth shut."

"I know, and I knew if I healed him it would get out. I just did not want to cope with this. I am glad for him. I think we will see him again. The good news is not just about healing for the individual. I am afraid these healings are a distraction, an impediment, to what our main job is, yet for the life of me I could not refuse him. I cannot refuse any of them when they approach me. They have prayed, they have besought the Father to help them, and then I come and I am bidden to answer their prayers, John, what if I am just that, an answer to their prayers?"

Back in Capernaum the next day, we cleaned up from the dust of the journey, had a meal prepared by Simon's wife and settled down for a quiet evening. As I expected, Jesus was nowhere to be found the next morning. Simon and I looked at each other and shrugged and sat down to breakfast of dried fish and bread. They would fish tomorrow. Simon said, "Oh, to be back on the water: no crowds, no pushing and shoving, but just the wind, the sea and a wet, heavy net to haul in."

A delegation of five Pharisees appeared while we were staying with Simon. We recognized them from our days in Jerusalem. It seemed their purpose was to foment dissention. One day Jesus invited Alpheus, a tax collector, of all things, to join the rest of us for dinner. The next day we heard about it from those Pharisees. Not only did they attack Jesus for keeping company with tax collectors and sinners, but they accused us of not adhering to the sanitary rules, of not fasting and many other crimes against Israel.

I confess that when we had been on our way back the last time, and passed through fields of wheat which were waiting for the harvesters, we plucked ears of the grain, rubbed them in our hands until the grain came loose and blew away the chaff—without washing our hands first. How many times had we done that as kids? It was one of the rituals of harvest time. That was one of my fondest memories of my childhood.

What a bunch of killjoys those Pharisees were. All Jesus said was, "You cannot gather fruit from thistles." Prickly characters, they were.

Jesus quoted chapter and verse at them, scorned their understanding and generally gave them a bad time. This was one of a very few times his anger showed; however, he said one thing that stopped me cold.

"The Sabbath was made for man, not man for the Sabbath, and the Son of Man is Lord of even the Sabbath."

That sent the rest of us scurrying for cover. Who was The Son of Man? Was Jesus talking about himself? Was he claiming identification with the figure described by the prophet Daniel? Was he simply referring to any man as head of his own family?

I've just had reports on the whereabouts of that Nazarene. Seems he has escaped our net and appears now in Galilee. I would have thought he would be keeping his head down, but no, he is developing quite a following. Is there any harm in that? The Baptizer is in prison, but he is still in conversation with his followers, and they are receiving encouragement and instruction from him. Here in Jerusalem there are definite groups that pursue his teachings and live by his tenets. What is the connection between these two movements?

Think it time to get rid of the Baptizer permanently. Removing him will at least simplify the situation. Herod will not willingly execute him. He is Herod's pet prophet, full of dark sayings and scurrilous judgments. That idea I had about Queen Herodias needs revisiting. John called her a whore, a scheming prostitute. She hates him, and, though for once I agree with the Baptizer, I think I could persuade her to do the job.

Secrecy is absolutely necessary. Who can I trust? I will ask Jonathon to check her whereabouts and itinerary if we have them. Normally, we do not bother with her, but maybe for our purpose we should revise that. She might make a good agent for other purposes if we could compromise her with this one.

Now what to do about this Jesus fellow? Maybe mobilize the pharisaic community? Some of them were enamored of him, but a fair slice of that party was definitely affronted by his teaching. In fact, they are quite stirred up against him. Maybe some of them would be willing to do a fact-finding trip to Galilee. I could even get Caiaphas to pay their expenses. That may cause tension in the Pharisees' ranks. I like that.

I can't move against Jesus openly from here. He is under Herod's jurisdiction, and if that superstitious character suspected my interest he might place him under his special protection. No, for the moment we need to not risk that possibility. After all, if Jesus were to generate a power base in Galilee, Herod could use that to make trouble for us here. Jesus could become a weapon Herod could direct at us, without even appearing to. I can imagine him wringing his hands in regret, and laughing up his sleeve at us. No, we watch.

Apparently Queen Herodias will be in Caesarea for some celebration or another this next week. That is a good neutral place to approach her.

What approach to take with her? I know John has been outspoken about her marriage to Herod. He calls it incestuous. Maybe if I expressed my concern over reports I've received of John's intent to discredit her and have popular demand force Herod to set her aside? Not a likely scenario. I think that if I play up John's influence over Herod, and infer Herod had made inquiries at my office about the religious legality of their situation, then I might get her to act. Intrigue is their most popular pastime, and paranoia a family trait.

Just to cap it off, I think I will stress Herod's religious instability and that under John's malign—no, EVIL—influence he could have a desperate change of heart and become a religious fanatic. Maybe I could emphasize she is the only person I can trust with my concern, and that for her to take action would be the fulfillment of her moral duty.

No, that is laying it on a bit thick. She is no innocent in these matters. She will wonder what my slant is and why I am helping her. I think the idea is sound, but maybe I should keep the message simple. The rumor is the weapon of choice here. She can clothe it in her own fears and give it certainty from her own suspicions. However, my messenger can of his own accord convey broader concerns, for example, about Herod's mental state and emotional stability.

I know the very man for the job. It will cost me, but like before it will be worth it. He is an oblique bastard. He enjoys nastiness. Twenty or thirty talents and travel expenses on top of that should be enough. I wonder if I could get the Temple to pay for it. No, it must not appear on any records, not even here.

Two days later

Well, that's done. My agent is off to Ceasarea. He jumped at the chance. I think I could have gotten him to do it for fifteen talents if I had tried. No, twenty was good; that little bit of generosity buys a bushel of silence. I must remember he is not loyal to me, or anyone else for that matter. Cash buys his silence.

Now the fact-finding expedition by the Pharisees is next. The conservative Pharisees I have in mind could be strategically useful. They could disrupt the Nazarene's meetings and challenge his teaching. Better still, they could sow doubts in the minds of people.

My concerns are that he is another false prophet, and he is secretly an agent of Beelzebub or some other evil presence. I think we will need to stress the danger to the nation, and give those Pharisees we ask to go on the fact-finding mission a sense of their superiority. If I approach them, they will only suspect me. They will wonder about my motivation. I can't say I blame them for that. No, this is where I work through Caiaphas. He has some good contacts among the more conservative Pharisees. I will also suggest he make it semi-official business of the Sanhedrin and even provide some travel expenses from Temple funds.

I can get this launched today. Caiaphas is due over here this afternoon. Maybe I will enjoy this week's meeting for a change.

29

DISCIPLES' DISCUSSION

One night Simon, John, James, Thomas, Andrew, Alpheus, Judas and I sat with a skin of wine provided by Alpheus and mulled over what we had heard. I described as well as I could the reference to Daniel.

James piped up, "You mean Jesus was saying that he was the man in Daniel's vision?"

"Yes, and if that is so, what does it mean?" I asked.

Judas said, "It means he is claiming to be something more than a prophet and more than a teacher."

"You think he is claiming to be the Messiah?" asked John.

Judas said, "I don't like where this is taking us. We've seen him in action, and when you're with him he makes all the sense in the world, but he is not Messiah."

"That's right. I just don't see him taking on the armies of the evil one and defeating them as you would expect the Messiah to do. He is a teacher, a prophet and yes, a powerful healer, but the commander-in-chief of an army, no!"

I resisted the temptation to blurt out what I knew, and I kept the confidence Jesus had shared with me, so I sat out the rest of the discussion. I watched as the rest of them rationalized their positions.

Judas went on, "My main concern is not whether or not he is the Messiah, but does he think he is? If he is thinking he is this 'Son of Man' from Daniel then I am worried about what's going to happen."

"You mean the authorities will take him?"

"No, they would if they could right now. That's why we left Jerusalem. I'm worried that if Jesus believes himself to be this 'Son of Man' figure from a dream, for God's sake, has his success gone to his head?"

"You think he is becoming enamored of his own strength, and that he is being carried away by his success?"

Alpheus stepped in, "Wait, wait, wait, you are jumping to conclusions. He said the Sabbath was made for men. Just think about that for starters. I've never heard that before, and you know, when you think about it, he is right. So you could say all of us sons of men are Lords of the Sabbath in our homes and in our souls."

"If you put it that way, he wasn't making any sort of claim, is that it?"

"As you listen to him, he had the audacity to state as fact that the Sabbath was made for men and not the other way around. He was speaking as if he had the authority to say what he said. He was not expressing an opinion," murmured Thomas.

"So what this comes down to is a question of his authority. Right? Why not out with it? Tell us plainly that is who he is."

Thomas answered, "No, I hope he never does. I don't want to know. I've been with him five, almost six years, and I just like him the way he is. He has changed, though, and I think this 'Son of Man' thing describes the change."

Judas said, "I would agree with you. That's why I think he's taking himself too seriously."

Andrew said, "Or maybe he has finally come to the point when he has to move on and take the authority given him. I sometimes think he has been loathe to take on that full responsibility."

Simon looked over to his brother, "You mean, like he said, the time has come! But that for him, 'the time has come' refers to his taking hold of that authority."

Andrew went on, "We have to acknowledge his power and not deny it. I don't know what this 'Son of Man' figure is, but I am his man. I've seen what he can do, so I say we go for it."

Thomas studied his own fingers for a moment as if he read in his palm an answer that surprised him. "Here we are, asking ourselves the question of who he thinks he is, but what if he has been asking the same question and now has the answer?"

Judas spoke quietly but insistently from the shadows. "But what if he is wrong? What if he—well, maybe I shouldn't say anymore. I just don't want to see any of you get hurt, or for that matter see Jesus get hurt. Neither do I want to see you disillusioned."

Simon spoke in his deep voice, "In this life there are always risks. When I was first learning how to swim I had to take my hand off the boat. I immediately sank, but I tried again and again, and I learned to swim. That saved my life on at least two occasions since. Well, I think that same thing applies here. I think we will not know the answer to Jesus' authority unless we try to swim with him. Maybe that is just what he is doing. When you think of it, if he is identifying himself with this 'Son of Man' person, maybe he is really taking his hand off the boat and is swimming in really deep water."

James said, "You've put your finger on something there. Maybe that's why he wants us around. Maybe this is no picnic for him, and he knows the risks, and it is taking the stuffing out of him."

John asked, "You mean our presence, our friendship, is important to him?"

James continued, "Yes, without us, could he do and say what he does? I have wondered what he saw in us to begin with. Who are we? Look at us. None of us know much about the scriptures or our laws, beyond what we were taught by the rabbis, but yet he invited you, Alpheus, and he walked up to you, Simon, and said 'come on'. He takes us with him, but what good are we to him? We mostly sit there and help a little with crowd control. So I think we are important to him in quite a different way. Like Simon suggested, I think it's time we took our hand off the boat and swam with him."

Judas asked, "Go with his authority?"

"Yes," James replied.

Judas countered, "Are you saying we should believe it?"

James said, "No. Acknowledge it, and see what's back of it, way back."

Simon went on, "Ah, that is a good way of putting it; like a fish looking at the bait on a hook. Though the fish can only see the bait, and maybe the hook, there is a whole other world that it is unaware of; the line, the boat, the shore, and everything above the waves. Maybe the world Jesus is trying to introduce us to is like that. It is a whole other world that extends beyond the horizons that we are accustomed to."

James frowned. "I disagree about the bait. I see his miracles as the expression of God, not just belonging to him. I hear his teaching as words from our Father, the Father of us all. This comes to us from beyond the stars, beyond the blue sky, beyond our own understanding. Acknowledge it as such and accept it. Go for it wholeheartedly."

"Your idea is like Simon's idea of a whole other world. What you are saying is it will take us saying yes to it for us to be able to enter it or even see it," said Thomas.

Andrew replied, "I agree with you, our new life is centered on him. When he is with us, I feel connected, not just to him, but to where he gets his power."

"Yes, that is a good way of putting it. It's as if the gates are open all the way to the very presence of God. Maybe I am going overboard, and I am exaggerating. No, I don't think so. You know when he comes in and says, 'Shalom,' it's not just a greeting from him. He brings peace with him as he steps into the place and spreads it around to all of us. I can feel it."

Alpheus said, "All my life I have been frustrated with what is offered by the Temple. They talk about spiritual issues like holiness, the presence of God, and righteousness, but it is as if there was a well, and I had a bucket, but the rope was too short so I could never reach the water. I finally gave up, paid my Temple tax each year, and that was that. I find that Jesus is himself a well, and the rope for my bucket is plenty long enough."

Simon chuckled, "I like that. You might have a well and a bucket, but you will still die of thirst if the rope is too short."

Silence fell on the group. The wine skin went round again, and the plate of nuts that had been in front of Andrew for too long was passed around the group. The silence grew as we pondered what Jesus meant to each of us. For me, none of these thoughts were strange. I had been aware for a long time of the depths that were opening under us. I was surprised at how comfortable I now was with that idea. I was becoming at home in that new world.

Yes, I thought, Jesus was indeed that figure in Daniel, 'The Son of Man.' Had I not heard him in my own dream? Did not Jesus occupy that greater world that surrounded our own small awareness?

Judas wrapped his cloak about himself and got up. "I'm ready for some shut-eye. Thanks for the wine, Alpheus." With that, he flipped the curtain aside and left. I assumed he was going back to Simon's house.

Shortly thereafter I took off. The dark was unbroken by the moon's glow, and the stars were bright points above. I looked deep into the night sky. A light from there had come into the world and walked among us. We could say, "No way, nothing like that could happen. That has to be nonsense." Or we could say, "Really? Let's see, let's hear." And, "Yes, I see."

I tripped over a curbstone and nearly buried my face in the path. Instead I got up and dusted off the pieces of rock embedded in the palms of my hands.

So much for that. I really must keep my eyes on where I am walking. That was the second time I had tripped over a rock while my head was lost in the stars.

30

Parables of the Kingdom

"Talk to us about the Kingdom of God. You mention it all the time, but just what do you mean?" This request was called out from one of maybe a hundred men who pressed around us. Most of them were seated, and among them were faces we had seen more than once. Most of them were rough agricultural workers, with the marks of their labors all about them. Hard, weather beaten faces first reflected the deep suspicion that is usual among country people who are cut off from the ideas and changes that accompany city or town living. To these people, change meant hardship; interruption or intervention meant disaster. Now for the first time, the men were asking questions without the hostility and suspicion that first greeted us.

The man who asked the question was younger than most. He looked around him for others' approval and lapsed into silence. He sat cross-legged, holding his staff in his clenched hands.

"The Kingdom of Heaven is not about obedience or judgment of people, but all about what God does," declared Jesus.

"Are you saying the religious leaders have it all wrong?" asked a husky, heavily bearded, red-haired man standing at the back of the crowd.

Jesus nodded, "In a word, yes."

"So how are you different? You ask us to join you in launching this new Kingdom and believe what you say, but frankly we don't want to join any new movement," said a balding older man with gnarled knuckles and stooped shoulders.

"I agree. We've paid our taxes, done our best, but we have to work to keep our families going. We can't do any more," said another who was thin as a walking staff. His long fingers clenched and unclenched as he spoke.

"Yes, we appreciate your presence with us, but like Jodias said, we are doing as much as we can and creating a whole new kingdom is beyond us," added one of those men we had seen several times. He now assumed the role of unofficial spokesman.

"The Kingdom of Heaven is not about you trying harder. As I said, it is about what God does," repeated Jesus.

"But what does He really do, and what does He want in return?" asked a dour, hard-faced older man sitting among a group that had been least attentive and who now echoed his concerns.

"Yeah, what is the catch?"

Jesus nodded his head in assent, "You are suspicious that, like everything else, this is another con job, and you will be left with the responsibility for everything."

Jodias said, "Yes, I suppose you are right, but it always seems to happen that way. We've learned you can't trust anyone, and nobody does anything for nothing. Don't blame Danus over there; his son left with a city man, and he's not been heard of since. We don't get it when you begin talking about the Kingdom of God or Kingdom of Heaven. It sounds nice, but..."

"Let me put it like this: As you all know, when you go out to sow seed at planting time you have to be very careful where you throw the seed so you don't waste it."

"You bet. What I sow is wheat I had to deny my children when they were hungry during the last months before harvest," muttered one man in the front row.

"It was worse for me this year," said another. "I had to borrow from that money lender to buy enough seed for this year. Every grain counts, and even if we get a good harvest it's going to be close next harvest time. As you said, nobody around here goes throwing his grain around. How is that connected with the Kingdom of God?"

"The Kingdom of God is like a sower who took his bag of grain and proceeded to sow his whole property. Unlike you, he threw it all over the place. Some even fell on the path and the birds got it, some on stony ground where it wouldn't do too well, some fell among the thorns and weeds around the edge of the field. A lot fell on really good soil, and each grain brought forth several full heads.

"Still, some fed the birds, others produced only a small harvest of maybe twenty- or thirty-fold, while others brought forth sixty- or even a hundred-fold. God is pleased with anything He gets from the seed He sows, and He throws it all over the place.

"When you go to harvest your wheat, are you not glad for every handful of ears? Do you reject the ears that are small or the grains thin? No, you are grateful for it all. So God is pleased with the little response He may get. Rejoice with Him over the harvest of your hearts."

"You mean God really takes notice and rejoices over me? How can that be, why would he?" asked a young man sitting in the front row.

"What do you think? If you can be pleased to hold those ears of wheat in your hands at harvest, knowing many of them are thin and small, then how much more would be the rejoicing of God over all kinds of moments in your life?"

"If you are right about God rejoicing when I do something good, what happens to all the other moments when I didn't?" asked another man.

"Rabbi, he really needs to know this one, because he can't count all the times he has messed up," cackled an aging laborer on the fringe of the group. Laughter sparkled among the men, jumping from one to the other.

"Yes, what about Martius? If the Kingdom of God works for him, the rest of us are going to be okay," laughed a robust, dark-headed man on the left.

"All right, you guys, I'm trying to have a serious conversation here. Alphonsos, you were not doing too well last night. You can't talk," responded Martius.

"All right," said Jesus, laughing at the banter and good humor of the men there. "Let me put to you another story. First of all, what do you do if you've got weeds growing among the wheat you've just sown?"

"We pull them out. They compete with the wheat for moisture and goodness in the soil," responded a voice from the crowd.

"Right, but God is different. He is like a farmer who sowed good seed in his fields, and a few weeks later after the rains have begun, his servants come to him and say, 'Didn't you sow good seed in your fields?

There are weeds coming up all over the place. Do you want us to start weeding and get rid of them?'

"This farmer says, 'Hmm, some enemy has done this, and I am sure that telling you to go ahead and weed everything is just what he would like me to do. No, leave the weeds alone. You will only disturb the young wheat if you go pulling the weeds. At harvest time we will burn the weeds and the wheat we will winnow out and store in the granary. We are in the wheat-growing business, not the weed-suppression profession.'"

"Are you saying the good people survive and the bad are destroyed?" asked Alphonsos.

"Have you seen an entirely good man? Or have you seen an entirely bad person?" replied Jesus, "You are all made of wheat and weeds. God is only concerned with growing the good in you, so concentrate on the good in you, and give it room to grow, for it is of God."

"Rabbi, this is new teaching for us and it's not what we've been taught at all. If we do as you say and just take notice of the good stuff we do, are we not in danger of breaking the law? Then what would happen to us? Things are hard enough without more bad luck for breaking the law."

"No. The more you appreciate the good in yourself and others around you, the less room there is for evil. You've seen that once wheat really gets growing it crowds out the weeds. Let me tell you another story. The Kingdom of God is like a mustard seed. It is the smallest of seeds, but it grows and grows until it is a bush. Even birds roost in its branches.

"When you let the Word of God grow inside you and give it room to expand, it's like that mustard seed. It gradually takes over, and you live your life in its shade.

"Better still, the grace of God sown in you is like yeast a woman takes and mixes into a measure of flour. She mixes the yeast in until it is evenly distributed throughout the flour, then what does she do? She sets it in a warm place, and the dough rises until it's several sizes bigger. When the dough is baked it is light and airy. It is no longer dough but bread. The leaven working secretly throughout the dough changes the whole lump into something else entirely. The word of God, like the leaven, changes you inside; like the dough, you rise, expand and become fragrant like new-baked bread."

"Rabbi, are you saying all this happens without us having to do anything? When I look around I don't see that happening in many people. There are a lot of folk who are more like dough than loaves of bread," observed Marius.

"Good thought. Yes, there is something missing. God has and does sow your life with His Word. The Word of God in you is like good seed. Every little seed has life in itself and with a little moisture will grow, but the Word of God needs one thing from you. You have to want the good, and want it more than anything else. Then you will possess it.

"Let me give you another illustration. The Kingdom of God is like a pearl merchant who came across the most incredible pearl. It was large, lustrous and perfect in every way. He knew he had to have it. He went home, sold everything he could, and bought the pearl. Lit by its beauty and its perfection, he was delighted with it. That pearl was the one pearl he would never sell."

"So we are back again to us having to sell everything and buy this Kingdom of Heaven. Why don't you come out and say it—you do want us to buy this from you," said a narrow-faced laborer leaning on a staff off to the side of the group.

Jesus shook his head and gently but firmly said, "No, nothing like that. It's easy for you to miss the point of what I'm saying. The important point of the story is not the selling of everything. If you want the Kingdom of God as badly as the pearl merchant wanted that pearl, then you will do what you have to do to make it happen. That desire for caring, justice, mercy and generosity in yourself will result in you doing all those things naturally without too much effort. Your actions will be an expression of your desires."

"What about our commandments and the teachings of the prophets? How about all the stuff we've been taught since we were kids?" asked the man referred to as Alphonsos.

"This is something I can't answer for you, but here is another illustration. Fishermen down on the lake let down their trawl net, and haul it ashore. They have a good catch, so they sit down and sort the edible fish with scales from the bottom feeders without scales. There is no market for the bottom feeders, so they get thrown away. Similarly, you have to sort through for yourself the things you've been taught, the things you've been told, then throw away the useless stuff you have been fed and keep all the good stuff that really makes sense."

"Are you saying we don't have to believe everything we are told is in the scriptures or all the things we are taught by the scribes?"

"Yes, but, again, I caution you. You have to be like a wise home-owner that cleaned out his house. There were all kinds of junk and a lot of new worthless stuff he would never use. So he sorted it out. He found among the old, many things that were beautiful and had meaning for him. Of course there were new things he had bought because he needed them. All the rest was junk, new or old, so out it had to go. Similarly you have to allow grace to show you what is good and what is useless. Seize and hold fast to what is good. Hold everything lightly except the grace of God growing in you. Train yourself to recognize it and to want it so badly you can taste it.

"If you do this, you will see the Kingdom of God come alive in you and all those around you. You all spend your lives growing things and nurturing them. You know if you care for your animals or your fields, they will support you. Well, your spiritual life is the same. Nurture it as I have described, and it will support you and those around you."

21

FEEDING THE FIVE THOUSAND

Early one morning, Jesus asked Simon if he would take us by boat to a quiet place away from the crowds. "I need to have time alone, and I need time with you. There is so much more I have to teach you."

Gone were the long hikes between places when we could talk among ourselves without interruption. I was beginning to get restless, and I thought about going back to Jerusalem for a spell. I sensed Jesus was working towards a definite goal, and I didn't want to miss out on it so I had dismissed that idea.

Within half an hour we were in the boat and pulling away from the shore, leaving the early birds behind us. There was a little wind so we ghosted along for about three or four miles before heading ashore. Unfortunately some of the sharper-eyed characters among the crowd saw which way we had gone and by the time we landed, there was already a huge crowd.

I watched Jesus' face. I fancied there was momentary vexation, but as he gazed at the straggling column of people, his face softened. He shook his head slowly and stepped out to meet them. He welcomed them and led them over towards a sloping hillside where there was room for everyone.

The rest of us carried the few supplies we had hastily thrown in the boat that morning, especially the water skins and food. We looked at each other. There were shrugs all around, and Simon said, "Well, we blew that. We should have just sailed out on to the lake, maybe even over to the other side." With that we shambled after the crowd to the place where everyone was assembling.

Jesus was already talking with some of them. "I thought I could give you the slip this morning, but I was wrong. So what do you want?"

"Rabbi, the harvest is in, we have a little time before we begin again, so we can pay attention to other things," said a heavyset young farmer.

"Rabbi, I know we are slow to understand a lot of what you are saying, but it's so different from what we've heard before that it takes a lot to really accept it," confided a small, timid man who later turned out to be the local produce merchant.

"When we are with you we can see it, and it's easy to understand and even know what you are saying is true. We want it to be true. There are a lot of us that really want it all to be true . . ." sighed another.

"That's right, and so that's why we followed you. We don't mean to harass you and take up all your time. Could you just sit with us and talk about some of the things you've said? When we are with you we dare think these things, but when we are not with you the old demands of teachers, Pharisees and scribes come flooding back," admitted a genial older man who removed his headgear and rubbed a bald pate reflectively.

A young man who had pressed closest to us said, "Rabbi, when I am alone I begin to doubt what I've heard from you. I hear in my head the threats of judgment that have made me afraid since I was a kid. It's like all the demons come out to play just as soon as I leave wherever you are."

A dark-haired giant of a man, who looked like a blacksmith with his leather clothes, spoke in a low rumble, "I've listened to all the stuff these people have poured over me, and I've never cared about any of it. I never believed it, but neither did I find anything to believe in. I chucked the lot. I taught myself not to care about anything because there was nothing worth caring about. You have given me a second chance."

So the comments went on. Jesus sat in the middle of a growing horde of folk as more stragglers came in. Finally Jesus began to speak, and everyone immediately settled down to listen.

"You are right, what I am offering you is, indeed, the word of life. This is why I am sent to you, that you might indeed have life and have it more abundantly. You say you're beginning to get it, but how do you claim the authority to choose my words and reject the words of those who have convinced you otherwise?

"I am not asking you to believe what I say. There are all kinds of people, some of them well-meaning and others scurrilous deceivers who want you to buy what they are selling. Don't! Don't believe, but take into yourself my words and let those words grow in you."

"Not believe?" A voice came from the rear of the assembled folk. "But we believe you are a prophet from the Almighty. We believe in you!"

Jesus looked up from those with whom he was talking and gazed out over the crowd. The hillside area was filling up as more people drifted in. "No, you already believe enough," said Jesus to the man who had last spoken. "You believe in God, the Holy One, you know the commandments, the words of the prophets are known to at least some of you. So you believe enough. There is always the temptation to believe, and when you adopt beliefs of someone else, whether it is the Pharisees, Essenes or even me, you have surrendered your responsibility to respond to our Heavenly Father. He wants to talk with you; He wants to laugh and cry with you."

"Well, that is clear enough," said a weather-beaten man with thick, black, tousled hair and beard. "We don't have to believe the nonsense people try to pour over us. The Day of Judgment, the calamity of the last days and the destruction of the world, are to me just bad dreams someone had, or maybe they hate everyone so much they would like to see everyone get hurt. I heard this man, he was dressed like a prophet, and he was telling us about how the world was coming to an end, and we were all slated for the big heave ho. I told him he was full of shit, and he promised me a special place in hell. That was when I was young, but he was wrong; for here we are and the world is doing just fine. I tell you though, if this Heaven place is full of people like him I want nothing to do with it. Not believing those creeps is easy, but what do you mean by God wanting to talk with me? You said even cry with me? That's a stretch. I can't go there."

"Why not?" demanded Jesus.

"I am just not worthy."

"Who told you that?" challenged Jesus.

"Nobody has to tell me, I just know," muttered the man.

"Do you have children?"

"Yes, four. We lost two, but we have three boys and a girl."

"Which of them is worthy of you talking to them when you go home in the evening? Which of the boys is your favorite? Is your daughter good or bad?" queried Jesus.

"I can't answer that. I don't have favorites. They are all only children; they don't have to be worthy. I love them all. I talk to them all."

"And your daughter?"

The man smiled as he thought of her, and he said, "Especially her. I am afraid she twists me round her little finger. All of them are favorites," confided the weather-beaten man.

Jesus nodded, took a moment to let the words sink in, and went on remorselessly, "So, you are saying your Heavenly Father is less of a father than you, that He loves his children less than you love your own? That He is not moved by their hurts or interested in their joys? Neither does He think we are beautiful in His eyes?"

"No, I am not saying that, but—"

"Go on," prompted Jesus, "but what? What would your life be like without your children? What would it be like without any one of them? What do you think it is for your Heavenly Father without you?"

"I don't know. I can't say." The man gulped as if having to swallow a huge lump in his throat and let out a muffled groan, "Oh, God."

"You see, it is not belief at all, but recognizing your Father's love that makes everything different," concluded Jesus.

There was silence all around as people digested this. Some asked their neighbors what had been said, while others sat staring at their feet as if not wanting to believe their ears. A voice from the group of disciples off to one side asked, "Well, how do we do that?"

"That's what your prayers are for. You're going to have to learn to talk with your Heavenly Father."

"Would you teach us to pray? John the Baptist taught his disciples how to pray and meditate; would you do the same?" said James.

"Yes, but you realize that prayer is more listening than talking, more thanksgiving than asking. It's more about God's will than what you want God to do for you. Conversation with God has to be two-way. Promise?"

"Yes, but you must first teach us how."

Jesus was silent for a few minutes, and people sat expectantly. He finally said, "How to start? Start by addressing Him, 'Our Father.' Whose Father? Father of us here. Does that include that group of lepers sitting up there by themselves? What about the man who bought your land out from under you? Is God his Father too?

"Think in another way. Is he Father of all your ancestors going back to the beginning of Israel and beyond? Will he be the Father to all your future kin?"

"I had never thought of Him being God of my children's children, or even my ancestors for that matter. Of course He is, or should I say He will be and He was. Yes, I see," muttered a man sitting in the front row with his arms round his knees.

"So start with *Our Father*," Jesus continued. "You will notice that once you start praying there is no place to stop. Nobody is left out.

"Next, *Holy be your name!* This is the name Moses heard, and contains the very secrets of God's presence among us. Prayer is not a tiny thing but giant, and you are ushered into His presence with this prayer. Think of it this way: This whole world you see around you is no bigger than the world of the Spirit within you. Look within you and you will find there a Holy of Holies, just like the one in the Temple. Find in yourself that space and allow yourself to utter the name secretly within it. Before you go any further in prayer bow your self before the Name dwelling in you and in the light of that devotion you can dare to pray.

"*Your Kingdom come.* This is the first step to allowing yourself to be changed. Rather than seeing the world through your eyes, see them through God's eyes and welcome things the way they are, instead of the ways you wished they were. This piece is hard because the world is not very nice, nor is it fair. Nevertheless, you have to start with the way things are and not the way you think they should be.

"How about it so far?" Jesus asked the crowd.

"I can't get my head around it. This is too big," responded a farmhand from near Capernaum.

"If that is what you truly think, then there is real hope for you because these first few moments in prayer are momentous. Instead of trying to comprehend, let your mind be part of it all. Allow yourself to be instructed and let the enormity grow in you. Put no words to it.

"Next: *Your will be done here on earth as it is in Heaven.* Open up to all the possibilities around you and within you. How about nationally? Are you ready to listen for the Father of Israel to express His love for Israel during this time? Instead of trying to tell God how it should be done, will you allow Him to teach you and for you to become part of his solution? Will you take your place beside Him in continuing His work of creation rather than just being another problematic part of it?

"*Give us this day our daily bread.* You all pray this every day in the hope that you can get by another day, but who are you including in your prayer? Go back to the first words I used, *Our Father,* so praying to our Father to give us our daily bread includes all your neighbors, those lepers up there on the hill, the rest of the people in Galilee, and so on. You are also part of the answer to this prayer for everyone else; for you, in the company of the Father, are to be part of the answer to the prayer.

"*Forgive us our trespasses.* Here I want you to face your own violence as part of your society. How many of you think your anger is justified and reasonable? When you are in other people's faces or thrusting yourself into their space you do violence to them. You are trespassing with intent to destroy or devalue the other. How can you have respect for someone and at the same time actively attack them? How can you break in and steal from them, or how can you envy them or lie about them to others and not intrude or trespass against them?

"*As you forgive those who trespass against you.* Give others space. Respect, understanding and forgiveness are all part of what I mean by giving others space. Other people are not perfect, none of you are; and, therefore, accord others forgiveness, understanding and acceptance. You can't expect to be forgiven for your sin if you are unwilling to cut others slack. You can't begin to understand what you have done until you see the destruction or damage you have caused others. If you will forgive others, then you will be able to accept the forgiveness of your Father for those mistakes you mourn for. Your sins are forgivable, but you have to know what they are and understand the damage you have done. Forgiveness is not forgetting but remembering and being willing to remember ever more clearly.

"*Lead us not into suffering caused by the sin of others, but deliver us from evil.* You are surrounded by people who want to bring about the end times. They fancy they will be the survivors and be delivered by God. No! God will not deliver them. Pray to be delivered from those who want to usher in their idea of the Kingdom. They want to take you into war without end, and the suffering of you all will be terrible if you don't seek another Kingdom of God. Pray for deliverance from this evil of ideology and half-baked religious beliefs. Pray for deliverance from such rigidity now, and pray for your children to be delivered from the same evil that tempts every generation and always disappoints.

"*For yours is the Kingdom and the Power and the Glory.* Put all things into the hands of God. Open yourselves to His will, and welcome His way. Rejoice in His presence and let go of your fears. Let loose the bonds that bind you and dance out that freedom that you are given as His own."

The teaching continued as the afternoon sun dipped behind the mountains to our backs. The scene was idyllic as people made themselves comfortable on the grass and Jesus walked among them. He would respond to someone's question and to another's special needs or concerns. Some of the requests were simple and, I thought, trite, but he had infinite patience with them.

Simon, Andrew and Philip came up to Jesus. "It's late. Some of these folk have a long way to go. They have no more food and water is scarce. It's time to send them away," they urged.

Jesus looked up at the lowering sun, and back at the crowds. "Well, you have a point, but rather than send them away to fend for themselves, I want you to give them what they need. That's what we have been talking about all day, and yesterday and the day before that. They are part of the Kingdom. You need to take responsibility for their experience of the Kingdom, so provide for their needs. Feed them."

"What? How can we? There are five thousand people here. Where are we going to get bread for so many?"

Jesus continued, "We will feed them, and I will tell you why. I keep telling you that the Kingdom is not about what you do but what God does. I talk about Him feeding them. I want to demonstrate to them where their food comes from and where they can look for grace. So first of all, what have we on hand to start with?"

The three looked at each other. Philip said, "We will go and see." They went off towards the other knot of disciples that stood looking in our direction. Even from where I stood I could see the incredulity on their faces and in their actions. Nevertheless, Philip and Judas went over to the pile of things we had brought and rifled through them. They came up with what looked like a few crusts and a couple of loaves. Philip put them in a basket and climbed towards us. Just then one of the new members of our entourage ushered towards us a young boy carrying a basket covered with a cloth. The boy of maybe eight or nine years old handed the basket to the man and explained something in a voice we could not catch.

The man stepped up to us and offered the basket to Jesus. "This lad has just brought you this. Apparently his mother packed these for us, thinking we would need some help by now. The boy is not alone, but I think maybe it was the boy's idea in the first place."

Jesus took the basket and lifted the cloth covering. There lay five small loaves and two fish. There was certainly enough towards supper for our small group, but Jesus had other ideas. He smiled at the boy, who was half-hiding behind the man who had brought him forward, and gravely thanked the boy, then asked, "Do you want to wait and see what can be done with something that is offered to God?"

The boy nodded shyly. I think he also wanted to wait to take back the basket. Jesus gave instructions to his followers to get the people sitting down in groups. Some had been preparing to leave, but now they turned back out of curiosity and sat back down with friends or others they had met that day.

Jesus took the five loaves of bread and in front of everyone gave thanks to our God, the creator of the universe who had given bread to feed us and flesh to nourish us. With that, he broke the loaves in pieces and gave them to the disciples with instructions to distribute them to the people. I think we were all at a loss for words and unable to comprehend what he wanted us to do. There was not enough food for very many, and there were five thousand or so people out there. Jesus said, "Well, go on. Take it to them; here is some fish too. Make sure every group has some and let them share it among themselves."

We looked at the little piles of food, looked at Jesus and looked out over the hordes of people. Led by Simon, we each of us hesitantly approached a group with the pitifully small pile of bread and fish. Each of us carried no more than would feed one person, let alone the fifteen or so people in each group we approached. We laid it before the group and asked them to share it out between them. We got some funny looks and I found myself shrugging as if to say, "I don't get it either."

I went back for another supply and to my surprise received another small pile of bread and a piece of fish. I delivered it to the group next to the one I had served and out of curiosity went back to check on how the first group was doing. They were still passing the bread around, and I saw everyone had fish as well. I stopped to watch and I noticed one after the other share with others the piece of fish or bread they had. People were eating, and the food went round and round. Everyone was eating.

I saw one person bring out a piece of fruit and offered pieces of that. Another took out some dates and offered those. I looked over at other groups and I saw the same thing happening. They were chatting and laughing and passing to each other whatever was available.

I walked back to where Jesus stood, and as I came up to him I heard him say to one of the others, "See, all that was needed was a little to start with. God does not make something out of nothing; that is magic, not grace. Look what He can do with the gift of that young boy. There is even enough for you. Go on, sit down and share what there is."

Other disciples joined the rest of us, and we began our own meal. I took some of the bread and fish. There was not much but another disciple returned from delivering his last helping to the group of lepers on the hill. There was nothing left in the basket, and without thinking I broke off some of mine and gave it to him. I went to munch on what was left and found myself eating quite enough to keep me going. I still had enough to pass around. We looked at each other in puzzlement and a little fear. What had we just seen?

Jesus came over and joined us. Once he was sitting cross-legged on the ground, he looked around at us. "Do you get it? Look at what is happening. Once I blessed the food and you gave it out, several things happened. The people shared it, and found so long as they shared it, God kept dividing it to make enough. They are even having fun dividing their little portion just to see it happening all over again.

"This is what being part of the Kingdom of God is about. God will honor your generosity and bless it and multiply what you offer to make it enough to achieve what He wills.

"You also saw something else. As people received the food I gave them, so they felt free to share also what little they had brought with them. God took that and blessed it and made it enough.

"This is what the Kingdom is about, rather than armies and conquest and defeating the enemy. That never works and yet everyone gets carried away with the passion for vindication and supremacy. I say to you, NO. This is the way. The Kingdom happens within the hearts of people and among people. It is here in Galilee, there in Jerusalem. Wherever people come together and do what you see those folk out there do just now, there you will see the Kingdom of God. Is that clear enough?"

"But Rabbi, how can we do what you did? I gave out more than five loaves; where did they come from?"

That was what was in all our minds, but Jesus just smiled, shook his head and turned back towards the crowd that was preparing to

A NIGHT ON THE WATER

disperse. He walked over to them and mingled, bidding goodbye or giving a gentle touch. Finally, he came back to us. People were packing up their few belongings and moving off in little groups. Laughter and chatter wafted down from the line of folk as they made their way back to their various villages.

Jesus explained to us that he needed time to himself to reflect on a number of things. He continued, "What I would like you to do is take the boat, and I'll meet you back at Capernaum. I know you have a lot of questions about today, but maybe tomorrow we can talk through what you all experienced."

With that he walked away and began the ascent into the hills behind where we had all met. Simon led the other six of us back to the boat, packed things under the thwarts and made ready to push off.

Thomas hesitated with one foot on board and the other in the water and looked out towards the hills. He said, "Do you think he will be okay? It's almost three miles back to Capernaum. There is no moon tonight. Ought we wait for him?"

Simon grunted, "Three miles is nothing out here. There's starlight, and in this limestone country the path shows up white, even at night. He'll be fine. It's us I am worried about. We've got over three miles to row, and the wind is dead foul for sailing. By the time we get back, you will wish you had walked. Man the oars! Push off, Thomas. No, use that pole, or you will be in the lake. That's it."

Darkness wrapped around us, and we headed out farther into the lake to avoid the rocky shallows. The wind came out of the northeast and kicked up short, steep waves that smacked against the bow of the boat, knocking us off course. Andrew, Simon, John and James took the oars and rowed steadily for an hour. The boat punched through some waves but bounced hard over others. We who were less used to such conditions hung on to whatever we could to keep ourselves seated.

After about an hour, Simon called to Andrew and John to keep rowing. He got up, called Thomas from the bow and, to both of us said, "Your turn. We are going to make a sailor of you."

Thomas and I each took an oar and began to row. I had rarely rowed, and when I had, it was a tiny boat on calm water in daylight. I soon found rowing at night in the dark, among waves that slapped the boat back and forth, was impossible. Sometimes as a wave passed under our keel, I could not find the water with my oar and heaved back on nothing. Other times my oar snagged deep and I couldn't get it out to make my backstroke. I couldn't see Thomas, though he was next to me, but I heard some of the things he said, and I knew he was doing no better than I.

Time passed slowly as we pushed on up the coast. My hands felt raw. I thought they must be running with blood, but the next day all I had was a series of blisters that persisted for days. We changed seats again. Judas took over a bow oar with Simon at the other. Andrew and John came back to the stern to rest. James replaced me, and I dragged myself off the thwart and stumbled towards the stern platform. The boat staggered on up the lake.

Sometimes a particularly strong gust would stop our momentum, then, with the next oar strokes, we would regain it and struggle on. The wind plucked at our oar blades as we swung them forward. I swore I would never become a fisherman nor be tempted to go out at night with anyone who was.

We were going at a snail's pace and, worse, we couldn't see where we were going. Simon was quite calm about the whole thing and didn't seem worried. Every now and again he would look over to the west, grunt and bend to his rowing.

Off to the west, the loom of the land showed against the starlit sky. Only an outline of the hills gave indication of where we were. The crashing waves, the splashes of cold water that coursed over the bow and the howling wind created a sense of chaos. Our little boat was the only fixed point in a maelstrom of movement.

We struggled on for another two hours as Simon stood as a shadow in the darkness, studying the profile of the hills to our left. He said, "We've passed the headlands now; we can move closer in. The wind will be easier, and we will make better time. The wind will be off the shore further up, and that will help."

We eased towards the shore, and Simon was right. The boat was easier to control, and the oars beat together. I was again at one of the oars and appreciated the very slight improvement; maybe I had learned to anticipate the waves better.

We crept up the coast, feeling our way towards the shore, which was indistinguishable from the blackness of the water. Thomas, in the bow, cried out. Simon, who was at the other stern oar to me, craned his neck 'round to see what was wrong.

Moving along parallel to us was the faintest shadow of a figure, as if it were on the very waves themselves. I missed my stroke entirely and almost went over backward off the thwart. Simon stood up and studied the figure. I recovered my seat and stared hard towards where Simon looked. The waves at this point were off the shore and so gave us no inkling of how close we were to land. I just hoped Simon knew where we were.

The figure stopped as if aware of our proximity and a voice came over the thirty yards of water between us. "It's only me! Don't panic. I thought you would be there by now."

In the boat, confusion reigned. "It's Jesus!" "Where are we?" "What's he doing out here?"

Simon said, "Steady! Keep the boat heading into the wind."

We could see the figure now, and we could recognize Jesus well enough. We rowed closer, thinking we would pick him up, but we grated on the shore before we reached him. Over the side we tumbled to secure the boat and run it up onto the stony beach. We had arrived.

It was lucky Jesus had waited for us there, or we would have gone past in the dark. Simon carefully stowed the oars, and Andrew lashed down anything else that could come loose.

I was exhausted, and I think Thomas was no better. We were not accustomed to that kind of work. We hoisted our bags onto our shoulders and set out for the town, five hundred yards away.

The story went out that Jesus walked out to us on the water, but in the dark and confusion, our fear had been that it was some evil spirit threatening us. Simon and the other three fishermen knew roughly where we were, but the rest of us had no idea. We were, as far as we knew, still well out on the lake when we first caught a glimpse of that figure barely discernable in the starlight. I've seen what Mark and our brother Matthew wrote in their accounts, but the whole thing was a lot simpler than that.

Jesus wanted to visit the area across the lake from Capernaum. After several hectic days it was decided we would sail across and visit the area of the Decapolis. Everything went well to start with, and we sailed along before a nice morning breeze out of the west. Jesus fell asleep on the stern platform, cushioned on the canvas bag containing the carefully folded net.

Just after noon, the wind died away, and for a while we barely moved. Simon looked anxiously at the sky, made a comment to Andrew, and they both moved to bring in the sail. Simon looked out beyond us to check on the other boat belonging to James and John, with another six or so of our friends who had wanted to come with us.

I heard Simon say, "The wind is veering. It's going to blow from the northeast out of those mountains," and he nodded his head towards the brown hills off our port bow. "I think we are in for a blow. We'll get out the oars." He nodded to Judas and me. "Take the bow oars and keep our head to the wind. At least you know how to row." He laughed and called back to Andrew. "We'll have the sail all the way down and stowed."

The wind hit us before he could reach for the halyard. A gust took us all aback, then a solid wall of wind laid us over until water rushed over the side. Judas and I had barely taken our seats, and by the time we had oars in the water, we had been turned broadside to the wind.

I saw Simon dump the sail in one motion. Some of it went overboard, but he and Andrew furled it down and lashed it securely. By the time they had it under control, Judas and I had the bow headed into the wind. Simon and Andrew grabbed the other oars and heaved with all their might. From watching both of them, I realized we were in trouble.

The wind increased and shrieked through the simple rigging holding up the mast. We dug our bow into a wave, and it broke over us and washed down the length of the boat. Every third or fourth wave caught us and broke over us, until we had more than six inches of water around our feet. As we rowed, I could sense the boat getting heavier and lower in the water. Simon looked around in desperation and shouted above the noise of the storm to wake Jesus, who was still comfortably asleep on the stern platform.

He finally stirred, and Simon shouted for him to help. "Get the bailer. It is under the platform there. We are sinking. Bail as hard as you can. We don't have long."

Jesus sat up, looked around at the waves and replied calmly, "I don't do bailing." Then he stood up and did the most amazing thing I've ever seen: He raised his arm and shouted at the waves, "Still! Enough!"

Immediately, the wind dropped and, little by little, subsided over the next few minutes into a strong breeze. The waves lost their driving power, and we were left bobbing on a heaving sea. Waves no longer broke over us, and our oars finally beat in rhythm.

Jesus sank onto the stern deck again and smiled at Simon, "Is that better?"

I was behind Simon and could not see his face, but he looked at Andrew, looked back at Jesus and shook his head in disbelief. In mock disgruntlement, he remarked that the boat still needed bailing.

Jesus studied Simon for a few moments and laughed, "Okay, but we are not going to make this a habit." He found the bailer and tossed water over the side.

Judas bowed his head towards me and, with a look that verged on terror, muttered, "Did I see what I thought I saw?"

As the realization of what I had witnessed dawned on me, I sat in stunned silence and could not reply to Judas. I just shook my head as if to deny the evidence of my own eyes. "Tell me I didn't really see that," I whispered.

We rowed on in silence. Simon said, "Let's try the sail again. We have at least another hour to row. I think we can make the area of the Gadarenes with this wind. We will be close hauled, but that beats rowing."

Andrew and Simon raised the sail again, and we thankfully dropped our oars. I looked at my hands, and saw that the calluses that had developed after our last escapade of night rowing had protected my hands from further damage. I was rather pleased with myself and looked over at Judas. "Much more of this and we can take up fishing," I joked. Judas was in no mood for levity. He shook his head and didn't reply.

We climbed on shore and found our way up the low cliffs to the meadowland above. The village was off to our right, and we could see a grassy area by some rocks and stunted trees that would make a good place for us to dry out. As we settled down, I was racking my brain to figure a way to ask Jesus what had happened in the boat. Did he make the wind quit? Was it a passing squall? None of these questions felt right, and I had no idea how to open the conversation.

A few minutes after we were settled, and Simon lay on his back already snoring, there was a crazed scream behind us. We jumped to our feet wondering what wild beast was about to attack us. Out of the trees behind us came a naked man, brandishing a great chunk of wood like a weapon and screaming at us. Judas took his staff and went to meet him. Stepping around Judas, Jesus laid his hand on Judas' arm and motioned him to lower his staff.

Jesus raised his voice and commanded the evil spirit within the man to come out. The man exploded in a great spasm of cursing and shouting. Jesus took a step forward and again commanded the evil spirit to come out of him.

This time, the man's voice changed into a cackle. "We are many, that's why we are called legion. You cannot touch us." Jesus raised his hand and repeated his command a third time and wrestled with the presence we now all felt.

The man was wracked with convulsions. The voice of one of the other evil spirits spoke up, "All right, we will come out, but let us go. Send us into the herd of pigs over there. Do not try to destroy us."

Jesus allowed a wintry smile to play across his face, "Go! Leave him and never dare to return," he commanded.

With that, the poor man convulsed desperately and fell to the ground like a sack of stones. The pigs squealed in terror and, milling around at full speed, fled towards the cliff edge. One after the other, they plunged over.

The men looking after them jumped to their feet and took off in the other direction. I thought to myself, "That does it; we are going to have the pig owners here in no time. How will we explain this one? Who is going to clean up the mess down on the beach?"

I was intending to make a comment about what I thought was going to happen next when I saw Jesus help the naked man to a sitting position. Jesus asked, "Tell me, what was going on in you?"

The man covered his face and started to weep. He shook his head back and forth. "I cannot. It went on all the time; it's been years. It's as if I've been several different people all at once, and they have argued and fought inside me. They've done terrible things, and I couldn't stop them. Is it over? Have they really gone? They may be hiding and waiting for you to go. Oh, what is the use?"

Jesus spoke quietly with the same tone of command we had heard earlier that day when he spoke to the wind. "You are safe. They will not come back. Talk to me, talk to these others; there is nobody else but those you see. This is your world, not where you have been living these last few years. It is over. You are safe."

The man sat in silence for almost five minutes. None of us disturbed him. Finally he looked up and looked around. "The sky, the rocks, these trees are all real. I thought the only thing that was real was the voices. This is real; this is our God's world, not their world?" he asked. He bent down and started to kiss Jesus' feet.

Jesus put his hand down and helped the man to his feet. "It's over. This is the real world, and all the rest is lies."

Up the hill came a bustling crowd of folk, obviously from the village. Leading them were the men who had been looking after the pigs. We waited for them. Jesus stepped protectively in front of the man who had begun to tremble as the crowd ran up towards us. The first of them came, stood in front of us and eyed with alarm the naked man. I took off my coat and draped it over him, mostly covering his nakedness. "You've caught him," said one of the first there. "We will take him away with us, he is dangerous. He has to be chained up like a mad dog."

"No," said Jesus, "He is now as sane as you or I. He is over that terrible time, and now it's up to you to let him be himself. You will see that he will be as healthy as any of you here."

"What happened to the pigs? Where are they? Is it true you drove them over the edge of the hill into the water?"

He eyed the man sitting comfortably at Jesus' feet by this time. "Look, we don't know what you think you are doing, but this man is dangerous. The pigs are gone, I can see that. We don't want any more trouble. I think you should leave before anything else happens."

There was a chorus of agreement. "We do not want you Jews coming over here and upsetting things. We did not ask you to poke your noses into our business. Rasheed is a little strange, but he belongs to us. He is fine, so long as he is chained up. We can look after him, and we don't need people like you horning into our affairs."

Rasheed, as we now knew him, faced Jesus. "Please let me come with you. Don't let me have to go back with them. They will chain me up again, and it will be like it was before."

Jesus looked at him, and shook his head. "No, you cannot come with us, but stay here. You are safe now. Tell these people what I did for you. Don't let them remind you of what hell you have been through, but rather tell them what hell they helped put you through."

To the village people, he said, "As for you, you will not use chain to hold him. He is healed. Know, though, that what you have done to him is all part of the evil spirit I drove out. Listen to him. He is your hope, if you will know it. If you don't take him in and welcome him as one of your own, the evil spirit I cast out will come screaming through the wilderness and return. When he finds everything nicely cleaned up, he will go with glee and find many more evil spirits as bad as he, come back and enter you. Things will be much worse next time. Remember what happened to the pigs."

With that we passed through the crowd and made our way back to the boat. As we came down the path towards the shore, we looked at the mess the pigs had made. Their corpses littered the shore, some of them in the water but most on the shore itself. Jesus shook his head. "There is evil, and then there is Evil with a capital letter. Don't ever muddle up the two. These evil spirits were small-letter evil. The great

Evil has yet to emerge, and that battle has yet to be joined. Pray to be delivered from the sufferings of that struggle, when it comes."

He led us back towards the boat, and, and, without more ado, we pushed off, sailing with the wind out of the east, towards Bethsaida.

SERMON ON THE PLAIN

About this time, we saw an influx of people from Judea, even from the coastal areas of Tyre and Sidon. Word was getting out, and people were making their way to Galilee to hear Jesus. Most came because of his reputation as a healer, rather than a teacher.

Some came to disrupt, to heckle and to ridicule Jesus as a country bumpkin, a Galilean, and wine drinker. These were from Jerusalem, and we felt their presence as an organized opposition to what we were doing. They kept up a constant stream of heckling and ridiculing of whatever Jesus did or said. If he healed somebody, it was by the power of Beelzebub; if he said anything that was somewhat exalted, he had an evil spirit. They tried to cast doubt on his ministry and undermine the hope and understanding growing among the people. In the face of these sophisticates from Jerusalem, the crowd grew quiet, the joy ebbed out of them, and they clearly feared to speak up or ask questions.

Jesus was not a person to let things get to him, but in this case he became angry. When we came together one evening, he said, "This is intentional. It is at the direction of a malevolence that we have offended, and we will continue to offend. This struggle is not our struggle, but that of our Heavenly Father, and it is His war in which we find ourselves. What you see is like looking down a well that has been poisoned by an invading force. They throw refuse and dead animals down wells to foul them so that nobody can drink from them. When you listen to those clergy from Jerusalem, they are trying to do the same thing. They are poisoning the wells from which these people might drink. That clamor and ridicule clouds the people's judgment. This we smell here in Galilee is what we stirred up in Jerusalem. The evil I have spoken of has sensed us here and is growing alarmed. We must hurry on with what we are doing, because this evil is on the move. This comes from the Temple itself.

Judas asked him to explain further, and Jesus continued, "When we were in Jerusalem, everything we did was an affront to those who represented the spiritual power of the nation. We healed and disturbed their sleep, we taught and we disturbed their minds, and we raised from the dead and sent them screaming in panic to their councils. Now they stretch out their hands to deny God's Kingdom, and they place themselves between God's servant and His people. They are in a very bad place."

I looked at Thomas and nodded. He smiled back and mouthed to me, "About time."

Judas spoke up, "Is there more behind this?"

Jesus nodded. "Yes, these men are not the enemy. They do his will, but they don't know the evil one. They are bought and paid for, maybe, but ignorant of the gulf opening before them.

"Their way is to cast doubt, create fears and frighten people away, so that I become sidetracked and powerless. I know the struggle with the evil they have brought with them will not be fought here, but it will be defeated. This is God's fight, and these are only representatives of institutional evil that has always existed and always will. My job is to make evil of this kind impotent in the face of grace.

"Right now, I have to defend the people who have come to me looking for help. Many have come miles to get a little of what I offer. I will not allow those vultures to take even one of God's people from me. The people have come looking for the Kingdom of Heaven, and I say that it will be given to them. None of them will go without a vision of what it is. The old men will dream dreams about it, and the young men will have visions about it."

As time went by, another party of clergy became definable. These were local clergy and most of them were Pharisees. They served the local villagers, and taught the people the law; they even taught some to read. They were often present, listened intently, argued with Jesus and invited him to speak at the Sabbath meetings at the synagogues in the various villages and towns close by. When we first started, they were on the fringe of the crowd, listening intently and only sometimes asking questions. Now they stood or sat close in. Were they disciples like most of us? Some of them were, and in a few months they would come with us to Jerusalem and join that fateful procession into the city.

What had started so quietly in the square at Capernaum now embraced crowds of folk from all over. On the day after Jesus had warned us all about the true nature of the opposition, and a month after the event down the coast when we disciples had to try to feed all those people, many followers were gathered on an open pasture cropped short by sheep, waiting to hear Jesus.

As Jesus began to teach, I noticed that a man with a deformed arm was propelled out of the group of Jerusalemites and pushed towards Jesus. He turned back to them, but was waved on. Jesus saw the whole thing. He knew he was being set up. The man with the deformed arm would come forward and ask to be healed. It was the Sabbath and the clergy in that group from Jerusalem would go berserk. They would hoot and shout, condemn Jesus for breaking the Sabbath and revile him as an unclean person nobody should touch. As I watched, I felt someone stir beside me. It was Simon. He heaved himself up to a standing position, and I could tell he was about to launch himself at the man. I touched his arm and shook my head. "Watch."

Jesus beckoned the man forward, took his arm and looked at it, then looked at the man intently. He raised his eyes to the expectant bunch of clergy. "Tell me, is it lawful to do good on the Sabbath?"

Nobody answered, and Jesus waited and held their gaze. He stared that way until their eyes had slid off of his and were trying to find something else of interest to look at. The rest of the crowd was aware of the approaching showdown. As the silence wore on, the looks of outrage and condemnation of the clerics' actions grew among the crowd. Several men nudged each other and began to move towards them. In no time at all, the tension mounted to that flash point when violence could break out. The crowd had had enough.

Jesus explained to them, "Blessed are you who need help; the Kingdom of God is yours for the asking. Blessed are you who are now hungry, for you will find both food and satisfaction. Blessed are you who weep now, for you will laugh. Blessed are you when people hate you and ostracize you, when they insult you and slander your very name. Don't let it get under your skin. Rather, exalt and dance for joy, for it's clear you've made your point, and they smart from it."

Then he dramatically spun 'round towards the huddle of well-dressed, somewhat overweight clergy who exuded confidence in their own exalted station and lofty authority, and he began speaking in a low, ferocious growl that jangled our nerves.

"Alas, for you who are rich, you have had yours. Alas, for you who are well fed now, you will go hungry. Alas, for you who laugh at these my people, you will mourn and weep by the time this is all over. Alas, for you when everyone speaks well of you, and you believe them; for that is how the false prophets have always been treated. You are in trouble, and you don't even know it; like a cloud rolling towards you, there will be no escape as it overtakes you. You don't even know how sick you are, you and he who you represent. The day of reckoning is drawing near."

He waved his hand in disdainful dismissal at the departing clergy and to the rest of us standing there and ordered us to ignore them. "Sit down, relax." He returned his attention back to the man with the withered arm who stood there watching the conflict swirl around him. You could see he was utterly confused. Jesus said gently, "Now, let us see your arm. You did want me to look at it?"

"I am sorry. I did not mean to cause this trouble. They said I should ask you to help me. I didn't think about the Sabbath. I can come back tomorrow. I am sorry; they told me I had to come here. I didn't mean to cause all this." Then with a sob he sank down on his knees. He knelt there before Jesus for several minutes, then standing up and cradling his damaged arm with the other, retreated toward the way he had come.

Jesus tapped him on the shoulder. "You've forgotten something." "What?"

"Your arm still needs help. There was a good reason why you came here. Let me see it."

The man looked around at the crowds and looked over to the clergy who were by this time somewhat dampened in spirit and, still not able to meet Jesus' eyes, offered his arm for inspection. There was a sympathetic intake of breath by those close by as he displayed an arm which had been clearly mangled and which had set in a grotesque, twisted mess.

"An accident?" Jesus asked softly.

The man nodded and added, "My mule slipped, and when I was trying to free her she rolled right over, trapping my arm against a boulder. There was nothing I could do until my neighbor came."

Jesus gently extended the arm out towards him, ran his hands along the length of it, and gently pulled the hand towards him. He coaxed the arm with his other hand as if helping it to stretch. The man's face registered alarm at first, then marvelously he began to smile as if he could feel the healing taking place.

"It doesn't hurt anymore. I can feel my fingers. My arm feels hot. I can move it. It's okay!"

He dropped to his knees, but this time he bent down and kissed Jesus' feet as a simple act of thanks. He stood and raised his arm, gingerly twisting his hand back and forth. "I began to think maybe I didn't deserve my prayer to be heard, or maybe I wasn't doing it right. I can work again. I can put food on the table. I can hug my children and care for my wife. You don't know what it's been like. I prayed and prayed for help."

Jesus spun him around and gave him a gentle push towards a group of us standing off to the side. We took him, and as had become our custom, sat him down with us, and one or two of us put our hands on him. This reassured him and he settled down, like an animal that had been gentled and led to safety.

Meanwhile, Jesus stood in silence, and the people sat expectantly watching. The Jerusalem clergy began to make their exit, one by one.

When the last of them were gone, Jesus addressed the whole gathering. "I have talked to you about the nature of your Heavenly Father, I have spoken of His love for you, His wanting for you and His great invitation for you to join Him in His act of creation. This is a new path to holiness which must replace your dependence on sacrifice of innocent animals and birds to provide you with salvation. I've described the initial steps you must take, and the discipline of prayer you need to observe, but now I want to talk to you about what else is required of you.

"How many of you are seeking the Kingdom of God? "

I saw a forest of hands go up.

"When you give alms, do it secretly. Pray secretly. If you fast, do it so nobody else knows. Make everything you do an offering to the Father, and he will recognize everything you offer and respond. You make a practice of this and you will indeed be part of the Kingdom of God.

"Now, how many of you need to turn your back on what you've been?" A sparse sprinkle of hands showed. "Take control of yourself. Can one blind man lead another? No, they will both fall into the ditch. So you need to learn to see for yourselves the way to be and the way to tread. Look at it this way. If your brother has a speck of something in his eye, and he turns to you and you say, let me look at your eye, I'll get it out, and you don't even realize you've got half a plank in your own eye and can't see anything, you are in a bad way. You have to look at what kind of a person you really are and come to grips with your meanness, resentment, anger, anxiety or any other aspect of yourself that has kept you imprisoned. Don't bother to feel guilty, but call to mind in detail what kind of life you have been living and mourn over it. This will give you the desire to turn your back on where you've been and seek a new life. So, I say, blessed are the sorrowful, for you will be strengthened to become that new person.

"Now, this is a hard one. How many of you want to take responsibility, exercise power and be leaders?" Nobody put their hands up, but I saw a few glance at each other. "Nobody wants to admit he would like power, but you are called to exercise power and take responsibility. First, no one can serve two masters. You cannot serve God and money. Make up your mind which you serve. Don't worry about food and drink, clothes or other material things. Look around you. The flowers over there are more beautiful than even Solomon in all his glory. So derive your true richness from your Father. Set your mind on His Kingdom and His justice. That humility and desire to serve will fit you to exercise power in the world. So, I say to you, blessed are the gentle in spirit for you will have the earth for your possession.

"Who wants to feel satisfied and know you've done your best?" I watched as a few hands crept up, hesitant, but finally there they were.

"You have to want justice and right actions more than anything else. There can be no hypocrisy in you at all. If you are angry at your brother, get over it and admit your part in the dispute. Don't go on praying and bowing to God and yet be full of resentment.

"Let me give you another example of purity of heart. You all know that if a man divorces his wife, he must give her a certificate of divorce, and that is that. I tell you, if you divorce your wife in order to marry another you are committing adultery, and so is the woman you marry. You may be legally in the clear, but in your heart you committed adultery, and there is no escaping that reality. Pain, suffering and destruction will result from it. You've got to want justice more than anything else, or you will lie to yourself. You will never feel good about yourself because right inside you will know you are a cheat. I say, therefore, blessed are you who hunger and thirst to see right prevail; you shall be thoroughly and deeply satisfied.

"This next one is for some of you who have been treated unfairly, accused wrongly and have had a lifetime of being abused. Stop feeling sorry for yourselves. Become a friend and advocate for others like yourself. Listen to their stories, and you will know you have never deserved to be treated as you have. Don't hang on to the past, but know the sin for what it is, the sin of the world. Let it go, and lead others like yourself back to wholeness. If this is your particular road, let me say to you, blessed are you who learn to show mercy to others. Mercy will be yours.

"Who wants to see God?"

I saw hands shoot up. I could buy into this one myself.

"Now, if you are to see God, you have to be pure in heart. You've all been told not to commit adultery, but, I say, if you look at a woman with lust in your heart, that is just as bad, and you are committing adultery. You've been told to not commit murder, but I tell you, if you are angry towards your brother and criticize and belittle him, you are as good as murdering him—your heart is just as full of violence as a murderer's. Give up those feelings that you find so satisfying and seek God with your whole heart. I say to those who will drop all their own desires, blessed are you who are pure in heart. You will see God."

I was blown away, of course. The battle I had fought for years was really against my desires. How could I let all of them go and want but the one thing, God?

I had missed some comments but now I heard Jesus say, "Now, who wants to be called a child of God?" A number of hands went up, particularly of younger men.

"Where to start? If anyone wants to insult you and hits you on the cheek, trying to get you going, don't strike back, but instead turn to him the other cheek. No, I mean it. Try it, just turn the other cheek for him to smack. It won't hurt for long. If someone insists on taking your coat, offer him your jacket also. Give to everyone who asks you, and when you lend to another, don't ask for it back.

"Now, this is not the law but is beyond the law. If you will trust me and try this out, you will find it works. Love your enemies and pray for those who give you a bad time, and you will become a peacemaker. So, blessed are you, peacemakers, for you shall be called children of God.

"Finally I want to say to all of you, if you stand up for what is right and proclaim these truths you've heard, you will get attacked. So, I say to all of you, stand up for the cause of right wherever you are. You will be persecuted, but don't be intimidated. Stand firm, and you will feel ownership and responsibility for the Kingdom of God.

"You all seek the Kingdom of God, but you are in it, so take responsibility for it. You are the light of the world. You don't take a light and put it under a basket, but stick it on a lamp stand so everyone can see. That is your job: be a light to the world.

"You are the salt of the earth, and as you know, you don't need much salt for a meal, but food is much less tasty without it. There are not many of you in the world—there never will be—but you are to be the salt that makes the lives of people sparkle with light or be alive with flavor.

"Now, all of you call me *Rabbi* or even more exalted things, but if you are going to be a part of the Kingdom of God, then you are going to have to learn to take my words and adhere to them. Imagine a man who builds a house. He digs down to bedrock and establishes his foundation on the rock. Once the house is built, it gets lashed with wind, rain and even floods, but the foundation is solid, and the house is left unmoved. So it is for you, if you allow my words to live in you, and you allow yourself to be guided by them. Make my words your foundation, build on them and you will be all right."

This sobered the people listening, and questions started to fly.

The teaching went on for another hour or so. People got out the food they had brought, and this time they shared what they had. There was much wandering back and forth, greeting those they had met before and visiting with those they knew. Meanwhile Jesus was besieged with requests. The rest of us, who were his companions, lay back in the sun or propped on our elbows and watched everything going on around us.

Jesus finally rose from where he had been sitting on a rock and called out for attention. "I have invited you into the Kingdom of Heaven, and those who have got the idea and understand what I have showed you, now have a job to do. How many of you will give me a hand?"

Over seventy hands went up. "Good, now I want you to go off towards your homes, but I want you to visit the villages and towns all the rest of these people are from and announce the fact the Kingdom of Heaven is upon them. Tell them what you have seen; tell them the things I have taught you. Lay hands on them in my name, and heal them if they need it. Tell them about the love of God for His people. Tell them the Lord desires to embrace them, and then call them to repent, rethink their lives, turn and decide for the Kingdom of Heaven. Ask them right out to make that decision. Invite them in.

"I have just talked to you about being salt to the world. Well, this is how you can be that salt or that light."

Questions erupted again, and instructions were repeated, and a great stir occurred as they departed. All those of us from Galilee went off, and the crowds drifted away with the newly commissioned "ambassadors."

Two days later, the seventy members who went out met with us back at Capernaum. They were full of themselves. They had indeed tried healing people using Jesus' name. It worked. People welcomed them, much to their initial surprise.

Jesus came back from listening to all their stories and said with a smile, "I saw Satan fall from Heaven; you have scared the pants off him." There was laughter at this, but as I looked at Jesus' face I couldn't tell if he was serious. I frowned and asked if he meant it.

He shrugged his shoulders, smiled and didn't answer. Sometimes he could be infuriating. However, I had work to do. I was still wrestling with the idea that my inner problem was my desires.

That had burrowed itself into my mind, and now new understanding was opening it up, little by little. Still, there was only room for one desire, and I knew what that had to be.

VISITS TO TYRE AND SIDON

That night we were all still camped just outside of Capernaum, and Jesus came into the circle of disciples, helped himself to bread and a yogurt-and-cucumber spicy spread and sat himself down among us. Munching on the bread, he studied each of us in turn. We waited in silence for him to speak.

"We need to begin the next phase. We have to spread what you have all witnessed this last eight months or so. I am going to ask these people who have just come back to continue talking and telling others what they have seen. Meanwhile, I want to visit Tyre and Sidon, then strike east across to the area of Decapolis."

Those of us who were closest to Jesus looked at each other, then nodded to him. For the next two hours, we discussed details and Jesus shared more of his ideas. The local men left to tidy up things before leaving, and those from nearby villages went off early to pick up their things. Jesus dismissed the eighty or so others who had reported in after their work of visiting other communities. Things were beginning to move.

Later that evening, I was sitting outside the chattering group and listening to what was going on, when a man crept surreptitiously into camp. He came over to me and asked if I could take him to see Jesus. I asked him what it was about, and he said, "Its bad news. I have to tell Jesus himself."

I replied, "Look, Jesus is away up there somewhere, and he will be gone for a couple more hours. Tell me, and I will pass it on."

The man said no and sat down by the fire. He stared into the flames and began to weep. I went to him and laid my hand on him, "Tell us, we are all in this together."

He raised his streaming face to me and sobbed, "They have killed John the Baptist. Herod cut off his head!" He collapsed into uncontrollable sobbing.

I felt more than heard Jesus' presence behind me. He said, "So it has begun. Those people we saw here the other day are part of this, and now we see how far the evil is spreading itself."

He called to the other disciples. "Have you heard the news? John has been murdered. It's time for us to move. Time is getting short, and we have much to do.

"John was the greatest of the prophets in his own way, but I want you to know that any of you who are part of the Kingdom of God are, in your way, more fortunate, or even greater than he. Like so many, he longed to see what you see. Many have died so that you might be here with me this night. Now is the time for you to know of yourselves that you are in the Kingdom of Heaven. Lay hands on it and don't let it go.

"As for me, I must journey across the land and spread my call to as many as will hear me. I thought the time was getting short, but with this news, we must move. Darkness is coming."

The next day we set out towards the coast. We had not been walking long when Jesus fell back and walked beside me. "John, walk with me. No, don't talk. I just need to have you there, and for you to listen to me. I need to talk through some things."

I nodded, and we walked on in silence for awhile.

Finally, he said, "John was more than just a prophet, you know. He was my friend. We grew up together. I know he didn't get what all this is about, but he gave me his friendship over and over. You know what this means? We are alone, and we are next. I have mixed feelings about this next step. I don't see how to proceed. I don't know what is going to happen, and I don't understand what everything will look like when it's all over.

"We've come so far, and I'm pleased with what we have done here in Galilee, but Jerusalem scares me, and it is to Jerusalem we must eventually go. I've talked of the evil there. We will have to face it in all its naked strength. There is to be a battle of one kind or another, but as I have said, it is not between armies. This far I can see; for everything we do must be consistent with what I have understood and taught.

"Beyond the conflict, I have no clue. I know for this Kingdom to be run among the people as I have promised, I have to be available for them. The truth I have spoken cannot be maintained in my absence. This is what worries me. Those we have taught and healed and led need my presence. All the evil and violence of this world quickly overwhelms people standing alone. Whatever happens, I must come back, I must return for them. We cannot use them and abandon them.

"John, I don't see my way forward. I think we are done here, but what after the coast, what after Decapolis? There is no other place to go but Jerusalem, and I know that is where my path ends, one way or another. Caiaphas and his rabble don't understand what is happening, but there is an evil squatting there that does. I have alarmed it, and it is preparing to do battle. Eliminating John the Baptist is its opening move. I know it."

I wanted to object or say something comforting, but I kept silent and let Jesus go on. He spent his whole life listening, and now I would give him the only thing I had to offer, my full attention.

"I don't think hordes of angels are the Father's plan. I don't think some political accommodation is in the cards either. I tell you, the will of God is at play here, and it is as if I am the spear point that is being aimed at the heart of that monstrous presence. I don't know what I am supposed to do. So far, I have been led by my Father, and the Spirit has coursed through me, and I have been part of the wonder of these days. Now, though, we are entering a darkness that I have yet to penetrate. I do not doubt, but I can't see the way ahead. Stay with me, will you? Don't go back to Jerusalem just yet. We will all finish up there anyway. I think I need you here.

"Poor John. Murdered in the dark of that dungeon, and not knowing, or only knowing that God's intention was afoot and His end game running. Did he experience doubt at the end? I think not. No, I think he was given a vision of what this is all about. Maybe that is what is stirring up these thoughts in me. Did John know in the end, or did God use him and abandon him in that dungeon? Am I in the same position? Will I be abandoned at the last moment when I have done what I am supposed to do?"

I wanted to protest this thought, but I sat silently and allowed Jesus to follow his own thoughts.

"Can you see how insidious this temptation is? My love and care for John becomes a snare for me and tempts me to doubt. I am used to temptation. You don't think those smart-assed tempters I once described to you went home and never bothered me again? No, at the most profound level of my being, the Father and I are one in this. Do you remember me telling you about those temptations in the early days, and all I had left was the presence of God? Well it's like that now. I don't see, I don't understand but the strength of that presence has grown. The presence of the divine occupies all of me, and I welcome it ever more completely. In the middle of all this, including the doubt, I am at peace. There, that is bedrock."

Jesus seemed calmer, now that his fears were off his chest. We walked on for an hour. Finally we increased our speed and rejoined the group. We reached the coast late the third day and made camp in a wadi not far from the seaport of Tyre.

The next afternoon, Jesus walked by himself, wrapped in his own thoughts, and he was uncharacteristically and thoroughly uncommunicative. After we arrived, he drifted off alone. That night, the ten of us made camp and prepared supper over a crackling fire.

Thaddeus looked at me across the firelight. "John, what happened on the dock in Tyre? I missed what that woman said to Jesus."

I thought back to the moment and traced the change in Jesus back to that encounter. "Well, she asked him to heal her daughter. Jesus said no, and that he was sent only to the lost sheep of Israel. Then he said, 'It is wrong to cast the children's bread to the dogs?' The woman came right back at him, 'Yes, but even the dogs get to eat the crumbs from the table.' I think that is about it."

"She said that? How dare she talk to Jesus like that? She was Phoenician, I am sure, and a woman. So what did he say? He didn't seem angry, but afterwards he just hasn't been the same."

"What did he say? Just that her daughter was healed. She impressed him. He was not upset at her, but surprised by her answer. On the road tomorrow, we should ask him about it. My Greek is good, but maybe I missed something she said that got to him. Her accent was awful."

"What's he doing wasting his strength on Gentiles?" Thaddeus persisted. "There was that Centurion from Tiberius, and then there was that Gadarean madman. I am not sure how I feel about Gentiles horning in like this. We've got enough work to do with our own people."

Philip was looking through his satchel for something, and said over his shoulder, "There is a lot I don't understand. His teaching is great, but there is this whole healing thing." He pushed his bag behind him and leaned on it for support. "Do you remember when those characters broke through the roof and let that paralyzed man down right in front of Jesus? Do you remember what he said? 'Your sins are forgiven.' Okay, so he got the clergy going. That is always fun to see, but there are two things that I don't understand. The first is, why should Jesus talk about sins to a man that is paralyzed? He did not have the opportunity to sin. I mean, unlike the rest of us, what could he do lying there? The other issue is, how could Jesus say that to the man—'Your sins are forgiven'—and the man believe him?"

"So?"

"If I said to someone, 'your sins are forgiven,' they would not believe me."

"We all know why. Coming from you that would be quite a stretch."

Philip smiled at my attempt at humor and continued. "I know, but think back. Jesus was able to make the man believe he was indeed forgiven. Do you remember his face?"

I thought back to the event and replied, "Yeah, confused, disbelieving, and looking at Jesus, then looking at the clergy. Then he got up. I see what you mean. When he stood up, it looked as if whatever had been going on was over, and he knew it."

"Yes, you've got it. This time it wasn't the healing but the forgiving. Remember the question the clergy asked, 'Who can forgive sins but God?' What have we got here? I have been asking myself what this rabbi of ours is. Maybe I should say, I have been wondering *who* he is?"

Andrew interjected, "Remember that storm on the lake? I still don't know what to make of that. He could not have known that wind was just about to quit. I know those squalls go as fast as they come, but not like that."

"I think the thing that got me was the food thing the other day. We fed over 5,000 people. I know because I kept giving it out," added Nathaniel.

Matthias shook his head slowly, "I tell you, he is more than a rabbi. What do you think he is working on out there?"

Judas said, from his position just outside the circle of firelight, "That woman in Tyre messed with his head. He is figuring out something, and I bet you we hear about it tomorrow. As for your questions about him, I think it is dangerous for us to speculate about who or what he is. We will spook ourselves. There has to be an explanation for it all. He is our rabbi, and he has said he is teaching a new way, or path to replace sacrifices and all the nonsense that supports ancient superstitions. He has said that more than once. He has been encouraging us to come together, treat each other with respect and be a community as is described in our law. When you start talking like this, putting undue emphasis on some of the events that have happened, then I think we do him a disservice."

Simon, sitting with his great back to the dark and his arms around his knees, shook his head as he stared at the fire. "I don't know who or what he is, but for my money I am his. I have come to believe in him, and for the first time I can trust myself to someone absolutely. I love him. I would rather be here with him than catching fish."

Andrew hooted with mock derision at this brother's words. "I never expected to hear you say that. I am with you though. I feel the same way. I can trust him absolutely."

Matthew spoke up, "You mentioned forgiving, I experienced that for myself. You know what I was when he came along. That first time he confronted me, I felt myself being searched through. Remember that psalm, 'Search me out and know if there be any wickedness in me.' That is exactly what he did. He searched me out and showed me all the darkness in all the different rooms of myself. Yet, I didn't feel as if he condemned me, but because of his presence, all those demons hiding there no longer had a hold on me. I was most certainly judged, but his judgment was a relief."

"The light went on, not out. Being with him now allows me to keep hold of that new reality. I know I have not changed, and all the old stuff is still there, but every day I spend in his presence, I become more familiar with myself. As I do, that old self grows thin and dim. The more I remember, the more I feel the grace I have from God, but it is through him it continues to pour over me. I have nowhere to go—I belong here."

"Our families need us," said Andrew, "but what we did when Jesus sent us out has got me thinking . . . Do you remember how people really understood what we were offering, in spite of how badly we explained things? Then there were those moments when we laid hands on people. That blew me away. If that is how it is with Jesus, and he can give us that opportunity, then staying with him is more important than going back to fishing or anything else."

James nodded agreement. "I've never been so surprised at myself than during those few days we were out by ourselves. I was given authority. Who am I to tell someone he is healed? I did though, and he got up a different man. That scared me profoundly. I feel I have a lion by the tail."

Judas said, "I don't see it going anywhere. We could become itinerant teachers, and do more of the visiting of other communities, but the spiritual power base of the nation is not going to move over and give us a place. They have a lock on the spiritual life, and they don't want any help."

With Judas' words our exuberance died. The fire too, as if sensing the moment, collapsed in on itself. The chill air dropped down the wadi and prompted us to gather our cloaks about us. Someone got up and said good night, then, one by one, the rest followed. I was left staring at the fire and watching the red dull. I would wait up for Jesus.

I thought of my office in Jerusalem and hoped my manager was looking after it, but the hope was getting thin and vague. It would be nice if he were, but if not, oh well. I drew my cloak closer around me and settled against a rock for a long vigil. I felt we were all at a moment of decision. We were at a tipping point that would either take us forward or would sweep the whole endeavor away.

Through the mountains we tramped and down to the area of the Decapolis. Caesarea Philippi was our main stop. The city was heavily Gentile, and I noticed Jesus studying the inhabitants intently. He passed by the grotto of the Goddess Athena which he studied at a distance. I noticed he sought out other sites where the Gentiles gathered for business and worship. He lingered there, listening in to conversations and watching them go about their lives. Our people were present in large numbers, and Jesus was soon recognized. Crowds gathered, and Jesus taught and healed some of those who came to him. Just as he was gaining a following, he decided it was time to leave. We took the road south towards Bethsaida and followed the mountain ridge to the east of us.

We had made a good start on our journey. At the mid-morning stop, Jesus gathered us round him. "I need to bring you up to date with my thinking about the next step we must take. First, though, let me ask you, who do men say that I am?"

There was silence. Nobody wanted to be the first, but the replies eventually started. "That you are Elijah, a new Moses, a prophet."

"Who do you think I am?"

After our conversation last night, nobody was willing to speak out. We studied our fingernails and looked at the sky or found something fascinating on the ground before us. Simon finally blurted out, "You are the Messiah, the Holy One of God."

Everyone's eyes now fixed on Jesus' face. For a long moment there was absolute silence, as if everyone was holding his breath. For me, there was nothing new in Simon's statement. I had known it for a long time, but being so familiar with Jesus tended to make me forget how momentous that claim really was.

Jesus nodded. "The truth has been revealed to you. This is the solid rock on which everything else is founded. It is the rock on which the Kingdom's foundation rests. I think from now on I am going to call you Peter. For you who don't know Greek, the word means 'rock.' Simon Peter, bear this name in recognition that you were the one to whom this realization was given.

"Soon I will have to journey to Jerusalem and confront the forces there. Those of you who are willing to accompany me will be part of the struggle. I must warn you that as far as I can see, it will mean my final rejection by the powers that be, both Sadducees and most of the Pharisees who occupy the seats of power, and they will kill me. Don't look so horrified. That will not be the end. I shall rise and return to you. When I do, I will be indeed what Peter has said."

Simon, or rather Peter, grabbed Jesus' arm and exclaimed, "No, you can't let that happen! We are beginning to make progress. There are so many wanting to join our movement."

Jesus shook off Peter's grip. "Don't tempt me. You think I am looking forward to this? I can see no other outcome. There is no way forward but through the heart of that darkness we call the Temple. I have said I will pull it down and rebuild it. This is what we are about. Israel has to break out from that cruel and useless round of sacrifices.

"Some days ago in Tyre, something happened that you may have noticed. That Phoenician woman made a claim on me that I could not ignore. Since then, I hear in my head the echoes of her statement, 'But the dogs eat of the crumbs from the table.' Maybe God's Holy one is not just for Israel, but for many others outside of Israel. Gentiles have the same need as you do. Last night I resisted this conclusion, but eventually had to agree with it. The task of the Messiah is to draw out a new Israel, and like the Servant of Isaiah, he will be a light to the Gentiles. The Messiah's kingdom is of the whole world. There is no border, no safe place for Israel to exist for ourselves. We are His chosen people, but He has chosen us to be the light to the world. Wherever our people are, they are leaven in the dough of the Gentiles, and somehow His Messiah is to provide the means for that to happen."

I was frowning heavily, but though I didn't like what I heard, I was not surprised. All those queries about where he had been before I met him were never answered. I thought, maybe he has been avoiding the implications of his experiences until that woman interfered.

I looked across at him. "I have no idea how, but then none of what we have done so far has been my idea. It comes from the very heart of the Almighty. So here we are. Ahead of us we have a widening mission, an inevitable catastrophic conflict, but as yet I have no clear idea of how we can accomplish it. Are you with me?"

"Gentiles?" asked Judas, and the rest of us looked with uncertainty at Jesus. I could see doubt begin to spread. "What are you saying? I thought we were working on the Kingdom of God for Israel. Are you throwing the net too wide? After all, isn't Israel big enough? Why do you have to die? Nobody can complain about what we are doing or what you teach. Why can we not continue as we are? You are making a real difference in the lives of so many; why do you have to risk everything on some wild messianic gamble?

"At some point, you have to stop expanding your vision and accomplish something. Look at who we are: eleven or twelve men from different backgrounds, and none of us have an iota of power. Here you are, talking about Israel as having a purpose in the eyes of God, of Israel being that servant person of Isaiah. The world doesn't care about us. The nations are not going to listen to a group of backcountry Jews. The nations are happy the way they are, so why create a scenario that cannot succeed? If you die now, everything will blow away like a puff of dust in the east wind."

Jesus smiled and nodded. He got up and asked us, "Who is coming? We have a long way to go." Off we went at our customary distance-consuming pace.

Thomas sidled up alongside of me and asked, "What do you make of that? That woman has really messed things up. I can see this splitting our group, and all the efforts we have made will go down the drain. Jesus is right about the gang in Jerusalem. We should stay clear of the place. You know why we left in the first place."

"How many decades, even centuries, has Israel been waiting for the Messiah, and now we've got one, and he is telling us we have to wait until he comes back?" added Thaddeus, who had been walking with Thomas.

I had similar thoughts, but I had also gone over in my memory the struggle Jesus had in defining his mission, and how he was himself bemused by its continual expansion. "I think the final piece has fallen into place for him," I explained, "and he can see back in time and forward into the future the purpose God has been pursuing and will continue to pursue. For the first time he can clearly see the Kingdom's full extent and its function in the lives of all people."

"I don't think he knows how to get there from here. That's next, and it's going to be a doozy," I declared.

"How can you be a Messiah to a world that doesn't know it needs one?" asked Andrew. "Dying, though, is a contradiction, and this returning to somehow complete the job is beyond me. For the first time, I have doubts about where Jesus is going with this."

Thomas nodded up ahead to where James and his brother John were walking on either side of Jesus. "What do you suppose they are talking about?"

I looked and saw Jesus shake his head. He paused in his walking and looked at each of the brothers and again shook his head. Soon he put his arms on their shoulders and they all went on. Thomas asked again, "What was that about, do you suppose?"

"Whatever it was, the answer was no. What's the betting they were asking for a favor?"

"That is what it looked like. No doubt we will hear about it in good time."

The Galilean contingent had less trouble with these new developments than Thomas, Judas and I. We knew Jerusalem, and we had seen the rabid response to Jesus' words and actions. If we went back there, he would die for sure. Unless there was some divine intervention, they would stone him as soon as they got their hands on him. We had seen notices of the condemnation by the Sanhedrin. He had already been condemned to death for necromancy, of all things. That meant stoning.

25
Transfiguration and the Way to Jerusalem

Three nights later, Jesus invited Peter, James and John to go with him up into the hills for prayer. He usually spent hours kneeling in quiet, his arms thrown wide as if to embrace everything. With closed eyes, he seemed to behold another world that only briefly intersected with our own. We would watch, but after an hour or so we would all be asleep with our cloaks held tight around us.

They were not back for breakfast, and about midmorning the crowds began to assemble. We fielded their questions and engaged in discussion, trying the best we could to give support and help, as Jesus had taught us. After our recent arguments and Jesus' news, our hearts were really not in what we were doing. Why pretend to these people? If everything was going to be torn up, why mislead them and give them false hope was the unspoken thought?

A father brought his young son to us. The lad was about fourteen. He suffered from epilepsy. The father had walked all the way from Cadasa, the other side of the valley, and we couldn't help him. Instead we used platitudes to soothe our sense of failure. Half an hour later, Jesus returned and took charge of the situation. The boy was healed.

That night we heard from our three friends what had occurred up on the mountain. By the time they had gotten up there and found a suitable place, it was dark. The three of them watched as Jesus prayed. As so often happened, they fell asleep.

They woke to see Jesus still in prayer, but there was light emanating from him. He gleamed like a white wall under a full moon. They saw two other figures appear with him. James did not go into more detail but looked around at our closed, gloomy faces. "You are not going to believe this. Simon Peter, tell them what you heard up there towards the end."

Peter looked up at Jesus and gazed around the whole ring of faces. "At the end? Well, a cloud or mist drifted over where we were. There was this voice that spoke to us, 'This is my Holy One, listen to him.' I am sure the voice was inside our heads, for at first I assumed I had merely thought it, but James and John were both staring in terror at me. They had heard it too."

One after another, we asked questions. "What did Moses and Elijah say?" "Did you dream it?" "Maybe you were worried by our discussion of Jerusalem."

Jesus sat there looking at us and smiling indulgently at us, he shook his head in mock disbelief. "Now I have a clearer idea of what is to happen. Tomorrow we continue down to Capernaum. Then we will invite all those who can to join us for Passover in Jerusalem. We need witnesses to this. When I finally came to Galilee, I told you the 'time had come; the Kingdom of Heaven was close at hand.' Well, here we go. This is the end of that beginning. Will you all come with me?"

"What can we say? Of course we will come," Simon Peter replied. All around the group, heads nodded, if somewhat reluctantly. I looked over at Thomas, who had not moved, but stared at the ground.

Finally he raised his head, looked directly at Jesus and whispered, "I'll come. What is the timeframe for all this? We are not ready for Jerusalem and a confrontation with the powers there. We will need time to mobilize support."

Jesus looked calmly at Simon Peter and at the rest of us, "We will spend Passover in Jerusalem. We will ask all those we have touched to journey with us, instead of by themselves. We will be at the head of all those coming from this region for the festival. In other words, we will co-opt the Temple's own power to confront the misappropriated authority of that organization. Passover belongs to the people. We will take it back and give it to everyone."

"That is only four weeks away. How can we get organized by then? To rush this will be to imperil the outcome. We need to have some organization in place to follow through with the initial takeover," said Judas. "We must also have enough political stability and control to assure the

Romans that we are a viable and preferred alternative to the Sadducees. We need them to stay on the sidelines. It would be helpful if we made contact with them. Tell them of our intentions and give them reassurance they would not be the target of our movement."

"All that would take months," continued Judas. "We have done nothing to bridge the gap between those of us in Jerusalem, whom we have hardly seen or heard from for a year, and all these miscellaneous individuals from Galilee. There is no coherence to our movement. We have no organization and we will be picked off one by one without planned resistance. I know these people, and they have been playing this game for centuries. They know weakness when they see it. They will exploit it unmercifully."

Jesus heard everything Judas had to say before he started talking. "If armed insurrection were our goal, you would be right. Armed insurrection or revolution is not our goal, so we will act the week before Passover. The stakes are higher than ever, and everything is falling into place. Let's get to sleep. We have a lot to do and a long way to go tomorrow."

I looked over at Judas as he flung into the fire a piece of wood that he had been whittling and hung his head, shaking it from side to side. He felt my eyes on him, but gave another infinitesimal shake of his head, got up and went to turn in. Jesus had not answered his concerns. That was unusual. I felt Judas withdraw from us all. Was this what was going to happen to the rest of us? Judas had been with Thomas and me from the early days of Jesus' ministry, and now I thought I saw some moment of decision; a reluctant, disappointing finality. Judas had been a loner when he first joined us, and in the years we had been together I had grown to respect his pragmatic view of the world. He kept us anchored, and he also provided so much of the day-to-day logistics. If he decided to leave, I would miss him. His leaving would be a mini defeat, a loss of a vote of confidence.

The next day, the rest of the group walked close together, talking about the previous day's events. Judas was there, but walked by himself. Nobody wanted to keep Jesus company after the conversation last night, so I took the opportunity to walk along with him. At first we fell into step with each other and walked in silence.

Jesus finally broke the silence, "You have been with me from the beginning. Do you understand what we are now about?"

I thought for a long time as I reflected back over the years we had spent together and the way I had witnessed the growth of Jesus' vision. I remembered Jesus' words that there would be no war, no revolution, and no legions of angels, but that there would be a spiritual struggle fought on his terms. I sensed how everywhere the same conflict that existed at the heart of our nation also existed everywhere: in Rome, in Greece, even in the brothers of that company of Essenes by the Salt Sea.

Annas was no aberration; this time in our history was no worse than previous ones. The same protestations would be made next year, and the same oppression and exploitation of the populace would happen. There would be new dictators, new self-proclaimed saviors, and some even more depraved. As I thought of this, I had a glimpse of a world in which the evil that dominated us in so many ways was locked in battle with a new presence. What was it? A light shining in the darkness, an eternal denial of the substance of evil, reducing it to that imagined existence with no ultimate power. Always it must yield to the power of God. A thought flashed into my mind, the idea that His Holy One was the instrument, the one who would forever deny evil down the ages, and we who stood with him would be witnesses and partners. The issue wasn't just Israel; the present rulers were not the ultimate problem, but rather, the evil that continually tempted men, even good men, whole parties of well intentioned men, to become instruments of oppression and destruction.

I caught up with Jesus, who had continued walking, quite content to wait for the answer to his question, and I asked, "It's no longer just the Temple, is it? That was only the beginning. It's not just Annas and the rest of that crowd. They think they are your nemesis, but you are aiming beyond them to what is in the shadow behind. Your objective is not just for this time, it is for always, isn't it?"

"John, I knew you would understand. Yes, it is for all time and for all people everywhere. You remember the people in Capernaum saying everything I said made sense while I was there, but when I left, all their old fears came back? Well, I can't be there all the time, but I must be there for each of those people in some real way. Not just now and again, but for always. That was a major realization. Then there was that leper: 'If you want to, you can make me clean.' Of course I wanted to, I always want for every one of them. That desiring tires me out, it drives me on, but what they need is not to be recipients, but bearers of the very grace they seek from me. I want more for them than they can imagine. Did you see what happened to the others when I gave them power to heal and teach?

"The final piece fell into place in Tyre, when that Gentile woman asked for help with her daughter. I realized there were no limits to God's kingdom. You remember when I gave the bread to that crowd down by the lake? I am like that bread, and I am going to be available like that bread. Not just for the people of Israel, but for everyone; not just for this generation, but for all future generations."

This was too much for me. I stopped in the middle of the path, "No! Please, no, I can't bear the thought of what you imply." As I digested Jesus' words further, other questions came to mind. "Is this the struggle the Essenes write about? Is this the struggle between the powers of darkness and the children of light?"

"Yes, although they have never moved much beyond this temporal world with its warring elements. They do have a grasp of the fundamentals, but that is the easy part. Becoming the answer, being the sword point thrust at the heart of darkness is very different from dreaming and what-ifs."

"This is very difficult to grasp. You say that the doctors of the Essenes have some idea of what is to come, but in the next breath you say they have it all wrong. How do you expect us, the people who now follow you, to understand something like this?"

"That is a good question. They will get hold of the wrong end of the stick often, but you forget the point of all of this is that I will be there for them. If they get some of these ideas wrong or mistake what I say, that will not matter because the real objective is for them to experience me, then they will live my way, whether they have it all correct or not."

"But you keep saying you will be dead. I don't get it. How can you be there for any of us?"

Jesus nodded in resignation. "John, I know that is what will happen, but I don't know how it will work out in practice. I can only go step by step. The next step is to return to Jerusalem, face off against the powers of darkness and their representatives, and inevitably die. There is no more to be accomplished here. The next step has to be taken."

"You make it sound easy. You are talking about your own death. Dying is hard, and some of those same people in Jerusalem like to make it worse than it need be. Do you really want to go through with this?"

"John, these last few nights I have lain awake and been almost overcome with dread. I don't know that I can go through with it. The next thing I do is pray, and there is the conviction all over again. The other night on the mountain, I was able to think this through with help from our Father. Moses and Elijah came to me. They showed me what must happen. That helped enormously. This whole thing is not my imagination, a sick need to suffer or a need for self-glorification. Yes, I have thought of all those things. If you are sane, you have to consider the possibility of your own self-deception. I am not alone in this. This is not my idea, but the will of my Father. John, I don't want to do it. As we walk, I feel the sun, and I look out over this land and see the hills and the people. I really don't want to leave all this. Can you understand that? I love this land and all of our people. I don't want to go. I want to see the light glinting off the lake, or see the children playing in the shade of a tree. I want to hear the rain splashing down and see new shoots springing from the earth. The thought of leaving this is almost too much to bear. I love it so."

I could not answer this cry of agony. As I walked I found myself praying, "Our Father, who art in Heaven, Holy is your name, thy kingdom come, thy will be done on earth as in Heaven." The prayer he had taught us meant so much in that moment. His father and my Father, his God and my God. Could I let him go through with this? Could I pray that prayer, "Thy will be done"?

I looked at him and caught his eye as he turned his face to me, and I began to weep as we walked. It was all too much. The thoughts were unbearable. I thought of Mary, Martha and of others who loved this man. How could this be? I put my arm across his shoulders as we walked, and he squeezed my hand in appreciation.

From Capernaum we took the road by the lake, heading south towards Tiberius and beyond. Three miles north of Tiberius, Jesus asked how I was.

I shrugged, "You were right to forbid any weapons. Our appearance as an armed threat would have given the authorities excuse to put us down without a hearing. However, even if we can begin a dialogue with the High Priest or Sanhedrin, I don't see how we can hope to persuade Caiaphas and his whole family to give up their monopoly. I know only too well they are murderous and have no scruples about removing anyone who is a threat. They have all kinds of ways of doing it. I wonder about John the Baptizer. I think they wanted him dead, and he died. There are sicarii and intelligence operatives around us. I know everything we do gets back to them. They know we are coming, or will by the time we are halfway there.

"So how do I feel about everything? I am scared to death. I don't want to lose you. I don't want it to be all over. You are everything to me. I mean everything: Your dream for Israel, your clarity in making sense of the tangle of our religion and above all, the proximity of the divine when I am with you. Even when I sleep it is as if you are there, and even in nightmares you stand guard. I know that sounds fanciful, but that is what I experience.

"More and more, I am overcome with the sense of dread, a sense of gathering darkness. So how am I? Just fine. Like anyone walking into a trap or an animal climbing the altar steps to be sacrificed."

I looked across at Jesus, and he smiled faintly at me. "Well, that makes two of us. You have got it right. I know this is the right move. When we came north after Lazarus was raised up, I knew I would have to go back. I see this clearly now. As you and I have said several times before, there will always be people like those in Jerusalem who want to hold people to ransom and try to be gatekeepers between the people and God, but I am going to erect a gateway for any of our people. They will not need someone to do it for them; they will have me as their guide to present them directly to the Father. To those who are heavy laden, worn down and desperate, I will say, 'Come to me, I'll look after you. It's okay', and I will conduct them or even carry them into the presence of our Father.

"The whole of Israel is my flock, even those who seem to be far off, and no longer part of our nation."

His brave words didn't make me feel any better. "You did say earlier that there would be others from outside Israel. What of them?"

"Israel is the light of the world, that's why God made agreements with Abraham and Moses. You don't think all that was so we could be like spoiled children stuffing our faces with rich foods and taking no notice of those around us? No, we are the light to the world, and out of us comes a real beacon of hope for the world. Unfortunately the world doesn't know it needs one."

"But how? You know and I know those Temple people will either have you murdered quietly, or arrest you, or have you condemned on trumped up charges and stoned to death. They could even imprison you forever, lost to us and to everyone."

"That will not happen. I do not intend to leave them any wiggle room. They will have to declare themselves. The butchers will make one more sacrifice. I will be it. I mean what I say when I say no more sacrifices. I am going to stand in the stead of all those innocent animals, and if anyone wants purity, forgiveness or sanctity, it is to me they must come."

"Jesus, if anyone else said that to me, I would think they were crazy. How can you ever stop those sacrifices when most people still believe in them? Don't throw yourself away".

"If people think that a dead animal can do anything for them, and eating its meat can restore them to some other state, then we have to offer them our new way, that path we have been teaching. We have to offer them something better, as well as something they will understand. Maybe a final sacrifice, to end all sacrifices. If that is what is supposed to happen, then you bet I will have something to say about their state of grace."

"What do you mean grace?"

"My word to any person who comes to me in humility will be like olive oil on dry and cracked skin. You know I can do that because you have seen it often enough. Well, now we are looking at the day when that grace, that soothing presence, becomes available to anyone who seeks it. A peace that passes our understanding or conscious selves and brings wholeness and health to our feeling center, our souls and hearts. That is worth the effort."

I couldn't reply, I looked up and saw Tiberius not more than a half mile away. I said, "When you talk like this, all my fears go away. I am aware of standing in the presence of God, and knowing that this is His will. I can let go for now, but only just for now."

We went on in silence for maybe a hundred yards before I said, "Jesus, would you consider playing the whole thing quietly? Kind of keep a low profile and not be inflammatory."

Jesus smiled at me, "The fears didn't stay away for very long, did they?" I smiled tearfully at him. "No, I'm scared to death."

We came to Tiberius late in the afternoon and the people split up, looking for places to stay or food to buy. Most would find a place to camp in the fields outside the town. Jesus inevitably attracted a crowd of townsfolk who, knowing his reputation, came with people they wanted healed and questions for him to answer.

Soldiers were clearly present, including squads of uniformed and armed men.

One young man came, knelt before Jesus and asked what he had to do to gain eternal life.

Jesus raised him up from his kneeling position and motioned him to sit beside him. Then Jesus asked, "What does the law say?"

The young man thought for a moment and replied, "Well, thou shalt love the Lord your God with all your heart and with all your soul and with all your might and, love your neighbor as yourself."

Jesus nodded. "Do that and you will be all right."

"I have been doing that as hard as I can ever since I can remember, but there has to be more."

Jesus looked at him for a long time, searching his crestfallen face. Tears were not far away. Jesus shook his head a trifle and put his hand on the young man's arm. "You need to sell all you've got and join us on the way to Jerusalem. To really understand the Kingdom of God, there is something you need to see."

The young man looked stricken for a moment. Then he got up from the bench, mumbled a thank-you and went off through the crowd that parted before him. Jesus looked over to us and gave a little shrug of his shoulders as if to say, 'See, it's hard for some of them.' Then he went on with his message of hope to everyone that their sins were done with, and that they could find peace for themselves without killing, without more death.

We tried to keep the people from pressing in on him, for we were aware of a very real danger of violence as we headed south. An assassin's knife was not a far-fetched concern. Jesus went out into the crowd and embraced all kinds of people. Finally, he came back and sat on a bench under a spreading shade tree. We gave up trying to keep people away and just did as much crowd control as we could. A bunch of snotty-nosed children, drawn by the excitement, ran about, wriggling through the crowd until they were in the front row. Some of them even crawled between people's legs.

Jesus put his hand up as we tried to grab them and stop them from crowding him. "No, don't do that. Let them come to see me. Don't you know that none of you can enter the Kingdom of Heaven unless you are like one of these?"

I saw Simon Peter almost choke as he grabbed one little urchin, who gave him a huge smirk in response to our attempts to intercept him. Soon there were at least fifteen boys around Jesus, all scruffy, unkempt and wild. He welcomed them and started to talk to them gravely, and in response they began to ask questions. The townsfolk that stood around groaned at the questions, embarrassed and fearful Jesus would be insulted. Instead, he and the boys were in a discussion that Jesus was not leading. He just prompted them, and from them flowed a constant, excited jumble of ideas and thoughts.

James pushed through the crowd and passed Jesus some dried fruit. Soon the kids were eating and passing to each other the snack that James produced. Everyone grew quiet and relaxed. Jesus went on with his teaching about the place of Israel and how each of them was valuable in the eyes of God, each one of them a child of God.

Every time it happened I was amazed all over again. The crowd became joyful—even playful—in their participation, and Jesus basked in their warmth as one might bask in the winter sunlight after a cold night.

Suddenly there was a disturbance at the far edge of the crowd, which opened to allow a man through. He was wearing a splendid toga thrown over his shoulder. This was a Roman soldier, a Centurion, and the crowd sensed trouble. The people fell quiet; even the children withdrew. The disciples all stood up, not knowing whether to take up a defense of Jesus or try to give assurance we were a peaceful assembly.

Jesus alone stayed seated. The Centurion was saluted by the soldiers who had been standing observing us and who now assembled as a support squad behind their officer.

The Centurion stood before Jesus and asked, "Please help me. I have had reports of you being able to heal people, and I desperately need your help. It is not for me, but I have a servant who is going downhill fast. We have done everything we can but he is failing. I apologize for intruding like this, but we don't know what else to do." A townsman who had been watching everything quietly pushed through the inner fringe of the crowd and whispered to Jesus, who nodded and thanked him.

Jesus paused for a moment and said, "Of course I will come." He stood up and nodded to those around him.

The Centurion held up his hand. "No, I am a Gentile and I know you do not like to enter a Gentile's house, so just heal him from here. I am a man of authority, and I say to this person 'go,' and he goes, and to that person 'do this,' and he does it. You have similar authority, so just say the word and the sickness will leave, and my servant will be healed."

Jesus looked around him at the crowd, and finally looked at us, his disciples. "Now, that is faith. I have not met a better description of faith, not even in Israel." Turning to the Centurion, he continued, "Between us, we will make it so. The young man is going to be okay. Thank you for taking care of him and coming to find me. Your servant is better. Go in peace."

The Centurion stepped forward and took Jesus' right hand in his and shook it, as was the Roman way. He smiled, "Thank you," and made his way back through the crowd that opened before him. The crowd, which had been somewhat guarded, visibly relaxed; remarkably, there was a smattering of applause. The Centurion bowed a little in recognition of the crowd, made his way through and disappeared. I wondered what happened to the servant, but it was a long time before we heard of him again.

The people were delighted and I could see that, for a moment, Jesus was able to shake off the menace with which he was weighed down and allow himself to enjoy the contagious joy and good humor of the crowd.

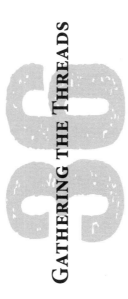

GATHERING THE THREADS

As we were making our way down the Jordan Valley towards Jericho, Annas sat in his palace and mulled over reports, thinking through scenarios and gauging the tempo of Jerusalem. In his diary, Annas kept a step-by-step account of how he stalked and trapped Jesus.

I have been revisiting the reports on that Nazarene's friends here in Jerusalem. Even those around the Lazarus family don't show any activity that I view as suspicious. Given their political leanings and their proclivity for being outspoken critics of Temple administration, I can only view their silence as suspicious.

Another report I have from my agent embedded with the lay Essene group here in Jerusalem has more promise. Their opposition to our administration has never wavered. However, I do see that they are incorporating some of that Nazarene's teaching in their discussions. They are a small but dedicated community that I know he has strong connections with. They also know many of the players on the list of those who support Jesus. In fact it was through Jesus' work they became connected. That is significant.

Most disturbing is their view on sacrifices. They, of course, do not honor our sacrifices at the Temple, but I see here there is discussion about all sacrifice. Otherwise, nothing to be alarmed about. I see they are observing the monastic vows of having everything in common: they observe all the excessive purity requirements. Nothing in any of this that surprises me.

This note at the bottom, though, gives me pause. "There is a suppressed excitement about the imminent arrival of the Messiah. There is no discussion of who, how or where this will happen." Now that is enigmatic. Do they know something we don't know? Why no speculation? It's this damned silence again. Nobody is saying anything.

My latest report from my agent shadowing the Nazarene in Galilee isn't as much more forthcoming. He speaks of the crowds, the teaching about caring for each other, upholding the law and fulfilling its intention rather than the letter. Nothing new there. I don't like the healings. Lepers, blind people and now epileptics.

Here is something. "His followers, who until now were over flowing with enthusiasm, are now beginning to question Jesus' leadership and direction." Now that is interesting. "Since the news of John the Baptizer's death, Jesus has changed direction and even warns his disciples about his own death." He doesn't have to be a prophet to see that coming. I think we can help him there.

"He has stated that in the event of his death, he will return to complete his mission." Yes, right, that I would like to see. I think our tougher stance with John is paying off. It has quite obviously unsettled those around him. He is clearly trying to buy them back. Do I see disintegration of his movement? Not yet, but maybe that is the way this will play out. In which case, we allow things to take their course and let him become another wandering windbag, uttering his pronouncements and being enjoyed for his entertainment value. That I like.

Still, there is more to this than is obvious at first glance. I think it is wishful thinking to believe this will all blow away. He has something else up his sleeve, but I don't see it. All along, his teaching has been within our accepted norms, but yet, I know, I just know, he is up to something. Why did he run away to Galilee after the Lazarus affair? Maybe he did not run away, but went to raise support from among Galileans. Thousands have been turning out, if this report is correct. Those damned Galileans are always ready to revolt against us here.

I remember his words from early on, almost seven years ago now. "Tear down the Temple and I will rebuild it in three days." I wonder what he meant by that? Whatever it was, I know he has not forgotten; he has it in for us. There is not much to do while he is in Galilee. Herod is likely to become one of his followers if I involve him.

His wife was useful in the case of John, but I don't want to go to that well twice. I know a couple of sicarii who would quietly murder him while he is up there in Galilee. They come cheap, and with other jobs I have asked them to do they were discreet, so I will get in touch with them. The other thing is to send word to my agents to keep tabs on the other players here in Jerusalem. If there is an upsurge in activity, that will give me warning.

I would prefer all this to blow over, but that is not realistic. I just know he is a serious threat. I wish I knew what he was after. I just don't get it. Then there are the dreams. Night after night he is there in the background. I know it is him, but I can't quite see him. He appears closer each time. Even in my dreams he is both a threat and not a threat. I must not let him get under my skin; I must not become obsessed with him. I wish I could get someone else to look after him. Maybe the Romans will. That would be the answer. They could deal with him, and I could wring my hands at Pilate's persecution of a good Jewish rabbi. Trouble is, he hasn't done anything that Pilate is interested in.

One thing I might do is check with Pilate's office. He hasn't come up from Caesarea yet, so Silvanus might be more forthcoming and give us more details of their surveillance. I know for a fact they have shadowed his work in Galilee. After all, Herod is their surrogate. I will send young Jonathon over there tomorrow. It is too late today.

Since that Lazarus thing, I have not looked forward to sleep. I must admit that Nazarene disturbs me, and when I sleep I am more vulnerable to his touch. Why did I say touch? Enough of this foolish thinking! I must get rid of him, there is no other way.

Four days later

I have another report from my agent up north. They are on the move. They have been sweeping up support from those coming to the festival and even encouraging others to accompany them. So that is his timetable. Let's see, Passover is in three weeks. Full moon was last week, so yes, three weeks.

There is no indication from this report of which way he is coming. That would be useful. Plenty of time for that. I bet it is the Jordan valley road. My two sicarii should meet up with him in the next week. I would rather it happen up there. Once he is in our area, an attack on him would set off just the kind of violence I am trying to avoid. Without him, though, we could weather any such storm well enough. I am not sure of the Romans. Would Pilate take advantage of any riots and weigh in with his troops to save us, then turn round and extract more concessions from us? That is a good point. We should do nothing to precipitate violence once he is past Jericho, if he comes that way. I am glad now that I had the forethought to tell those two to do the job north of the Galilean border or not at all.

Do I involve Caiaphas? I think not. I will wait until I hear from my sicarii. If they are successful, then that is an end to it. Caiaphas can't keep his mouth shut, and in any case, I would not like him to have anything to hang over my head. When I consider how he has recently been less amenable in our discussions and more independent, I have wondered whether he is thinking of making a break with me. Maybe even getting rid of me permanently. I would not put it past him. Maybe I should watch my back. That's my imagination; he doesn't have the stomach for anything like that. That is why I have had to do everything for him. I just love to see him fluttering his hands when we have to take some dramatic action.

However, I may just have to get rid of him and have somebody else take over as High Priest. I can work on that later. If someone has to take the fall for what happens to that Nazarene, then Caiaphas would be my candidate of choice. I like that. Maybe Pilate could be the tool whereby that would happen. What I would really like to do is stick it to Pilate, but there is no way I can get the Romans to do the job. I will have to be satisfied with Caiaphas. I am not sure how I am going to finesse this. There are supporters of the Nazarene in the Sanhedrin, and the majority of its members are Pharisees, so I do not see how we will accomplish what is necessary through the normal legal channels. I have time though. I think we have at least two, if not three weeks, so we can do a lot in that time.

Now the waiting is over, I feel better. Maybe I will sleep tonight. I wonder if little Tamara is still available. I haven't thought of that for months. That is a good sign. I

Damn, I've just had a note from the sicarii. They were too late. "Met up with target near Alexandrian. They are two hundred plus in the party. We have tagged along, but at your direction, avoided contact. We are now at Archelais. Subject is still gathering support. We will continue with him as far as Jericho."

Maybe I should have let them deal with him when they first met him. I know that would have been messy, but maybe less dangerous than letting him loose in the city. Having those two with him is comforting. Do I tell them to finish the job? It's too late. No, they will be at Jericho and have broken contact. The message has taken three days to get here; my reply would take another day or so to find them. No, by now the Nazarene will be in Jericho. I will probably hear about his arrival tomorrow, if not late this evening.

I was really hoping those two would finish it. He is coming. Damn, I should have just told them to get rid of him.

Next Day

I've just received another report from my agent in his party. My agent says, "He has as much as admitted he is, indeed, the Messiah." The report took at least five days to get here. I wish I had gotten it sooner.

Look at this! "So the secret is out. Ten days ago, on our way back from the coast, he asked us who we thought he was. One of us blurted out, 'You are the Messiah,' and just like that, he agreed. He definitely said he was. He is no longer talking in vague terms about the 'Son of Man,' not that any of us were taken in by that. I do not know what his intentions are. I think he is telling us one thing and planning another. The sanity of his teaching has given way to disturbing and contradictory statements. I no longer understand what he is about.

"Since his admission that he is the Messiah, he has been talking about how we must now come to Jerusalem. We should be there for Passover. We are joining pilgrims coming for the festival and persuading many others to join us. We are on the way down towards Tiberius right now. It looks as if we will pick up some more there.

"I've had difficulty finding a courier. I will try again tomorrow. There will be someone in Tiberius, I am sure."

Messiah! There it is in black and white. I definitely don't want to share that with Caiaphas. He would wet his pants, or worse, he would spread it around, and Jesus would have all the publicity he needed. By the time he got here, everyone would be in the streets waiting to welcome him. They have not forgotten Lazarus and all the other people who claim he healed them.

Is he the Messiah? Could he be? What have I been sensing all along? I knew he was dangerous, but is he, indeed, the Messiah? Do I, deep down, acknowledge or recognize him? Is that why he has alarmed me so for so long? Is that what the dreams are about? No! He can't be. From Nazareth? He has nothing, he has no power, no program, no timetable. As far as I know he has only attacked the Temple that once, and that was several years ago. Then there are the miracles. Some of them are probably true. There are other wonder workers, though. None of my advisors are worried about him; why am I so sure he is trouble? Some of them think I am senile. Some of the looks that pass between them when I speak of this issue tell me they think I am obsessed. Too right, I am obsessed.

I wish I had listened to him myself. I could have judged better what was going on. Instead, I relied on these reports from so-called reliable sources. Who is he?

I don't want to go to sleep tonight.

What is he up to?

I looked at those last words and smiled bitterly. I thought, "Annas, you blew it. You never figured it out, did you?"

87

THE LAST WEEK

I sat there on Patmos with the pages written by that poisonous person. I groaned aloud at the memories his writings brought back. From what he had written, I saw a profound awareness of the deeper issues at stake. If only he had grasped the moment instead of trying to stamp out the inevitable!

He is in Bethany. I just got word from one of my old friends with a villa there. Now what? The time is short. We are only a week away from Passover. Not even that. Two other reports have just come in. This one is from the Essene group here in Jerusalem. Their leader received a message this afternoon from the Nazarene. They expect him tomorrow. Plans are being made to meet him with a welcoming procession.

This is it. He is going to attack us. I knew it.

How many men at his disposal? Are they armed? Why does nobody report properly? All I have is that letter from the sicarii, that he had upward of 200 people, but that was a week ago.

This other report is much the same. "He is planning a triumphant entry and has arranged to rent a donkey for the day."

A donkey? That was King Solomon's mount when he rode to his coronation. Let me look it up. Where is that scroll? Here it is ... "And Zadok, the High Priest, took David's donkey and put Solomon on it. Solomon rode on David's donkey to the Temple and his consecration." He intends to be proclaimed King! That is his plan. His followers don't know it, but the mob will do anything he says, without thinking of the consequences. Pilate will go ape. Maybe not! What if Jesus has made contact with Pilate, and they are plotting to get rid of me? What if Rome has told him to get rid of me and establish a new priestly regime?

No. I would have heard. They would not do that. I am their best bet, and I give them valuable information about Herod and Philip and other activity around the area. I am too valuable to them. I could have gone over Caiaphas' head and made a deal with Pilate. Well, it's too late now. Perhaps it is for the better. It is not good to ask the Romans to do anything for you. You offer them your hand, and the next thing you know, they have swallowed your arm. No, we can handle this.

King? If Pilate does not know anything about this, then he might be interested to know what is going on. Maybe I should go see him tomorrow. No, he would do nothing, just to spite me. Better to leave him out of it for now; but if this Jesus fellow gets proclaimed King, I think we can use Pilate. I did notice a comment in one of the letters that none of the people were armed. So, he doesn't intend a violent rebellion, but he must be hoping for a rising of the general population.

Dammit, here we are on the verge of confrontation, and there is no indication what the plans. We can't arrest him if the crowd proclaims him King, but if he accepts, then we can move. Pilate would be there ahead of us, probably. However, if the people all proclaim him King, and he does not positively accept, then where will we be? He has to say it out loud in front of witnesses. What can I do?

First, I will have at least four people watching him at all times. I will need at least two clear witnesses who have unambiguous memories of what he said or did. There is another possibility. What if he manipulates the crowd to proclaim him High Priest to supplant Caiaphas? King is a huge stretch when you think of Roman politics, but would Rome be pleased to supplant Caiaphas, and, by inference, me also, with this upstart? He has been careful to not preach against the Romans. Pilate would go for a more moderate leadership in the Temple, for sure. There is no evidence for this. It's my overheated imagination. Maybe or maybe not, the answer is the same: we must get rid of him.

What is this? A note from my man in Pilate's office. Damn! Those sicarii have been picked up by the Romans. Apparently they were recognized and wanted for another crime. Will they keep their mouths shut? I wonder what Pilate had on them? Not that other job I asked them to do? No, I am safe there. This is a little unsettling. Pilate will string them up probably,

Caiaphas could look into it legitimately, even talk to Pilate about the case and wring his hands over them. I will just sit back and let everything take its course. I will only have to mention it to Caiaphas; he will jump at the chance to look inside Pilate's palace. Maybe he should bring it up when he goes to retrieve the vestments for the festival. What am I doing? I am just going to let things take their course.

This Messiah thing has really got me stirred up. Even a little thing like this gets me thinking and planning. I don't need to do it. I must disengage and let him come to me. Let him show his hand. I must take my time. Nobody else sees it.

Yesterday we headed a triumphal procession into Jerusalem. I am not sure what I expected, but there was no overt evidence of the Temple squads. Roman troops turned out, but since we did not appear to either be armed or intend to disrupt the peace, they stood aside and watched. Jesus took up his post in the Temple courtyard and people gathered around.

Philip and Andrew walked the donkey back. A mess of palm branches littered the road up towards Bethany, and as I watched, a swirling wind idly tossed some of them about, as if erasing the part they had played in the procession. I determined to look up Jonathon later in the day. I would visit his parents just before dinner time as I used to do; unless things had changed, he would be there. The occasional reports I had received from Jonathon had not told me much.

I wondered how my business was going. I had heard reports off and on during the year, and, as far as I could judge, it was still doing all right. My manager was more than willing to keep it going. No doubt he was doing a little business on the side on his own behalf. I noted my detachment about the store. My future lay elsewhere. I sat with my back against the wall of the portico, half listening to Jesus and keeping note of the crowd.

After an hour, Jesus got up and signaled to his disciples that we were on the move. I hastily got to my feet and began to tag along. I didn't hear the first comments, but one of our group from Galilee expressed surprise at the size of the stones and the incredible beauty of the Temple itself. I tended to take it for granted. I had lived with it for almost thirty years. I looked at the soaring walls and thought to myself that Herod had done a good thing. The whole place was beautiful and its proportions perfect. I felt pride in the place well up inside me again, and I thought that this was what made us Jews. This building, perched high up above the city, was the one thing we could be proud of. We had so little. There was no king, no royal palace except the Roman fort, and that didn't count. The Temple was a symbol to all of us in Jerusalem that there still was an Israel, and we still had a center.

It was then that I heard Jesus say, "All of this will be destroyed. All will be thrown down, and there will not be left one stone upon another."

What had been said? I tried to recapture the conversation, but I realized I had been thinking my own thoughts. I suddenly felt the rush of alarm at the thought of the destruction of this beautiful building, and I made sounds as if in protest.

Jesus, of course, heard me, although I was a good twelve feet away. He shrugged, "No, it is not God's will, and no, I am not going to contribute to it; but this whole place will be thrown down, and the nation will be no more, at least as we know it today."

"When will this be?" piped one of the men from Galilee.

"There are those standing here among you who will see it. It will be in your lifetime. You ask what the cause is for its destruction; the cause is hardness of heart, stiff-necked self-confidence, and stupidity. I've said this before: you can't turn the months and years back to another time long gone. We must carry the new Israel onward through these growing pains. Don't you see the signs of that day? The work of a few troublemakers keeps the pot boiling now, but when more powerful leaders use the anger of those men to enlarge the conflagration of the crowd's passion, then war will break out. Can't you see the signs?

"It's no different when you look at the sky and see a blazing red sunrise, and you say, 'There is a storm coming,' or if you see the changes in the season and you say, 'Summer is coming.' Well, in the same way, read the signs of the times. People make their own futures, and this generation is crafting its inevitable demise. I am their last chance but they will have none of me. What pains me is that the people who will suffer will be those who always suffer: the wives, mothers and those who are expecting will suffer the most. The poor and those who have no way to escape the chaos will pay the initial price. I tell you though, that when the fire has consumed all those, it will not stop until the whole nation is consumed, and those belonging to the Temple will be gone, all those who take up the sword will die, and even those Essenes who look for the day of the Lord will be swept away.

"Religious folk, in their folly, will mislead the people with their prognostications, superstitions and ideologies. None of them speak for the Almighty. People believe them, and they forget what they have heard from me. Only those who reject the violent course of action will survive. So, I tell you, when that time comes, leave the city. Don't think of tidying up or selling off your belongings. Get out. Leave. No second thoughts. Don't even go back for your coat."

I had heard similar warnings before, but today, back in Jerusalem after so long, I felt overwhelmed with sadness as I looked at the city through Jesus' eyes. I felt his frustration, his grim far-sightedness that seemed to see and hear the actions of men not yet born. Dread settled over me.

Jonathon was waiting for me at his parent's house. I felt relieved to sit in an ordinary house with friendly ordinary people who were glad to see me. We hugged each other with delight and sat down with a cup of wine and some delicate pastries to nibble on. I began to describe what I had seen in Galilee, but decided to just say we had returned for the festival. There was no way I could explain Jesus' expectation of his death and somehow ushering in the Kingdom. If it didn't make much sense to me, it would only confuse Jonathon. I certainly couldn't explain it.

Jonathon began to fill me in on developments in Jerusalem. "You may have been buried up there in Galilee, but, I assure you, old Annas has been following you every step of the way. Be careful. He intends to get rid of Jesus. I know it."

"He thinks Jesus intends to make a move, during the festival, to be crowned King or High Priest. He thinks Jesus will use the crowds to achieve a bloodless coup without the Romans getting involved. He is obsessed with Jesus.

There is another thing that you should know. He wrote to Herod's wife to get rid of John the Baptist. That whole episode from John's arrest to his death came out of Annas' office. That is not all. He has had Jesus shadowed all the way down from Galilee by at least two sicarii. I dropped their names to Silvanus in Pilate's office as wanted criminals. They are now out of the way, but I think their orders were to murder Jesus if they got the chance. That is how serious things are. Annas does not intend Jesus to survive the festival."

Our conversation stopped abruptly when Jonathon's mother came in from the cooking area and began laying out dishes. With what Jonathon had said, and the expectations Jesus had expressed, my hopes plunged. Jesus was right. The conflict was inevitable. Jesus would not run, nor would he fight, but stand there like a sacrifice waiting to die.

28
ANNAS' QUANDRY

As I read these pages I at least get some satisfaction from Annas' frustration. I wondered what would have happened if Caiaphas had told Annas to go back in his hole. Would things have turned out differently?!

I've just about had enough of Caiaphas. He came in today alarmed and all of a flutter over the arrival of the Nazarene. What does he think I've been trying to tell him about for twelve months?!

"What should we do? What if he marches against the Temple? Do I think he is the Messiah?"

Damned fool, we get rid of him, if he is! Caiaphas is fine at running the place, but he has no grasp of what we face here or how finely balanced everything is.

The Nazarene came into Jerusalem riding on a donkey as if he were Solomon riding to his coronation. All the crowds went out to cheer him into the city.

I must hand it to him, because he was so careful to have no display of weapons or rebellious rhetoric. There was nothing one could latch onto. Poor Caiaphas is bewildered. Well, I am not. Tomorrow he will be smack in the middle of the Temple, teaching, preaching and pulling his miracle tricks. He is not going away this time. He has come to stay. He will exert constant pressure, wearing us down by his law-abiding reasonableness. There will be no sign of rebellion or criticism of Rome.

I can just see it now. Week in and week out he will weave a web around us here that will be full of sweet reasonableness, but in the end the people will either pull us out of this place and murder us all, or, worse still, ignore us. They will refuse our services; no more sacrifices, no more taxes, no more respect and no more fear of us.

No! We must act fast. Our mistake last time was we let him call the tune. He kept escalating the pressure, both in his teaching and his healings. Finally he did that raising of Lazarus. I still think he faked that.

He will do the same again until he has the whole of Jerusalem in his hands. He could do it by Passover. I am sure his timing includes using the festival. There is a reason he happens to come back just in time for it. We cannot let him get into his stride. The question is how?

My two sicarii are out of the game. They will be lucky if Pilate doesn't string them up.

No, I think that a surreptitious accident would not be politic. We have to do it openly and spin the reasons afterwards. Wringing of hands, regret, no doubt an imposter, in league with the evil one—that kind of rumor should be spread. I think it important that many different reasons are given, so that there is no one thing to be refuted. We create uncertainty, so that there will be a cloud of doubt surrounding him.

If I give it some thought, we can have everything in place by the end of the week. Tomorrow, I will talk with Caiaphas. I will tell him he was right to be concerned, and having thought things over, I agree we should take action.

I think I will set it up so Caiaphas can take full credit for his quick action and the fall, if things go wrong. Maybe it's time he just took the fall. I have a lot to do tomorrow.

Next Day

So the Nazarene is following the path I expected. He is doing lots of teaching and healing but making no big political statements. Nothing to upset Pilate, though I bet he's had full reports by now.

Tomorrow I will go and listen to him. I want to see him with my own eyes and listen to what he's got to say. I should have done this before. I will go disguised and be a part of the crowd. I'll take some muscle with me just in case.

I must give him a chance to either utter blasphemy or come out with criticism of Caesar. My preference is to use Pilate, if I can. If we go the blasphemy route, there will be a trial, there will be arguments for the defense, long drawn out deliberations, and the Pharisees in the Sanhedrin will never vote to get rid of him. That would all take at least a week, and who knows what the people would do in that time. That could precipitate the kind of disaster we must avoid at all costs. We must not leave anything to chance, or he will wriggle out of our grasp, and the next time will be even harder. This has to be final.

Pilate can get the job done quicker and cleaner. He hates me, suspects me and will do nothing to help. After the games I've played on him over the last seven years, and the way I have embarrassed him, I cannot expect him to co-operate.

Rome is too far away. We need this resolved soon. Herod might be useful. He will be here this week.

Second thoughts? I don't think so. Stories are that Herod is still haunted by John the Baptist. I doubt whether he would be willing to do that again. No, Herod has a superstitious streak in him; he could fall for Jesus, and where would we be?

Murder is still the easiest to set up, but the consequences would be uncontrollable and, in any case, I would be in the power of whoever I got to do it. Even if I were two or three places removed from the actual deed, I know responsibility would be laid on the Temple steps. Caiaphas and others would know who was responsible, and it might give them the weapon they need to hold over my head. However, that might be a risk I will have to take.

My best bet is to listen to the man himself, and I can better gauge what I need to do. Strange, all this time I've worried about him, studied his moves, even had reports on his teaching but I've never met him. Well, at least not in real life. He has been in my dreams more than once. I wonder if I will recognize him from that?

No! I don't need to go down that path again.

29 Teaching in the Temple

The second morning we were back in Jerusalem, Jesus led us into the Temple precincts and we settled in our familiar corner.

Within minutes a small crowd had gathered, and a typical interchange began. There were questions, and Jesus carefully and respectfully taught from those openings people gave him.

Into this familiar and warm meeting of minds intruded a file of clergy. By their dress they appeared to be Temple Sadducees. There was a lull in the conversation as they picked their way through the crowd and halted in front of Jesus. In the silence that followed, looks were exchanged between the clergy, as if to signal their leader to take the planned action.

Their leader stepped forward and began, "Rabbi, we have heard you teach there is a resurrection of the dead, and we would like to ask you to clarify some concerns we have over how the resurrection works."

Jesus settled back against the wall and nodded. He looked from one to the other and I noticed a very faint smile of anticipation flicker across his face. "I am sure you do have questions. What is the particular concern you have?"

The leader took a deep breath, looked at his compatriots and began, "There was a man who had seven brothers. He was married but had no children. He died, and, as is our custom and law, his brother married the widow to raise up children to his brother. He also died before there were children, and so the next brother married her. Each brother died in turn. Finally, after marrying all seven brothers, the woman also died. Our question is, at the resurrection, whose wife will she be?"

The young man looked around at his friends with barely disguised glee. They all smiled in anticipation at Jesus' humiliation. They should have known better.

Jesus said, "At the resurrection, she will be nobody's wife. There will be no marriages. Women will stand before God on their own account. They will not need husbands or other relatives as mediators before our Heavenly Father."

There was silence all around as the assertion sank in, then there was a hubbub of conversation between individuals as the significance of this became obvious. One of the young Sadducees started to ask a question, but Jesus silenced him with a slow shake of his head, saying, "Women will not need men to intercede for them. Sinners will not need you priests to intercede for them, nor will the people need you to declare them clean. They will all stand before the Almighty in their own right and not need your help.

"Everyone who understands this and takes their freedom in their own hands will be free. If anyone hears my voice and understands what I am saying, and lets it be so for them, they will appear before our Heavenly Father on their own account, whether they are men or women, sinners or righteous, rich or poor. You are not needed anymore."

These last words were directed at the file of clergy. Incredulity darkened the faces as the full import of Jesus' words dawned on the priests. One of them strode purposely off towards the Temple offices. The rest, nonplussed, made their way through the crowd. Smiles and gibes by people in the crowd grew to general laughter and derision at their discomfort.

Jesus sat surrounded by people. He said, "There was a man who built a vineyard from scratch—walls, terraces, tower, and wine press—then planted it with vines. He let it out to a company of men who would look after the vines, harvest the grapes, make the wine and give him a fair return on his investment. Everything went fine until the second year, when there was a good harvest. His servant returned empty-handed and reported a bunch of excuses from the company tenants for not making any payment. So the owner sent two others. They came back, having been beaten up. This went on for a while, and so finally he sent his son, thinking they would listen to him.

"The stupid tenants said to themselves, 'This is the heir. Let us kill him, then we will inherit the place.'

"Any one of you can predict what the owner of the vineyard would do. He took a squad of his men, cleaned out that nest of no-goods and found someone else whom he could trust to take over the lease."

The Sadducees, who had withdrawn to the edge of the crowd, said, "Surely not!"

Jesus said, "Yes, you've heard the expression 'the stone which the builders rejected has become the cornerstone, that stone on which all else is aligned and leveled.' Well, you're looking at the new cornerstone."

A couple of hours later, a delegation of Pharisees assembled before Jesus. Our friend Nicodemus was among them. I think they had heard about the rout of the Sadducees, and now they came with their own concerns. The senior of them made three attempts to get started, and finally, as if with an apology, asked, "Rabbi, we have this problem regarding taxes. We have to handle Roman money, and we have to collect the taxes for them. Our people are asked to acknowledge the overlordship of Caesar. The Romans even talk of Caesar as if he is a god, and they would love it if we would sacrifice to him as they do. We cannot and will not do that, but should we be even paying taxes to Caesar, especially with their idolatrous images on the coinage?"

There was silence in the crowd as everyone considered the possibilities and consequences. Jesus finally spoke, "Anyone have a denarius? Thank you. Now tell me, whose head is this on the coin? Yes, that's right, it's Caesar's head. What I tell you and tell everyone, 'Give to Caesar what is Caesar's and give to God what is His.'

Nicodemus stood there with a smile all over his face as if to say, "I told you so." The rest took a moment to digest the idea, then, one after the other, began to smile. Finally the old Pharisee who had been their spokesman said in relief, "You've spoken well."

The people in the crowd turned to each other and exchanged comments. A noisy hubbub arose, and the tension among the people diminished. There were smiles and nods. They understood.

However, noticeable among them were some individuals who were clearly upset at the idea of giving anything to Caesar. There was a knot of men who looked anything but pleased. One of them asked when the

Messiah would come and lead everyone in to the war that would bring this age to completion and introduce a new kingdom.

Jesus said, "Listen, you go on looking for that day, and it will come. I told my disciples this yesterday. Look around you and all that you see will be thrown down because of the stupidity and hardness of heart of religious bigots. There are those among you who will see it. When that day comes, you don't want to hang around. Leave! There are those among you who long for that day. Well, they will get it. They will bring it upon themselves. There will be such suffering that it will be worse than when the Babylonians destroyed the city. There will not be a stone left on another.

"There is no Messiah coming that will lead you in battle. There is no day of reckoning for the other nations. There is only the hardness of heart of those who would lead our nation into temptation, into suffering and destruction. The Kingdom of God is not of this world. How many more ways do I have to say it? Violent and dogmatic men will try to force their way into the Kingdom. It's no good talking to them, for they hear but they will not listen. They read the prophets and use them to buttress their own desires. They think that if they make a big enough mess, God will justify them and come to their aid. God will not! Listen to the prophet Amos. 'You want the day of the Lord? Well, you will get it, but it will be a day of darkness, of deep darkness and not light.' Put these hopes far from you."

The knot of men who had attracted my notice began to withdraw, pushing their way silently through the crowd. Jesus glanced in their direction and sorrowfully shook his head. "How often do you think your Heavenly Father has sought to bring you home to himself? Always some stiff-necked religious zealot leads everyone in the opposite direction. When someone comes claiming he is the Messiah, don't believe him. If someone says the Messiah is in the house or over there, don't believe it. Many will come who think they are the Messiah, and they will try to convince everyone else that they are. Don't follow them!"

Later that night we withdrew to Bethany. I accompanied Jesus as he went out into the dark hillside for his prayer time. He said to me, "You know, John, people don't want war. They don't want rebellion. Did you see how those crowds reacted today as I responded to the Pharisees' question? These people have suffered enough. Our people have suffered enough. The people don't care whether they have to handle Roman coins. I doubt whether many of them would mind taking some oath of loyalty to Caesar. What matters to them is that they have peace and can see their children grow up.

"The real enemies are those who want to ignite the passions of our people and then manipulate them. The crowds are easily frightened, angered and led to take actions that cannot be undone. The consequences pile on consequences until circumstances crush the people once more.

"Within your lifetime, all that," and he waved his hand towards the Temple silhouetted on the horizon, "will be swept away. There are ideologues and intemperate people who think they know how everything should be, and they will lead the people into suffering the consequences of their stupidity.

"Oh, John, I am crushed by what I see coming. I am their one chance for peace and a new beginning, but they will not listen. The various leaders and factions will bring upon themselves destruction and suffering worse that anything Israel has seen before.

"As for me, I must be got rid of. I told you my death was necessary. Now you can see that my death is part of the blindness that afflicts these people. I cannot be different. Like the waves battering a headland, these various contingents of religious ideologues are going to try to overwhelm me. They will, for a moment, but like the rock emerging from the waves, I will rise once again."

Silence gathered in the darkness, and I looked out over the Kedron Valley towards Jerusalem, which sprawled over that historic mountain. Beside me Jesus muttered, "I am the cornerstone they will stumble over, the rocky headland that breaks the waves into wild spray. I am the light, I am truth, and I am like the pascal lamb of Passover: gateway to freedom, doorway out of this perpetual nightmare people are forced to live."

"But—" I began.

"No buts, John! Yes, they will kill me, but I will be back. They will kill many who follow in my footsteps down the years, but all those will be mine too; they will be mine forever. Now I must pray. Sit here and watch for me."

With that he turned away, knelt between the rocks and began his nightly prayer.

So this was what Annas saw when he met Jesus! I turned the page and read on. I smiled to myself at the memories of Jesus running rings round those sent to argue against him.

Wednesday

I met him yesterday. I was just another old man on the edge of the crowd. Nobody seemed to know me. I don't know whether I am pleased about that or upset that I am now forgotten. What I saw today is alarming and puzzling.

I watched one of our young lawyers take him on. The Nazarene had been expounding on the notion of loving your neighbor. Personally, I think I would have told the imposter that we already had that all laid out for us in the book of Deuteronomy, and we didn't need help with it, but the lawyer had to go on and on with him about it. Finally he asked, "Who is my neighbor?"

I thought that was a reasonable question, because it narrowed the issue down to a specific application or should have done. Instead, that confounded man began to tell the story of some fool who on his way down from Jerusalem to Jericho got himself rolled. One of our priests came by and saw him. Quite rightly he avoided any contact with the man and went on his way. A Levite also of the Temple did the same. I could see where this was going. He didn't mention their need to keep themselves clean for their duties, or explain at all why they had to avoid possible contamination by a dead man.

Instead, he introduced a Samaritan who took the victim to an inn, paid for him to be looked after, and even then said he would be back to check on him. On the face of it, it is a nice story about what the people should do. But, no! He has to make it an attack on us. Here we are trying to do our job, and he makes our rules an occasion for ridicule. Worst of all, he all but said out loud that even a Samaritan knew who his neighbor was, and by inference, we don't! In other words, our lawyer didn't know who his neighbor was and had to ask a question to which even a Samaritan had the answer.

He asked the poor fool of an attorney, 'which of the three saw the man on the ground as his neighbor?' I wanted to scream at him not to answer, but I couldn't draw attention to myself.

"The Samaritan," he mumbled. Could he not see that this Jesus, by inviting his collusion, got him to undermine our authority? Jesus couldn't have made it worse if he had said that the Samaritans know the law better than we servants of the Temple. Those people all knew what he was saying under cover of that story. At least they laughed as if they understood.

I heard him tell the people that the spiritual authority centered on our Temple will be taken away from us. Others will take our place. The intimation is that the Almighty will do all this. Who does he think he is?

My conclusion is that he does not intend to offer us the opportunity of putting down a rebellion. There is nothing that would stand up in court, or that would stir the Romans to take action. However, he constantly attacks our credibility and essentially denies our integrity, authority or function. This can't go on.

He is building support. All his teaching is down-to-earth so that the riff-raff can understand it. I watched the faces of the people. They were not whipped up or angry rebellious faces, but thoughtful. I've just put my finger on what is disturbing me. If he was talking civil war I could handle him, if he was talking civil rebellion I could deal with that, but teaching the people to think is dangerous indeed. We have to do the thinking for them. What does a crowd in a town square know of the intricacies of our religious duties? I can see that, if we don't put a stop to him, he will indeed destroy our whole edifice. We've spent centuries erecting this edifice of law, rites and practices. People will think for themselves and no longer respect our authority. How to stop him?

I saw some of our people try to argue with him. He ran rings round them. Worst of all, the people laughed. They dared to laugh at the young priests even though they were dressed so that nobody could have mistaken who they were. This will ruin us. He appeals to common sense, but how can the thoughts of the herd aspire to understand the unknowable mysteries of the divine. He spoke with familiarity of things that should not be mentioned.

Even the Pharisees are eating out of his hand. They don't understand how he is undermining the whole foundation of our national identity. What center will there be left if the Temple loses the respect of the people and no longer can command their obedience? What would we have if everyone were expected to do what he thought was right?

If I understood him correctly, he also advocated the destruction of the foundations of our culture. 'Women will not need a man to stand before God for them'. I even saw women in the crowd listening to him; as if they could possibly understood what he was saying! There was a couple of beggars sitting, listening and nodding away as if they understood.

This popularization of our belief is treasonable. Gone will be all the commands and customs with all their intricate requirements. Instead we will be faced with a demand to serve the people. Instead of them serving us, we will be expected to pander to their needs. The people are there for the sake of the Temple, which, in its turn, is there to honor the divine.

If we let this happen we will lose the lynch pin holding our nation together. We don't have a King nor are we in command of our own existence. We are at the mercy of Gentiles, who deny our existence as a nation. They allow us to worship in our own way because we make too much trouble if we are stopped. If this Jesus has his way, the heart of who we are will be taken away, and the little identity we have left as a nation will be lost. Jerusalem will become one more city and not the city of the Most High God.

Those Samaritans would like to see that.

I am glad I saw him. Now I understand the danger I have sensed all this time. He is not crazy like so many of the doom and gloom club, neither is he using the base instincts of the people, but calling them forth in a different way. What was the phrase I heard . . . "responsible for their own salvation," was it? At least he called on those who had understood his rigmarole to take responsibility for their actions before the Almighty. That would not last long. You have to have spiritual control over the population, or else everyone is worshipping as they want. Soon your have every weird abomination of the Gentiles, sharing the honors with the God of Israel.

When I think of it, he is much worse than John the Baptizer. I should have got rid of Jesus and not him. People would have got tired of John's tirades, but I can see people do not get tired of this man. At one point he looked right at me. We have never met, so that he could not have recognized me, but I am sure he knew me. He recognized me in some way, and he invited me to understand him. He wanted me to go along with him. I think he knew me as his enemy, but he still invited me. Later on in the morning I noticed he looked for me again and sought my response once more. I am not imagining this.

Why would he invite me to understand him or to hear what he is saying? I would have thought he would try to hide his agendas, but this morning when he looked at me it was as if he was inviting me to see everything as if he had no secrets, and what he was saying was what he meant. So what is he hiding? I think he is like one of those Egyptian magicians, they ask you to watch one hand carefully and then do the trick with the other.

Maybe there is another layer to this. He must know we are capable of getting rid of him. Why is he so open? What happens if we lay hands on him tonight or maybe tomorrow, and he unleashed a horde of angels on us? That is a stupid thought and nothing more than superstition. I refuse to accept this wanderer from Galilee is any kind of Messiah. He has been at it for almost seven years. He is here to stay unless we get rid of him. That is the bottom line. Tomorrow, I must put in motion plans to look after the Nazarene. I need evidence of some kind. Pilate is the only one to be able to carry out a quick sentence, but to accomplish that I have to come up with evidence of treason. I have to build my case around his admission he is the Messiah. We've got the entry into Jerusalem, that would have to be explained in three letter words to that fool Pilate, but even he cannot ignore the implications of what was being portrayed. I need more evidence of treason, and that he is claiming to be King of Israel. Pilate could never allow any such challenge to Caesar to go unpunished, and there is only one sentence for treason. Not only that, but for such a crime, there is no waiting period. The sentence is carried out immediately, unless he is a Roman citizen. There is no appeal or excuse for people like this impostor.

The next thing is when and how. It will have to be at night. There must be no hint of what we are planning. Maybe I will not even tell Caiaphas. If he knew, then half of Jerusalem would know. I must look after this myself.

Next, we get him back here, have a hearing that provides us with public accusation by witnesses that he claims to be the Messiah, King of Israel, and I give him to Caiaphas with instructions to march him off to Pilate. We provide Pilate with the witnesses and the accusation, then he will have to do the rest.

I must stay in the background, for if Pilate got wind that I was involved, he would not go along with it. I like this. I get Caiaphas to front the operation and get Pilate to do the final deed. The Nazarene will be gone and I will wring my hands over the untimely death of a son of Israel. I like it.

All I need is evidence. I will have to work my contacts tomorrow.

40

Final Preparations

Jesus beckoned me, and again we walked down the slopes of Gethsemane to the olive groves. This evening, Jesus led me to an olive press, perched himself on the wall and in the darkness began to speak.

"John, I am not sure I can go through with this. You heard me today talking about the suffering and pain that would result if the nation continued on its present path. Well, they will continue. I know it. There is no stopping their slide to disaster. Our people are going to be butchered, and everything will be destroyed.

"I have not reached them. There is no turning back for me, but I have not convinced them,. Why did I think I could?

"John, there is a part of me that so desires to save our nation, but the other part of me knows I cannot. All those visions by the Essenes of the Almighty coming and rescuing us and establishing a kingdom centered on Jerusalem are nonsense. Yes, nonsense! There will be no kingdom set up. There will be no Jewish King. That is all vain nostalgia for days long gone.

"My kingdom is not of this world. I don't know what it is to be. I don't know how to describe it to you any better than I have already, but the fools here don't get it. There is no hope for any of us according to our old dreams and hopes.

"There is a new Kingdom all right but the one I am talking about is for everyone who will bend their knee in worship and love of God and serve every person everywhere. It's a kingdom of the soul.

"Tomorrow night I want to eat Passover with everyone. My mother, Mary Magdalene and the other women, Lazarus and his sisters, Simon Peter and all those from Galilee should be there. I want to have you all with me. I know it isn't Passover until the next day, but I will not be here. Could you look after the arrangements for the room? Why not ask Tendratus. His group of Essene followers has a good-sized room they assemble in. Don't tell the others about it. If Tendratus can let us have the room, I will have others put the meal together. My mother and the other women will help, I am sure, but I don't want Simon Peter and the rest of them to be involved.

"The Essenic brotherhood can be trusted to keep their mouths shut, but others cannot. Don't ask Judas for the funds, talk to Lazarus tonight. He can give us what we need, and the women can shop for everything in the morning. In fact, we should be getting back if we want to catch Lazarus before he goes to bed."

We got up and began the ascent back up through the garden to Bethany. The ancient olive trees hung their feathered, silvery branches along the path and caressed us as we passed. The moon was just about full and was rising behind the villages to the east, silhouetting them, but leaving us still in shadow. Our path was a faint ribbon of white in the darkness. Protests and questions swirled around my mind, but I could not contest Jesus' resolution or defy his will. I went on in silence, climbing behind him and in the darkness followed the faint gleam of his clothed form. Looking back over the years since that moment, I realize I have been following that same shape going on ahead of me, year in and year out.

In my hand I have more pages of Annas' scribblings. As I read them I realize with crystal clarity the intricate trap Annas wove, not only to ensnare Jesus, but to use Pilate and to leave Caiaphas to hold the bag. It was diabolical.

I think I have my answer. My agent, who has shadowed the Nazarene, made contact last night. He was definitive. Jesus has claimed openly to his disciples that he is the Messiah. In fact he has described himself as the Holy One of God. Not only that, but he has spoken openly about establishing his Kingdom.

My problem is Judas does not want to stand as a witness. I've got enough background evidence of his stated intent to destroy the Temple, and also we can stretch some accusations to give a little more solidity to our charges than might otherwise be deduced. That will not be enough. My only hope is to get him to confess. Maybe, if I set him up, he would make the claim in front of everyone. I will have to pressure him to admit that. If he just stays silent, I will have difficulty making the case.

Thinking back to what I saw yesterday, I think he might rise to the bait if I challenge him. If I came right out and asked him if he was the Holy One of God, His Messiah, he would bite. There is that episode in our histories when David is praying, and God replies and promises David that his son would sit on his throne, and he would be God's son and God would be a father to him. I wonder if I could use that to describe his relationship with the divine. A whiff of that kind of talk would get me to my first objective. I can depend on everyone to condemn him right there.

With the family behind me, I will have him sent on to Caiaphas, who should not be at the trial, I think. Best if I give him a heads up; I will send Jesus to him, already condemned for blasphemy according to our law. That way I don't think Caiaphas will have any scruples about taking the next step. If I can get the family to come together behind the condemnation for blasphemy, then he will feel confident about going to Pilate.

Now, the charge Caiaphas has to make against the Nazarene must be that he is claiming to be King of Israel, that he intends to lead a coup against Pilate and to set up his own Kingdom here. It is revolt against Caesar and Roman rule, no less. That's it.

I think I can trust Caiaphas with that. The trouble is, there is little extant evidence that Jesus has made such a claim publicly. My extraction of that confession is going to be key. Armed with evidence obtained publicly, Caiaphas can make the assertion well enough. The whole company of clergy who witness his confession will go with Caiaphas and give evidence if needed.

What happens if Pilate asks Jesus outright? He will. He will have to. He will have to ask whether he pleads guilty or not. This is the crux of the whole exercise. If he believes he is the Messiah and King of Israel, then he will have to say so. If he says no and denies it, we are able to discredit him. In other words, he ducked and lied. Of course, if he wants to go that route, we let him scurry away with his tail between his legs. That would be just as good as having him executed. We could make him a laughing stock to the riff-raff, and totally destroy his credibility.

There is the probability Pilate will examine Jesus more closely than we would like. If he gives Jesus the opportunity to explain his position, maybe Pilate will throw the whole thing back in our court. There is the danger he will say it is a religious matter, and we should deal with it. If that happens, we are back to square one. There will be a long trial, witnesses for the defense, the Pharisees involved and his powerful friends will weigh in. There is no certainty we could even get a conviction, let alone a death sentence. No, we cannot allow Pilate to duck out.

Pilate has been declared a "Friend of Caesar," I know that means a lot to those professional bureaucrats. He has received recognition for his work here, in spite of my efforts. Quite clearly we can make the point directly to Pilate that he would be allowing to go free a seditious and dangerous figure, who was endeavoring to claim the throne of Israel for himself and supplant Caesar in the area of not only Judah but the other Tetrachies. We can make the point that he has preached and created support organizations in each of the four political areas. Now, that would be regarded as a serious threat to Rome, since we lie athwart the trade routes to the east.

I think if I instruct Caiaphas to remind Pilate that if he doesn't look after Jesus permanently, Caesar will hear about it, and that it will be a real blot on his career. Pilate will get the message. So that is the way this whole thing needs to go. Everything will hinge on me getting a confession from him in public. I think with plenty of witnesses we can push this thing through. I was really annoyed when I heard Pilate had been honored with that title, "Friend of Caesar," but now I think it could be the leverage we need. I must tell Caiaphas to keep it in reserve.

This is a good night's work. That information was well worth thirty talents. Judas' co-operation will not be needed after tomorrow night. Insisting he lead us to Jesus will tie him to us more tightly. I don't want him changing his mind once he sees what we propose to do. Telling him we were going to arrest the Nazarene in order to have a series of hearings and a public trial was a good idea. That man has changed these last few years. Five years ago, none of this would have worried him, but now I really think he is concerned about what will happen to Jesus. He just wants Jesus stopped. "He has gone too far," was his way of putting it. Well, whatever his reasons, I think we need to keep him involved and tied to us. We could have one of our people follow Jesus tomorrow night, and just beat down the doors wherever he is staying and arrest him. Getting Judas to lead us to him will mean he has taken the first public step in setting all this in motion. A tender conscience in a traitor can be dangerous. If he proves a problem, we can always get rid of him. I wonder if Jesus has got to him? Did he really become a disciple and not just pretend?

I think I have put together a plan that should achieve what we need and leave us with little responsibility for his death. There will be rumors, but they cut two ways. I think a thorough campaign of disinformation about him needs to accompany all of this. He was in communication with the powers of darkness; he was a fake. The healings were faked, with people pretending sickness. That kind of rumor will go a long way in mitigating any major public outcry. They don't have to be true, so long as there are many of them; that way a cloud of suspicion will defuse any attempt for opposition to coalesce around his death. Maybe an official declaration that we acted just in time to thwart serious rioting that would have brought the Romans down on everyone.

That is enough for tonight. The time is set for late night tomorrow after everyone is off the streets. Judas will be here and do his part. Tomorrow all I have to do is make sure Caiaphas is on board and knows his part. That's it. Now I must get some sleep, but I fear I am too wound up for that. Maybe if I read some of that material the Essene brothers have been writing I would drop off. What a bunch of nonsense. I wonder what their response will be to us disposing of Jesus. I know some of them are thick with him and his followers. Enough! I must let it go. Who cares what they think. I can deal with that tomorrow.

Annas left nothing to chance. As I read the lines of his scrawl, I realize all our agonizing was pointless. Annas had set the wheels in motion of a monstrous plan, and none of us could have done anything, even had we known.

41

The Last Supper and Jesus' Arrest and Trial

Last night—Wednesday—we spoke to Lazarus, and as usual he quietly and efficiently provided us with the resources to cover the cost of the Passover meal. After everything was settled, I walked back into the city and to my apartment.

The next morning, I could view nothing with pleasure. I was not hungry. I could not face the bread and fruit I had bought the previous day. Neither did I feel inclined to wash or otherwise prepare for the day. I had to talk myself through the ordinary habits of the morning.

My first task of the morning was to get the room settled. I felt I was slogging through the mud found down by the Salt Sea. We had told the women with us about the plans for the evening. They would know what to do without any guidance from me or anyone else. I remembered from last night their excited concurrence when we announced the plans for the Passover feast to be celebrated this evening. I groaned to myself as I realized afresh that they did not know. They had no idea what was coming.

Judas had retreated into himself and was not communicating with anyone. I fancied he understood more about what Jesus had been talking about for the past month, and he now anticipated a disastrous ending to our work together.

He had gone off alone last night. He wanted no one's company. I saw him plunge on down the hill, and I even thought to call out for him to wait for me, as I was also returning to the city. I was too late. He was gone.

Now—fifty years or more later—as I think back to that night and the next day, I still wonder whether it would have made any difference if I had walked with him down across the Kidron Valley and up into the city. Maybe he would not have made those fatal arrangements. I think I still mourn Judas. Our present followers are all taught to hate him for what he did, but I cannot. I don't think the Master did either. It was not in Jesus' nature to hate.

Judas was with us from the start. I had always been aware that he was not like the rest of us. He had a cynical attitude to the world, which was at odds with everything he heard from Jesus. He hung on for over six years as a faithful companion. He tirelessly coordinated all the logistics for our enterprise and took delight in arrangements to look after us.

Yet, even now, I refuse to believe that Judas was indifferent to Jesus. I believe he came to love Jesus as did we all. I think he thoroughly enjoyed Jesus' profound insight into our world and relished the discussions that Jesus stirred up whenever we were together. Maybe Judas was an intellectual at heart and saw clearly the full implications of what Jesus represented. I think Judas saw but could not believe the evidence of who Jesus was. If only he had waited.

Instead, I think he jumped ahead of the moment and got everything wrong. There arose in him such a conflict that he could no longer contain his own suspicions, but he had to report them. Jesus, in Judas's opinion, had gone over the edge.

But that night, and the next day as we prepared for our feast, these worries were not uppermost in my mind. I got on with the job I had been given and forgot about everything else.

I was still operating in a fog but dealing with mundane issues helped pull my mind into the present. I made arrangements for the room. I met with some of the Essene brothers, and I got from them all the necessary details of where everything was. We got the oven started for the lamb. The utensils for over twenty people had to be borrowed from somewhere. Everyone had a job to do.

So the morning was spent, and I climbed back up to Bethany to report to Jesus. I found him ensconced with Mary and Lazarus, talking in low tones. They fell silent at my approach.

Mary rose to welcome me and made a place for me. I sat between Jesus and Lazarus. After a quick glance at her brother, Mary smiled forlornly at me. "Jesus has told us he has to leave us. He believes we will not take up our own responsibility if he stays."

Lazarus shook his head slightly. "We will be there tonight. We can all come back here and maybe take our leave in the morning. I realize things can't go on like this. There is a growing opposition to the Master. Sooner or later we will be attacked, and, of course, Jesus will be the focus of it.

"The last time there was a hunt for Jesus, followed by a trial or hearing in his absence, and he was condemned to be stoned. Since then I have heard from at least two sources that there was money on my own head. We have to take this threat of violence seriously."

I looked back and forth between the others, and I realized Jesus had not told them that he expected to be arrested or worse. He had left the question of his departure wide open to interpretation. He and I had talked about his fear and expectation, but none of the others really understood what was coming.

I was relieved when Martha came in with a tray with lemon water, a bowl of dried apricots and some cracked walnuts. "I thought I saw you come in, John. The Master has been telling us he must leave us again. I really don't know why. We have only just got used to him being here. Can't you persuade him to stay for another week at least? Why go now? Passover will be starting in a couple of days, and we could all have such a nice time together."

"Maybe it is time for us all to think about the next step in taking the road the Master has laid out for us. We have to stand on our own feet. If he is here we will be content to bask in his presence and have a nice time but not really change," I said.

Mary looked up from her meal. "But what are we to do differently? The last time the Master left, we kept to ourselves and went about our business. How will this time be different?"

I thought for a while and looked over at Jesus, who gave no indication of helping me out. Instead, he was clearly waiting to see what I would come up with.

"Well," I began, "we are like every other nation. Most of the people want someone to come along and set up a strong stable kingdom that we can all shelter in. We never think beyond an Alexander who will win battles for us and defend us from outside interference."

I felt flushed with my own eloquence and plunged on. "Our idea of the Kingdom of God has been that His Messiah will come and do just that. Then God will reign here in Jerusalem, and we can all live in the shadow of His throne, secure from the outside world. As I understand the Master, that is not going to happen. The Master has said, 'We are to be in the world and not of it.' In other words, we are to become his teaching and allow others to be drawn to us."

We all looked at Jesus, who nodded but said nothing.

Mary said, "I still do not see what we are supposed to do. Everything will be just the way it has always been. There will be those frightful clergy at the Temple, those grumpy old Pharisees, and the place always teetering on the verge of erupting into violence. Are we going to change all that? Don't you see, you make them afraid. They take you seriously and they may well be willing to negotiate with you, but no one is going to negotiate with us."

Lazarus glanced at Mary with gentle tolerance. "Mary, I think the Master sees it all well enough. I think I understand what is needed. I am not really ready for it though. Then, I will never be ready to step out. I am like the rest of our people, ever ready to follow, but I am never prepared to be my own authority in the world. We talk endlessly about how the world should be, and how people ought to be different, but that is all we think is required of us. I believe the Master is going to make us talk with authority to the world. Until we take upon ourselves the task of being teachers to the world, we will not learn for ourselves what we have already heard and now possess."

"That reminds me of your parable of the mustard seed," I said, looking up at Jesus, sitting there with his attention focused on us. "You described how one small seed can grow into a bush, and it provides a place for birds and shade for animals to hide beneath. Once we begin to take upon ourselves the responsibility to act on what you have taught us, everything you have taught us will start to grow in us, and, like the mustard seed, provide shade for everyone around us. Your teaching will take on a life of its own and that will be the Kingdom of Heaven."

I was flushed with my sudden insight and looked to Jesus for his confirmation, but he looked back and gave no sign of either approval or the opposite. I realized he wasn't going to help, and from now on this was what it was going to be like. We were on our own and had to make our own judgments. Like children who always looked to their parents for confirmation, we looked to Jesus. Now, as I sat there hoping for his approval, I knew I was not going to get it and that he wanted me to find in myself my own conviction and truth.

Looking down at my clasped hands, with sudden clarity I saw afresh why Jesus' death was inevitable. This time it was not just an abstract idea, but, with a jolt, I felt the imminence of his death. Tomorrow, Jesus would not be sitting here among us.

He nodded very slightly, as if he knew what I had just intuited. I could not look at the others and, instead, examined my clenched fingers with interest.

The room in which our Passover supper was being prepared was a space created by ten stone archways. Twelve heavy stone pillars supported the arches and beams which held up the flat roof above. I looked around, and there were herbs in pots, several plants and even captive lemon and olive trees. I had come early to check that everything was ready, and now I leaned on the balustrade surrounding the roof.

I gazed out over the city in the gathering dusk. Not more than five hundred yards to the east, the Temple loomed. Smoke rose from the courtyard, and I thought of the sacrifices that had been offered that day. My mind filled with the memories of all the butchered animals I had seen burned to honor our God. I thought of the countless thousands down the centuries that had been herded up that hill, only to be butchered, burned and eaten by the priests and all their hangers-on. What benefit had all that wasted life conferred on anyone? What good had all that waste served? I thought of all the gullible and simple people trusting their precious offerings to that army of rapacious clergy who assured and authoritatively claimed efficacy of their actions.

This evening was our last hope. A choice would be made, or maybe it had already been made, that would take the nation on the road to destruction. I shouted at the city rooftops before me in my agony of frustration, "Listen to him! He is your last chance." I pounded the balustrade with my fists and screamed in my anguish, "Listen to him!"

Silence mocked my inner tumult. Dusk gathered the deepening shadows and obscured the Temple's base. The Temple's silhouette was now dark against the brightening moonrise. Huge and orange, the top arc of the moon showed itself just to the left of the Temple. It hefted itself above the horizon and swelled to an enormous size, as if in its fullness it demanded primacy.

My thought went to a grimmer time, when the ancestors of those men who now fed the fires of the altar, actually fed the fires of Moloch, the moon god who demanded human sacrifices. How many firstborns were dropped into the flames? How many people were sacrificed to head off disaster or to save the nation? Why didn't the priests offer themselves? Why did it always have to be someone else? Why was it—so often—the young?

I looked again at the great globe of a moon and screamed at it, "This is your night and you've come for your last sacrifice, you bloody face of sanctimonious evil. Tonight you will meet Him, and He will puff out your dead fires with a blast of his breath."

Hammering at the balustrade, I pointed my finger at the moon. "He will stand between you and all of us. You will have no more sacrifices from us."

I sobbed in rage and grief, and I beat the balustrade again.

As my anger ebbed and the tears of grief dried on my face in the cool night air, I felt Jesus' presence behind me. Wrung out, I spoke quietly, "I can't believe the pain of so many for so long. Why do we do it, and why do we believe the nonsense we have been fed?"

"John, you were right, there will be no more sacrifices. From now on, if there is to be sacrifice, then I will do it. Nothing else needs to die."

He placed his hand on my shoulder. "Come. Let us drive this terrible darkness away with the light of the Passover candles."

We all lounged around the tables that had been assembled for the crowd and waited for the first moments of the Seder to begin.

Jesus got up and went over to the foot bowls and, taking one of them, approached us. "On this night, we wash our hands before we eat, but for this moment, I desire to wash the feet of each of you. I don't expect you to understand what I am doing; in fact, I don't expect you will understand very much of what I will do and say tonight, but you will at least remember my words and actions."

Peter let out a muffled cry, "You are not going to wash my feet! I can't let you do that."

Jesus looked at all of us sitting aghast at the idea of him demeaning himself in this way and said, "You have all come in here with the dirt of the street clinging to you. Worse, you have come here tonight with the sin of the world inundating you: the violence of others, the fear in which you live, and the dishonesty and corruption that stalks our every institution. I am going to wash all that away. I am going to cleanse you from all of it and, for tonight, you will be clean."

With that, he began with Lazarus and moved on through the community of his disciples gathered at the table. Peter reacted to Jesus' attempt to wash his feet, but Jesus was adamant and none of us was willing to go against his demand. I watched as Judas' feet were washed. He showed no emotion as Jesus took care, washing the dust from his feet. Did I imagine it, or did Jesus spend a little more time on him? Looking back now from the vantage point of several years, I cannot say, but I like to think Jesus did make one last attempt to save him.

We lounged around the table. The women came in with the platter of matzo and lit the candles. Mary, Jesus' mother, lit the one in front of her son. Mary Magdalene set the platter of matzo before him and poured him wine. We bowed out heads over our plates, and the blessing over the matzo and the wine were intoned.

The story of our nation's beginning unfurled. Time and again, we had heard the story, and each little wrinkle in the telling was noted. For that short time, we were one with those who set out by night to escape from the slavery of Egypt. For a moment, we were there, huddled 'round the table, preparing to leave for the unknown as soon as the word came to our house.

As I listened to that familiar story, I forgot my own fears and dread, and I relaxed into that old bond which this story of our origins invoked in our people everywhere.

The story concluded by the time we poured the second cup of wine. Our host, Tendratus, brought in the roast lamb and others brought in the dishes that always accompanied this special meal. We drank our third cup of wine with our food. I tucked into the lamb and gave myself up to the joviality that ran among us.

Jesus took out the napkin-wrapped afikomen, the half of a matzo that was placed in a napkin after it had been blessed. It was symbolic food for the journey, as on that first Passover when our ancestors hastily wrapped the unrisen dough in cloth and carried it with them to give them sustenance during their initial flight.

Jesus stood, moved behind the place we had set for the prophet Elijah, and waited for our attention to focus on him. As usual, he took the matzo, raised it and led us in the blessing. We all joined in.

Seeing him take position behind the place setting of Elijah worried me. I wondered what was coming.

Looking around the table at us, Jesus took a deep breath. "This night I am giving you bread for your journey. Unlike the bread our ancestors took with them, the bread I offer you is myself. This bread is my body, eat it! I want you to do this to remember this moment and to call to mind my presence with you."

In the silence that followed, he passed the broken pieces of bread around. This was not part of the story, I thought. Where is he going with this? We all looked quizzically at the pieces of bread in our hands. Jesus urged us, "Go on, eat it."

Peter nibbled at his piece and slowly the rest of us followed suit. We looked at each other but nobody asked what it all meant. Above all, we were paralyzed by the bizarre departure from the customary account of that Passover event long ago.

Jesus was not finished. Our cups had been filled with wine for the fourth time, and we waited for the blessing of this cup. The matzo was hard going by itself. Jesus ignored his own cup and slowly reached for the cup that had been set for Elijah. We were transfixed, for every one of us knew that cup was poured for the Messiah. The old tradition associated with that cup explained that, when the Messiah came, he would take that cup and declare his arrival. It was a way of proclaiming our nation's expectation and keeping hope alive. Every Passover someone at the feast even opened the door for him to enter.

Jesus, holding Elijah's cup, quietly but forcibly declared, "Yes, I am here. I have come. I take this cup intentionally. I offer it to you—no, not as you all expected—but as a symbol of what your Messiah has to become.

"This is my blood of a new Covenant, a new understanding between you and your God. There will be no more sacrifices; no more animals have to die for you. Your Messiah will do the dying. So this is my blood, and it is shed for you and for many, for the forgiveness of your sins. Drink it so that you will remember this night."

I protested, "But your blood? We cannot."

"Everyone of you knows how the blood of the sacrifices is poured out. We believe the life of the animal is in that blood. We surrender the life of the animal by pouring the blood out onto the ground or putting it in the fire so that, in the smoke, the life of that animal will ascend to God. The life returns to its source.

"Thus, we Jews have always demonstrated our belief that all life is sacred and that it belongs to our God." He looked each of us in that room, "I am saying to you, this is to be for you, my blood, my life. This is a life not going back to God, but it is to remain here among you. I want you to take my life, into you. So drink up. Share this Elijah's cup between you. You don't understand this now, but I tell you, just do it. Take bread and wine and bless them. Do it to remember this moment. Remember what blood is to us. Don't fail me in this!"

We sat frozen in place. Jesus broke the spell by offering us the cup. As we passed it among us, I was aware how gingerly we all sipped at it. When it was my turn, a thought sprang unbidden to my mind. "If this was a life not going back to God, then what?"

I held the cup and looked into it dubiously. I handed it to Peter. "Drink a little. It still tastes like wine to me. Look, we are all in this together, and I think Jesus is trying to leave us something so that later we will understand what is going on."

Jesus looked at the cup traveling round the group. When it came back to him he handed it to me. "Finish it." To the rest of the people there, he explained, "I will not be drinking wine again until this is all over, and I can drink it fresh in the Kingdom of God. Yes, this night is it."

Later that evening, we walked back towards Bethany. Some of the others slipped away. I guess they had had enough for the day. Peter, James, John, Andrew and others followed on as we entered the Garden of Gethsemane. The olive press stood in silence. We entered the walled enclosure and sat on the stone walls in the moonlight. Now the moon rode—high and pristine—in the dark vault of heaven and turned everything to silver. Gone were my rage and despair, and in their place I felt a tired fatalism.

Jesus motioned to four of us, and we walked off with him deeper into the olive grove. Ancient trees took on fantastic stricken shapes as if bowed down with sorrows and witnesses to grim events for centuries. What terrible events had these denizens of Gethsemane seen? Were they waiting in expectation of another chapter in their lives?

Jesus stopped. "Wait here. I badly need to pray tonight. Keep an eye out. You had better pray for yourselves too." With that he walked off making his way to a grass-covered stone he had used on previous evenings. He settled into a quiet stillness that he gathered about himself like a robe. I had been privileged to be with him on many nights like this, and I never tired of seeing this transformation. It was as if he slipped away and left his body there to stand guard.

Tonight, though, as he prayed, I noticed that stillness had deserted him, and he slipped to the ground as if in agony. I rose to help him, but I paused as he cried out in pain. Clearly the terror of what he saw advancing on him had now become real, and he took the assault like a boat in a mountainous sea. He looked submerged by it.

I thought of that moment on the Sea of Galilee when he stilled the storm, and I wondered if he would do that tonight. I got up and moved a little closer, hoping to watch over him. My heart was breaking to see him so inundated by what he now clearly saw approaching. Two hours later, he said aloud, but not to me, "Okay. Not my will, but your will. I am ready to drink that cup I passed around at supper. I am ready to do it."

More time passed and I shifted uncomfortably on the hard ground. Jesus stretched, stood up and sat back down on his rock. Looking around, he noticed me. "Come on, we have to hurry. I must get back to the others."

He helped me up, and we roused Peter and James where they lay dozing. Jesus walked quickly on ahead of us, back to the olive press.

Up the path from Jerusalem a column of men climbed rapidly. I could hear the clink of metal and knew them to be armed. Among them were Temple police uniforms. I ran to catch up to Jesus, who now stood in the gap between the stone walls of the olive press. He faced those who came.

My heart sank. There, in the front rank, was Judas. The cold moonlight made torches unnecessary; Judas knew exactly where he was going and what he was doing. He strode up the hill to Jesus and embraced him, giving him our customary kiss of greeting. Jesus glanced at him and murmured something in too low of a voice for me to hear.

Three men grabbed him and Jesus braced himself against their force. "Who are you after?" he called.

The reply came in the form of a question from a haughty young man off to one side. "Jesus of Nazareth?"

"I am he," Jesus announced as he shook off the hands that had held him. Head high, he calmly stepped towards the column.

Many people in the column drew back, and I noticed some of them found shelter behind the ones in front. I wondered how many of them were wetting their pants. After all, they knew who he was and had at least heard accounts of what he could do.

Jesus gave himself up and told them to let the rest of us go. Peter was, by this time, struggling with two of the guards. All my attention was on what was happening to Jesus, but out of the corner of my eye, I saw Peter draw an old rusty sword from under his cloak and hack at one of the men who had now grabbed Jesus.

Jesus whirled around and shouted, "No, Peter. Put away your sword. That is enough."

42

THE TRIAL

They marched him away. We stood by helplessly, allowing them to hustle him down the path towards Jerusalem.

We looked at each other in dismay. Shame covered the faces of some, but it was Peter who galvanized us. "Did you see Judas? He has betrayed us all. He showed them which of us they had come for and that by a kiss. If I get my hands on him, he will wish he had not been born."

He grabbed my shoulder. "John, you know more about this city than the rest of us. Where will they take him? We have got to be there. We must speak for him. We have to do something."

We retraced our steps to the city. I hurried to my apartment, hoping Jonathon would know what was going on and leave me a message like he did before we went off to Galilee.

When I arrived I found a young boy busy banging on my door. The time was late for any boy this young to be out, for it was at least midnight. I recognized him as one of the Temple pages. He spun around at my approach and called out to me. Jonathon had sent his messenger.

The message was simple enough. "They took Jesus to Annas' palace." I had expected them to take him to the Temple and keep him in a cell there until they could bring him before a court for a hearing. What did this mean?

I asked the boy if Jonathon was at the Palace and got a nod. I sent the child on ahead to ask Jonathon to meet us by the gate to Annas' palace. Full of urgency and importance, the messenger disappeared down the narrow street.

This was odd. Why Annas' palace? "Peter, I don't know what this means. If he is not at the Temple and held pending a hearing before the Sanhedrin, I don't know what they are going to do with him. They surely will not murder him. Let's get over there and see what we can do."

Jonathon met us by the steps outside Annas' palatial house and led us round to a rear entrance into the courtyard. Peter stuck out like a sore thumb. He was challenged at least twice before we managed to get into the courtyard.

We stood in the shadows behind all the retainers and servants who littered the place. We waited by a brazier, and Peter was accosted once more. "I don't know the man; I was never with him." It was that moment when the earliest of the cocks heralded the approach of dawn.

We spotted Jesus, who had been led into the inner courtyard. He looked out over the heads of the gathering crowd and found us. For a moment he looked at Peter, who stopped—paralyzed and struck dumb. With a muffled cry of anguish, Peter turned away and pushed through the curious onlookers, heading for the doorway and the street.

Over time, much has been made of this event, insinuating that Peter betrayed Jesus, but I can understand. It was such a small thing—to deflect the curiosity of those in the courtyard—and something any of us could have done were we in his position. After all, Peter had come with me into the very palace of Annas. He had rushed with me to the city. The rest of the followers were all in hiding. They were not even there to witness what happened.

Unfortunately, Peter could never brush that denial from his mind. When others who knew him, heard about it, they dismissed it and rightfully so. But Peter never forgot and would not allow Jesus to forgive him. A long time later, when persecution dropped like a cloak over all the disciples in Rome, Peter stood and confessed to knowing "Christus," as the Romans called Jesus by then. I think, with that confession, he finally laid to rest the pain of that one thoughtless moment in the inner courtyard of our enemy's home when he blurted out, "I don't know him!"

Once Peter fled from the courtyard, I worked my way through to the front of the crowd. Jesus was restrained between two guards. His hands were tied, and he was disheveled but otherwise unharmed. I breathed a sigh of relief. Obviously things were under control, and there was no intention to murder him or make him disappear secretly like so many had done.

We waited for almost an hour before the officials began to file in. I noticed right away that these were all Temple clergy. There were members of Annas' family: his sons Jonathon and Matthias, and the younger Annas were all present. I looked for Caiaphas; as the High Priest, I expected him to preside over the hearing.

Annas finally walked in behind two retainers carrying torches. They sat in a crescent with Annas in the middle. Still I waited for Caiaphas to make his entry, but there was no Caiaphas. What was this? Annas had no official status. He couldn't hold a hearing.

Annas stood and asked for Jesus to be identified. "This person has been brought here, and we have been called to hear the complaints from people disturbed by his teaching and accusations. Let those who have anything to say, stand and tell the rest of us what you have heard."

Annas sat down and waited. There followed a succession of men who repeated in garbled form some of the things Jesus had said over the course of the years: He had talked about destroying the Temple. He had attacked the priesthood and office of the High Priest. He had denied the efficacy of sacrifice and the Temple's cleansing rituals.

I listened and began to feel easier in my mind, for none of these things were serious reason for concern. The witnesses laid themselves wide open for any defense attorney to drive a loaded camel through their accounts.

Annas was growing impatient. He too saw the futility of entertaining these complaints. I noticed that the old accusations from a year ago when Jesus raised Lazarus were not reiterated. Obviously no one wanted to remind people of that event.

Finally Annas stood and asked if there were other witnesses, but there were none. Jesus had said nothing the whole time. He appeared relaxed but alert. He was waiting for something else. All my fears returned. What had just occurred was window dressing. What were they after? None of what we had heard was actionable, so now what?

Annas spoke to Jesus directly, "You have heard all these accusations. Do you have anything to say?"

Jesus replied, "You know I have taught openly in public. Yes, I have spoken out against the venality of the Temple administration and the misplaced reliance by our people on the usefulness of your sacrifices. Everyone knows that, and you saw no reason to arrest me during the day. People have found healing and relief from my work. For which of these acts have you seized me and brought me bound to this place? Why did you seize me secretly and at night? Are you afraid of the people, or is the night and darkness your natural time?"

The attendant on Jesus' right swung around and hit Jesus full in the face. "Curb your tongue!"

Jesus did not flinch, but absorbed the blow. "For which of these things I have said do you strike me? Is this the treatment anyone can expect at the hands of the Temple's staff?" he asked.

Annas advanced a step towards Jesus. "No, we do not treat our people like that, but you must admit you try our patience with your unbending attitude towards all that we do here at the Temple." Then he addressed those who had attended him and constituted the Temple clergy present in the courtyard. "This hearing is not because this man has spoken out against the Temple, although he has done that constantly over the years, and in spite of our forbearance, he has continued to undermine our work among the people. There is a far more important question to be answered this night, which cannot be aired to the mindless masses, but must be attended to by you who are appointed to safeguard the religious interests of the nation."

Turning dramatically to Jesus, he asked, "Jesus of Nazareth, are you the Messiah, the son of the Blessed?"

There was an intake of breath all around the hall, and a deep silence fell as Jesus stood in thought for a long moment. Finally he said, "Yes, I am, and you would see proof of that all around you if you were not so blinded by your own closed minds. You don't want to see, but you will because you will look up and there I will be, at the right hand of the Almighty".

A gasp was heard throughout the room and Annas nodded, allowing the significance of the statement to sink in. Dramatically, he seized his light undergarment visible between folds of the heavy outer vestments, and tore it apart, exposing his chest. He cried, "You have heard it with your own ears! How do you describe what you have just witnessed?"

"Blasphemy!" called out two or three people, then a shout went up from all the rest in the room, and a great roar of outrage sounded the cry of "blasphemy!"

Annas let the noise continue for a full minute, but it felt like half an hour to me. Annas held up his hand to still the uproar, and when it had subsided, dolefully and with feigned regret, he said, "You all heard his words, you are witnesses to what he willingly uttered. You heard from his own lips the claim that he is the Messiah, son of the Blessed.

"Our duty is clear. We must present your evidence to the High Priest, and because of the seriousness of this man's claim, we should do so right away. A full trial and public hearing must ensue at the earliest possible time. Until then we must hold him and not let him slip away as he has done before."

With that, the whole entourage—with Jesus in the middle of several retainers—headed through the crowd and out of the courtyard in which we were standing. I was left puzzled by what I had just heard. I understood that a brief hearing before Caiaphas was necessary for Jesus to be formerly arrested and held for trial, but why now when there was only a hint of dawn showing in the east?

My first thought was that a trial with proper hearings would be very much in Jesus' favor. We had a lot of friends on the Sanhedrin, and among the Pharisees there was no love lost for Annas and his malevolent gang.

But, why the haste? Why did Annas look flushed with success and anticipation? There was something very wrong here. Annas had his witnesses. All of them were eyewitnesses. They all heard Jesus make a willing and voluntary answer to a legitimate question.

Jonathon nudged me. "I can't get us into Caiaphas' rooms. I think the best thing is for us to go back and find as many of our friends as we can. We must be prepared to pack a public hearing later today. Right now none of them know what is happening. We must find Peter and get him to round up all those from Galilee. Go to Nicodemus, alert him to what is happening, then tell the Jerusalem Brothers. We need to get the word out so that right from the start Caiaphas will see what he is up against, and he will tread very carefully. He has no strong stomach for public outrage, and he will want to avoid any rioting. Believe me, if we wanted to, we could bring out the crowds in Jesus' support. They all love him and have reveled in his miracles."

"I hope you are right, Jonathan. I think there is something else going on here. Whatever the issue, we need to do as you suggested. We must get the word out. It's early yet. I know where most of the followers will be, and Nicodemus' house is not far away. Let us meet there in an hour."

I headed off to the house of the Jerusalem Brotherhood, in whose upper room we had supped the evening before. Was it only last night? Jesus' words echoed in my head, "This is my blood that is shed for you and for many." I hoped not, but . . . .

The whole Brotherhood community was already roused, for Peter had come with the news an hour ago. I quickly filled them in on the details of the hearing. There was food left over from the evening before, so while we passed bread and some of the meat around, everyone began to talk and ask questions.

Peter said, "We have to think about organizing protests, and we must make sure the authorities know they cannot sweep this under the rug. I think we should call as many of our friends together as we can in say, two hours, and organize ourselves. There are people we know who can tell us how to go about this. Those of us from Galilee have no idea just how we should proceed or what rights we have or who to apply to for help. We need someone who knows the law, for starters."

I was relieved to see Peter taking charge; in spite of what happened three hours before, he was thinking and acting as a leader. Joseph of Arimathaea, Lazarus of Bethany and several others were named as people who needed to be alerted. Peter sent Philip to Bethany to tell Lazarus. I sent Thomas off to find Joseph of Arimathaea, and I set out for Nicodemus' house.

He was hardly up by the time I got to him. As gracious as ever, he invited me in and offered me some breakfast, which I refused. Suddenly I felt sick to my stomach. First I told him of last night in the Garden of Gethsemane and afterwards at Annas' palace. Then I told him of the questioning and the procession to rouse Caiaphas in order to present the facts to him.

Nicodemus listened with a grave look on his face. "You say Annas was collecting information, and when Jesus made his statement they all agreed he had uttered blasphemy?"

"Yes, at least half a dozen men got up and made complaints about what he had said at various times. Some of the things mentioned had occurred years ago."

Nicodemus asked, "Was any mention made of that affair of Lazarus and the Sanhedrin's concern at that time?"

"None," I said.

Nicodemus paced up and down the room for several minutes. With his hands clasped behind his back, he stopped in front of me and declared, "Annas has another plan up his sleeve. He gave Jesus to Caiaphas, all nicely packaged. Witnesses, agreed testimony, and all in a controlled space. I have never known Annas to give Caiaphas anything for free. I think he is setting Caiaphas up. You have to realize that where most men like and love other people, Annas hates others.

"Would you go to Joseph of Arimathaea and ask him to come see me? I think we need to find out just what is happening. I have had no notice of any action of the Sanhedrin, nor have I heard any noise in the streets. Of course it is early yet, and nobody is up except you folk who never went to bed. You said there is to be a meeting in a couple of hours at the Upper Room where we met last night?"

I nodded and he continued, "On second thought, I will get dressed and go visit Joseph. My suggestion is that you go back to Jonathon and ask him to find out what is happening."

With Nicodemus informed, and obviously as concerned as I was, I began to feel better. My anxiety and sickening dread diminished. We parted, and I went to Jonathon's apartment but found no one there. I thought of his parent's house, but I knew he would not be there. I retraced my steps to Annas' palace.

With caution I entered the outer courtyard and proceeded to the offices I had visited long ago. A servant girl went in search of Jonathon, and soon he stood before me. He ignored those around us and took my elbow to lead me out into the gray light of early dawn. "I've been expecting you. Annas came back half an hour ago looking pleased with himself. He ordered breakfast and is sitting in his study contentedly chomping away. He hardly ever eats a large breakfast. He usually leaves half of it and then starts roaring for his servants."

"You mean he is in a good mood?"

"That's it. He is never pleased with anyone, but right now he seems very pleased with himself. It is as if he thinks he has been especially clever."

I dismissed the thought of Annas having breakfast and said, "I need to find out what is happening to Jesus and report back to the others. We are getting together in about an hour to decide what we should do. Is there any way you could get into Caiaphas' place and find out about any public hearing? If there is one, we need to be there. Nicodemus and Joseph of Arimathaea are alerted, and they will be heading towards Caiaphas' offices."

Jonathon nodded. "Let's go. I can invent some reason to get by the retainers at the door. I also have a couple of friends there who I can ask without them running and telling their master. They probably have Jesus in the cells underground."

Jonathon returned after about twenty minutes. He appeared grim, and as he approached me, he shook his head. "He is not there. They brought Jesus over earlier. Caiaphas met with a number of witnesses, conferred with Annas for at least half an hour, then ordered Jesus to be manacled. Caiaphas, the witnesses and other family members left for Pilate's offices with Jesus in tow. They threw a cloak over Jesus' head so nobody would recognize him."

Jonathon paused. "John, I don't like it. Pilate has nothing to do with our religious issues. He keeps out of our business, preferring us to beat upon each other. If they have taken Jesus to Pilate, none of us can reach him, not even our friends."

I was utterly confused by this turn of events and alarmed beyond measure. Under our Jewish law there would be hearings and even a trial before the Sanhedrin. We would be able to organize and develop a response to Jesus' arrest. We had friends who would help, and we could count on the support of hundreds of others who knew Jesus and had received help and care from him. All we needed was time.

Now, with Jesus in the hands of Pilate, I was unsure of how we could help. Pilate was not someone to bow to crowd pressure or even back-door pleading, I thought frantically of bribery, but set that aside for now. I realized also that Jonathon was putting himself on the line. Long the servant of Annas, Jonathon was now clearly exposing himself politically.

I said, "Jonathon, this could cost you your job and maybe more. We have not talked about this for years, but maybe this is why you stayed in place all these years. What I am going to suggest may well expose you, and there may be no way back for you."

Jonathon nodded, "We knew this might happen, and now anything I can do, I will do. I will count it against everything I have had to endure. What do you need?"

I replied carefully. "I think I should get back. We have to tell Nicodemus and the others about this new development right away. I will go there, but Jonathon, do you think you could get in the back door of Pilate's offices and look up your friend Silvanus? He may be able to tell you what is happening."

Jonathon nodded and turned away without a second thought. I ran towards the Upper Room, hoping that by the time I got there Nicodemus would have arrived.

As I ran down the stone-flagged streets, I dodged the few people who were preparing for their day and elicited strange looks from some as I hurried by. I thought, "You would run too if you knew what was at stake."

Nicodemus and Joseph both registered alarm at my news. Nicodemus said, "If they have taken him to Pilate it means they are going to hand Jesus over to him, and the only reason Pilate would be interested in Jesus were if he were accused of treason, or a violent threat to social good order. That does not fit Jesus. He has been around, and no doubt he has been watched by the Romans for years. John, tell me again what Annas asked Jesus when he questioned him."

"Annas asked whether he was the Messiah, the Son of the Blessed. Then everybody got upset and hurled charges of blasphemy at him."

"Annas—that scurrilous dog. You know what he got Jesus to admit?"

"To being the Messiah, the blasphemy charge will not stand. He clearly claimed to be the Messiah, though. He stood there and responded to Annas' question with "I am.""

Nicodemus nodded. "We know what we mean when we say Messiah; a holy servant of our God. There is another interpretation that he is the rightful and God-appointed King of our nation. I think Annas really wanted that admission from Jesus' lips. I doubt he was concerned about the blasphemy business, except to send all the witnesses into an outrage. No, I think he wanted the confession from Jesus' own lips that he was the Messiah, and he will now interpret that word to Pilate as a pretension to the throne of Israel and therefore treason against Caesar."

"But Annas is sitting in his offices eating breakfast. He is not involved."

Nicodemus began his pacing again. The rest of the brothers and followers from Galilee were anxiously waiting for orders and had fallen quiet. All eyes were on Nicodemus as he worked through the details of what he had heard. Nicodemus turned to Joseph. "What do you make of this?"

Joseph stroked his beard thoughtfully, "I think it was you who said Annas is setting up Caiaphas. I wonder whether he was indeed setting him up, not to absorb the ire of the people, rather, setting him up as the one who would be the instrument to force Pilate to do what only Pilate can do. Pilate hates Annas and would not do anything if he thought Annas was involved or even in favor of it. I think that is why Annas is eating breakfast, and Caiaphas is keeping Pilate from his."

Nicodemus let out a loud groan, "Oh, no. If you are right, then you know what the outcome of any well-attested charge has to be."

Jonathon said soberly, "Summary execution. There would be no real trial, just the witnesses, and the sentence carried out immediately."

Nicodemus nodded. "That is why Annas is so pleased with himself. He has everything worked out. Caiaphas, the High Priest, no less, is making the accusation. There was a room full of witnesses, and the only thing the Romans know about messiahs is that they all aspire to be King of Israel. What is worse, Pilate will ask Jesus if this is true, and no doubt Jesus will say it is."

As this possibility sank in, despair settled over all of us. Now I felt horribly afraid. We were no longer talking about a long battle, but the death of our friend and rabbi in a matter of hours. Summary execution meant today, immediately, within a few hours. I felt within me a rising tide of horror and despair. I felt my chest tighten, and I could hardly breathe as panic flooded through me. I cried out, "No!"

Joseph and Nicodemus looked at me with sorrow filling their eyes and nodded. "Yes," said Jonathon, "I think we now see the whole stinking plot. Everything will be decided before we can marshal any support and before most of the people of the city are awake. In fact, by now they may have Jesus before Pilate. It may already be too late." He looked back at Nicodemus and said, "We have to act and right now. We don't have time to think this all the way through. Our only hope is that Pilate will smell a rat. If he at least suspects Annas is behind this, he will dig in his heels. We may be too late, but I think I can get an audience with Pilate and lay the whole thing before him. I know he doesn't care two pence for any of us, nor would he think twice about executing anyone who just might be a problem, but if he thought he was being manipulated by Annas, he might not go through with the execution and may even order a full investigation."

I looked at Nicodemus and asked him, "Would you be willing to go with Joseph and support what he says?"

"I will do my best. Come Joseph, we must do it now. There is no time to lose. Caiaphas is at least an hour ahead of us."

I watched them go and, turning to the others, said, "There is little we can do. If we tell everyone what is going on, word will spread and hundreds of people will come out in support of us. If the Romans see our efforts as rioting in favor of Jesus and support for any claim as King of Israel, we will do more harm than good. We could confirm the charges Caiaphas is making and goad Pilate into deciding against Jesus. Our only hope lies with Nicodemus and Jonathon. I will go over to the Palace of Antonia and wait for Jonathon. I suggest, Peter, you remain here with everyone and wait for our word on what to do."

The Palace was more like a fortress and housed the Roman garrison. I entered the area reserved for public hearings or announcements, and I found it filled with the clergy and attendants of the Temple. They were clearly waiting, milling around, gesturing and excitedly talking together. There must have been almost a hundred men there. Excitement and anticipation animated their faces, and you could see humor flare between individuals as comments were exchanged. How I hated all of them for their insensitivity and blindness.

Jonathon was nowhere to be seen. I must have waited half an hour. Finally, there was a stir as attendants ranged themselves on a dais backed against the wall of the inner courtyard.

Pilate, wearing his official toga and the decorations of his office, stepped onto the dais and motioned for silence. He looked around at the raised faces and, as if taking pleasure in disappointing them, said, "I find no substance to the accusations you have laid against this man. He is like many of your race—stubborn and possessed of a religious fanaticism that characterizes so many of your teachers. We have had our eye on him for years, but he has not posed a threat to public order. Therefore I have had him flogged for his stubbornness and the obstinacy of his opinions. Bring him in." These last words were addressed to two attendants who remained by the door leading into the fortress.

They motioned to others inside and made way for a horrific procession. Two leather-armored soldiers half carried, half dragged Jesus between them as they approached the lower steps of the dais. There they turned him around so we could all see him.

They had jammed a crown of thorns on his head and blood ran from the wounds the thorns had made. His arms, bare chest and legs were crisscrossed with welts from the scourging, and I could see deep wounds where the knots and pieces of metal tied into the flagellum had torn the flesh. Blood trickled from scores of wounds. He bowed his head as if trying to stay on his feet. His face bore the marks where someone had obviously punched him.

The sun shone on my back. I felt too hot. I began to feel sick. Tears welled up and I felt I was dissolving inside. I whimpered like a child. I found the wall to lean on. For a moment I thought I was going to pass out, so I bowed my head towards the ground. Someone touched my shoulder; I looked up and there was Jonathon. I grabbed him and clung to him and began to sob.

He said, "John, it's going to be okay. It's a flogging. He will be released now."

I pulled myself together enough to listen to what was now going on. Pilate advanced to the edge of the dais and waived toward Jesus. "Here is your so-called King. I find no evidence of treason. He has not been heard or seen to conspire against Caesar, neither do I have any evidence of his inciting others to do so. Since today begins your festival, I will release him."

There was a stunned silence in the courtyard as the meaning of what he had said sunk in. I saw Caiaphas turn and urgently exchange words with two other men beside him. He approached the dais and said, "Your Excellency, you do not understand. This man has not only usurped the name of Messiah, and thereby King of Israel, but he has also claimed to be the son of God. That is blasphemy in our law, and he must die."

Pilate acted as if he had been slapped and looked with alarm at the battered form of Jesus. He walked down the steps of the dais and warily approached Jesus, stopping a few feet short of where he stood, still supported by the retainers. Pilate lowered his voice, but the sound carried around the walls of the courtyard. "Where do you come from? Who are you? You said your Kingdom was not of this world, then what world?"

In the gathering heat, I saw flies settling on the oozing wounds of Jesus' head and legs but he paid them no attention. He tried to raise his head as if to take a breath, but pain etched his face as his battered chest and back tried to move under his shift. He finally gave an infinitesimal shake of his head and lapsed once more into immobility.

Pilate said, "Speak to me. Don't you know I could have you crucified? Tell me, where are you from? Who are you?"

Jesus raised his head and looked up towards Heaven and managed to say, "I am not of their world. King is your word. Do what you must. This is between them and our God. You can't do anything."

Pilate looked with alarm at Jesus. With a decisive swirl of his toga, he stepped back up on the dais and declared, "I find no fault in this man. I normally let go one prisoner on this day, and so I am going to release him."

At this a cry of protest rang out. "No," cried Caiaphas. "We don't want him released. Release someone else!" He bent over to hear a suggestion from a colleague who stood at his elbow. Straightening, he said, "Give us Barabbas."

Several men around Caiaphas took up the chant, "We don't want him. We want Barabbas!"

More joined in the shouting until there was a foot-stomping, dust-throwing crowd shouting for Barabbas to be released. Pilate backed up onto the highest step of the dais. I noticed a file of soldiers enter the courtyard to reinforce the retainers already there. Pilate had a word with a retainer who promptly left the dais and entered the fortress door behind them.

Pilate once more advanced towards the front of the dais and waved his arms to command silence. "I have sent for Barabbas. You asked for him, and I will release him to you. This disturbance you have raised must stop. I will not be dictated to by a herd of malcontents who seek the harm of an innocent man. Roman law is often judged as harsh, but it is also fair."

Barabbas was shoved through the door and had his manacles removed. Silence fell for a moment and Pilate spoke again. "There he is, take him away." Then, to Barabbas, he said, "If we arrest you again, you will be crucified."

With that he turned away and was in the act of ordering Jesus taken back into the fortress when Caiaphas spoke up, "What will you do with Jesus of Nazareth?"

"Do?" snarled Pilate. "I will keep him until I decide what I will do with him. You don't want him. You see what a wreck he is. Are you not satisfied?"

Caiaphas glanced at those near him, "You should execute him. You should not let him go. If you let this troublemaker go, we will all be back here in a little while, and we will have to go through this all over again. You need to have him crucified."

Pilate stalked back to the front of the dais and snarled, "Crucify your King? Is that what you want? Are you telling me that just to support your precious beliefs, you are willing to have someone crucified? Is that why you brought him here, to have me do your dirty work for you? I will not be party to your gross insult to the gods. If you want him dead, do it yourself. I will not have anything to do with his death. You can take him away."

Caiaphas stood his ground and folded his arms under his vestments. He rocked back and forth on his feet and said, "We can't put a man to death without a lengthy trial, hearings and long defense. No, this needs to be done now, and you need to do this.

"Let me put it to you this way. You have received the honor, "Friend of Caesar." You are a professional civil servant and Caesar values your loyalty. We have brought before you this man, who we know to be a pretender to the throne of Israel. He has said as much in front of witnesses who are here to give their evidence again if you wish. If you don't take action and convict this man, even let him go, what will Caesar think when he hears our account of what transpired today? Here is a man turned over to you, proven to be claiming the throne of Israel, supplanting Caesar and proposing to commit treason, and you did nothing about it. Throughout your empire there is one law that none of you question: the person guilty of treason must die. Do you believe Caesar will not hear of this? I can assure you he will hear that those of his loyal subjects responsible for the people's Temple and observance of their religion turned over to you someone who sought to supplant Caesar. We are loyal to Caesar and we prove it through our actions. We are saying that we have no King but Caesar."

Pilate looked out over the crowd of assembled Temple clergy and their retainers and asked in a raised voice which rang round the stone walls of the courtyard, "What shall I do with this man whom you call Jesus of Nazareth?"

Three or four voices rang out, "Crucify him!" Then more joined in until the whole courtyard erupted as men stamped their feet and with raised fists screamed at Pilate, "Crucify him," and, "Away with him, crucify him!"

Pilate stood there staring at Caiaphas. Finally he understood the net that had been woven round him. He stole a look at Jesus, who stood there quietly, seemingly indifferent to what was being said. Pilate angrily barked orders in Latin.

I was recovered enough to advance to the edge of the crowd of clergy who now pressed around the dais. For a moment I had begun to hope Pilate would prevail, but now I saw clearly the devious plot Annas had concocted. Jesus' death was intended and sought from the beginning. The hearing in the middle of the night, the establishment of clear evidence heard by multiple witnesses, the enlisting of Caiaphas, the subverting of Pilate—these were not haphazard or fortuitous events, but carefully orchestrated, one built on another. This had not been dreamed up in the middle of the night or even yesterday.

My thoughts went to Judas, who had been our companion for so long. I thought of the question Annas had asked of Jesus that finally set this whole catastrophe in motion: "Are you the Messiah, the son of the Blessed?" How did Annas know to ask that question?

The final piece fell into place. Judas had talked. He was the only one who could have given Annas that piece of information. I wept, "Oh, Judas, why?"

Jonathon stood beside me, his face like a stone. He looked with hatred at the crowd, then put his arm around my shoulder and held me. Even in the heat of the warming sun, I felt cold. I could hardly breathe, and I felt the crushing weight of what now had to be the final word that would destroy my Lord.

Servants brought a huge lavar and jug of water and held them in front of Pilate. By now there was a crowd of onlookers gathered around the great doors of the fortress. Jesus stood motionless, his eyes closed. Pilate plunged his hands into the bowl and ground out between his shuttered teeth, "You want this man crucified. I wash my hands of his blood. He is innocent. May his blood be on you and on your confounded Temple. You do it; I will have nothing more to do with this matter."

Pilate stalked away. The rest of the gathering stood in silence eyeing their victim. I noticed some of them begin to express some discomfort. Jesus was finally escorted away, disappearing from my sight.

I seized Jonathon by the shoulder in panic. "We must tell the others." We pushed through the crowd of onlookers and made our way across the city to the house where most of the brothers were staying.

They gathered around us and waited for me to speak. I could not say the words. I opened my mouth but nothing came out. I just stood there, looking at them. Aghast.

42
THE CRUCIFIXION

Peter cried out in a voice that rumbled round the room, "For God's sake, what has happened?"

My eyes filled with tears, and they erupted down my face.

Jonathon spoke. "He is to be crucified."

I nodded my head. I could say nothing.

A chorus of denial filled the room as the men looked frantically at each other. "They can't crucify him just like that. There has been no trial. We have been working on a defense for him. Tell us what has happened!"

Words finally spilled from my lips. "It's no good. There will be no trial. There was never intended to be any opportunity for his defense. Caiaphas wants this done today before the city is awake. People are out on the streets now and they will be hearing about it, but the decision is made. There is nothing to be done; even now, they are preparing for his crucifixion. We can't object or have any hope of bringing about a delay. There is no time left."

Nicodemus pressed forward. "The Sanhedrin could be called together for an emergency meeting. The majority of us are against capital punishment and Jesus has a lot of respect among the members."

I shook my head. "The convener is Caiaphas. He was the one who pushed Pilate into agreeing to Jesus' conviction. He provided the witnesses, and he made the case against Jesus. The execution detail will be getting everything together right now. Caiaphas and the rest of the Temple clergy do not intend any delay, nor will they allow any opportunity for public demonstration or outcry to develop. Word will have run through the streets, and the markets will all be full by now, but there is nothing to be gained by rioting, attacking the Roman forces or pressing Pilate to reconsider. His hand was forced. Believe me, he hates those clergy. Above all he hated being outmaneuvered by them. I don't think for a moment he cared about Jesus himself, but he knows he was used." I looked around at the stricken faces. We could only be there at his crucifixion. There was nothing left for us to do.

"Then what now?" asked Thomas.

I said dejectedly, "I don't think there is anything to be done. This was very carefully planned and choreographed. I must tell his mother. Where is she? Has anyone told her of his arrest?"

"She knows he was arrested last night, but nothing else. There has been no news, so we thought it best to not worry her with our own fears," said Philip.

The next hour was one of the worst hours I ever spent. I went to see Jesus' mother and found her sitting calmly and ominously quiet in the shadows of a cool inner sitting room. With great reluctance I told her as much as I knew, as well as my speculations. I continued the explanations until she placed her hand on my arm to stop me.

"John, thank you, for telling me. I know you have loved him, and you have been with him for many years now. I can't cry yet, but my tears will come. I have lived with the knowledge this would happen ever since he began his ministry. We, his family, all knew that to speak as he spoke, and to act as he acted, would eventually bring him to this day. There was a time when his brothers tried to talk him out of it. They called him mad and challenged his emotional balance. How stupid. Jesus was the only sane voice in this whole insane world. Jesus knew this day would come, and although he never said as much to me, he knew I understood."

I watched as she gathered her strength to finally say all she wanted to say.

"You men! How many other mothers have woken up to hear such news of their sons? All down the ages we bear you, we nurture you, and this is all you know how to do to each other. I know despair right now because there is nothing I can do, but there is a worse despair beneath my own sorrow that is for all mothers. When will this stop? Is there any point to our sacrifice? Would it be better for us not to bear you men and so end the human race? All the good my son did, his teaching, the words of comfort and strength he offered, the healed lives he left behind him wherever he went—is it not all a waste? What has been achieved? Everything is being wiped out, like someone with a sweep of his sandal erases words written in the dust."

I saw in Mary's face a dryness like the summer heat. There burned behind those eyes a white hot anger that surprised me. I sought for words of comfort but none came. I thought to somehow explain the evil of our world in a phrase or two, but the thought died as I understood the vast sorrow she had tapped into. Mary was not sorrowing for herself, but bore in herself the suffering of so many mothers for so long. Every mother who had lost a son to war, to strife or to violence was present in that room before me.

I again had that suffocating feeling that I had experienced in the courtyard. A dim memory stirred of that horrifying image of evil from my dream, threatening to overwhelm me. I felt my breathing paralyzed with the old fear. All around me, I now felt that same image pressing in and surrounding all of us. I had felt it last night in Annas' house, I felt it in the courtyard, and now here that terrible presence had come to mock and to celebrate its victory.

Mary looked at me as if reading my mind. She nodded. "Despair is all I have left right now. Oh, yes, I know he will rise again at the resurrection, and we will all be united. Spare me any such hollow consolation. I want to feel my anger. I want to shout it to the world so all you men hear it. How many more sacrifices must be offered at the altars to your vanity and search for power? I would suffer this gladly if I knew this was the last sacrifice you demanded, but his sacrifice is not the last. You men will go on, forever killing in God's name. Do you not realize the evil one would have no power, no presence, without the sacrifices you constantly offer it?"

I stood before her unable to defend any of us from her indictment. I waited, for she was not finished.

"Last time Jesus spoke to me in this room, only yesterday afternoon, in fact. He came and took me away from the kitchen where we were all busy preparing food for the evening meal, and he sat me down right there." Mary pointed to the low divan mounded with cushions. "I now realize he had come to say goodbye. He spoke of the approach of the Evil One and talked of a coming struggle. Last night at supper he tried to tell us all over again when he took the bread and later Elijah's wine. I don't understand what he meant, but he knew the end was near. Whatever he had planned or whatever he expected was in his words, 'the will of The Father.' He said once this was another moment of creation, a next and necessary action."

Mary suddenly fell silent and then began to crumple. I took a step to her and hugged her to me as she cried. "Why, oh, why does it have to be my son? Is God another male caught up in this macabre dance?"

I felt her tears wet my chest through my shirt. I didn't know what to say, so I just held her as the horror of what was unfolding came to her. Jesus' words from a year ago came back to me, "Do you not think the Father knows the suffering of his creation? Do you think he doesn't feel the agony of all those sacrifices at the Temple?" For a fleeting moment I wondered if the One who Jesus so often called Father would now feel the agony of what was about to happen to his most faithful, obedient and trusting servant?

With that thought, a great presence filled every cubic inch of the room and, by its presence, expelled that triumphant, mocking shadow that had drawn around us. Mary's sorrow and the sorrow of the many she had spoken of eddied around us, made all the more real by the weeping of a frightened and despairing mother.

My own horror of earlier felt as nothing in the face of her despair. What was I losing in comparison with her?

I took a breath. It was as if the presence that had filled the room entered me. Strength flowed back into me. I said, "There is much to be done. I don't want to distress you more, but by now the soldiers will have everything ready. I must be there. I will stand by him as close as I can, just like he once told me to stand, and not let myself run for fear. This is that moment all over again. Do you need to be there? These events are horrible, and I think you should wait here."

Mary pushed away from me and shook her head, "No, I cannot wait in this stifling room and listen to the distant shouts. I would rather see and know what was being done to him than sit here and imagine everything."

I left the room and went in search of Mary Magdalene and the other women who had accompanied us from Galilee. I found them in the kitchen area cleaning up after the Passover celebration. I thought for a moment about what had happened since. It was not much more than twelve hours since we had risen from table and took our leave of each other. I met the eyes of the women there and explained what had happened. Mary Magdalene held her stomach as if I had punched her, then turned away, supporting herself with one arm on the wood countertop. The others covered their faces.

I had thought to ask Mary to go in to be with Jesus' mother, but now I hesitated, for she was in great distress. "Mary, I know you love him. I know what he did for you."

"No, you don't know." She howled. "You have not suffered the indignity and rejection I lived with for years, nor have you lived in fear of arbitrary and unexpected violence. You know why I love this man? He knows. He intervened, and here I am. I owe him everything. He reached down into my hell and drew me out. He gave me my sanity and confirmed me as whole in my own eyes. The world is crazy, not me. Now you bring me the ultimate proof. The world of men is ruled by something other than our Father, the God Jesus introduced me to. You destroy anything that wants to grow, deface anything that wants to be beautiful in its own right, deny anyone who wants to exist without your permission."

Mary took a deep breath, then plunged on. "This is the ultimate folly. You don't know what this means, do you, John?"

I opened my mouth to say something reasonable and calming, but nothing came to mind. There was no reason to be calm. Mary wasn't finished.

"I know how much he means to you," she continued, "but you don't understand what your world of politics and power is about to do. He is my shield, my one fixed point. I cannot live by myself. I will not go back to where I was, but how can I maintain myself? He is always there in my thoughts when I start to descend into the nightmares of where I was. Do you think those memories are gone? No. Hell is just below the surface, and I startle like a frightened animal at every sound I recognize from before. All I have needed is to hear his voice say my name again, and I am inviolate, protected from the demons that lie in wait for me. Do you understand? When I hear him say 'Mary,' I cannot be touched: those demons have no substance, they have no power over me. Now what am I to do?" she shouted.

There was nothing I could do or say in response to her tirade.

She continued, "It's not only me. When he is gone from the world, what happens to the rest of us who have taken shelter in his shade? Do you remember his story of the mustard tree, how birds and other critters found a haven in its branches? They are intending to cut down the mustard bush, John. You don't know what evil is. I lived with it, tried to crawl away from it, tried to die even, but I was held down, suffocating, until I crumbled into dust, and my mind began to disintegrate. He brought me back. He holds me together. Now I see evil has again reached back into my world just when I have thought myself safe. Evil is out there right now going about its daily business of destruction. Evil has no reason for its actions, no motivation but the desire to destroy anything good, to deface anything that would show its independence, and kill anything that would grow."

I looked at the other three women in the room, and they nodded very slightly as if in confirmation of what they had heard. I lowered my head and looked at the cut, scarred surface of the wooden preparation block. In the face of Mary's experience and the accusations of Jesus' mother, I felt shame for all of us. I hated the world I inhabited. Memories of Jesus' ministry over the years came back to me, and I wondered if this was what it has been about from the beginning. I pushed all those thoughts away and appealed to her, "Mary, you are right, but for the moment we need to set all this aside. There is a lot to be done."

Mary looked at me with scorn. "My heart is breaking, and you say there is much to be done. Ha! What is there ever to be done when evil does its dance?"

I did not know what to say. There was nothing that would give comfort, no reason to contradict her view, and no way of answering her angry assertions. Finally, I said, "It's Jesus' mother. I think she needs you right now. The rest of us can say the right words, but that is not going to be enough. You know better than we what is happening for her right now."

"Oh, God, Mary!" she cried and dodged past me, heading down the passage towards where Jesus' mother sat.

I went out into the main room. I looked around and noticed Nicodemus was no longer there. Peter and Andrew had also left.

One of the brothers from this little community of Essenes who had welcomed us as guests yesterday came in, "John, you have eaten nothing." He brought bread from last night and some nuts and dried figs. "Today is going to be a long day. Eat something."

I nodded. I felt suddenly tired and slumped down onto the low divan we had reclined on the previous evening. The brother came in with the food and set it before me. I ate the figs and reached for the nuts. They were almonds, both bitter and sweet. What a message for today.

The bread was from the thick matzo we had used at the table. I took the whole piece in my hands and weighed it and considered whether I wanted to eat it. Finally I put it back on the plate. What ran through my head was Jesus needed my help. He had nothing to give me now. I needed to be there with him.

I looked up and saw Thomas eyeing me. "Peter and Andrew have gone to Palace Antonia to find out as much as they can. They will be back as soon as they have any news. Nicodemus has gone to speak to Pilate. They think they might get him to postpone the execution until after the festival. I think their idea is to use the time to gather the Sanhedrin together and have the charges discussed, then voted on by the full body of the Sanhedrin. Pilate might listen to them if they give him an excuse to do so."

I nodded. "Good. That is our only chance. Listen, I want to go back to the Fortress. I want to be there when they bring him out."

Thomas nodded, "We all want to be there. Right now, Peter is down there, and he will tell us as soon as he sees anything happening. I went down there a few minutes ago and apart from a crowd of clergy standing around with the usual onlookers, nothing was happening. Let's wait here until we get word."

We lapsed into silence, listening to the noise of the city that seemed to me comfortingly normal. Half an hour later, Joseph of Arimathaea came in. He had told Lazarus and his sisters, who were now on their way. There were others that came in and asked questions then left or stayed on, talking quietly. Soon the room was full of anxious, angry and bewildered men.

Andrew burst into the room. "They are starting!"

The room emptied as men bolted through the door. I was swept with apprehension that some of our people were hot-headed enough to try to intervene. Pointless sacrifice was unthinkable and I wished I had cautioned them against any rescue attempt or creating a riot. The well-armed contingent that turned out for the execution was large enough to deal with any kind of force that they might meet and they were accustomed to hostility. They were hard men who had carried out this duty in countries across the world. Executions were part of their job as the occupying force.

I went into Jesus' mother and told her the news.

"John, I want to be there, but not yet. I don't want to watch those terrible men do to him the things I have heard of. I could not bear to see others smash what I have so loved and cared for. Would you take me along there in a little while? I want to be with him. Will they let us close enough so he will know I am there?"

"I don't know. I think they encourage his friends and relatives to be there. The Romans think such a terrible death will deter others. That is the whole point of their cruelty."

Mary Magdalene stood over the mother of Jesus and rested her hand on her shoulder. "Do you want me to come too?" She looked up at me and said, "John, we three love him in different ways for different reasons. Each of us has to be there. Mary is right. We have to get close enough so he will know we are there. Will you help us?"

I replied, "Of course I will. Nicodemus has gone to see Pilate. He wanted to try to buy us time by getting the execution postponed until after the festival, and maybe by then raise support to petition Pilate for another hearing. He was obviously too late. Let us wait for him to return. As a Sanhedrin member, his authority will get us through the crowds, and the soldiers will listen to him."

Simon Peter, Philip, Thaddeus and several others set out right away for the execution site. I intentionally waited and let time pass. I did not want to expose Mary to the terrible process of crucifixion. Nicodemus came back, having been refused an audience with Pilate, and joined us who were waiting. When I judged we could leave, we made a sad procession through the streets, through the gate and up the path. There were hundreds of others going to view the crucifixions. Word was out that Jesus was one of the victims, and a long procession of silent people who had encountered him followed us. I was absurdly grateful for their support.

Golgotha was a bald mound of weathered limestone. Years ago it had been a quarry. Jerusalem buildings were, in part, built from its stone. During the last century the good, consistent rock gave way to softer, fissured and poorer rock, unfit for building purposes. Grass grew in the crevices of the rock.

Permanently dug into the limestone at the top of the hill were the sockets into which upright posts were driven for the purpose of executing those who fell afoul of the Roman occupation. The spot was ideal from the Romans' standpoint, for even from inside the walls of the city, everyone could see the crown of the skull-like outcrop and see the bodies of those executed and exposed there for days.

Nicodemus led us through the crowd until we were within a few feet of the cross on which the soldiers had nailed Jesus. Two other men were crucified there. I was surprised to see them, as if somehow this event belonged solely to Jesus, but I realized this was an unremarkable day for the Roman Empire, and they unburdened themselves of whoever was held on capital charges.

The soldiers had evidently gone about their business as impersonally as ever, and by the time we got there, they had tidied up their tools, bagged the clothing of the men now hanging on the crosses, and were settling down to wait out the long time it would take for the men to die.

At least six heavily armed soldiers stood guard around the area of the crosses, while the others made themselves comfortable. I noticed at least one managed to produce a bottle of wine from under his mantle, and it was passed round. Another brought out some dice and they began to play a game to pass the time.

Wind whipped up the dust and blew it around us in little clouds. The women had covered their faces, but now drew their garments tightly around them to keep out the dust.

I would prefer to go on describing the storm clouds forming along the hills to the north and the various people who stood around the central cross, so I would not have to remember what they had done to Jesus.

Arms outstretched, his wrists were nailed to the wood of the cross-beam. The helmet of thorns some soldier had forced on his head was still in place. Blood smeared his hair and face, rivulets ran down his arms from the nail wounds in his wrists, and the cross-hatched marks of the flogging were now evident all down his body and legs. His feet were held together and nailed by one huge spike that pierced both feet.

When we first arrived, Jesus was hanging mostly by his arms with his head drooping forward, and I thought maybe he had died already. After a few minutes he raised his head and painfully pushed upwards to take his weight on his nailed feet. He eased himself there for a while, and I heard him say a psalm to himself. I only caught a few words here and there, but he went on, minute after minute, psalm after psalm.

Eventually his strength gave out or the pain overcame him, and he slumped down. His head dropped forward again, and he hung there. Just as I wondered whether he was unconscious, he raised his head and, in great pain, tried to take a deep breath. My breath caught in my throat, too, and my heart froze as I saw him struggle to push himself up so he could breathe again. A second trickle of blood flowed from the nail wounds in each of his wrists, running down his arms and dripping in the dust.

At last he raised his eyes in our direction and focused on our little group. I saw incredible pain cross his face as he realized who we were. I saw a look of deep gratitude for our presence. He gave us an infini-tesimal nod to acknowledge our presence and redirected his attention back inside himself to battle new waves of pain. He closed his eyes and set his face against the agony. He sank down again.

Involuntarily, I stepped forward, not even knowing what I intended to do—maybe touch him, maybe to speak to him. A guard forced a jav-elin pole vertically against my chest and barked in a hard voice, "Back!"

So the hour passed. I had never been present at a crucifixion and now I saw the slow rhythm by which the sufferer descended towards death. Earlier, when I had seen Jesus standing in the courtyard of the fortress after he had been flogged, he could hardly keep upright. Now the accumulation of trauma to his whole body took its toll. He could hold himself up to breathe for shorter periods each time, and he hung motionless for longer stretches. Every time he struggled to raise himself, I could see the toll was greater and the struggle harder.

He was dying! I couldn't believe it. *No!* I wanted to scream, but I only hung my head as his fell forward once more.

The other men crucified with him were in better shape. One of them raised himself up and stood on his nailed feet and looked desperately about him. He looked across at Jesus and shouted, "Okay, miracle worker, get us out of this. We saw you save others, so save yourself and us. For God's sake, try, or we are done for."

A jeering voice from a group of Temple clergy standing to one side shouted, "Let's see you do that. Come on down from your perch, and we will believe you."

I grabbed Peter's arm as he started towards where the jeer came from. "No, Peter." He was sobbing with rage. Unfortunately, the only emotion he knew how to express at that moment was anger.

Someone else joined in. "You saved others; let's see you save yourself." Other taunts came but Jesus was insensible to them all. He hung there, inert.

The third crucified man turned his head to the first criminal and barked, "Knock it off. We knew what we were doing; we just got caught. Do you remember what we saw him do? He healed, and he had a word for anyone. He even saw us. He knew why we were there. Leave him alone, for he should not be here with us." He paused, and then in a soft voice I hardly heard, "Jesus, remember me when you come into your Kingdom, okay?"

Jesus made a huge effort to raise himself up so he could take a breath. Painfully, he turned his head to look at the man to his right. Barely audible, he said, "Today you will be with me in that Kingdom." He looked out over the crowd, down at us who stood almost at the foot of his cross, and slumped down again. It was a long time before he moved.

A soldier said something to the officer in charge of the detail and received a nod in return. The soldier very soberly took a javelin, stuck a sponge on the end and dipped it in some of the wine the soldiers had with them. He held it to Jesus' mouth, who took a little and then shook his head.

Jesus heaved himself up again, perhaps making one final effort. There was a hush among those around us as they recognized this struggle was close to his last.

He looked down, locked eyes with mine and croaked, "John, look after her," and he nodded towards Mary clinging to my arm. Infinitely, painfully, he said slowly, "Mother, take him as your son."

He looked at Mary Magdalene and said simply, "Mary."

His gaze rose over the crowd to the city and the arid ridges beyond and he smiled a thin little greeting of love.

With great effort he took another painful breath, looked up towards the sky and cried, "It is done, Father. Into your hands I entrust my spirit. It is finished." Jesus lowered his head and gradually slumped down exhausted.

Every now and again he moved his head slightly, and he continued to breathe. Once he strained to raise himself up again, but he could not. After that effort, more of his weight hung by his arms. He took little, shallow gasps, but they grew less frequent until they stopped altogether.

Mary buried her face in my chest, clung to me and cried great shuddering sobs that shook her whole body. I wrapped my arms about her and forced myself to watch the last moments of life drain from my friend.

We stood there for what seemed like an eternity. There was nowhere else for us to go. Mary finally pushed away from me, uncovered her face and stared at the now lifeless form of her son. She gazed up at him steadily, as if wanting to remember him there as completely as she could.

I heard the officer in charge bark an order for the men to get up. "Right, you know what to do. We've got to get these down before nightfall, so let's get started."

I watched as two soldiers picked up a huge wooden mallet and went over to the first condemned man. He still groaned but was conscious. He saw what they were going to do, and he struggled to right himself, but it did no good. The soldier with the mallet swung it and broke the bones of one leg, then the other. We all heard the bones break, and in spite of the horror of the day, this final brutality sickened me afresh. They came over to Jesus, looked up at him and said to the officer, "This one's dead already," and walked over to the last man.

The officer took the javelin from one of those who had been standing guard and advancing to the foot of Jesus' cross, thrust the point expertly into Jesus' rib cage. There was no movement, no response. As he withdrew the weapon, a gush of blood and clear fluid flowed out.

I stood there, unable to believe what I had seen. I thought everything would somehow right itself if I just stayed still. I couldn't move. After about fifteen minutes, I thrust off my paralysis and gave Nicodemus a little shake. "Nicodemus, now what? Can we look after the body? Who do we have to see to bury him? I am not going to just leave him there."

Nicodemus said, "Yes, I mean, no. Oh, dear, I don't know. You are right, we must do something. Let me ask the officer there." He walked over to the officer and spoke in hushed tones.

On his return, he said, "I am going to see Pilate. He has to give permission for us to take the body. It will be another hour before they get the bodies down because the others will take a while to die. I think we should get what we need to wrap him up, and also we have to find somewhere to lay him for tonight. We will bury him properly on Sunday. Why don't you leave this to Joseph and me, and you take his mother down to the house."

The crowd was thinning and drifting away. The storm that had been threatening for most of the afternoon suddenly let loose. Rain poured down, and the wind lashed the little mound where we all stood. I took one last look at the still figure on its cross and led Mary away, down the hill towards the city.

Simon Peter, Thomas, and Thaddeus caught up with us as we made our way back to the house we had been meeting in. I explained to him what we were planning. At the house we met Lazarus and his sisters. He looked as devastated as the rest of us. He produced a parcel, which he thrust into my hands and said, "I brought this. Maybe we can use it to wrap his poor body in."

I took the parcel, which was a bolt of linen cloth. It would be enough to do what we had to do. How strange it was that, after such a horrific day, the ordinary tasks like preparing the body for burial should restore us to normalcy.

The linen shroud was not all we needed. I explained, "We will wrap him and, with help from a couple of other men, we can carry him back here. It is too late to do much else. First thing on Sunday, we will find a place to bury him and do everything we need to do then. Right now we will need a lot of spices and other herbs to help keep the body from deteriorating too quickly. With the festival starting in a few hours we don't have any other option. We can hardly carry his body through the streets as everyone goes to their Passover gatherings."

Simon Peter and I retraced our steps through the city, out the western gate and up to the mound where the soldiers were lowering the body of one of the other crucified men. Nicodemus was already there, and he had taken charge of the body of our friend, our Lord, our teacher. "Pilate gave us permission to look after the body. The officer has clearance for us to remove it when we can," Nicodemus informed us.

Nicodemus eyed the linen we had and looked at the bag of spices. I told him of my plans. He nodded, "That will work. Joseph of Arimathaea came with me to Pilate. He will be back in a minute. Right now he is checking out the garden down there," tilting his head towards the quarry bottom where a garden had been laid out. "There are tombs down there belonging to various families. He thought there might be one we could use. I don't see how, because once they are in use they are sealed and nobody is going to thank us for disturbing their family's ancestors."

We stretched out the linen on the ground. All of us stood around the body of our friend and, lifting together, we carefully moved his body onto the linen.

Just then Joseph appeared, climbing up the last few feet of the slope towards us. He was a little breathless and took a moment to collect himself. "There is a tomb down in the south corner of the garden, down there." He pointed off to the right. "It looks as if it is new, so the stone is rolled back and there is nobody there. I don't know who it belongs to, but right now it is the best we can do. If we leave him in that tomb until Sunday, we can move him elsewhere then. Right now we have little time left."

"I think you are right," I agreed. "Let me go look at it. If we can leave him there, the temperature will be cooler. We should have no problem getting him down there." I climbed down the path into the garden.

There were a number of tombs there. All had the stones closing their entrances rolled into place, and seals attached to them. I came to the one Joseph had indicated and immediately saw the advantage of what he had suggested. We did not know whose tomb it was, but if we were up early on Sunday, we could remove Jesus' body before anyone was awake. Until then, we could roll the stone into place to secure the gravesite from animals.

I scrambled back up the hillside and found that Jesus' mother and Mary Magdalene had rejoined us. They had brought more spices.

I looked inquiringly at Mary, who said, "I am going to look after him. I tended him as a little boy, I nursed him as a baby and I carried him within my womb. All that is left for me is to carry him in my mind from now on. It is all I have left."

Simon Peter and I took the head, and Nicodemus and Joseph of Arimethia the feet. Lifting together, we took the weight and slowly and carefully headed a short procession across the barren hill.

Gone were the cross bars, and now all that was left were the sockets into which the towering vertical timbers were sunk. I was too occupied to look back as we descended. Once we were down, I did manage one last glance but the angle was wrong. Maybe I didn't need to see that accursed place again.

Here on Patmos, and over there in Ephesus, there are followers who've journeyed secretly to visit that place I thought was cursed. I've never returned, but those who go, come back blessed, and they know it only as a holy place.

As I write these words, I cannot but think of my own friends who were murdered in Ephesus. Jesus' death, their deaths—they are all cut from the same piece of cloth. Man can desecrate, but only God makes holy that which is profane.

44

The Burial

We four men carried the body between us down the path. Stones rolled beneath our feet, and the limp form was difficult to hold. Once we were down on the floor of the garden, we pushed along until we staggered to the doorway of the grave. The doorway's lintel was low, and we had to stoop to enter. With the weight of the body between us, we carefully carried Jesus into the carved outer chamber.

We found there a rock bench carved out as a preparation table and laid Jesus on it. There was not enough space in the cramped cave for all of us, so Nicodemus, Simon Peter and Joseph ducked out and waited for Mary, his mother, and I to complete the necessary rituals.

Mary entered immediately. I braced myself to deal with her complete collapse into uncontrollable weeping and wailing. Certainly I could not have censored her for that. Instead, Mary took the limp body of her son in her arms and sat on the rock bench. There was hardly enough height to allow her to hold him in her lap but she clasped him to her.

With closed eyes, she raised her head and intoned the prayer for the dead. I joined in. Mary finished the final prayer, opened her eyes and gazed at the body of her dead son in her lap.

She looked across at me and held my eyes with her gaze. "Why?" she demanded.

Her authoritative question required an answer. She didn't speak in the soft and reasonable tones I expected from her, but in a hard voice made up of countless mothers' voices down through the centuries. She was speaking, I knew, for all of them: mothers whose sons and daughters had been offered as sacrifices in days long past, sons wasted in battle or broken by endless toil, and sons who disappeared and no word was ever heard of their fate.

As I looked into her eyes, I saw the aggregate of violence we men visited upon each other and consequently upon the women who gave us life and sustained us through their love. I had no answer then, but I have spent my life since that moment trying to understand her question and provide an answer.

She sat and wept. I now know she was not only weeping for herself but for the world and the suffering we men inflict on each other. She closed her eyes. Tears squeezed out and ran down her cheeks. She cradled her dead son, and her lips moved in prayer for the world, for the suffering and waste we inflicted. Mary prayed in words I didn't understand, but her pain poured out as sorrow and mourning for all of us. In later years, she never lost the love for us all that, she explained, came to her during those moments in the tomb.

At last her tears dried, and she started to get up, twisting out from under Jesus' limp weight. With my help, she laid him down on the stone slab and carefully arranged his body.

Mary moved with a certainty of years of knowledge and practice as she straightened his limbs and carefully rearranged his hair to cover the worst of the wounds to his face and head. She was a mother saying goodnight to her sleeping child. She touched his forehead with her lips, then rose and stepped back from the table so I could complete what little preparation was left for me to do at that time.

The square of cloth that had wrapped the linen I tied firmly over his head and under his chin to hold his mouth closed. I withdrew from my pocket two drachma coins to weigh down his eyelids. Pilate had issued the coins. Jesus' words, "Render unto Caesar the things that were Caesar's and to God the things that belonged to God," came to me. I blinked away tears. The irony of using Pilate's coins swirled around my head.

I stroked his eyes closed and placed a coin on each eye and combed his hair with my fingers to cover the headband. His hands I placed together over his abdomen. For a long moment I held his hands, and I, too, bent and kissed his cooling forehead. Covering his body with the linen, I tucked the last foot of it under his heels. As the sheet settled upon him, I saw the stains of blood from his wounds show through the linen, marking it as a map of his sufferings.

I stood up and moved to the entrance. With one last look of farewell, I bowed out of the entrance to the tomb, leaving Mary with her son.

Mary Magdalene appeared on the path to the tomb carrying a large bouquet of flowers she had gathered from the surrounding garden. She ducked into the tomb. I stood in the entrance and watched as she gently laid the flowers on the linen shroud and knelt on the rough rock floor before the body of her savior.

After about fifteen minutes she rose, and, in the tight confines of the tomb, the two women embraced. They slowly and reluctantly emerged into the failing light outside. Hand in hand they walked down the slight slope towards the city gate and the house we had made our home for the last week.

I bent down and removed the blocking rock from the massive round stone intended for a door to close off the tomb. Peter and I levered the stone along its track until it closed off the entrance.

We clumped downhill towards the city gate. Simon Peter snuffled beside me. All down the path, I alternated between grief that swamped me and rage that sent a scream into my throat. Halfway down the path, I felt the weight of Simon Peter's thick arm rest across my shoulders and he pulled me to him as we walked.

Caiaphas was just here. He gave me a glowing report of how he outsmarted Pilate and forced him to do what we needed to have done. Ha!

I was very good: I congratulated him and even went so far as to praise him for his planning of the whole thing. I laid it on so thick he got my point. I don't know what my daughter sees in him.

So the Nazarene is dead. That all worked as I predicted. From what Caiaphas said, and what my other sources have reported about the morning hearings, Pilate came close to letting that Jesus fellow off. I am glad I gave Caiaphas that clincher. "Friend of Caesar" Ha!

I must remember that. Leverage—it's all about leverage. Now what?

Nicodemus of the Sanhedrin is a nuisance. Do we need to pursue him and any others who followed this man? I can think about that later.

I am worried about my secretary. I hear he was helping Nicodemus and the others who were trying to stop the proceedings. That is disloyal. I just can't stand disloyalty. It would be a pity to lose him; he is very useful around here.

The Sabbath begins in half an hour. I can finish the rest of my notes tomorrow evening. I will sleep tonight after being up all last night. It was worth it.

Saturday morning dawned red and stormy. Wind whipped the streets. The Sabbath was no joy to us.

Pointlessness and powerlessness stalked my thoughts. I fancied that old image of evil chattered and laughed at me, mocking all my hopes. I had to confess that I had indeed had dreams of a kingdom without the evil I now saw triumph.

If Jesus could not overcome it, but only be destroyed as he stood against that terrible image, what hope was there for any of us?

I thought of the miracles of healing, and I sought consolation that at least those people had benefited. They had been give a better chance, but I found myself bitterly rejecting them as the justification for all the life Jesus had poured into all of us.

Mary, Jesus' mother, came to me. "John, would you talk to Mary? She is losing control. She has done so well until now, but I fear for her. She could slip back to where she was when she came to us."

I went in with her and sat on a low stool. What was there to say? Mary sat with her knuckles in her mouth, her face white and eyes restlessly moving from the high window opening to the door and back to the room. She was disheveled. Her hair fell down her face, partly hiding her from view. In the corner of the room there was a torn shirt, as if she had torn it off herself sometime during the night. Now she sat hunched against the world. This was how she had been when we first met almost a year ago.

Mary's eyes flickered over me and returned to the window. Finally she said, "John, I thought I was safe. That demonic presence has reached right back into my life, and he has snatched me back. All I can see is the great gulf opening before me, and I am slipping towards it."

"Mary, do you remember what Jesus said? Nothing can touch you. 'Stand and do not be afraid.'"

Silence filled the room and I hoped she was thinking over what I had said and fortifying herself with my words.

Apparently not, because she shook her head. "John, you do not understand. You think the evil one is just an image you can dismiss or laugh away. He is not finished yet. He never is satisfied, but must always seek our destruction. He is not satisfied with Jesus' death. John, why did we leave him there all alone in that cave? We should have brought him here. We could have kept watch over him. We could have protected him.

"Tell me, what will happen if the owner of the tomb hears we are using it to hold Jesus' body? What if they send someone over there, and they find him lying there in the tomb? What if they take him away and throw him in the valley of Hinnom? That evil presence is never done; it will savage even his poor dead body."

"Mary, Mary, think about it. This is the Sabbath. We left him there last night when everyone else had gone back to the city. In any case, nobody will do anything until Sunday morning. First thing tomorrow morning we will move his body and have a proper burial. Last night, Joseph said that he would find a place."

Mary looked wildly around her and shouted, "No, you will see. Evil is never satisfied to conquer, but it must squash us under its heel. That is the way it's been for me forever. Just when I think I am safe, that's the moment he comes back. Jesus is alone in that tomb. He is defenseless. Just when we think it's all over, when he is safe, that is when the Evil One will celebrate and demonstrate his power with revenge."

I got up, stood over Mary, took her hands in mine very gently and assured her, "Mary, Jesus is safe. Tomorrow we will do what little we can. Maybe you and some of the other women would like to get together spices and the other things you need to prepare his body for burial. We will all come and take him to where we can bury him.

"Mary, you are safe with us. We understand what you have been through, but remember what Jesus himself taught you. The Evil One cannot touch you. You are safe."

Mary shook her head. "I was safe in his presence. Him being there was my bastion against the darkness that continued to chatter and gibber at me from the shadows. Now he is gone. John, it was not what he taught, but who he was. He was a rock on which I was unassailable. I no longer care about myself. With him gone I have no future. My only vulnerability is through him. That is why I fear for him. I watched him become powerless like I used to be, and now that evil will want to destroy even what is left. It is always that way for me."

For the rest of us, shock was giving way to grief. I was far from being able to comprehend what had happened. We sat in the house, looking at each other and listening to the pounding rain. Simon Peter strode restlessly around the central room, complaining about the city with its walls and dirty streets. I fancied if he was back in Capernaum he would be out fishing. That is where he would be most at home. At one point I tried to engage him in conversation, but he cut me short with a shake of his head and a mumbled, "John, I betrayed him." He withdrew into himself, hiding from the rest of us behind a restless, angry exterior.

I grew more anxious about Mary Magdalene, for when I went in to see her again, my impression of her was a wild animal caught in a trap. She had pulled at her hair, and there were scratch marks on her face. I went to find the other Mary to get some help.

Not five minutes later—just about three o'clock, the hour Jesus had died—I saw Mary Magdalene go to the cooking area. A moment later a loud crash was heard throughout the house. Everyone ran to see what had happened, and we found her sitting on the floor, weeping, surrounded by shards of a large earthenware pot.

Mary screamed at us, "Why did we leave him there? He was with us in life—could we not have been with him in death? Have we not abandoned him?" she sobbed.

Jesus' mother came in and gently took Mary Magdalene by the hand and helped her up. "Mary, don't blame them. They did what they thought was right. Let us get things together for tomorrow." We filed away, one by one, sheepishly avoiding each other's eyes and went out from the cooking area. Each found a spot to be alone.

Saturday evening after the Sabbath ended, men arrived from other houses where they had been staying. Lazarus and his sisters appeared. Some brought food. Others brought wine.

We said kadesh, our people's prayers for our dead, for Jesus. Nobody wanted to leave. We talked about Friday and exchanged our views of what had happened.

Later someone began a mournful lament—a haunting song of loss. Others joined in the slow cadence and soon a ring of bearded men began a slow dance, linking their arms together. Their stomping feet oscillated back and forth as the circle of men slowly circled about the center of the room.

We broke up and each of us drifted off. Some went back to where they were lodging. I sat up, staring at the wall. I was empty of all feelings and thoughts.

Everything I had hoped, everything that I held dear, was gone. Not only was everything lost, but intentionally desecrated.

Perhaps Mary Magdalene was right after all. I wished we had him with us. I could at least watch with him, like I used to when he went out to pray.

Saturday evening

The Sabbath is over. Everything is quiet today. I would expect that. Getting that Nazarene looked after just before the Sabbath started was a stroke of luck. First John the Baptist, then him. That should discourage any more rabblerousers.

Might we have trouble with the Sanhedrin for going around them? Maybe. I should brief Caiaphas about how to deal with that if it happens. It would be just like Nicodemus and a few other liberal Pharisees to ask questions on the floor of the Sanhedrin. They can't bring that Jesus fellow back—he is dead—so they can complain all they want.

I can't help thinking about Jonathon. I always thought of him as such an honest and open young man. Has he been deceiving me? Was he a secret disciple? I find such duplicity despicable. I must make inquiries before I do anything. Judas is another one who surprised me. Yesterday morning when he realized we were going to have Jesus executed, he came and threw his money at us. Damned arrogance of the man! Now he has gone off somewhere to nurse his conscience. Ha! A bit late for that, I would say. He never had a conscience before, why would he bother now. So we saved thirty talents. I should make a note for Jonathon. We need to use that money for something other than normal Temple needs. It cannot go back in the treasury.

That's enough for now. Too much excitement, all in one week. We can tidy up any loose ends later.

Last night that dream was back. That man from Daniel appeared again. This time he looked more like the Nazarene than ever. Funny thing what the mind can do if you are overtired. Those nightmares should go away now we've seen the last of him.

45
THE RESURRECTION

The next morning I was awakened by screams and someone banging on the door. By the time I got up, others had opened the door to admit Mary Magdalene.

She was disheveled and frantic. "I told you so! They have taken our Lord away! The tomb is empty! The body is gone! I told you so. I knew we should not have left him there!"

Peter and I looked at each other across the room and together plunged through the door and headed towards the tomb. Dawn had hardly broken when we set out. We both ran, but I outran Peter who lumbered along as best he could. Out through the gate we went and found the path to the garden. When I came to the tomb, I pulled up short.

It was open. I stooped down and looked into the dark interior. Jesus was gone. Where his body had lain, there was only the dim outline of the linen shroud. "No! Please don't let it be true," I whispered to myself.

Peter came puffing up, saw me and blundered on. He ducked his head to enter the tomb and crouched inside, bent almost double. He looked around, mystified. I followed him in . . . . .

I hunted through the clothes I had hastily thrown on to find my flint and steel. There was an oil lamp left by those who had excavated the cave and who had worked in the dark there. Once I had success-fully struck a spark from my flint, I saw the lamp wick smolder. I gave it a couple gentle puffs, and the spark became a flame.

In the dim light of the lamp we looked around the cave but there was little to see. I picked up the cloth napkin I had tied round his head to hold his jaw closed and examined the cloth more closely. The knots were in place. Everything was as I had tied it. I was perplexed. How could this have come off? To remove it, one would have to untie it.

I showed it to Peter. He picked up the shroud itself and folded it together roughly, I said, "Peter, why did they not take the body the way we left it? Why didn't they take the shroud to help carry the body? How did they get this off?" and I pushed the napkin under his nose. "Why would they want to take it off? By now rigor mortis would have left the body, and everything would be loose and the body would be leaking its fluids. They would need these clothes to keep the mess together."

We looked around the tomb and ducked out through the entryway. Mary Magdalene had followed us, and she now stood beside the great stone that had been rolled back. More coherent now, she explained that she had been unable to sleep and that she had finally woken two of the other women and convinced them to help her. "We made our way through the gate and up here to the tomb. On the way we realized we would not be able to move the stone. It was barely dawn so nobody would be around to help us. When we got here, I knew immediately what had happened. I told you so. We should not have left the body here!"

"Did you see anyone? I asked.

She shook her head. "The owner of the tomb must have heard about it and taken his body away. John, where would he have taken it?"

"Mary, we will find out," I assured her. "You were right, but now we have to get to work and find who the owner is, and where he has taken the body. We can do nothing here."

As she spoke, her voice had risen, words tumbled out and her tears fell. I thought she was going to start screaming again or lose control entirely; but she sat down on a nearby rock, hugged herself tightly, rocking and crying bitterly. I looked at Peter for help, but he shrugged his shoulders helplessly. We couldn't carry her down to the city, but we ought not to leave her here by herself.

Mary saw my concern. "Leave me here for a while. I will be all right. I will come down when I am ready. You don't have to worry about me. There is nothing more anyone can do for me."

I looked again at Peter, who nodded, gathered up the folds of linen more firmly and turned to go. I said to Mary, "I will go back to the others, let everyone know what is happening and come back. Mary, I am terribly sorry. You were right, but . . ." I could not finish. Instead I said, "I will be back in half an hour."

Back at the house everyone was awake. Peter stood in the middle of the room displaying the shroud and told everyone what we had found. I added my observations and told them of my puzzlement. "Why did they not take the body wrapped in the shroud? Why did they take the headband off, and how did they get it off without untying it?"

Thomas broke in, "But who would do this? The only person who might have done it was the owner of the tomb. Could we not find out who that is and get him to tell us where he had the body taken? What I don't understand is why he would have had the body removed on the Sabbath. Nobody could move a dead body through the streets on the Sabbath. There would be a ruckus, and they would have been stoned. Besides, we would have heard about it."

"Well, going to the trouble to remove it at night is as problematic," I argued. "Whoever they were, they would have had to arrange for the city gate to be opened. They would certainly have been challenged if they had tried to lug a dead body through the streets in the middle of the night. Someone must know about this."

As we considered the possibilities, the conundrum became more puzzling. We decided to split up and fan out to look for any information available. We had to find the body!

Two of the brothers associated with the house we were staying in offered to visit the valley of Hinnon where most of the garbage from the city ended up. Nobody else wanted to even consider that possibility. I thought I would find Jonathon and ask him about any involvement of the authorities. For the life of me, I couldn't imagine why anyone would want to take Jesus' body. They would not want to display it or otherwise maltreat it, for any such disrespect towards the dead is profoundly antithetical to our beliefs. Even Caiaphas and his staffers would have no desire to do any such thing. To do so would bring about public revulsion, and certainly nothing would be gained by it.

That brought me to the question that had been at the back of my mind since I left the cave: Who would want the body to disappear? This was in nobody's interest. Even the owner of the tomb would not want to be accused of desecrating a corpse. There is no way to get rid of a corpse secretly without a lot of time and planning. Somebody must know.

For the second time that morning, there was banging on the outer door, and Mary's voice raised in agitation. I ran to the door, but by the time I got there, someone else had opened it. Mary Magdalene stood there, wide-eyed. "I have seen the Lord," she said.

The line of people behind me made way for her to enter the room. Mary took the center of the room and repeated, "I have seen the Lord." We all stood there frozen in place, eyeing her with alarm. What on earth now? She answered our questions before we could ask them.

"Soon after you were gone, John, I sat there on that rock trying to get myself together. It must have been at least five minutes, when I sensed there was someone there. I looked around and there was, indeed, a man. I immediately thought it must be the gardener. I said to him, 'If you have taken the body away, please tell me where you have laid it, and we will take it away and look after it.'

She stopped and looked around at all of us. "Then he said, 'Mary.' I knew his voice. I have heard it so many times in my head and in my heart, I would recognize it anywhere. It was him. I looked up, and indeed Jesus was right there in front of me. I wanted to run to him, but he held up his hand, 'No, don't cling to me. I am not yet ascended to the Father. Mary, go tell my disciples and all my friends that I have been raised. I am back.'"

"When he left I came here as fast as I could. Oh, John. What does it mean?"

A whisper was heard in the silence, "It means it is not over." We all looked towards the back of the room, and there stood Jesus' mother. She repeated herself a little louder this time. "It means it is not over! Come, Mary." She tenderly led Mary Magdalene to their room. The rest of us were left looking at each other.

"Mary is still in shock," someone ventured. "She has been blaming herself for leaving him there in that tomb. She couldn't wait to go there this morning. Maybe she is just wishing it were so."

"Maybe it was his ghost," another offered.

For the first time I felt I had to take the lead and address the others. "No, I believe Mary. Think! Why would anyone remove Jesus' body? The owner of the tomb has not had time; it is still very early in the morning after the Sabbath. He might create a stink and go to the authorities, but quietly and secretly remove it without anyone knowing? Not a chance.

"The authorities wouldn't want to muddy the waters. They are celebrating their victory. The Romans gave us permission, and in any case, they would do it with a procession and big public display just to make the rest of us feel bad.

"There is no one who would want to remove his body, but it is gone. Who would take away his body and leave the shroud behind? Surely anyone intent on moving it would use the shroud to carry it in. And another thing: the napkin I used to tie around his face was just the way I left it. The knots were still tied."

I paused, expecting comments, but everyone waited for me to go on. "He said on more than one occasion that he would return, and he spoke of being raised up to complete his work. None of us understood what he meant. Now Mary has said she has seen him, and he told her to announce his presence to the rest of us. I don't know what to make of this, but I believe Mary, and I think all we can do is wait. Anyone got a better idea?"

Philip broke in, "Maybe he was not dead. Maybe he came to, in the cool of the cave."

"Be reasonable." I replied. "That Roman officer stuck his javelin into Jesus' side and it went in at least eight inches. I saw it. The point must have penetrated the heart. Think of the injuries he had sustained from the scourging and the crucifixion itself. Jesus was on the cross for at least three hours. No one would be walking about forty hours after all of that."

Another asked, "What does it mean?"

I shrugged, "I don't know. I think we believe Mary, for a start. She was not hoping to see Jesus. She was absolutely convinced she would never see him again. In fact, these last two days, she has been worse than upset because she would not see him. Think back to this morning, how Mary was distraught when she banged on the door, but look at her now. She is as amazed as we are. All she knows is what she has told us. We need to trust her."

Someone muttered, "That is all very well, but she has had mental problems before."

"Defeated, despairing, anxious beyond belief and without any faith in herself, yes, she has been through all of that. You saw none of that as she stood here before us. His mother had it right. It's not over," I declared.

A great hubbub broke out. I left and went in search of Mary. She and Jesus' mother were sitting together in silence. I asked Mary to tell me again exactly what had happened. She did, and afterwards she asked, "John, do you believe me, or do you think I am just a crazy woman?"

"I believe you. I think Jesus is raised from death, and it's not some ghost or demon. It is not only what you have reported, but there are other things that can only be explained by his being raised."

She reached across and took my hand in hers. "Thank you. I had begun to doubt my own experience. Nothing this good could happen to me, and I still cannot believe it. Whenever something good happens to me, I just know there must be something wrong about it that I don't know. This is not like that. Jesus is back."

We did not know what to make of the reports. The room emptied as men drifted away. We were bewildered. On the one hand, we still felt the horror of Jesus' crucifixion, while at the same time, there was a faint hope that maybe Mary's experience was real: he had somehow risen and was back.

As the day wore on that possibility receded, and the blank sense of defeat and disillusionment returned.

Peter turned to me at one point and asked, "Now what?" I shook my head. "I don't know. I don't understand what is happening, and I have no clue what we are supposed to do now. Without Jesus, I don't think we have much to offer."

Peter nodded his bushy head. "Yes. It's over, unless...."

"Yes—unless. I don't think there is anything to do but wait. Some of the others are heading home. I don't blame them. I will return to my apartment and hole up there for the moment. What about you?"

Peter looked around the room, "I can't stay cooped up here. I must get out. I don't care if they do pick me up. Maybe I will get the opportunity to knock a couple of heads together." He hesitated. "John, remember what happened at the High Priest's house? I didn't mean to deny Jesus. I was caught off guard. I wish I could do it over."

"Peter, I was there. You were trying to avoid attention."

"But I said I didn't know him. Oh, God, I wish I could do it over. I must get out of here. I hate this city."

I looked at Peter, and I saw the raw pain he felt at failing his friend and lord. This great bear of a man so often had the right instincts but lousy timing. "Peter, there is nothing wrong with your heart, but it's just the way you are. Let it go."

Peter shook his head.

"I want to find Jonathon. He may have some news or at least a reading about the intentions of the Temple authorities. Why don't you come with me?"

We slipped out and mingled with the usual crowd that by then had filled the streets and market places. Everything was normal. People were going about their business, buying supplies and chatting with each other. We made our way towards my apartment. I checked for messages, but there was nothing. I had not been back there since Thursday night. Why had I elected to stay with the others when I could have hidden here? I wondered. I looked at Peter standing halfway in the doorway and felt for the first time real affection for him and the others. The emotion had been there, growing slowly, but now I recognized them as my family.

I explained to Peter, "There's nothing here. We will go to Annas' house, but since you are a little obvious maybe I should go, and you stay here."

Peter nodded. "Yes, we don't want me saying stupid things again, do we?"

I tried to think of something to cheer him up, but there was nothing. I left him there and made my way to Annas' offices. The maid, with whom I had become familiar over the years, said, "I suppose you want to see Jonathon. He is in there," she nodded towards the inner rooms of the complex, "but he may be busy. They have some kind of problem."

Jonathon's message was, "I can't break away right now, but I will see you later."

There was no indication of when or where. I explained to Peter when I got back that Jonathon could only mean his parents' place and before the evening dinnertime. I found some stale bread, some goat's cheese that smelt as if it still had four legs and the usual assortment of dried or salted meat. We chewed on the food and made halfhearted conversation.

Finally, I asked Peter, "What do you make of Mary's report?"

He munched for a moment and said, "I think he is back. I think he is back to finish what he started. He never did set up the Kingdom we all wanted when he rode into Jerusalem a week ago and now, maybe, having risen—when everyone thinks he is dead—is going to be his way of taking power without bloodshed. When he appears before everyone and confronts those who did this to him, there is nothing they can do. He is just going to step right by them."

I weighed what Peter had just said. "But Peter, Jesus said his Kingdom was not of this world, that it was within us and that it wasn't to be centered in Jerusalem or anywhere else. How many times did he say that to us? We need to forget all that stuff John the Baptist preached. It is not going to happen."

Peter looked up. "Poor John. Do you remember how he harangued us? They got him in the end." Peter shook his head, "If Jesus has been raised, what will he say to me about the other night?"

There was a knock at the door. Peter and I looked at each other in alarm. I got up and called out, "Who is there?" Jonathon answered, and I threw the door open. He came into the room. "I got your message. I have an errand to run, and I hoped maybe you would like to come with me."

We looked at each other as if no one was willing to begin. I didn't know what question to lead off with, and Jonathon held back because of a sense of despair he assumed we felt.

"I am sorry I could do so little. On Friday, by the time I got to Silvanus, there was nothing that could be done." He waited for me to comment and when I didn't he went on, "Annas got the full report this morning. I very nearly quit right then. I was sickened by his pleasure at what he had done. Then reports came in that you were spreading rumors that Jesus was alive, that one of you had seen him, and that Jesus had given you instructions. Annas immediately sent out word to have the rumors run down. He has sent me over to Silvanus to check on the facts about his death. Would you like to come?"

My first response was to refuse, but I thought that if there was any information, Pilate would have it, "Okay, but I think Peter should stay here."

We both left for the fortress and, after passing the guard who looked at us with indifference, found our way to the office of Silvanus. He came out immediately and welcomed Jonathon, who explained the High Priest's order. Silvanus thought for a moment and replied, "Maybe we should listen to what the officer in charge of the detail last Friday has to say. We can ask around for any other information."

He looked inquiringly at me, and back to Jonathon, who explained my connection and my interest. He nodded, and said, "I am sorry, it was a bad business. Maybe we can talk after we've spoken to the officer. There are a couple of things you might be able to help me with." He led us through to the barracks and sent for the officer.

I recognized him as the officer in charge of the crucifixion detail, but in his clean uniform and in this environment, he was the epitome of solid, dour professional soldiery. "This is a debriefing for the Governor and just routine. Do you have any comment about what happened on Friday?" Silvanus asked.

"Not really, started out like any other execution. That guy Jesus, though, was different. I didn't like doing it to him. Some deserve it, some don't matter either way, but with him it shouldn't have happened," replied the officer.

Silvanus asked, "You mean you disagreed with the verdict?"

"We don't question verdicts. Orders are orders. No, it was something else. It was all wrong. It was like everything else were wrong, and he were right. All that we do and make and build were all wrong compared with him," reflected the soldier.

Silvanus asked, "Do you regret it?"

The man said, "Soldiers can't afford regrets. Though I would have liked to talk to him. No, funny thing is, if it had to be anyone I'm glad it was me. When you get 'em down on the cross most curse you. He didn't. He was already pretty far gone from the whipping. It was like I was helping him rather than executing him.

"No, I don't regret it. Funny, but I don't even feel sad, no. No regrets. I tell you, though, that guy was one of the gods, or one of their sons.

Normally you just want to get drunk after executions, but this time it's different. It's like I'm waiting for something."

"Waiting for what?"

I watched the officer search for an answer. He rubbed his bristly chin and shrugged his massive shoulders. Finally he confessed, "I don't know. I'm getting too old for this kind of thing. You start thinking, you've seen too much, killed too many. Maybe there are too many ghosts in the past. No, I don't regret Friday; it's all the others I regret. Time I went back to Rome and quit this life."

Silvanus nodded sympathetically, "The reason for my questions is that there have been rumors that he has been seen alive. Is there any possibility he was not dead that he came to in the cool of the tomb where he was kept overnight and walked away?"

The officer gave a short laugh. "Nobody is going to get up and walk when we do the job. Believe me, that guy was dead. As I said before, I've done too many to be mistaken. In any case we can't afford to make mistakes. That is why I lanced him in the chest. He took at least eight inches of steel in his chest, through the heart. If he hadn't been dead before then, he would have been dead afterwards."

Silvanus thanked the man, and we returned to his office. Jonathon asked about Pilate and why he had signed the execution order. Silvanus shook his head, "Pilate did not sign any order, and when he was asked by the High Priest not to advertise Jesus as the King of the Jews, he refused. He told them that they could explain to the people why it was necessary to seek the death of their King. Pilate was furious."

Silvanus went on, "When he heard there was a rumor of Jesus being alive Pilate smiled for the first time since Friday, 'Serves the bastards right,' he snarled, 'I wish he were alive, how I would like to see their faces. No doubt the cowards would come running to me to do it all again. Fat chance.'

"Normally Pilate never swears. He is a cold fish and doesn't show what is going on inside. He hates being used. You know we had kept an eye on Jesus for some time. We never came up with anything that really concerned us. We thought he was a player, and we even considered approaching him. Pilate had speculated about Jesus being an alternative to what we have right now. I had talked to Pilate about making contact, but that is all too late now." Silvanus looked at me and asked, "You were a friend to this man? Is there anything you can say about the rumors he is not dead?"

I shook my head, "No, I have not seen him, but one of our people claimed she has. You know how at these times things can be misinterpreted or even imagined."

Jonathon nodded. "Well, if anything develops let me know. Maybe it's his ghost or spirit. These things do happen."

We thanked Silvanus and outside the fortress I took my leave of Jonathon. As I walked back to my apartment to pick up Peter, I thought bitterly about the lost possibilities. What if Pilate had talked to Jesus? What if Jesus had gone to see Pilate when he arrived in Jerusalem last week? I remembered one of the temptations Jesus had told me about. He had been offered all the Kingdoms of the world and turned them down, so we would have finished up in the same place even if Pilate had made contact.

Why did the Messiah have to suffer? Well, I didn't get it. My friend is dead, I thought, and I would rather have him alive and no Messiah. As I walked, the tears fell, and I could hardly see my way down the rough stone streets. I wanted to scream at the sky, but it was empty.

I found Peter asleep on my couch. I awakened him, and we made our way back to the others. Gone was the wild hope generated by Mary's words that morning, and now a pall lay over all our hearts. The women busied themselves preparing food for the dozen or so people who now crowded the meeting room.

It was late evening when, for the third time that day, there was a banging on the outer door. Cleopas and his friend Matthias entered. We crowded around as they told a wild story of how Jesus had appeared to them on the road to Emmaus, their home village.

Jesus had caught up to them on the road, they explained, and walked with them and discussed the Messiah. They walked on for an hour, and when they got to Emmaus, they invited him to join them for supper. Until that time they had not recognized him, but at supper he took the bread, blessed it, and broke it just like he had done on Thursday evening. At that point they recognized him. It was definitely Jesus, he was not a ghost or anything like that, but himself. The moment they recognized him he was gone.

Doubt, hope, fear and pessimism characterized our responses to Cleopas and Mathias. What was going on?

The women came in with platters of food. Mary laid her platter down on the table that ran the length of the room. With her arms crossed, she said, "You didn't believe me this morning, and most of you dismissed my experience as wishful thinking. You thought I had imagined it. Now I hope you will begin to realize something is afoot. Jesus is not dead, but he is out there." Mary nodded her head towards the door.

I sat down and others followed suit. I had nothing to say. Peter had told me about a dream he had that afternoon, while he was napping on my couch, in which Jesus had appeared to him. He assumed he had been dreaming, but now as he sat down beside me, he brought up the dream again, "Do you think he appeared to me this afternoon, and that was not just a dream?"

A hush abruptly fell over the room, and I looked up and nearly spilled the wine I had just poured myself.

Jesus stood there in the middle of the room, right beside the table, and looked around at each of us. "Peace be with you," he said. Some drew back from him; I struggled to my feet while Peter stood, immobilized.

Jesus faced us all in turn and lifted his hands to show us the wounds on his wrists. "It is me. You want to see more?" He lifted his outer garment and showed us his feet. "No, I am not a ghost or some spirit. Let us all sit down," he said gently. He sat down in the same place he occupied on Thursday evening. Gingerly others sat too, but they ranged around him in a half circle.

He repeated his greeting, "Peace be with you." Those closest to him edged further away. The rest of us paused in whatever we had been doing and collectively held our breath.

Jesus said, "I promised you I would return, so why are you fearful? I understand, for only a few hours ago you could only believe what you saw with your own eyes on Friday. Everything you hoped for was dashed to pieces, and you grieved for me and for all we had talked about. Well, I am here to establish the reality of all I talked about.

"My Kingdom is not of this world. Our Father has raised me from death, and now you see me and know me as the Christ, the Messiah you have all sought. You have heard me describe the Kingdom of God as within you, now you see the first step in bringing that about. When we talked about the future several of you said that what I taught made sense, but when I was not there you became muddled and doubted the authority I had offered you to break free from the old ideas that have enslaved our people for centuries. This is the first reason for my resurrection, that I might be with any one of you wherever you are. I see you there, Cleopas; we met on the road to Emmaus and I stayed with you for a meal, and here we are now. Do you all understand? I am to be available and in support of you wherever you are.

"I also gave you power to go out and preach and heal in my name. You came back amazed at how it worked. People listened to you when you bore witness to me and what I was teaching. There will be a time when I will again send you out, and you will go forth only to find me already there before you.

"As you discovered, without me you could do nothing, but through me you will again amaze yourselves. Imagine a vine . . . during the winter all the branches are pruned off, and the vine looks like a dead stick. That is how everything looked like to you yesterday. In the spring the new growth begins to happen and new branches thrust out in all directions. This moment today is the beginning of that spring time. I am the vine, rooted deeply in God our Father, and you are the branches. Just as I am rooted in our God, so you must be connected to me. As the Father is the source of all life, so for you I am the immediate source of that life. What I give you comes from the Father, what I have taught you, comes from the Father. As I shall never be separate from the Father, now you must not be separate from me."

I looked around at the others. Most of them were nodding, but with bewildered looks on their faces. As Jesus paused, they looked at each other for some confirmation or agreement about what they had heard. When we looked back Jesus was gone.

Mary stood in the archway leading back to the food preparation area and, walking into the room, said, "Now you know what I learned this morning. Since then I have been filled with that same inner certitude he gave me when we first met, and he drew me to him. On Friday I thought I had lost that. I now own it forever. I have known hell, but now I know Heaven, and it is the power of the Most High. That power has raised Jesus from death, to be a Messiah in ways we could not imagine. This is the genius of our God."

We stood round the table, not knowing what to do. Nobody wanted to leave, but none of us had anything to add.

We had no idea what this meant or how we should interpret what Jesus had said.

An hour later, Thomas came in. By then we had recovered and told Thomas what we had experienced. Of course he couldn't believe it and said as much. I don't blame him. He was like the rest of us. Lost in our grief, we had no way to accept such an unlikely and wonderful surprise.

Thomas asked, "Was he real? You say he came through the door when it was barred? Nobody saw him leave? Was he a ghost?"

We looked at each other with alarm, but Peter said, "No, he was my friend, my rabbi, and I would know him anywhere. He stood here," and he motioned to the spot where Jesus had first stood, "and he sat right there. It was him and no ghost."

Thomas shook his head, "Oh, God, I want it to be true so much. If I could see the wounds in his hands and feet and even the wound in his side, maybe I would be able to accept it. I saw him dead. His death was so utterly wrong. I can't let it go. I have been in this despair for two days now. How can this be? I saw him dead, so dead."

Thomas sank down on a bench and dropped his head into his hands and wept.

The next Sabbath we met again to eat the Sabbath meal, and we had hardly lit the lamps and said the blessing over the bread, when Jesus was there with us. Thomas rose from his seat, and Jesus addressed him, "Thomas, look, here are my hands. Look at my feet. Reach here and touch the wound in my side. I am back."

Thomas uttered a strangled cry of pain and threw himself at Jesus' feet with a cry, "Oh, my Lord, and my God."

"I am with you only a little longer, then you will see me no more. You will look for me, but I cannot be only here. I give you a new commandment: Love each other as I have loved you."

Peter asked, "Where are you going?"

"Where I am going, you cannot follow now, but you will eventually. Do not let your hearts be troubled any longer, believe in God, and believe in me. I go to prepare a place for you. I will come to you and take you to myself, so that where I am you will be there also."

Thomas, who had recovered and had sat back on the bench beside the table, asked, "We don't know where you are going, so we cannot know the way."

Jesus spoke in that emphatic way he had when he was making an especially important point he wanted us all to know. "I am the way, the truth and the life. No one comes to the Father except through me. If you know me, then you will recognize the Father as well. From now on you will know Him, and that is as good as having seen Him."

Philip stood and, shaking his head, said, "Lord, this is very confusing. Show us the Father and we will be satisfied."

Jesus threw up his hands in mock distress. "Have you been with me all this time, Philip, and yet you still don't know me? Let me say it again, anyone who has seen me has seen the Father. Have you not grasped that I am in the Father, and in another way, the Father is in me? The words that I speak I do not speak on my own account, but they are from the Father who dwells in me.

"Above all, love one another and keep my commandments and teachings. For each of you who desire to do so, I will ask the Father, and the Holy Spirit will be your companion for ever. I am talking of the very Spirit of Truth that will abide with you and will be in you.

"Thus, I am not going to leave you orphaned but I will come to you. The world may not see me, but you will, and not with your eyes, but with your hearts. You will know I am with you through the coaching of the Holy Spirit that I have described.

"All of this is confusing for you now, but remember the bread and wine I asked you to eat and drink as my body and blood; it is as simple as that. Take me into yourselves. The Father and I will reside in you, and you will recognize us, for you know very well what I am like."

46 GALILEE

The city had become an alien place to all of us. The horrors of Golgotha cast a pall over us all, and the Temple with its grandiose architecture appeared to us as the very source of evil. Of course it was not, but we all felt its sinister, lurking presence overshadowing us all. Peter decided that he would return to Galilee, and the rest of the party from there immediately elected to go. The city had always been home to me; now I wanted to escape from its embrace, for its indifference to everything that had happened there was itself a threat. It was a place where abuse of power and the violation of people went on unnoticed. I found relief in the idea of going back to Galilee, but above all I did not want to be alone. I needed the others, and admitting it was a relief.

We had not been in Galilee for more than three days when we were all restless. Now what were we to do? On the way there we had hashed over the events of the previous weeks and gone over things we had heard Jesus say, but none of us had an idea of what to do next.

Peter finally couldn't stand it any longer and announced he was going fishing. We were all so relieved to have something to do that we got into the boats and spent the night out on the lake. As so often when I went with them, they caught nothing all night. However, none of us had our mind on fishing. By morning we were ready to go back, and the boats made one last cast, encircling an area of water and pulling the ends of the net together. There was nothing.

In the dawn's light, the lake was calm and reflected the shoreline features becoming visible as the mist withdrew. We had fished the shoreline for about half a mile and were taking the net onboard to stow it its canvas bag, when we heard someone hail us from the shore.

We looked up from our work and there was a figure on the beach. He called out, "Have you caught anything?"

Peter replied that we had not. The man called back, "Cast the net to starboard. You should catch something there."

Peter looked out over the water in the direction the man had suggested, shrugged, and motioned to the other boat to take the net in the other direction. As we hauled in the purse net, we found we had netted a small shoal of fish that jumped and splashed as we drew the net tighter. Peter and the other fishermen went to work hauling them on board, but there were so many there was a danger of them tearing the net and escaping.

I was not part of the team corralling the fish, for that took experience. All I was good for was the occasional bailing and taking my turn at the oars. I looked out towards the figure on the beach and I rose in shock. "It is the Lord," I said.

Peter looked up from his work and gazed at the figure. "John, you're right." He immediately plunged into the lake and swam towards the shore. Two of us took the oars while the others secured the net. We couldn't fit it in the boat, so we towed it ashore.

Jesus was there to meet us. We took some of the fish and busied ourselves with cooking them on an improvised fire. None of us knew what to say to Jesus, or what to say to each other. He looked like he always had, but his outward appearance was not what we recognized; it was his inner being that announced his identity. None of us were in doubt, and we all knew we were in the Lord's presence. What do you say to someone you know, yet don't know? Since the first time Jesus appeared to us, we had all taken to referring to him as Lord. We no longer thought of him as our friend and familiar companion Jesus. He now possessed an authority far beyond us and a reflective attitude that kept us from questioning him. I, who knew him better than most, could not frame in words the questions I wanted to ask.

Typical of Jesus' gravity was the exchange with Peter after we had eaten. Jesus looked over to Peter and asked, "Do you love me more than these do?" He indicated the rest of our little group.

Peter, somewhat flummoxed by the question, replied, "You know I think the world of you, Lord."

Jesus again asked, "Simon, son of John, do you love me?"

"Lord, you know how much I admire you. Why do you ask?" replied Peter

Jesus asked a third time, "Simon, do have affection for me?"

Peter said, "Lord, you know everything. You know I have affection for you."

Jesus paused, "Feed my sheep." Then, almost sorrowfully, he added, "Follow me."

He turned to the rest of us. "As the Father has loved me, so I have loved you. Dwell in my love. I have appeared to you so that you will know me and recognize my energy and liveliness when you encounter me in the future. That joy or vitality is what I want you to entertain in your very souls, so that you may know completeness and wholeness. Remember what I said about the vine. You will be a branch growing and flourishing with my life and bearing fruit, not of your own, but of God."

Jesus upended an empty fish basket and sat among us. "See, I can even sit. Surprised? Now, during the next few weeks, seek my presence within you, and I will prepare you to receive the Spirit. I have already mentioned this. The Spirit welling up in you will show you what to say and do. The Holy Spirit is not your leader, but your guide. You have to take responsibility to be my representatives. Trust the Spirit to show you all that is true, right and beautiful. The Spirit will empower you to act out on your own the will of the Father. When you enter a new place or speak to those who desire to hear what you have to say, I will be there ahead of you preparing the ground. The Spirit will give you the words needed. Don't try to figure it out now."

"But—" I objected.

He broke in, "No buts, John." He smiled at me—that irresistible smile that had never allayed my fears and worries—but called me to follow him in spite of them.

I laughed and nodded my acquiescence.

"Your job will be to extend an invitation to all who want to enter the Kingdom of Heaven and welcome me as their own guest," he explained. "You are no longer my followers, but now you are to be my representatives to the world. You speak for me. Now that you know me as I am, you will no longer see yourselves as merely part of this world. You can never go back to being the way you were. There will be plenty of people who will persecute you, as they did me, but there will be others who will hear and understand what you have to offer them.

"My parting gift to you is peace. A peace which is found only in my presence. From now on, let everything go. Believe in me and in the One who sent me. Go back to Jerusalem and wait for the Holy Spirit, who will continue to teach and coach you as I have been doing. You will know very well when the Spirit comes, and you will understand what I have told you this morning and everything else that has happened. You are not supposed to understand all this now, so don't try. Just keep your eyes, ears and hearts open."

He got up from the fish basket. "Call to mind what I have taught you of The Way. It is a pathway for your feet among the nations of this world. You will find my presence within you wherever you travel. It was necessary for you to go through these last weeks so that you can tell others how this works. Many have prayed for this day without knowing what they looked for, but you now know for yourselves and you must witness to this new work of the Holy One of Israel, the Almighty. This is His doing, and the only way He can show anyone the extent of His care for all His creation."

That was the last we saw of Jesus as one we would recognize with our eyes.

Afterwards we sifted through what we had seen and discussed on the road back to Jerusalem everything we had heard.

I asked Peter what that betrayal with him for the rest of his life, and he refused the solace of our Lord's forgiveness. Gone was that ebullient, impulsive, well-intentioned youth, and in his place was a powerful figure who would dare anything to prove his love for his Lord. Only his own crucifixion expunged his sense of that one failure.

I asked Peter what that exchange was all about—when Jesus had asked him whether or not he loved him—and Peter ruefully said, "I guess it was a test. I failed again. I just couldn't say I loved him. Not because I don't, but because I betrayed him that night. How could I do that and love him?" He turned his shaggy head to me, paused in the road and protested. "But I do love him. He is everything to me. I just couldn't say it. He wanted me to, but I couldn't. Then he gave up."

Peter bore the marks of that betrayal with him for the rest of his life, and he refused the solace of our Lord's forgiveness. Gone was that ebullient, impulsive, well-intentioned youth, and in his place was a powerful figure who would dare anything to prove his love for his Lord. Only his own crucifixion expunged his sense of that one failure.

So our "coach" came, and the Holy Spirit was all that our Lord had promised. We went out and told everyone how the Messiah had come and, in spite of being put to death, now lived. We proclaimed, "Our Lord lives!"

So the Christ entered the world and is loose and beyond the reach of evil. Now that the light of the Christ is thrown upon it, evil no longer can exist without being recognized for what it is. No longer does the world reside in darkness, but can walk in the wisdom of God's love for His world.

This great gift to the world comes from our nation, from Israel, that has herself struggled with the burden of its own calling as the People of God. The Christ—the Holy One of God —is fulfilling that old promise to Abraham: "Through his seed all the nations of the earth would be blessed."

The Christ is loose in the world, and he will do everything the Father has ever intended.

Epilogue

I stood facing the rising sun on the island of Patmos, and I thought of Jesus' words so long ago, "You don't take a light and put it under a basket; no, you stick it on a lamp stand. If salt loses its saltiness, what good is it?"

I thought again of my friends, remembering how they stood firm and refused to bow to the demand to worship the very image and face of evil. I thought, "Yes, we are the salt of the world. We are the light for the world. There are not many of us yet. But we are like Spartans without spears, the thin red line in the forefront of the action. Our mission is to announce to the people of this beautiful world the call of its creator."

There is, in the world, that which will not recognize any such call and recoils from any such hope or possibility. All that evil knows is the mindless need to deny and destroy. It builds nothing, nor creates anything worth the material it is made from, but it spreads suffering and death to all it touches.

My Lord took me by the hand and showed me over again what I had known and what I had been part of. It was nothing short of the salvation of the world. Gone is my anger and hatred. Even in myself I can feel how that grotesque presence reached out to me to corrupt my soul. I was filled with its bitterness. I was brought to the brink of being utterly consumed in rage and hatred.

Last night I had another dream. This was different from the others I suffered regularly six months or so ago. In the dream, the angel carrying the last of the incense bowls from the altar of God took me to a mountain. There I saw this incredible city descending from Heaven. It was Jerusalem, the Holy City, and it settled over the ruins of the old.

The new Jerusalem shone with the glory of God. By the light from the city, all the nations of the world functioned in their myriad ways.

In the dream, I saw a river flowing out from the center of the city, carrying the Waters of Life, and on its banks on either side grew trees of life, the leaves of which were intended for the healing of the nations. Everything that was accursed and born of evil had disappeared, and the people walked in the light of the Almighty's presence. My people were there. I also saw thousands upon thousands more from every nation, and people who bore on their foreheads the sign of the Christ's name.

This morning, remnants of the dream still cling to me. I stand again on the patio looking out towards the mainland, but my heart is full. I begin a chant of all the names of those who died in the persecutions just over the horizon in Ephesus. This time, I see them in the company of the crucified, and I hear his words again. "They are mine, all mine."

I feel that old peace he always brought to us as we traveled with him. I know to not turn around to look for him, but I turn inside, within myself, and find his presence there. I understand the long purpose of the Almighty is in progress. My people added their own contribution to His mighty tapestry. Their own lives were now woven into the whole. Nothing was wasted, nothing was left out, but everything about all those friends is there, holy and vital in every way.

About the Author

Peter Snow grew up in England during WWII. As a member of St. John's College, Cambridge, he studied academic theology and graduated with both a bachelor's and a master's degree in that subject. He was ordained a priest of the Church of England in Birmingham, where he served as a parish priest.

Snow moved to the United States with his family in 1967 and has subsequently served churches in Santa

Barbara, California; Jackson Hole, Wyoming; and Redmond and Mukilteo, Washington.

While in southern California, the author experienced the full force of the cultural revolution during the early '70s and subsequently helped develop alcohol treatment programs, battered women's protection and assistance programs, and post-traumatic stress studies. He also worked on minority youth issues and youth ministries.

Insights gained from these activities, along with a lifetime of immersion in the study of the historic Jesus and his ministry, came together to illuminate this book.

In introducing people to a believable Jesus of Nazareth, Snow has always sought to create a path for people to find their own way to faith.

The author presently resides with his wife in Seattle, Washington.